Somethin'
Extra

Patty Rice

Simon & Schuster
New York London Sydney Singapore

SIMON & SCHUSTER
Rockefeller Center
1230 Avenue of the Americas
New York, NY 10020

SIMON & SCHUSTER and colophon are registered trademarks of Simon & Schuster, Inc.

Book Design by Ellen R. Sasahara

Epigraph: Nikki Giovanni, "Fascinations," in *Cotton Candy on a Rainy Day,*
copyright © 1978 by Nikki Giovanni. Reprinted by permission.

Manufactured in the United States of America

10 9 8 7 6 5 4 3 2 1

Library of Congress Cataloging-in-Publication Data
    Somethin' extra / Patty Rice.
      p.   cm.
    1. Young women—United States—Fiction. 2. Afro-American women—Fiction.
    I. Title: Something extra. II. Title.

PS3568.I2927 S6 2000
813'.54—dc21   99-054747
ISBN 0-684-85340-X

Acknowledgments

All honor and glory to Jesus Christ, my savior who directs my path and pen.

Thank you to my daughters, Tonja and Pamela Rice; my siblings, Janice Leak, Joyce Cooper, Olivia Pulley, Michael Massey; my special niece, Tiffany Leak, and especially my parents, Curtis A. and Betty Massey—your love and support are necessary to my existence.

John Inscoe—you are my soul mate, my keeper. My esteem and love for you are ineffable.

My agent, Nina Graybill who believes—I love you, Nina; my editor, Dominick Anfuso—Yes! We share the same vision; Laurie Chittenden—you infused me with enthusiasm.

Duane Conley (my kindred spirit) and Sandra Price (sister of my heart).

Sharon Conn, Tracy Schoenleber, Greer Nelson (I can never fully express the depth of my gratitude, but let this work serve as a reminder of the irreplaceable bond we share).

Dear friends: Starlene Joyner Burns (your love and guidance sustain me), Hana Almodemeigh, Amber Waller (God sent you to me).

Wonderful others: Ed Costello, Ann Scherer, Jim Troxell, Kim Lewis, Karla Howard, Tom Mazzuchi, Michael Duffey, Bobby Austin.

Tony Robbins and Dennis Kimbro—your work said, let there be light and there was!

John Harrald, once my mentor, treasure, and friend. This particular work would not have been possible without you. The hard lessons you taught have greatly enriched my life and have proven the old saying "When it is dark enough, you can see the stars."

**This book is for every woman
who has ever suffered, but
was strong enough to learn
to love herself.**

if you were a pure bolt
of fire cutting the skies
i'd touch you risking my life
not because i'm brave or strong
but because i'm fascinated
by what the outcome will be

—Nikki Giovanni
from "Fascinations"

The Genie Gatlin Theory on Men

Tina Turner said, "What's love got to do with it," and damn if she wasn't right. For some crazy reason it seems nobody but me really listened to Tina's good advice. 'Cause every woman I know is still out looking for love and Mr. Right. I'm not about to waste my time. I refuse to allow myself to get strung out on that love shit. That's one of life's phases that I will never go through. It's too dangerous.

I mean, think about it. When you allow yourself to become immersed in some man, you run the risk of losing your identity. And I'm telling you, it can be devastating to wake up one day and be forced to try to remember who you were as an individual. And how to exist without the person you've committed yourself to. I've seen it happen too many times. That's why I intend to keep my heart to myself.

I have to be fair, though. It isn't all a woman's fault that she can become strung out on love. The search for perfect men to give our hearts to is something that's ingrained. As little girls we're told fairy tales that teach us how bleak life is until the prince steps into the picture.

Later, as grown women, we're still spoon-fed the same shit to keep us panting after love. Only it's repackaged and sold in formats that we can *relate to as adults. Check out movies like* Pretty Woman *and* While You Were Sleeping. *Typical Cinderellas.*

Then there's the television soap operas and talk shows—all featuring women who will do anything to get and keep some no good man. And I swear, magazines are the worst of the media bunch. Every time I turn around, Cosmo *and* Redbook *are giving tips on becoming a better woman in order to keep a tight hold on some man, with article headings like "Ten Surefire Ways To Please Him" or "Easy Recipes That Will Win His Heart."*

First of all, I'm more worried about whether the man will please me as opposed to what I can do to please him. And second, why do I need his heart? I can't pay my bills with it and I damn sure can't trust it.

The only thing that love does is alter your personality. In fact, if a woman isn't careful she'll find herself doing all sorts of things she normally wouldn't do. Like allowing the man whose heart she thinks she's won with easy recipes to treat her like the dog that HE is. She'll most likely find herself becoming the queen of excuses to try to gloss over what is glaringly obvious to every friend she has (and Stevie Wonder): that she is being used and abused. Then, after many tears are shed and her heart is broken, that so-called love won't have done a damn thing but shown the poor woman what a fool she's been. That's what love will do for you. So I say the hell with it, and I stick to this theory I came up with: The Genie Gatlin Theory on Men. Let me really break this down for you.

You see, there are two things that men are good for: what's in their back pants pocket and what's behind their zipper in the front. All the rest is fluff. It can be taken or left. If the man is a good conversationalist, then go ahead and talk his ear off. If he loves spending time with you, great. Have a ball. If he's sensitive and attentive, lucky you. If not, so what? As long as the wallet and the dick are accessible, there shouldn't be too much of a problem.

As I've explained to a lot of women I know, I think we can capitalize on my theory by telling these men up front, "Hey, brother, I know what you want from me. While you're getting yours, I expect to get mine too." If he's with it, then both parties are happy. No nonsense and no expectations. An amicable, noncontractual business arrangement with safe sex as the rule. Another thing I personally insist on is no games. I can't stand for a man to think he can put one over on me. If we can agree to brutal honesty concerning our arrangement, then I'm cool.

I came up with my theory back in '89. Since then, I've never been happier with my life. After testing it a few times I realized that there was another facet I should add to my loveless living that would keep my relationships a little more controlled. Married men. Men who are married and looking for a little spice to add to their humdrum lives are a perfect complement to a single woman's life 'cause there's less risk of emotional attachment on their part. Now I strictly date married men. The single ones are less respectful of my arrangement, so I gave them up. The important difference between a married man and a single one is that a married man is a dog with a leash around his neck. I'd much rather deal with the leashed dog than with a pound puppy in need of an owner.

I guess you could say that my relationship with the male species is a love/hate kind of thing. Because the whole time I'm accepting their gifts and their declarations of how they just can't get enough of my sweet sweetness, inside I'm sickened by how weak men really are. They're all on the same ego trip, wanting a woman to praise everything from their fresh haircut to the ugly tie they just bought. And the married men I know all use the same tired lines to justify why they're stepping out on their wives. Like, "my marriage is in name only," or "we stay together because of the kids," and my all time favorite, "my wife doesn't understand me." What the hell is there to understand? Women should know by now that there is no complexity to men and that the real reason men play these games is to make up for their own lack of depth. And this will never change. Men will always be insecure about one thing or another. Unfortunately, women will always try to cater to those insecurities, in turn hurting themselves. Hmm. Not me. I learned the hard way that it's better to lease a man than own one.

The two subjects that I studied to come up with my theory were two of the best: my mother and father. Contrary to the beliefs of women I know, my theory for loveless living did not sprout from some shallow and insignificant seed. It grew instead from years of observing the relationship between the two people who gave me life. My mother Maxine was from North Carolina. Mama was a strong woman. A diva, too. Her hair was dyed burgundy and she wore it in a body wave that fell dramatically over one eye. She had some pretty brown eyes, too. Mama wore a ring on every finger, and had this ruby lipstick she wore even to bed at night to match her beaded silk bed jacket. She was funny and smart. She had a temper that could match the devil's, but she always made sure my sisters and I had everything we needed.

Yeah. Mama was a strong woman. But she had her weakness too. For her, the sun rose and set on Edward Gatlin—my father, who wore expensive clothes and loved his liquor and other women. It was like Mama would look at him and everything seemed possible to her. Her eyes wouldn't allow her to be in the same room with him without satisfying their hunger on his "godliness." She might have been a real tough as nails hell raiser with us headstrong girls, but when Edward was home, she was all woman. And I remember how she called him "lover." Not honey or dear, but lover. "Hey lover," she would say whenever he walked through the front door.

I was curious about why she called him lover, and I remember one day I asked her, but she just looked at me with this funny smile and said, "One day, Genie, you'll know the answer to that." Then she laughed real strange and walked away, leaving me more confused than before I had asked the question.

I didn't truly understand until prom night, when I was at the Holiday Inn with my date Tommy White. Things had gone further than I had thought I was ready for, but after it was over I had seen the light. And as I lay across that double bed propped up on two fluffy pillows, I heard myself breathlessly say to Tommy, "Come here lover, let's do that again." But I digress.

Mama was enamored of my father to the point of worship. Her devotion to him made me sad and angry because I knew what he was doing on the side.

Sometimes when he took me out he'd bring along his latest sidedish. He would buy me a Cherry Smash and a Slim Jim and call me his favorite girl. Then he would ask me not to tell Mama that the woman had accompanied us to a movie or to Burba Lake at Fort Meade. I would swear to him that I would keep my mouth shut. The only reason I didn't tell on him was because I didn't want to hurt my Mama. I remember sitting in the backseat of his car eating my Slim Jim, promising myself that when I *grew up I would be happy. I'd be out with some man like my father's women were instead of sitting at home lonely like Mama must have been. I felt so sorry for her. And I began to hate my father for making me an accomplice in his cheating.*

I didn't know until I was eleven that my father was the one who couldn't keep his philandering a secret. I'm guessing he would come home to Mama's worshipping eyes and feel guilty, 'cause each time he was unfaithful he would order her a dozen long stemmed red roses to make up for his infidelity. It got so every few weeks, Mama would receive those roses. They would arrive with a card that said, I'm sorry. *The reason I know this is because one summer me, Mama and my two older sisters were in the kitchen baking brownies when the doorbell rang. Mama went to answer the door while my sisters and I peeped around the corner to see who it was. We knew the delivery man from the flower shop on sight since he came so often. After he'd leave we always wondered why Mama would get so quiet. But this time was different. This time when she saw who it was, she snatched the box out of the delivery guy's hands and tore off the red bow. My shocked sisters and I stood in the kitchen doorway, watching Mama take the roses out of the box, throw them to the ground, and crush them under her feet. She grabbed the poor man by his shirt and told him that if he ever delivered roses to our house again, she would get my father's .38 and shoot him. Then she slammed the door in his face and ran to her bedroom in tears. I was the one who went down to the front door to clean up the mess. I found a little white card on the porch with a picture of a flower on it. Printed in my father's neat handwriting was,* I'm sorry.

That episode was the beginning of the end of my parents' life together, 'cause Mama was different after that. She stopped calling my father lover and moved into the guest bedroom down in the basement. She stopped dyeing her hair burgundy and let it return to its natural dark brown. She took the rings off her fingers. She stopped wearing her ruby lipstick. She stopped laughing all the time and started crying more.

But what was happening to Mama came about so gradually that none of us really paid attention to the fact that she had stopped everything that was part of her. All we knew then was that my sisters Marilyn and Tess were busy planning for college. They both moved away and grew busier with their studies, and then their jobs, and then Marilyn's baby boy Keith that she was raising on her own, and Tess's many financial problems. All I knew then was that I was too busy trying not to be lonely in that big house with nobody really close to me to explain why my body was changing so fast. And why boys were starting to make me feel sick in my stomach like something was pulling in it that kept taking my breath away.

Though Mama showed me the mechanics of tampons and told me what birth control pills did, nobody told me what it felt like to have somebody special holding you close. Or that nothing in life is as it seems. That everybody has an agenda, or that you had better make damn sure you take good care of yourself because baby, when it comes right down to it, nobody else really cares about you. Nobody told me these things. Not Mama. Not Marilyn or Tess. Not even my second mother, Sister Lettie in the 10–14 Girls Club that I belonged to at my church, where I learned all about how we must keep our dress tails down and that makeup was worldly. Sister Lettie taught us to coat our armpits with Secret deodorant and smooth Vaseline Intensive Care lotion onto our young brown skins, and she gave each of us a bottle of Love's Baby Soft perfume. We taught Sister Lettie a few things too. Like how to jump double dutch and play hand games like Miss Mary Mac. And whenever Sister Lettie left us to check on the Sunday programs or make fruit baskets for the sick and shut-in, we 10–14 girls went around the side of the church and did cheers that Sister Lettie would not have approved of, like Party and Sexy Ida, wishing we could wear tight pants or short shorts and swiveling our hips, hoping the older boys across the street playing basketball would see us and notice that we were on the verge of something big.

When I outgrew the 10–14 Girls Club, my father signed me up with the YWCA for swimming and karate lessons. Around that time Vonetta Long, an older woman who lived up the street from us, began giving me piano lessons. I became much too busy to be lonely. So busy that I didn't have time to notice that my own mother was slowly dying.

I wanted to believe she was losing weight because she wanted to. Not because she wasn't eating. While I went about my busy little life filled with pep rallies, cheerleading, boys, yearbook staff and swim team, Mama stopped getting dressed altogether. She finally gave up without anyone around to pay attention to her. Somewhere, in the back of my mind it seems, I knew she was taking pills for whatever was going wrong with her mind, but I was too busy living to stop her from letting herself die. That is, until I came home from a date one night and found her dead on her bedroom floor. I felt like I had all the time in the world for her then.

It hurts me so much to know that Mama killed herself because of a man. It really hurts. She stole my chance to get to know her. I wish she could have told me what she was feeling before things got so out of control. Maybe I could have helped her find her way back to life again. Maybe I could have shown her how to fill your days with so many things that you don't have time to think about anything else.

Mostly I've tried to shut those thoughts out of my head because they're too painful, but sometimes I can't help but wonder what went on in Mama's head while she was trying all that time to love my dumb-ass father too much.

Was she silently asking us for help when she went down into the basement bedroom all by herself without her lipstick and her dyed hair? Was a man worth that much, Mama? Does a woman have to give a man the power to control her happiness? Was a man worth your life, Mama? I asked her those questions when I saw her for the last time at her funeral. She couldn't tell me what she thought, but I knew what the right answers were. Just like I know the answers every time a man proves my theory right. That's why when any of my girlfriends ask me, "But Genie, what about love?" I don't hesitate to refer them to Miss Tina's words of wisdom.

David Lewis's Advice on Life

I'm getting old. Tired. Worn the hell out. I turned fifty-two last August. That means this August I'll be fifty-three and shit, it's January already. I was just getting used to the idea of walking around in this fifty-two-year-old body. Now I have to prepare for fifty-three. Before I know it I'll be sixty.

I don't know what's happening to me. Here I am looking in this mirror at what I used to think was a pretty good-looking guy. It wouldn't be so bad if I had to deal with just my hair graying around my temples. When I ran a comb through my hair a bit the other morning I noticed that it's thinning on top.

How can this be happening? It seems like everything about me is changing for the worst. My middle has gotten a little thicker over the past few years. Nothing too bad, but even when I work out it isn't as tight as it used to be.

I stand at the window sometimes and watch my two boys, Mark and Devin, doing their Jordan moves on the blacktop across the way, and I get a bit jealous. At sixteen and seventeen, they can't know how lucky they are right now. I would give anything to be able to run and jump around like that without getting tired. What's funny is that it seems like yesterday I was able to do those things. Football, basketball, baseball, soccer. I was into everything. Now my knees ache when I spend even a half hour on the court with my boys. I get so winded sometimes I have to sit on the bench to catch my air again. And sweat? Seems like as soon as I get into doing something active I start to sweat.

I remember a time when I could make love to my wife every night, sometimes two or three times a particular night, and still lie awake talking to her into morning. I'm lucky now if I get in twice a month.

I wanted to believe all this was caused by the pack a day I was smoking, so I quit, only to discover it isn't the cigarettes at all. I'm just not the man I used to be. I don't even feel like I look as good in my clothes as I used to. Last week I took the boys up to Potomac Mills for some Sunday clothes because my wife, Monica, was spending the day with her sister Carolyn who was up from Charlotte for a few days. Devin convinced me that my problem is that I am not, in his words, wearing the right kind of gear. He also told me that he was going to "hook me up." So I came out of the store with a pair of CK jeans and two Donna Karan shirts that cost me an arm and a leg.

I had planned to leave that stuff right on the racks, but when I tried them on, the salesgirl's eyes lit up with a look that I hadn't seen in a while. Man, I went on ahead and bought that stuff quick and even picked up a couple sweat suits, a new pair of basketball shoes and this unisex cologne Devin told me I needed by that Calvin Klein guy called CK One. I thought it was impossible for a woman and a man to be able to wear the same cologne, but I bought Monica some too and it works.

I haven't worn any of the clothes I bought yet, but I plan to put on one of the sweat suits today. I was just thinking about bootblacking my hair to go with the new look. Now I see I may have to join the hair club and get a couple plugs on top before I do anything else to it. I don't know. Maybe I'm overreacting. I should probably wait a month or two and see if any more comes out first, because it really isn't that noticeable yet. I mean, with all the gray gone and these younger clothes on, I really won't look half bad, to be truthful. Now if only my kids could show me where I can buy me some of their energy I would be okay.

I can't stand this getting old shit. I feel like I need to know I still got it, but I'm beginning to think that maybe my "it" has deserted me forever.

I thought I would feel more alive when I traded in my Volvo about a year ago, and bought myself a Mazda RX-7. That bad boy is nice. For a little while, speeding up the highway blasting the Temptations with the windows down felt good. Real good. Took me back to when I was a different man than I am now. Back in my early twenties I had nothing on my mind other than making some money, listening to good music and chasing every good-looking woman I saw. Yeah, that car took me back for a minute. But that's worn off now. And I've still got to get out of this rut I've gotten into.

My biggest problem is that I have too much time on my hands now. We moved up here to Maryland from Atlanta because Monica received a big promotion and was transferred to the D.C. headquarters of the consulting firm she works for. It was a sweet deal for her. A v.p. position that meant a huge salary increase, a plush office and some real input into the management of the company. There was no way she was going to turn it down, and no way I was going to ask her to. She suggested we have one of those commuting marriages. But that's too unorthodox for me. And too lonely. No, when Monica got this gig, I quit my job as editor of the city paper and we bought a house in Cheverly. And I do like this house.

We live on a quiet, tree-lined street that reeks of history. Our house is a three-story brick colonial with a Florida room that catches every bit of the sun, and there's a brick fireplace in the master bedroom. I love that touch. I love everything about this house. But I think I've been sitting in it too long. That's why I've gotten so depressed. I'm too much of an active man to have gone seven months without a job.

Seven months. I don't think I've gone without a job since I was a nine-year-old kid working my neighborhood paper route. If I only had some direction, I could figure out what to do with myself. The only thing I was sure of when we moved up here was that I don't want to go back to editing. I spent those first few months kicking around a few story ideas, thinking that maybe I'd do freelance writing for a while in order to replant myself in some creative soil. But writer's block can be a bitch. You work something out in your head and it sounds great. You put it on paper and it stinks.

It took me four months just to realize that I've been editing so long that my creative juices have turned to stagnant water. Now I don't know how to get my creativity back, in addition to my youth. I can't go back to editing, though. But I don't know what else I can be good at yet. Can you believe that? More than middle-aged, and I'm still trying to find my niche.

So, these last three months have passed by without me so much as having a blink of an idea about what to do. Monica's been great about it. Take your time, she says. Breathe a little while and everything will fall into place. In one sense that's fine advice. But in a way I'm starting to feel like a kept man. Sure I get my little pension from the army. But Monica covers the house note and damn near everything else, which is fine with her, but a man needs to feel useful and I don't anymore.

On top of that, I don't have a soul in this town to talk to. People around here aren't like those in Georgia. They're so busy. So standoffish. Even my neighbors who've seen me puttering around out in the yard for months barely wave or nod.

Seems like all I do during the week is sit in the den, staring out the window or watching the cursor on my blank computer screen wink at me while I wait for Calliope to climb up on my shoulder. She never does. Not one creative thought runs through my mind, other than whether a rhododendron will look better in the front or the backyard come spring or how that certain cloud up in that milky gray sky seems to have taken on the shape of a unicorn. All these days that have run up a tab of seven months have me bored to death.

Even my weekends, when the rest of the family is around to make a little noise, are pretty routine. Like today for instance. I already know that every Saturday morning, sick or well, Monica wakes up at seven and starts cooking turkey bacon, grits and eggs, and she makes herself a pot of orange spice tea. I can smell it now.

I normally get myself out of bed and go a half hour on the treadmill or go for a run if I feel like it, then I take a quick shower and turn on the Today show while I wait for Monica to join me in the bedroom with our breakfast trays and the newspaper. Monica always reads the metro section and hands me the sports page, and with the TV going, both of us find out what's going on in the world. Then she finishes her eggs first and we talk about the boys and she tells me what her plans are for the day.

Most of the time her plans include dropping the boys off for basketball or football practice, shopping, going in to the office for a few hours and

*then sharing a quiet dinner with me. I tag along with her when she's
shopping, and sometimes I convince her to take in a movie with me, or
stroll through the park on a nice day. Then we have church on Sunday,
which is an all day event. And that's my life in a nutshell. Monica and
I have downshifted into comfortable. I have no job. No excitement. Nothing to really get this old dick hard anymore. I swear, I need to get out of
this damn rut. I've got to make some changes in my lifestyle in order to re-
gain my flow. No more sitting around on my ass feeling sorry for myself.
I'm finding a job in tomorrow's* Post *that will not have a single thing to
do with editing, but will have everything to do with challenge and personal growth. Those things are important at any age. I tell my boys all
the time that life does not make a person, a person makes a life. I think it's
time for me to take my own advice.*

Phase 1

Genie

Hell yeah I was eavesdropping. I wanted to see what Eric's ass was up to. I crept up on him and stood out in the hallway with my hand cupping one ear in a half-c, so I could catch the whispered conversation coming out of my bedroom. Just in case I needed to nail him.

I can always tell a man is being sneaky when he talks like that. His voice gets extra low and he speaks real slow like maybe he's had a few drinks to relax him. And laugh? It gets all soft and deep, with each note of laughter standing on its own. Heh. Heh. Heh. That's how Eric sounded now. Sneaky. And I didn't like it one bit.

I leaned over as far as I could without being seen. I cursed myself for having turned on Tom Joyner's morning show on the radio, because all I could catch of Eric's telephone conversation was a few words here and there between that funky Brothers Johnson baseline on "Strawberry Letter 23."

I'm not prone to eavesdropping. It's not something I like to do. Normally I wouldn't care one way or another what Eric was up to. But this Negro came all the way down the hall to the dining room to get his cellular when a perfectly good phone was sitting on the night table beside my bed. That's what made me curious. I'm glad I was too.

'Cause what Eric's ass was proposing to whoever "Sweet Thing" was on the other end of the phone, sho 'nuff set my teeth on edge.

I couldn't believe this boy would even think about breaking one of my commandments, knowing what the consequences were. I looked down at the lacy peach nightgown I was wearing. I'd run up to Vicki's Secret earlier to get it. Paid a pretty penny for it too, just so this fool would get a thrill that he couldn't get at home. I felt so stupid. It's bad enough that I don't trust men as it is, but sometimes even when I'm straight up with them, that shit backfires too.

When it seemed like Eric was about to end his little conversation, I stepped back away from the door. I picked up the small wooden coffee tray with two large hand-painted mugs on it. I had deposited the tray on the floor when I tiptoed up the hallway. I was so mad I had to relax, relate, release four times just so I could calm down. I decided not to get ethnic with him just yet. Let him play out his little game of hangman.

I walked into the bedroom just as Eric clicked off his cell phone and directed his long brown legs from beneath the beige paisley comforter and to the floor. He sat up on the side of my bed wearing nothing but a smile and scratching his sides. Fine bastard.

"Mmmmmm. Thank you baby," he said. His fingers closed around the handle of one of the mugs. He blew into the mug and sipped at the strong, ebony coffee carefully while his sleepy brown eyes followed me. I set the tray down on the dresser and walked over to the window.

I know Eric gets pleasure looking at me. I'm easy enough on the eyes. At least I like to think so. I'm what my Mama used to call "mo-lasses" brown. My eyes are brown too and my hair is in a short bob that I'm trying to grow out. I hate my lips because I think they're too big, but men seem to love them. I think my best features are my hands and my legs, though. I have these long "piano" fingers and well-shaped hairless legs I inherited from my mother. I'm about average height and kind of willowy, but thank God when I turned twenty, I finally grew myself a black woman ass.

I could still feel Eric watching me. I'm beginning to think he's in love with me. Those ugly tell-tale signs are starting to show. All of a sudden he's been wanting to see me every day. He's canceled quite a few meetings just to be with me. He buys me gifts up the ass, and when we're screwing and it's getting real good, you know, when the brother is hitting that spot and I feel like I just want to slap somebody's mama, he tells me to open my eyes and he looks at me like he's begging me to let him see into my soul. And sometimes he asks me these probing questions about myself and about my life that make me feel like he's a private eye or something. I just tell him, "Baby, it's fine for us to get up close, but let's not try to get personal." That's not happening over here.

I opened the jade miniblinds to slits, and peeked out to see what the weather was like. It had snowed hard half the night, covering everything with sheets of white, including the dingy mounds of glistening snow and ice from a storm the week before.

Overnight, the plows had run through the main strip that I live on twice, making parallel wet gray paths in either direction. Mini mountains of snow were piled up so high on either side of the road that they blocked driveways and cars parked against curbs in front of the houses. It had begun to sleet now, and when I felt a hot breath of heat shoot evenly out of the vent near my bare feet, I was so glad to be warm and inside on such a treacherous day.

Eric took a few more sips of coffee, then set the mug down on its saucer next to the clock. He turned the radio down once the reporter finished the weather report and moved onto traffic. I moved away from the window and sat in the mauve leather armchair opposite the bed. Dipping a spoonful of creamer into my coffee mug, I stirred gingerly, waiting for Eric's first move. I didn't have to wait long.

"Babe," he said, "I know I said I would stay the weekend, but I've got to go."

I didn't even flinch. If Eric had seen my eyes, he would have known I was pissed. But my face was half hidden in the bowl-wide mouth of my mug. When I lowered my cup, my eyes followed.

"Oh?" I said. I calmly stirred more cream into my cup.

"Yeah, babe," he said, pushing his weight into his legs as he got to his feet. "I completely forgot I told a friend of mine I would show him some houses this morning. He's moving down here from Jersey in a month. I promised him last week that I'd dig up whatever the M.S.L. has in his price range and take him out today. I had forgotten all about it." It was a bad lie and it made me want to throw up. I hate a liar. Why did I ever stop taking Karate? I could have jumped up off my chair and Bruce Lee'd his ass.

Instead I opened my bottom dresser drawer and pulled out a pair of pink Deerfoam socks to put on. I needed something to do while I spoke.

"Why are you really leaving so soon, Eric?" I said, smoothing the socks on my ankles. My voice was as hard as the ice falling from the sky outside.

"I just told you, babe. Ralph's a friend of mine from way back. I forgot I promised to show him a few houses around town. I'm doing this as a favor."

He left the room before I could say anything else. That was alright though. When he came back, if he didn't tell me the truth, he was going to find himself cut from my life like a head full of hair.

A minute later, I heard the gush of the shower spray behind the closed bathroom door. I moved over to the bed and put his half-empty coffee mug back on the tray, then began stripping the brass king bed of its comforter and white silk sheets.

My bedroom is small, but it seems smaller because of the tasteful clutter I've carefully sprinkled throughout. I have this compulsive thing for filling empty space. Every inch of my room is filled: a high square bed, pine double dresser, matching chest of drawers, a night table and a short nutbrown bookcase lined with my hardbacks and cooking magazines.

The stucco ceiling and walls are blinding white, but the wall above my bed is mirrored with beveled strips that can't possibly do the job of providing imagined spaciousness because the room is too full. I went through this serious pottery-making phase after I saw *Ghost,* so now I have ceramic pots everywhere, with ferns and spider plants on the dresser and hanging from ceiling hooks. I have a few cactuses, and geraniums arranged in large floor pots, and Mother-in-law tongues trailing lush green leaves across the top of the bookcase and my night table.

I heard the shower water stop. I gathered the bed linen and fit it into the wicker hamper beside my CD player at the foot of the bed. The bathroom door opened, and Eric soon emerged through the bedroom door with a long bath towel sarong-wrapped around his hips. Lord knows how I love to appreciate a fine man, and this lying wonder definitely fit the bill. Eric's mother is a Sioux Indian, so his facial features are fine-boned and distinct. He's very chocolate, and he has a body that's built to accept all my sins.

His muscular arms were glistening with water. So was the soft triangle of dark hair on his chest that trickled into a thin trail down his flat stomach. I waited while he used a second towel to dry his hair and face, then he reached for his leather shaving kit and found his Speedstick beneath a clean pair of socks and BVDs.

"Are you going to tell me the truth, Eric, or what?" I said finally.

He turned away from me and sat down on the bed, fitting his legs into dark blue slacks. I wasn't about to be ignored. I went over and stood in front of him with my arms folded across my chest, gazing down at him like a soldier.

"Truth about what, Genie?," he said like he was tired.

I sucked my teeth and turned away from him with a quick wave of my hand and said, "Eric, come on. You know as well as I do that nobody is interested in looking at houses in all this snow. Who in their right mind wouldn't want to stay cozied up inside somewhere? Plus it's sleeting out there right now, so stop tripping and tell me what this is really all about."

I was trying to be nice. If Eric admitted the truth, I would straighten him out but still let him come over for dinner next week.

Instead he chose to stay on the same flow. I watched him button his crisp white shirt and attach his gold cuff links, then he shrugged into his blazer and buckled his belt.

"Genie, nothing is up, baby. Why do you always think a brother is up to something?"

Now what kind of question was that? I rolled my eyes toward the ceiling impatiently. I couldn't believe he was standing here keeping a blatant lie going like this, knowing what our arrangement was.

"Listen," I said, "every man I've ever known is either up to something, soon to be up to something or has just been up to something. So what's going on with you, Eric?"

He checked his appearance in the mirror and smoothed his mustache then turned again and had the nerve to grip my shoulders, wearing his best sales pitch grin.

"Aw, come on, baby. I don't know why you believe I would skip out on a passionate weekend with you without a good reason. I really am on my way to the office and I really am going out to show Ralph some houses this afternoon. No kidding."

I nudged his hands off me. I could feel my face growing warm. For a moment, I thought I saw my father staring down at me instead of Eric, and all of a sudden I was so mad at myself I wanted to spit. How could I have ever allowed Eric into my bed? If he had only told me that he'd found a new diversion because he wanted to stop himself from falling head over heels for me, it wouldn't have been a big deal. I'm a big girl. I know the rules. But that's just it. Eric knew the rules too, but here he was breaking the one rule most sacred to me. Brutal honesty.

"What was the phone call, Eric?"

He straightened his collar and pulled his tie into a deeper knot. He pulled his coat off the hanger and draped it across his arm.

"I already told you that Ralph—"

"Okay. So you mean to tell me," I said, folding my arms across my chest again, "that when I was in the hall and I heard you whisper, 'I'm on my way as soon as I can, sweet thing,' that you were talking to Ralph?"

Eric looked surprised. Then he looked kind of scared. Yeah, dickhead, I thought, how you like me now?

"See baby," he began shakily, "that ain't even right. Naw. That ain't right. See, I was talking to my daughter. You know, I always—"

I put my open palm up to his face.

"Save it. I distinctly heard you call sweet thing by the name Beverly, and I dare you to deny it, you lying son of a bitch."

Eric's eyes got bigger and a vein in his neck seemed to grow and pulsate. He changed his strategy.

"What were you doing eavesdropping on my conversation? What kind of shit are you trying to pull here, Genie?"

I almost laughed. His voice had risen at least an octave or two. I knew it was time to set him straight.

"Look Eric, I am not your wife. I thought you knew that it wasn't necessary for you to feel you have to lie to me. You and I were cool just as long as you understood that you cannot play with me the same way you play with my pussy."

I watched Eric's face change again as he stood staring at me for a moment, looking like he was trying to find the right words. Then he shook his head like he couldn't believe what I'd just said. He was definitely shocked.

"I swear to God, woman, you are one cold-blooded chick. You know, you should have been a damn man."

"If I were a man, we wouldn't have been able to have the fun we had last night, now would we?"

He set down his coat.

"I could stay, you know. Matter of fact, I think I should stay. I mean, we did plan this and all. Sometimes I can be a real jerk. I'm sorry, baby."

He leaned into my face and kissed me on the lips real slow and sensual, which was a surprise because he never came near me before I brushed and gargled. I almost felt sorry that I had to quell a sudden feeling of revulsion that welled up in my throat. I knew then that I could never allow him to touch me again.

"No, Eric," I said when the kiss ended, "you go on ahead. You have an appointment to keep. Enjoy it."

"Genie, I really think I should stay. Lemme make it up to you, sweetheart."

"Bye, Eric," I said.

He looked at me real hard for a second then said, "Alright, baby, I'll call you later."

Over my dead body, I thought. He picked up his coat to leave but I stopped him at the bedroom door to clarify for him that he was history.

"I have a better idea," I told him. "Why don't we both forget we ever met."

He cleared his throat. He looked hurt as hell. He reminded me of a damn hush puppy.

"Don't you think you're tripping over this, Genie? I said I was sorry. I told you I want to stay."

"No, Eric. *You* broke the rule, not *me*."

"Come on, Genie. We have a good thing going. Don't spoil it, baby."

"Goodbye, Eric. Go."

"Come on, baby. You're being irrational over this. Don't be so mean." He was beginning to sound like a true punk. I mean, the brother looked like he was about to get down on one knee and do a Keith Sweat imitation. I couldn't take it another minute.

"Look, now," I said, "what part of the word *go* didn't you understand?"

Eric hung his head and said, "Aw, come on, Genie," trying to put his arms around me. I pushed him away with so much force that he almost lost his balance and crashed into the doorframe. He recovered quickly. He didn't say anything. He just stared at me with hurt and anger in his eyes, rubbing his shoulder. Then he turned and walked down the hall, muttering under his breath.

To be honest, part of me was going to miss Eric. It's funny how easy it is to get used to a person and a routine in a short time. I met Eric six months ago at a surprise birthday party for Evelyn, one of my girl-friends. I remember I was standing by the punchbowl minding my own business that night, adding Sambuca to my cup from a silver flask I sometimes carry in my purse, when over walks Mr. Thing, gabardine suit and all, asking me for my name.

I had noticed Eric earlier in the evening and had been told that he was one of Evelyn's coworkers at Re/Max. I hadn't paid him much attention after my corner conversation about him with my best girl-friend, Paulette. I had just gotten my period that afternoon and was feeling a little cranky.

But hey. He approached me and I was looking alright in my black wool pantsuit, so I decided to go for it. When Eric told me he was married and said he hoped I didn't have a problem with that, I thought to myself, Bingo! You've hit the jackpot again, Genie. Little did I know then how big that jackpot would be.

Eric is not only the finest brown brother I have ever seen, he's also the best sex I've ever had. The man can go all night. He even looks like he was made for the bedroom, with his sleepy brown eyes and those soft rumpled waves in his hair.

Eric makes love as if it is an art. He always made me feel like I was a canvas and his hands and mouth were painting these abstract pleasures into my body. Before Eric, I always thought that sex was supposed to be ugly. You know, sweaty people groaning, bodies humping, hands and fingers groping with a lot of sucking and licking that sounds more like feeding time at a pig farm than two people fulfilling a desire for each other. Good sex, but ugly nonetheless.

With Eric, sex always had to be a classy event. He refused to even begin lovemaking if it looked like all we might have time for was a quickie. Eric only performed when the mood and the ambience were completely in sync. Lights down low, soft music, a good bottle of wine, me, all perfumed and dressed in something sexy.

He'd spend an hour on foreplay alone (I timed him twice). Thirty minutes of that just kissing. Not just on the mouth. We kissed each other's entire faces—foreheads, eyelids, cheeks, chins, noses. He would even kiss my hair. The first time he did this, I admit that I thought he was insane. I kept trying to take his hands and place them on my breasts, but he was adamant about teaching me how to make love his way.

"Please Genie, a woman needs complete adoration during lovemaking," he said. "I have to pay attention to every inch of you so that not one area of your body will feel that it hasn't been loved. Let me adore you, baby."

And he did. He adored my ass on the dining room table, on the hood of his Lexus parked in my garage, on the kitchen floor and in the Jacuzzi in his secret little condo in Alexandria. I swear the man is talented. But all of that is past tense right about now, since he was bold enough to think he could feed me a tired lie like that.

After I heard the front door close, I stood in my window watching that fine Negro who had taught me how to ride a man just the right way walk down my driveway. I know I'll have to find a replacement. But right now all I want is to listen to some Mariah Carey and a glass of Sambuca.

Phase 2

It's been a month since I kicked Eric out of my life, and now I'm so lonely I could die.

I was standing against the ironing board, smoothing out the wrinkles in a pair of stone washed jeans, mad because it was Saturday night and my phone hadn't rung. It could be a bill collector or one of those irritating telemarketers wanting to do some survey, for all I cared. Just being able to talk to somebody would help. Damn. Where is a Jehovah's Witness when you need one? Better yet, where'd all the men go? I swear, I must be jinxed or something. Maybe Eric put a whammy on me. 'Cause I have never known it to be this hard to find a replacement.

Of course, all the snow hasn't made it any easier. A desolate January gave way to this unforgiving February that dished out a first-week ice storm and a heavy snow storm right after that brought all of civilization to a halt. Barely nothing has moved outside. Everything has been buried in thigh-high snow, and the only wheels that are turning are on the snowplows and, of course, the humvees.

I hear either a snowplow or humvee blasting up the road every once in a while, and I keep wishing that I could flag one of them down and pay the driver to take me with them. Especially since I have cabin fever so bad.

I've spent the past two weeks eating and reading and watching soap operas and stuff. Since it's Black History Month, I caught two good movies about Martin Luther King, Jr., and Ossie Davis and Ruby Dee's African-American network showed *Cabin in the Sky* and *Carmen Jones*.

My time away from the television has been spent doing housework mostly. When I got bored enough to scream, I started mixing and matching recipes to see if I could come up with new dishes. At first it was fun to have so much time for myself. Now, it's just a burden.

I want me some male company so bad I can taste it. I want a pair of strong arms wrapped around me tight, and a pair of strong hands filled to overflowing with my hips. I miss the smell of a man, you know— that mixture of woods, muscle and sharp, sweet soap. Lately I've lain awake at night in my gigantic bed with my body pillow pressed against me, just so I can pretend someone is lying next to me. I swear, this is just too much. Now I know how Jack Nicholson felt in *The Shining*—and he even had his wife and son with him!

My thoughts had wandered so far away from what I was doing that I burned my thumb on the damn iron. I jumped back, cursed and sucked my thumb to ease the burn. I shut off the stupid iron, deciding to leave it for later and went into the kitchen to put some Country Crock on my poor thumb, but that shit didn't hardly help. My thumb still felt stunned. Like me.

What I really needed was a drink. That would do the trick. I reached into the bottom cabinet of the china closet in the dining room and found an almost empty bottle of Sambuca. I poured out a small glass of it and downed it in one gulp. That was a mistake. The burning sensation in my throat made me gag, and I had to race back to the kitchen for a bottle of Evian. Sipping, I sat at the kitchen table to flip through my phone book again to see if I had missed anyone I could call. I hadn't. There were more names crossed out in my book than not, and the ones that weren't crossed out were mostly men who do things for me.

Samuel Cox, the pudgy little white guy that mows the lawn, trims the shrubs, and cleans the gutters when they get full of dead leaves. Jeffrey Lucas, my maintenance guy. He replaces fuses, cleans the furnace, and changes washers on the faucets and stuff. Then there is Michael Wiggins, the floor man. He's the one who installed the rose pile carpeting for me after I lived through a month of floor-dust hell when I first moved in.

Shit. I wasn't used to having time on my hands like this. I had already cleaned the house from top to bottom, done the laundry, and alphabetized everything in the pantry. I read all of my good books a second time, and it was getting dark, so I couldn't go back out to try to build the snowman in the front yard for the three kids next door to dress up like I'd promised I would do yesterday. I didn't feel like cooking, not nare 'nother thing either. Then I remembered that even if I wanted to cook, there was no one but me to enjoy it.

Something inside me trembled. My throat was tightening and I felt so cold that there were goose bumps on my arms. I felt like just frigging giving up. I laid my head in the crook of my arm on the table and did something I haven't done in a long while. I cried my heart out.

I remembered how terrible the quiet was when my sisters, Marilyn and Tess, went away to college. Marilyn's six years older than me; Tess, five. I was almost twelve when they left home. I was small for my age, with braces and long black pigtails. There were pencil-point spots of acne across the bridge of my nose that made me self-conscious, and my slack hips felt like nothing but bone when I put my hands there to dish out attitude.

My sisters seemed so graceful and diva-esque to me then. Marilyn with her slender neck and wicked sculptured cheekbones. Even Tess, plump as she was, had a clear, buttery complexion, black doe eyes, and a smooth pair of legs that were made to be seen. They both had lots of boyfriends hanging around the house and ringing the phone off the hook for dates.

Their weird girlfriends with their arched eyebrows and double pierced ears were always sitting up in their bedroom polishing their toenails, watching music videos, and talking about boys. The record player was always spinning the S.O.S. Band, Angie Bofill, Kashif, Phyllis Hyman, the Gap Band.

There was always so much noise in the house that I didn't worry too much about the silent war between my parents. I would sit back quietly in a corner of my sisters' room when they got in from school and watch them practice how they would dance at some party, finger popping and doing the prep and the happy feet or snaking around the room.

Even after Mama moved down into the basement bedroom, Marilyn and Tess made up for the quiet with all of their racket. When Marilyn graduated from high school, she took a receptionist job in a law office, just so she could wait for Tess to graduate so they could start college together. I would listen to their plans until late into the night.

The day they left was the saddest day of my life. I refused to go out to Dulles and watch them get on the plane headed for California. I couldn't watch them leave me like that. Just before they left, I sat up on the yellow velvet piano bench with my ankles crossed, crying and biting what was left of my fingernails. Marilyn sat down beside me and put her arm around my shoulder. Tess couldn't fit, so she stood in front of me, pulling my hand away from my mouth and holding it tight. I knew things would never be the same again.

I remember walking around that solemn house after everybody left for the airport. But what was worse was when Mama and Edward got back from the airport, 'cause Edward retired to his bedroom with the newspaper and Mama . . . well, Mama disappeared into her dungeon with her shoulders hunched, clutching that blue flowered housecoat she hardly took off. My life was a complete nightmare after that until I met Paulette in seventh grade. You see, I believe that God always sends you somebody. I don't care who it is—a pet, a friend, a child. There's always someone to turn to just when you need them. Paulette is my someone.

My sobs turned to sighs and the tightness left my throat. I pushed my chair away from the table, reached for the cordless phone sitting on the breakfast bar and went into the living room to call Paulette. She answered on the first ring.

"Hello, Beardsley residence."

"Hey girlfriend," I said, trying to sound light and happy.

"Genie, girl, what is up with you, honey?"

"Nothing much, girl."

"Well, chile, what man has got you sounding like all your people dead? And don't say it ain't a man, 'cause I know that ain't your PMS voice."

I laughed a little too loudly. The heifer knew me all too well.

"Mmmhmm," Paulette said knowingly, "whenever you're laughing all nervous, then something is wrong. Especially since you've been avoiding me forever. I've been trying to reach you, bored as I've been stuck up in this house with Robert. The man is on my last nerve, girl. So what's been going on with you?"

I felt so bad I couldn't even speak. I just burst into tears.

"What am I going to do?" That was all I could say. I pushed the coffee table aside and lay on the floor with my feet propped up on the sofa.

"What happened, sweetie?"

I tried to explain to Paulette how I felt, but I couldn't. How could I admit that I'm scared when I'm supposed to have everything under control? How could Paulette even understand what being alone is like when she has her job and her husband and baby to fill up her time? All she ever talks about is wanting to have time to herself.

"Look," Paulette said finally, "I'm on my way over. Be comprehendible when I get there."

I switched off the phone without saying goodbye and lay on the floor, wiping my eyes. I looked over at my kissing fish, Porgy and Bess, gliding together around the rigid little plastic diver in their fishtank, puckering their mouths at each other. My fish had it better than me. I heard a noise and looked quickly around the room, but realized that the sounds came from the tall mahogany grandfather clock dividing the living and dining rooms. It was times like this that I regretted having so much space. It's hard to find enough things to fill up all the vacant corners. If I had settled for a one-bedroom condo like I had originally planned, it would have been easy. Paulette was the one who convinced me that buying a house was a better investment.

My house is a two-level brick. The flagstone porch is two steps high, with massive ceramic pots of red geraniums set like bookends against the wrought iron stair rails that I painted blue to match the shutters framing the windows. Inside are two bedrooms, a living and dining area, an eat-in kitchen and a basement with a laundry room. I have a nice deck out back that overlooks my vegetable garden, and a grapevine that snakes around and through the silver fence separating my yard from my neighbor's.

The living room is my favorite room in the house besides my bedroom. It makes me feel safe. It's small like my bedroom so it was easy to fill up. The only things I don't like about it are the nine-foot ceilings and the way the room flows into the dining room.

I have an overstuffed, mauve leather sofa, chair and ottoman set. On the antique cherrywood coffee table are family pictures in gold and silver frames. Above the brick fireplace is a painting of Mama, the way she looked before she got sick—smiling and laughing out of her sweet brown eyes, a young woman untouched by grief.

I glanced at my watch, wondering what was taking Paulette so long. Frustrated, I sat up on the sofa and grabbed a deck of playing cards off the coffee table. I shuffled them and started snapping the cards out onto the table so hard that I bent the edges of some. I was so pissed with myself. Why in the world had I cut back all the other brothers once I had gotten comfortable with Eric? Why? Shoot. I knew why. It was because I'm basically a monogamist. I don't need more than one good lover at a time. Eric was free with his money. He knew how to please me. We enjoyed each other's company. There was no fore-seeable reason to be with any other men. Until now.

Here I was, playing solitaire on a freaking Saturday night with nothing to look forward to but finishing off the rest of my Sambuca. What's worse, I was so horny I wanted to die. Matter of fact, I was so horny that the short, overweight married deacon from church who had been worrying me for a date, was starting to seem tempting. I remem-bered that I still had the crumpled tithe envelope he wrote his home office phone number on, somewhere down in my black patent leather church purse. I wondered if I should find it and call him. Although he isn't much to look at, I was sure he had something to work with below that successful round belly of his.

The doorbell rang. I thanked God for Paulette's timing. Another minute and I would have been on my knees. Not praying, but sitting in front of the closet digging in my purse for that phone number. I jumped to my feet and made for the door.

"Wooo. That snow is a bear, girl," she said. She crossed the thresh-old with a brown paper bag under one arm and slammed the door.

"What took you so long, Paulette?" I asked my best friend, who only lives a few blocks away. I winced because I sounded like a sad lit-tle girl.

Paulette gave me a once-over and drew me into a mothering hug. "Poor boo," she said.

"Take off those boots. You're gonna track up my carpet like that."

"I see now that you ain't feeling *that* bad, huh?"

I would never feel so bad that I wanted her to mess up my three-thousand-dollar carpet. Paulette unzipped her wet boots and left them sitting on the coarse woven "Welcome" rug in front of the door. She took off her red woolen hat and gloves, and her earmuffs. Her long auburn hair, achieved through Dark & Lovely was pulled away from her face into a secure Barbie doll ponytail. She wore jeans, a heavy but-ton-down sweater under her thick brown leather bomber jacket, and beneath the sweater, her husband's baggy Morgan sweatshirt that was at least three sizes too big.

"What took you so long?" I repeated.

"Genie, you know that snow is hip high out there," she said, shiver-ing and bustling toward the kitchen.

"It was all I could do to stay upright. Man, G, let me borrow some-thing to put on. I feel soaked through."

She reached into an overhead cabinet and pulled down two bowls, then got spoons out of the drawer.

"What's in the bag?"

"Something I pulled out of my freezer to cure what ails you," she answered, then scooped Heavenly Hash ice cream into the bowls and set them on the kitchen table.

"Only you would bring me ice cream in the dead of winter. And look at you, shivering."

"Well it is our favorite ice cream and I wouldn't be shivering if you would get me something to put on like I asked for in the first place. Hell, Heavenly Hash always makes me feel better after a fight with Robert."

I just shook my head and said, "I'll be right back."

I dug out some jeans, some thermal leggings and a gray thermal shirt and put them on the bed.

"Here you go, Paulette," I yelled down the hall.

"Okay. Be right there."

We passed each other in the hallway. When Paulette returned a few minutes later, I pulled the large oak table away from the wall and freed the other chair so that she would have a place to sit.

"So what's going on, Genie?" Paulette asked, spooning up some ice cream.

On cue, tears sprang to my eyes and I had to look away.

"I don't know, girl. I just feel all alone, that's all."

Paulette's delicate hand covered mine.

"What do you mean all alone, sweetie? You've got me."

A tear skated down my cheek and fell into my ice cream.

"I'm talking about my love life, Paulette."

"What about it? To hear you tell it, love ain't a part of your life."

I sighed and looked away again. She just didn't get it.

"I got rid of Eric."

Paulette shrugged.

"So?"

I looked at her sharply and almost knocked over my bowl.

"What do you mean, So? My life is falling apart and all you can say is, So?"

"Wait. Hold on. Are you trying to tell me that Eric meant something to you? Because you never gave me that impression."

I shook my head like a child and chewed a chocolate chip.

"No. But I did get kind of comfortable. I thought we had the perfect little arrangement until he lied to me. He was supposed to spend a weekend with me, but something better must have come along, 'cause I overheard him on the phone sweet talking some chick. Then he jumped up and tried to act like he had to go see a client. I don't know why he tried to play it like that. Girl, I didn't have any choice but to give him the boot. Now I don't have anybody, Paulette—and plus, the dream came back."

My fingers wove a pattern through my hair. I wanted to pour myself another drink, but thought better of it, since the bottle was near empty. If I had the dream again tonight, I was gonna need those last few drops later on.

"Girl, I even called up a few dudes I know I don't want to be bothered with, but they're tripping too. I even tried calling Nick."

"That jerk? Tell me you didn't."

"I wish I could."

"Girl, you know you need to stay away from him if anything. What did that fool say?"

"He didn't have time to talk. Said I should page him later. Girl, I get so sick of these bastards and their pagers. What ever happened to them answering a telephone?"

"They're too busy trying to be player player to do that. That would just inconvenience their lie. Then they wouldn't be able to tell you they didn't get your page or they left it at home or turned it off. But Genie, this is exactly what I mean, girl. You are so much better than this. You have so much more to offer a man than laughter and loving, and I wish you could see what I see. You're beautiful, you're talented, intelligent. You own your own home. Got money in the bank. Got your own business. You have goals in life. Do you know how many men, how many single men, would love to have a woman like you?

"And here you are wasting your time on men who belong to someone else. It ain't worth it, girl. It just ain't worth it, 'cause you know good and well if these married men are doing it with you, then they damn sure will do it with someone else just as easily."

I was silent. I'd never be able to make Paulette understand. Paulette had a perfect childhood. Her mother is the black Donna Reed and her father is an Italian Ward Cleaver. Last year they retired and relocated to a sprawling home in North Carolina on two acres. Paulette's an only child and never even got one whipping growing up. She'll never understand what I've been through.

I picked a strand of hair out of my ice cream, and reached for a hairclip on top of the microwave. I twisted my hair up and away from my face and clamped it tight.

"What you need to do," Paulette was saying in her usual authoritative tone, "is see a psychiatrist, girl. You have some major issues that you've never worked through."

I thought about it a moment, but dismissed the idea.

"Paulette, you know how I feel about that mumbo jumbo. I don't want anybody getting into my head. I'm just going through a bad time right now. Wasn't for all this damn snow, I'd be in the swing of things. I swear, girl. Business is so slow because of this horrible weather. Not that I've minded, because you know how bored I'm getting with catering, but I have to get out and about again. What I need to do is find a quick replacement for Eric and start looking for a full-time job to keep me busy."

"Okay. Have it your way. No head doctor. But you know, they could probably help you figure out where those dreams are coming from, if nothing else."

"No, Paulette. That shrink stuff is the kind of thing white people get into."

"Genie, that's not true. Robert's mama goes to one, and she swears by her doctor. There's no use in you labeling getting professional help as a white thing just because you don't want to do it. I'ma leave that issue alone 'cause I respect your opinion on the matter. But at least let me fix you up with one of Robert's single—"

"No way, Paulette. Uh, uh. Not interested."

"Why not, G?" she asked softly.

"You already know the answer to that."

"Hold up. You call me 'cause you don't have a man to be with and I'm sitting here offering to fix you up with a handsome man with a car and a job and you wanna turn me down? You know, sometimes I think your brain is on empty."

"I don't care. I'm not interested in a relationship and you know it."

"Genie it's one stinking date. I swear your ego is bigger than anything I ever saw. Why do you always think every single man out there is interested in a relationship with you?"

"I don't, but knowing a man is free to think about getting serious with me makes me uncomfortable. Sometimes I wonder if the single guys I've dated wanted to get all serious with me just because they knew that's not what I wanted. I know that's what Gregory's problem was."

"Okay, Gregory was a case. A nut case. But girl, you need to realize that there are good men out there, and one of them could be yours if you would stop looking in the wrong category. I can hook you up on a date, and instead of sitting in this lonely house you can be out having a good time."

That sounded too good. I leaned back in my chair and forgot all about how after Gregory had stalked me, I'd had to get Michael the carpet guy to teach him a lesson. I had sworn off single men after that. But I was too on edge to think about that vow right now. I needed to be touched badly. Just thinking about going on a date with someone made my body tingle. I thought about the last night I'd spent with Eric and how good it was. You better believe that memory was just enough to make me vulnerable.

"Okay," I said, knowing I would regret it later, "I'll let you set me up this once. But let it be known that this is a one-time affair, Paulette. You've got to promise me that if it turns out to be a disaster, you will never bring this subject up again. Okay?"

"Okay. But I'm sure you'll like him."

"You already have someone in mind?"

"Mmmhmm. James Caldwell. A good friend of Robert's."

It occurred to me that since Paulette's husband Robert was a high school teacher, his friends would most likely be in the same profession and have the same lackluster personality. Not that Robert was boring, but boyfriend did have some nerdy characteristics.

"Oh God. He isn't one of those schoolteacher types is he, Paulette? You know some of Robert's friends are boring as hell. You've even said so."

"Jimmy is not boring at all. He's a musician."

"A musician? You wanna set me up with a broke brother?"

"He's not broke. He's very popular at a lot of local clubs. He plays Blues Alley all the time."

"Blues Alley? Really?"

My eyes lit with instant interest and Paulette grinned triumphantly, knowing how much I adore jazz and blues.

"Yep. He's really good too. Me and Robert saw him at the Vegas Lounge last year. He's something else."

"Vegas Lounge. Wow."

"See. I knew you'd be impressed," she said.

"Where have you been hiding him? I've never heard you talk about him. What's he play?"

"Sax. And girl you should hear him. Branford ain't got nothing on this brother. You haven't met him before 'cause he hasn't been around much. He's newly divorced, which means he almost fits your type."

"Shut up, girl," I said, finishing my ice cream, "only other thing I wanna know is if he's fine."

"Honey, with a capital F. He's as tall as Robert, has a nice fade, pretty brown eyes and that sexy kinda mouth on a man that makes a woman pray he's the type to go downtown, if you know what I mean."

She gave me a sidelong glance.

"Ooh, Paulette. If Robert heard you talking like that he'd be too shocked."

Paulette sucked her teeth and tossed her hair like she always does when she could care less.

"Chile, please. Just 'cause I'm married doesn't mean I've lost my sight and sense. I can truly say that if Robert wasn't in the picture, James Caldwell would definitely be on my 'get' list. Are you feeling any better?"

I smiled, suddenly realizing that I did feel better. The hell with Eric. Life is too short for tears when there are dozens of men waiting to be discovered.

"I do feel better. Thanks. I knew I kept you around for some reason."

"Girl, please," Paulette said, tossing her hair again. She wiggled her toes. "You want me to stay here tonight?" she asked.

"Would you? I mean if Robert doesn't mind."

"Girl, Robert went round the corner to Melvin's house to see some Tyson fight on pay-per-view. He probably won't make it home till after midnight, and then he'll wanna make love, which I'm not in the mood for. And anyway, you know his mama has Telaysia for the next few weeks, so I'm a free woman. I'll just leave him a message on the machine."

As usual I felt a small pang of jealousy when Paulette mentioned her daughter, Telaysia. Telaysia was two now and cute as a button. And so smart. When she was born and I first saw her tiny little face through the nursery window, I thought about the baby I'd willingly aborted at nineteen. When I was pregnant I didn't make a connection between the growth in my belly that sent me to the bathroom every morning and the real live babies I see all the time. But when I saw Telaysia . . . If man could only figure out how to go back in time and change the past . . . I wonder what my baby would have looked like, felt like in my arms. I damn sure wouldn't be lonely like this.

"*Roseanne* is coming on in a little while," I said, " so why don't you go make your call and I'll pop a couple of Budget Gourmets in the micro."

"What kind?"

"Chicken Marsala. I think I might have some Sutter Home in the fridge, if you want a glass."

"Sounds like a plan," Paulette said and went into the living room to make her call.

I put the remaining ice cream in the freezer, removed the frozen entrees and put them in the microwave to be zapped. I pulled out two wineglasses and filled them almost to their rims.

"Girl," Paulette exclaimed as she walked into the kitchen, "for you to be a caterer, you sure put that microwave to good use pretty often."

"I know you ain't talking. You are the only woman I know that makes boil-in-a-bag turkey cutlets for Thanksgiving dinner, and if it wasn't for my famous homemade sweet potato pies, Mrs. Beardsley's Christmas pie would be Mrs. Smith's."

There was ice cream on the counter, so I pulled the 409 out of the sink cabinet and started cleaning. When the microwave beeped, I turned the dinners at different angles and reset the timer.

"Okay, fine, but Robert knew I couldn't cook when he married me. I have gotten better though. I can at least make toast now without burning it. But girl," she said, rolling her eyes toward the ceiling for effect, "did I tell you the latest about Sheila?"

Sheila was a tiny brown mouse of a woman who worked with Paulette at the Little Tots Day Care Center.

"No, girl, but do tell."

The microwave beeped again and I retrieved the dinners. The aroma made my mouth water.

"Chile, she had to call the police on Marcus again."

"Again? What happened this time?"

Paulette moved between a cabinet drawer and the kitchen table, placing silverware on the peach linen napkins on the table.

"If you can believe it, he beat her up for wearing makeup to the store this time."

"Makeup to the—that scene is getting overly ridiculous. Sheila needs some help. 'Cause if that was me," I said, placing the Marsala and wine on the table, "and that bastard dared draw back at me, you know he'd be dead or crippled. That's one thing I don't play about."

We high-fived each other.

"Ain't that the truth, Ruth," Paulette answered and cut into her chicken.

"So did the cops arrest that fool?"

"Yeah. But she didn't want to press charges. She believes it won't happen again, and he came up to the school to pick her up yesterday. The sight of him made me sick."

"Mmm. That girl probably won't see her situation for what it is until it's too late."

"You're probably right. I told Robert if he ever thinks about doing something like that to me, me and my baby will be gone. Right after I pull a Lorena Bobbitt."

I chuckled and said, "I know that."

Paulette put up her wineglass for a toast and we clinked glasses. Then I clicked on the television with the remote and we laughed our way through the next half hour watching *Roseanne.*

In bed that night, I prayed that God would take care of Mama up there and me down here. "Please, God," I said, "have mercy on me." I hoped with all my heart that He heard me.

Phase 3

It was Wednesday, and a simple dinner party that I catered for twenty people at Glenarden's town hall turned out to be a major fiasco because the guest of honor arrived two hours late. By that time, the roast duck was rubbery and the chocolate mousse had turned into one big milkshake. I did so much running back and forth to the kitchen trying to salvage what had been a beautiful buffet that my feet were on fire. The hostess apologized at least fifty times and sent me limping home with a fat check in my purse. But even with the bonus, this fiasco just underscored all my feelings about catering. I was getting tired of it. As far as customers go, there was no continuity. One month I'd be so busy I could barely handle the jobs. Then, all of a sudden, I'd be twiddling my thumbs. It was the busy times, though, that were getting to me. Over the last several months, cooking has started to seem like a chore and not an enjoyment. The whole thing has gotten so boring that I barely cook for myself now. That's why I know it's high time for me to earn a living some other way. I put my car in the garage, and all I wanted to do was immerse my battered body in a tub filled with hot water and start reading my new Colleen McCullough.

When I got inside, I played back my messages on the answering machine. There were only two. Paulette called asking if I wanted to get my hair done on Saturday because she was going to call our joint hair-dresser, Arleeta, for an appointment for herself. The other caller was James Caldwell, wanting to know if I would have dinner with him at Jasper's on Friday.

I was still a little apprehensive about going on this blind date. What I felt like doing was backing out of my promise to Paulette and finding a man on my own. But the reality is that something is mal-functioning with my aura. The snow was almost gone and I still hadn't attracted any possible replacements. There was no other option but to make do with this James character—the one man that's rung my phone in what felt like ages.

Tiredly I deposited my purse and coat on the chair in my bedroom and popped a Harry Connick CD into the diskplayer. The music was soothing and Harry's sultry voice immediately put me into relax mode. I stepped out of my shoes and sat on the edge of the bed to massage my aching feet and checked the clock. It was after ten. My pantyhose were more than a little uncomfortable. I stood up and unbuttoned my skirt, letting it fall to the floor, then I peeled off my sheer black hose. That felt much better. I found my nail clipper hiding behind the telephone, and clipped a ragged toenail. Then I pulled out a bottle of Sally Hansen and a bag of cotton balls from my bottom drawer and started taking the faded strawberry polish off my toes.

Something wasn't right. The room still seemed too quiet. I reached for the remote and turned the music up a little more just as Harry started scatting like an auctioneer. I couldn't wait for the warm weather to come. As much as I hate the outbreak of raucous noise from the rowdy neighborhood kids who hold court on the corner after mid-night, it's better to hear them than to hear plain silence.

I put away my remover and picked up the soiled cotton balls, toss-ing them into the trash on my way to the bathroom. I placed the stop-per in the drain and turned on the water full blast and dashed in a few capfuls of Skin-So-Soft and a squirt of Ivory Liquid.

The telephone rang just as I slipped my hand beneath the nozzle to test the water, so I limped back into the bedroom to answer it.

"Hello?"

"Genie?"

"Tess?"

"Mmmhmm."

I sighed. I didn't feel like getting into a long, drawn-out conversa-tion with my sister.

"How are you, Tess?"

"Alright. You?"

"I'm fine. Hanging in. Talk to Marilyn?"

"Mmmhmm."

"When?"

"Yesterday."

"How's she doing?"

"Fine."

"And Keith?"

"He's fine. Bad as ever."

"That's my baby. I've got to call Marilyn and tell her to send me some more pictures of him. I know he's probably grown a foot since I last saw him."

"Mmmhmm. That's what she said."

"How's the weather down there? I heard on the news you guys got a lot of rain this week."

"Mmmhmm. Sure did."

"Well, I'm glad the snow's finally clearing up here."

I wondered whether my bath water had reached the rim of the tub yet.

"You still seeing Darryl?"

"Nope."

"Why not?"

"He's too fat."

Tess weighed over two hundred pounds. No diet known to man—be it Bahamian, Slimfast or Jenny Craig—had ever helped her lose weight, because of the endless supply of Twinkies beneath her bed. Tess has always had a weight problem. As a little girl, she always wanted the biggest portions of food. Tess hoarded snacks like I hoarded Barbies, and her dependency on food has grown worse over the years. Any small problem sends her on an eating binge. So I was very surprised to hear Tess call anyone too fat.

"Too fat? What do you mean?"

"He's too fat, Genie. I need me a skinny man."

I laughed, picturing my sister smothering a poor skinny man.

"What?" I managed to spit out. "Why would you want a skinny man?"

Tess sighed like she was about to lose patience with me.

"It's hard for two fat people to make love, Genie. Real hard."

"But Tess I thought you—Hold on!"

I almost tripped rushing into the bathroom to turn off the water. The suds were dripping down the side of the tub. I unplugged the stopper to let some of the water out, then rushed back to the telephone.

"Tess?"

"Mmhmm."

"Sorry. I was running my bath water and forgot about it."

"Oh."

"Anyway, back to Darryl. Girl, I thought you loved him."

"Not really."

There was something Tess was leaving out.

"Yes you did, Tess. Now come on, tell me the truth. What'd Darryl do?"

"Nothing, really."

"What really did he do then?"

"Nothing."

It was my turn to use Tess's favorite non-word.

"Mmmhmm."

"Really, Genie."

"Alright then. Well, where are you going to find this skinny man you're looking for?"

"I don't know yet."

I looked at the clock and rolled my eyes.

"Okay, Tess. Look, I'll try to call you next week. My bath is calling me."

"Alright. Bye. Take care of yourself, Genie."

"See you later."

I shed the rest of my clothes, pinned up my hair and brushed my teeth. Then I eased into the bathtub. The water was perfect. I relaxed for about half an hour, reading and listening to Harry Connick croon to me from the CD player. The weariness was fading from my body. The steam surrounded me like a curtain of fog, making my flesh tingle. I felt good and weak at the same time, and all of a sudden didn't feel like reading anymore. The words seemed like they were beginning to run together. When I reached up to set the book on the counter, my breast grazed the side of the tub and I groaned. My poor deprived nipples stood out like twin antennas. I tried my best not to think about it. Instead I tried to think about what kind of job I was going to look for now that I'd made the decision to do the catering part-time.

Aside from the fact that cooking professionally has started to bore me, the monetary issue is another reason that I've come to the conclusion to get a nine-to-five. Most months, because of overhead, the money I make isn't enough to do more than buy the groceries and pay the light bill. Thank God my house and car are both paid for. I don't want to spend more of my mother's money than necessary. I want to hold onto as much of the twelve thousand dollars worth of certificates of deposit that I have left. Mama's will specified that my sisters and I each receive four CDs. I took part of my inheritance from her life insurance money and bought the house and my car. Nobody in the family knew she'd even had any investments, let alone where the money had come from. That's one mystery I doubt we'll ever solve.

Lying there thinking in the tub, I didn't realize that I was massaging my breasts. When I did notice, I closed my eyes because it felt so good. I leaned my head back against the suds cloud, matting my hair. The black cherry candle I'd lit was giving off a rich, pungent aroma. Harry had sung his heart out and now Luther picked up where he left off, making his voice weave like magic thread in and around the music.

"Oh God," I said. I couldn't stop picturing myself beneath Eric. Above Eric. Eric behind me. He was such a dynamite lover. That familiar twinge in my stomach and the warm water lapping at my body every time I moved made me want to burst out of my skin. That's when I thought about the box on the top shelf of my closet and opened my eyes.

I hand-searched the water for the pearl pink bar of Caress and finding it near my ankle, closed my hand around it. It had softened like butter in the hot water. I lathered with it and loufahed briskly, hoping to scrub away my arousal, but that didn't work. All it did was intensify the sensitivity of my skin. I rinsed, pulled out the stopper and stepped quickly out of the tub, splattering water all over the floor and my book.

I couldn't fight the overwhelming feelings. I walked quickly toward the bedroom closet and drew out the brown, plainly wrapped small box. My heart was beating so fast I couldn't think straight. I carried the box over to the dresser and set it down gently. Then I reached over and switched off the CD player. This wasn't something that Luther should take part in. The box was sealed with heavy brown mailing tape, so I grabbed my purse and dug out my keys to slit the box open. It was cold in the room. I stood over the dresser, shivering and dripping wet, goose bumps popping out on my arms and legs, but I didn't care.

The content of the box was swathed in plastic bubble wrap. I was almost ashamed of myself but too horny to care. I withdrew the little joy toy and studied it like it was a foreign object that I couldn't figure out how to operate. Seven and a half inches of pure pleasure was how the ad had described it. It was made of shining black plastic, thick and inflexible. It reminded me of the handle of a hairbrush.

I bought it on a dare from Paulette four months ago, but I never felt a need to use it. Me, Paulette and Evelyn—acting all giggly and silly after five of the loaded daiquiris Evelyn's heavy hand had whipped up—checked out this *Playgirl* magazine that Evelyn showed us. When we got near the end where the ads were, Paulette leaned over the magazine with her index finger on the ad for a vibrator and said, "I bet you wouldn't order one of those." I said, "Girl, please. I get my share. I don't need that mess." Evelyn had gotten sick and rushed to the bathroom. Paulette jabbed the ad with her finger again and said in slur-language, "I ain't talking about using it, Genie. I mean, you ain't got the guts to call up right now and order you one. And if you do have 'em, I will personally give you," she reached into her purse and pulled out a crisp $100 bill, "this. You game?" I laughed and said, "Since you're dumb enough to give away your money, heifer, I'm smart enough to take it. Hand me the phone." And I tucked the money down the front of my blouse.

When the box came two weeks later, Paulette and I just stared at it, too embarrassed to open it and look inside. So I stuck it up on my closet shelf between a book about the Holocaust and my *Webster's* dictionary.

I removed two batteries from my dresser drawer, slipped them in through the bottom of the toy and turned the thing on to see what it sounded like. It started whirring like a mixer. I liked the way it massaged my hand. Nick had a foot fetish, and he used to rub kiwi massage oil on my feet and use a hand massager. It was so erotic when he did that. But this was a whole different story. This was inserting a foreign object into my pride and joy. What if it hurt? What if it got stuck? I pictured myself calling 911 and then riding in an ambulance, trying to explain to the EMTs what happened. Shoot. I was kind of scared. I looked at myself in the mirror.

"Okay, Genie. Go for it, girl. Nobody's here to see you do it. Hundreds of lonely women out there use these things every day. They even use them in those movies and nobody ever had one stuck."

I worked up enough nerve to put it on my thigh. It felt good there. I figured I should probably lie down, but just when I was about to, the telephone rang. I didn't realize I'd been holding my breath until I exhaled loudly. I set the vibrator on the dresser and dove onto the bed, catching the phone on its second ring.

"Hello?"

"Hello. Is this Genie?"

"Yes, it is. Who's calling?"

"Hi, Genie. This is James. Rob's friend."

He sounded sexy and he temporarily rescued me from simulated sex. Two points already.

I pulled the comforter up over my shoulders and snuggled into the warmth of my bed.

"Oh. Hi, James."

"I was calling to see if you got my message."

"Yes," I said, shifting my body more comfortably. "I had planned to give you a call tomorrow."

"Oh. You know, I must admit that I was somewhat anxious to talk to you. I've heard so many wonderful things about you from Paulette and I haven't met anyone in quite a while."

Hard up like me. That was three points.

"Well, James, I've heard a lot of great things about you, too. Paulette tells me you're a musician."

James thought that was funny. He chuckled awkwardly for at least ten seconds before answering.

"She told you that, huh?"

"Yes she did," I said suspiciously. "Was that untrue?"

"Oh, no, no. It's just that although music is my passion, I teach high school. I guess I'm both a teacher and a musician."

I gripped the receiver tighter wishing it was Paulette's skinny neck I was wringing.

"Wait a minute," I said. "Paulette told me you play professionally. She didn't mention anything about teaching. Matter of fact, I asked if you were a teacher. Even though she didn't say you weren't, she made it seem like you were simply a musician."

There went that laugh again. I wanted to tell him to shut up, but decided I should be nice.

"She didn't exactly lie. I play backup with a band called Shadows at a few clubs in the area. But it's not how I make my living. It's more for enjoyment than anything else."

"So you're a teacher."

I said it with such disappointment he got offended.

"What do you mean by that?"

"By what?"

"You sound as though you have something against teachers. My job is very fulfilling, Genie. Especially when I can get through to some of my tougher students. It makes me feel good to know that somebody's son or daughter was inspired by something I've said and will want to apply themselves. Don't get me wrong, I love my music, but making an impression on a young mind is more important to me."

I felt about as tall as an ant. Here this man was making a difference in children's lives every day, and I get upset because he's not sweet-talking crowds in smoke-filled rooms with his sax every night.

"I'm sorry, James. That wasn't fair of me. I agree that you have a very rewarding career."

"It's alright. 'Musician' does sound more exciting than 'school-teacher.' Hey, is something wrong with your phone?"

I glanced at it and shook it, thinking that there might be static in the line.

"No, I don't think so. Why?"

"You don't hear that strange noise? It sounds like the hair clippers they use at the barber shop or something."

I looked toward my dresser and my jaw dropped.

"Hold on!"

I jumped off the bed and grabbed the vibrator off the dresser and turned it off, then stood staring at the telephone for a full minute wondering if James somehow knew what I had just been up to. When I finally picked up the telephone, I cleared my throat.

"I'm back. It was something on TV. Some drag racing commercial. I turned it off."

I caught my embarrassed expression in the mirror and was glad James couldn't see me.

"Oh. Well, Paulette told me you weren't too hot for this blind date business, but I'd really like to meet you, Genie. So how 'bout us getting together this Friday?"

"Jasper's, right?"

"Yeah, so how about it?" he asked expectantly.

I looked over at the vibrator on the dresser and couldn't believe this was what I'd been reduced to.

"It's a date," I said.

"Great. Seven okay?"

I could hear the smile in his voice. It was nice that *somebody* wanted to take me out.

"Seven's fine. I'll meet you there."

"I'm looking forward to it. Have a good night's sleep."

"Same to you. Bye."

The hell with vibrators. I tossed it back in its box and put it behind the Holocaust book, where I wouldn't have to see it. It could never substitute for a man anyway. It didn't have warm hands and a warm body to go with it. It couldn't kiss me or tell me that I'm beautiful or call out my name, so what's the big attraction? I had a better solution for handling my hormones. I took a quick, cold shower. Then I scrubbed out the tub with Comet, lotioned myself, put on my favorite Snoopy pajamas and gave myself an avocado facial.

When the mask was so stiff that I felt like I'd just had a facelift, I loosened it with my fingers, then washed it off with a wet cloth. Then I put on my moisturizer. I picked up my book and shuffled through it to find the page where I'd left off, and went down the hall to get myself a brownie and a glass of milk.

The phone rang again, and I almost answered it without checking the caller ID in the kitchen first. It was Eric. His name and number flashed across the tiny screen and I counted the rings, hoping he would just hang up before I lost my backbone and invited him over. It was so tempting. It would only be one night. I could handle one night with the lying bastard just to get my rocks off. Couldn't I?

I snatched up the phone and heard a click in my ear that sounded almost like someone cocking a gun, and I sighed. If I called him back, I would have to let the phone ring twice then hang up. Then I'd have to wait five minutes and call again and let it ring twice more. That was our signal. Going to all that trouble would probably give Eric the wrong idea. It was just as well. I would have hated myself later. I set the phone in its cradle, wondering why I even bother with these married men anyway.

Through the open kitchen shutters I saw Mama's face in the painting, caught in a mixed stream of moonlight and streetlight. I felt like she was looking at me. My hands started shaking and I dropped my book. I picked it up and grabbed a brownie from the baking pan sitting on the stove. Instead of milk, I poured myself a big glass of wine and went back to the bedroom and turned on the TV. I drank the wine and fell asleep with the TV and the light on.

• • •

It's been a long time since I've dated a single man. Gregory Hemphill three years ago. Gregory was this mechanic who worked for the Honda dealer where I bought my car. I met him when I took my baby in for an oil change. Gregory was shorter than my normal six-foot type, and bulldog muscular. He sparred down at Sugar Ray's gym, so he was in tiptop shape, with a washboard stomach and powerful runner's legs. He was a reddish brown, like mahogany wood, and his hair was a jet-black birds' nest of short dreds. Not my type at all. But his hands were what attracted me. Looking back on that phase of my life, it seems silly that I was attracted to him at all.

He had big hands. Most of his fingernails were split and dingy with grease. His knuckles and creases were ashy. His palms were leather rough. At the time I had just gotten rid of this prissy, pampered surgeon named Vance. That man was so compulsive about his damn hands that it drove me insane. Always wanting me to rub them and put oils on them. That fool even talked to his hands the way most men talk to their penises. By the time I was finished with Vance, I vowed to replace him with somebody less tame. Someone without polish. So when I saw Gregory, I knew I had to have him. I asked him to have a drink with me and didn't even wince when I saw the disgusting black smudges appear on the business card I gave him.

Two weeks of Gregory brought me back to my senses. I stopped thinking it was funny that he called so much that his messages were the only ones filling up my answering machine. The Negro had a bad habit of showing up at my door unannounced, and I got sick to death of the smell of Murphy's Oil Soap in my bathroom and the black flecks of water and dingy bubbles left in the sink after he washed the filth off his hands.

When I told Gregory I didn't want to see him anymore, I didn't expect him to go off on me. The Negro went totally ape, cursing and pacing and shit. I calmly tried to remind him of our arrangement. That was a mistake, because he grabbed a knife out of the open dishwasher, pointed it at the side of my throat and said, "Bitch, ain't nobody ending shit around here unless you want me to put an end to your little ass." You know what I did? Shoot. I fainted.

When I came to, Gregory was gone but my apartment looked like the twister scene from *The Wizard of Oz*. It was totally wrecked. I was scared to death. The Negro had shredded everything. After I made sure he was gone, I packed up as much stuff as I could and drove over, despite my busted windshield, to Paulette's house. Paulette called her cousin Michael, who's a black belt in karate, and he and two of his tree-trunk friends paid a special visit to Gregory. I never heard from that lunatic again. I met Nick and he set me up in another apartment, and that was the end of my single guy dating. Gregory is exactly why I was so fearful of meeting another single man.

I tried to remind myself that not all single men are Gregorys. But I felt that old familiar fear creep up when James called early Thursday morning and told me I was on his mind. I sat at the kitchen table with a sketch pad and pencil, designing a two-tier wedding cake, and talked to James for two hours. James and I learned we had a few things in common. We were both the youngest in our families, we both liked Easy Rawlins mysteries, old movies, plays and cooking.

I was surprised to find him so easy to talk to. It made me realize how much I missed being able to really talk to a man. It was a far stretch from the two-minute conversations I had with married men. We always had to devise signals just to make a date. And sometimes I'd be interrupted in the middle of a sentence with "I gotta go!" And before I could respond I'd hear a dial tone in my ear. My conversation with James was much nicer, but I told myself not to get used to it. This was a one-time thing.

I spent the morning perfecting my cake sketch so I could bake it the following morning. It was going to be a southern strawberry shortcake with a bouquet of strawberries, kiwi and blueberries gathered at the top and trickling down the sides. It was a summer cake. I'd wanted to make something more in tune with the season, like a carrot cake or a black forest cake that would better reflect the mood of the sky and wind. But the bride was eighteen and silly in love. She said she didn't want somber colors anywhere near her wedding.

I dropped some overdue books off at the library and returned a videotape to Blockbuster, then I jetted downtown to Mario's Pizza Palace to meet Paulette for lunch. We people-watched from the long glass window near our table and ate slices of veggie white pizza with hot herbal tea and talked.

"Well," Paulette was saying, "I think you two will really hit it off. I mean, he's so adorable, Genie. And funny? The man has a real sense of humor."

"Okay, Paulette. I get the picture. You don't have to build him up to me anymore. He sounded really nice on the phone."

Paulette leaned forward with her elbows on the table.

"What did you guys talk about?"

"I don't know. Stuff," I said, shrugging.

"For two hours, Genie? The man had you on the telephone for two hours and all you talked about was stuff? What kind of stuff, girl? You know I want details."

"God, Paulette, you are so nosy. All we talked about was getting-to-know-you kinds of things. Like, Do you have sisters and brothers? What do you like to do in your spare time? Here, hand me the sugar please. This tea is too strong. Anyway, we just kind of chatted back and forth on that note. But you shouldn't get your hopes up though, Paulette."

I sampled my tea again and set the wet spoon on my napkin.

"Who said my hopes were up?" Paulette said, smiling and waving at a hefty blonde woman with badly drawn on brows. "And anyway, why couldn't my hopes be up if I want them up?"

"Because he's a Scorpio. Who was that?"

"One of my parents down at the center. He's a what?"

"You know, a Scorpio. And I'm a Libra. That means he's too fiery for me. Scorpios are known for their hot tempers, Paulette. Nick is a Scorpio, and I am not putting up with that type of shit anymore."

Paulette tossed her hair.

"Nick was just damned crazy, girl. And married. That's all there was to his story. James is a nice man, so don't worry about that sign shit. That stuff is bogus anyhow. Listen, I didn't tell you that Telaysia bit Evelyn's little boy yesterday, did I?"

I laughed.

"No. Why'd she do that? He make her mad?"

"Girl, we left them in the living room for a minute just so I could show Evelyn that new credenza we put in Robert's office, you know. We weren't gone but a second and heard Simeon screaming the house down. So we ran back up the steps to see what had happened—girl, my heart was in my throat—and Telaysia had left her teeth marks on his face. He said she acted like she wanted to give him a kiss. Girl, she had the nerve to laugh too and point at his face."

"That little stink. I'ma get her little butt when I see her," I said, laughing.

"That isn't all. Robert is trying to help me toilet train her, and when he tried to make her stay on the little potty, she bit him real good yesterday too. I thought the man was ready to cry."

We both laughed, and I glanced at my watch. I had to run. I motioned to the waiter for the check and Paulette laid a credit card out on the table and said, "It's on me this time, chick."

"Thank you Miss Paulette."

"No bother. Listen, what are you gonna wear tomorrow night for your date with James? You know first impressions are important."

"I don't know. I hadn't really given it any thought."

"Mmhmm, just as I suspected. You'll be home later this evening?"

"Yeah, I'll be in. I have a four o'clock appointment to get my teeth cleaned, but I'll be home the rest of the evening after I leave there."

I belted my coat and grabbed my purse from beneath the table.

"Okay. So I'll see you around seven tonight."

"What for?"

I counted out a few dollar bills and dropped them on the table for a tip.

"So I can supervise your choice of datewear. Why else? I'll see you at seven, girl."

I laughed and walked out of the restaurant. Hey. I had a date. I felt like skipping down the sidewalk to my car.

●　　●　　●

A heavy rain developed later in the day. The sky was a cloudless gray, and the remnants of ice that still clung to the street corners slowly disintegrated in the rain. I alternated between watching the downpour from my bedroom window and watching the news while I ate a dinner of steamed vegetables and rice.

I was on my health kick again. Trying to stick to foods that were good for me, cutting down on my alcohol intake and exercising every night. I swear, those news health reports that remind you that you shouldn't do this or that because you risk getting heart disease or hypertension always make me want to be more responsible with my health. At least for a minute, anyway.

The doorbell rang and I set my plate on the bed and went to answer the door.

"Hey." I ran my tongue over my teeth. My teeth always feel fake after I've been to the dentist for a cleaning.

"What's up."

Paulette shook out her umbrella outside the door and left it, then took off her bright yellow rain slicker and shook it out too.

"Chile. Think I broke my umbrella. It's not fit for man or beast out there. Oh, man."

She shivered and hugged herself. Her bangs were flat against her forehead. The bottom of her jeans were dark with water splashes.

"Lemme make you some hot chocolate to warm you up."

"No thanks. I'm in a soda mood. Got any Pepsis?"

"Here, give me that soggy raincoat, girl, and take off those shoes. I done told you about my carpet a million times. I'ma hang this down in the laundry room to dry. I think there's some soda in the fridge. Take all you find in there home with you. I'm off that mess for a while."

I held the raincoat at arm's length and walked it down the steps to the small laundry room. I put the coat on a hanger and hung it from a nail protruding from the unfinished wall. I took a section of old newspaper from the recycling bin and spread it out beneath the coat. When I got back to my room, Paulette had the nerve to be reclining on my bed eating my dinner and sipping soda through a straw.

"I see you've made yourself quite comfortable with my food."

"Genie, it smelled so good I had to taste it. When'd you get this new chair?" Paulette pointed at the chair in the corner.

"That's not new. Ms. Henley from up the street reupholstered it for me. I catered her bridge party last week, remember? It was such a small affair, I didn't charge her, so she took my chair down to her shop and rejuvenated it for me. What do you think?"

"It's beautiful. I was admiring it when I came in here. I think that floral pattern really works in here. Even though you need to give it to me, since you can hardly move around in this room as it is."

"Paulette, shut up. Listen, I went ahead and picked out some outfits for tomorrow, so tell me which one you think I should wear."

"Okay. Cool."

"Alright. The first one is this."

I held up a tight-sleeved China red silk dress that accentuated every curve. The neckline was squared and it belted at the waist. It was very long and chic, and wore well with my high-heeled, knee-length black boots.

"Naw. Too dressy," Paulette said, "You need something a little more casual."

"More casual," I said thoughtfully, and hung the dress back in the closet.

"So, what d'you think?" Paulette asked.

"What do I think about what?" I asked, looking for my black dress.

"About James, of course."

"Oh. I already told you he sounds nice."

I held up the black knit with its deep split. Paulette shook her head.

"Too ho'ish."

"You bought it for me," I said. "What does that say about you?"

I smiled and Paulette returned it.

"Says I shop for ho's."

"Oh. Okay. Okay." I licked my tongue at her and put the dress way in the back of the closet. Way back.

"Maybe," Paulette said, "you should wear slacks, or a nice pantsuit. That's all you think—is that he sounds nice?"

I shrugged.

"Do we have to go over this again, Paulette, damn. I can't form but so many opinions from a couple of phone conversations. I gotta get a look at the man first. Then I might say more. Until then, he sounds nice."

"Heifer," Paulette said.

"Hussy," I responded.

I held up a dark blue pantsuit.

Paulette nodded vigorously.

"That's the one. It says sexy but it also says smart."

"I don't know why you're tripping so damn hard. I ain't trying to impress, Paulette. It's just one date. So stop it."

Paulette tossed her head and opened the *People* magazine she had gotten out of the magazine rack by the bed.

"Oh yeah, and another thing I meant to cuss you out about: Why did you tell me that James is a musician?"

"He is."

"Paulette, he's a teacher."

She tossed her hair again.

"Teacher, musician. What's the difference? He's got a job."

"You are so full of shit, girl. I swear I could murder you sometimes."

"Well, Genie, in this day and age a decent looking brother with a single status, a steady paycheck and a running car is scarce. I knew you wouldn't be interested if I told you he teaches."

"Damn straight."

"But you still think he sounds nice."

"Yes, but I'm warning you now, if he ain't fine I'ma beat your butt."

"Fine. Here I am trying to do you a favor—"

"Paulette, shut the hell up."

She gave me the finger. I took out my low-heeled blue pumps and tried them on to see if they still fit. They did. I unbuttoned my cardigan and plopped on the bed to take off my pants. They were a little hard to get out of.

"Lord," I said, "I feel like I should have been greased up before I put these tight things on this morning."

With a little struggling I finally got out of my jeans. I tried on the suit to make sure I still looked like something in it. I hadn't worn it in several months. I closed the bedroom door so I could see my full-body reflection in the mirror that hung on the back of the door.

"I'm glad you decided to see James even though he's not a serious musician, 'cause he's really a nice guy, Genie."

"The only two reasons I'ma still go out with the man is 'cause I like his conversation and 'cause he called me last night at a weak point and saved me."

"A weak point? Tell me you wasn't gonna call no Eric or no Nick."

"Girl, no. Although Eric did call me, but I let it ring." It wasn't really a lie. "What I did was open that brown box up in my closet and put some batteries in that thing."

Paulette sat up abruptly.

"The brown . . . You did not!"

I smoothed the pants, wishing I had time to take the outfit to the cleaners.

"I did. Honey, I was armed and dangerous last night."

"Girl, you look too fierce in that outfit. So James called right when you were about to use that freak stick?"

"Just in time. I don't know, sometimes it feels like I'm gonna explode if I don't get me some soon."

"Well, girl, I'm glad he was there for you. You shoulda called me. Poor thing. How long's it been anyhow?"

"Too long. Six damn weeks."

"I feel for you, sister. Every night. When I gets mine."

"Oh sure," I murmured, "rub it in. But if things heat up between me and this James, I'll be feeling for myself, if you know what I mean."

"Genie, promise me you aren't going to hop right into bed with the man."

"Listen, Paulette. The way I feel right now, a promise like that would be a lie."

"Okay, I can't say that I blame you. But at least promise me you won't bring up that dumb-assed theory of yours."

"I beg your pardon? What do you mean, dumb-assed?"

"Come on, G, you know what I mean. I don't want you showing this guy your true colors just yet. He's a nice man. And he's Robert's friend."

"Okay. I promise I won't bring up my theory. But I did tell him I have one, so he may ask."

"Well, change the subject or something if you have to. Just don't tell him any of that hard-ass stuff, okay? His ex-wife has already taken him through more changes than a little bit."

"Yeah, he told me a little something about that. Alright. I'll play it cool with James tomorrow."

"Thank you. So I told you I made us a hair appointment for Saturday at ten?"

"Yeah. I may miss it though if this James is everything you say he is. So if I don't show up, let Arleeta know that it's a 'man thang.'"

"I hear you. But if you don't show up, call me with the blow by blow as soon as you can."

"You know I will," I said.

I unbuttoned my suit jacket and threw it on the bed. I leaned back in the chair and took off my pants then hung the set on the back of the closet door. I slipped on my robe and belted it tight.

"Paulette, would you cut it out. Leave it right there." I gestured toward the television. Paulette had discovered where I'd hidden the remote inside my pillowcase. She aimed it at the TV and was about to change the channel for a third time.

"You know I like to channel surf, girl. I can't control myself when I come over here and see cable. There's too much to choose from."

"Lord, chile. You are worse than a man with that remote. That's the very reason I hate for you to get your hands on it. Listen, did Evelyn get that job listing for me from Simon yet?"

"Oh. Oh yeah," Paulette said, zooming through the channels, "it's over there in my purse. Mmmm. I wish I could understand what they're saying on this Spanish channel. Some of their programs look so watchable."

"Take some Spanish lessons and watch them then. Look I'ma turn this thing off and cut on some music."

"Aw, Genie. Come on now."

I know she didn't think I would sit around listening to the channels change every few seconds. I hit the power switch on the cable box and queued Joe Sample's "Mystery Child" in the CD player. I reached for Paulette's brown leather Coach bag and opened the purse. It seemed like Paulette kept everything in that bag but her man, and she had a thousand pictures of him in there to make up for that. Somehow I found the job listings inside. I pulled out the folded set of paper clipped pages and put on my reading glasses to review the small print.

"Oh, now this sounds halfway decent."

"What's that?" Paulette peered over my shoulder, squinting.

"This one here." I touched a finger to one of the listings.

"Says a grade nine office assistant in the Facilities office. I can do that. Or maybe this other one in the English department. But it's for a secretary, and I don't think my office skills are all that great."

Paulette shrugged. "So. Try for it anyway. The only thing they can tell you is no."

"I guess."

"No 'I guess.' Go for it. You know how to present yourself and you do have the skills and some experience. You're a smart woman. Like the Nike commercial says, just do it."

"You're right. I'll go down first thing tomorrow and put in an application. I just hope they call me. I'm about sick of catering."

"I know you are. Something'll come up. Watch. . . . Hey, Genie, can we talk about something?"

I plucked an inkpen out of the mug on the dresser where I keep my odds and ends.

"Sure. What's up?" I circled the two listings.

"Genie, come sit down a minute."

"For what? What's this about?"

Paulette patted the bed.

"Just come sit for a minute."

I was very suspicious. Paulette only wrapped strands of hair around her finger like she was doing now only when she was nervous about something.

"Paulette, what's going on? Is there something you haven't told me about this James?"

She scrunched her face up but didn't say anything.

"I knew it! Alright. Out with it. What's wrong with him?"

"Ge—"

The telephone rang and made us both jump. Paulette almost rolled off the bed trying to turn at an awkward angle to answer it.

"Hello? No it isn't. Who's calling, please?"

She pressed a hand over the mouthpiece and mouthed, "It's Eric."

I shook my head and stood statue still, careful not to make a sound. Paulette put the receiver to her ear.

"I'm sorry, but Genie's unavailable at the moment. Is there a message? No, she isn't. Yes, she is busy. Listen, Eric do you want to leave a message or what? Okay, thank you. Mmbye."

She hung up.

"Genie, he sounds so pitiful."

"As well he should. He knew better."

"Mmmm. Well. I would feel sorry for him, but he shouldn't have been cheating on his wife in the first place. Anyway, there's something I need to say to you."

"Then shoot. This isn't one of your dumb lectures, is it?"

"No, this isn't a lecture. In the first place, I don't lecture. I educate and I advise. If you little people don't understand where I'm coming from, that's not my problem. But as I was about to say—please Genie, sit down—I have something, or rather someone to talk to you about."

"Who?"

Paulette drew in a deep breath

"Listen, can we talk about your dad for a minute? I ran into him this afternoon at Hechinger's and he asked about you."

I think the room started spinning, 'cause all of a sudden I felt really sick and wanted some air. I jumped up out of the armchair and turned away from Paulette. My eyes were itching to shed some tears. I wanted to scream. I wanted to do something. So I lifted a meshbag from the lid of the hamper and dropped three pairs of silk panties into it. I know I probably looked like a statue with my back all stiff and straight like that, but I couldn't help it.

"Genie?" Paulette was behind me.

"Why are you telling me you saw him? I don't care."

There was no emotion in my voice. But oh God, there was a pain in my throat and my chest that felt like I was being suffocated. Paulette put her hand on my shoulder.

"Genie, please. Why won't you see him? He didn't put those pills in your mama's mouth any more than you did. Why do you and your sisters keep blaming him for that?"

I had to put a stop to this shit. I put my hands over my ears for a second, then turned toward Paulette with a hand in the air.

"Hey. Let the shit go. It's not your business and I don't want you talking about my mother, okay."

"But Genie, this is—"

"Look, as far as I'm concerned the conversation is closed!"

I had to get out of that room, so I ran, knocking the plate of food off the dresser. I locked myself in the bathroom and turned on the fan, but left the light off. I retched, but nothing came out of my mouth. So I slid down onto the toilet seat and stuffed the end of a towel into my mouth, sobbing so hard that my face hurt. My throat felt raw and constricted and I felt this overwhelming urge to talk to Mama. I ignored Paulette's knock on the door. I was too busy asking Mama why she chose to run away. How could she have done it? I trusted her and she just left me there in that house to rot with pain. The bitch. I felt like sprinting down the hall to the living room and ripping that laughing woman off the wall because she wasn't real. She just wasn't real. What was real was the gray, old-looking woman she became, her saggy body made shapeless by that beat-up housecoat and her arm wrapped around a gallon bottle of Easy Jesus that she nursed all day long. That was my real mama. That was what Edward turned her into because of his filthy ways. He was as responsible for her suicide as if he had shoveled the pills into her mouth, no matter what Paulette thinks.

I heard the wind blowing fast and furious outside, almost like it was underlining my thoughts, making them feel tangible and sharp-edged to me. There was no place to put all these feelings. So I did what I've become so good at doing. I buried them. I stopped crying and let the towel slide down to the floor between my ankles. My nose was running so bad that I couldn't breathe, except by opening my mouth. I felt behind me in the dark and found the box of Kleenex to blow my nose.

I was so worn out that I closed my eyes and leaned back to rest. I heard Paulette leave finally, and I was so glad to be alone. I turned off the fan and cut on the bathroom light to examine my face. My eyes were red and sad. I washed my face clean and french-braided my hair, then I went out to the kitchen for cards and Sambuca. Paulette had left me a note on the back of a Safeway receipt, held against the refrigerator door by a black angel magnet. I read it, balled it up and trashed it. Paulette's always terrible with apologies.

I don't know. Maybe I'm crazy. I'd never admit it to Paulette, but I think sometimes that maybe I really should see a shrink. Easier said than done, though. It's just that I can't imagine letting some stranger dig inside my head like that, you know. It trips me out when people say that they want someone to listen to them, but will go as far as paying someone to do it. How could I want to talk about myself if the person sitting in front of me is being paid to listen? I'll bet five dollars to a doughnut that shrinks act like they understand where you're coming from just because they know that you have to write them a check. What good is that?

If Paulette knows what's good for her she'll leave me the hell alone about Edward. That's a subject that I avoid at all cost. Why can't Paulette see what a no-good bastard he is? I'm just too angry to even waste a whole bunch of energy on the man. Hell yes, I blame his ass for what Mama did. It was his whorish ways that caused it. I never ever want to see him again as long as I live. End of story. I should've said that to Paulette, but the hussy caught me off guard bringing him up like that. That shit was uncalled for. But at least I didn't break down in front of her. Thank God I made it to the bathroom just in time. All I need is her friendship. I don't want her pity. People's mothers die every day and they turn out just fine, so Miss Forgive and Forget can kiss my brown butt and stop trying to play mediator between me and Edward. I'm good and tired of her always sticking her nose into my business where it doesn't belong.

Paulette is still my girl, though. Correction: my sister. We've been through hell and high water together and we'll always be thick as thieves. It's just that ever since I've known her, I've had to reaffirm my individuality with her. Always.

We met in the seventh grade when we were both twelve, and even then she thought she was perfect. I remember the first day of school I wore these little Chardon jeans and a red and white striped shirt with a white tie on the side that I had saved my allowance to buy. Paulette had on the same shirt. She walked across the blacktop over to where I was standing by a high fence, blowing enormous pink bubbles from a wad of Bazooka in my mouth and she asked me if I was double-handed. I told her no. She smirked at me and said, "I like your shirt. What's your name?" I told her. Then she took me by the arm and said, "Genie. Cool. I'm Paulette, but everybody calls me Peaches. You think you could turn the jumprope for me?" I walked with her onto the blacktop and turned my heart out while she jumped a mean double dutch to Apple on a Stick. I was so happy. I needed a friend so bad after Marilyn and Tess left.

Paulette was the same loud-mouthed dynamo she is now, so she was always the center of attention. I was the little quiet one in the background, just like I was at home with Marilyn and Tess. That may be why we clicked so well. I could just sit back and let Paulette be the one to shine, and sometimes some of her sun rays would find their way to me. The problem started when she wanted to think for me and tried to get me to be the person that she is. She tried out for ROTC, so she wanted me to try out even though I hated it. She looked good in Shirley Temple curls, so she wanted me to wear them. I kept telling her my face was too skinny. She excelled in math, so she pushed me to take trig with her when we got in high school. I almost flunked. She liked boys with dimples and thought I was a nut for liking the dark ones. She's always trying to clone herself through me.

It's like Paulette wants me to live her perfect little life with the white picket fence and the minivan and the good-looking, obedient husband and beautiful baby, but I can't. I'm me. I have my own life to lead and my own goals to fulfill. *Paulette, please just understand that I'm me. Not you. So you can just try to fix somebody else's damn life. Okay?*

I found the cards and poured myself another nice stiff drink. I cleaned up the food I'd spilled in the bedroom and spent the rest of the evening sitting on the bed and shuffling cards for a game of solitaire that I couldn't seem to concentrate on. Those memories beat away at my mind, just like the winter rain beat against the house, with an urgency so harsh that only the clear liquid in my crystal glass could ever dull the pain.

Phase 4

My alarm clock was going crazy. I opened my eyes carefully to peer at the clock. It was four in the morning. The sun wasn't even awake yet. I turned over to hit the snooze button and winced. I had a killer hangover. I groaned and put my hands on either side of my head to hold the pieces of my brain together. I closed my eyes again and lay on my back, scratching my hip. When I moved my leg, a handful of playing cards fell onto the floor.

It was cold in here. I shivered and pulled the covers tighter around my neck. I had forgotten to turn the heat up. Probably because of the booze. In the middle of the night I had felt hot and sticky, so I'd stripped down to my panties and thrown my robe and pajamas on the floor.

The alarm screamed again, and this time I shut it off and made myself get out of bed. Every movement hurt my head more, but I fought it. I threw on my pajamas and robe and found my Isotoner slippers in the closet. I had to make the wedding cake early so that I could run over to Whitman University and fill out an application today. On my way down the hall, I turned the heat up full blast and went into the kitchen to make some strong black coffee and buttered wheat toast.

I sat at the kitchen table with yesterday's *Post* and a sketch of my best cake design. Half my work was done. I had already done my measurements the day before. The utensils were on the counter, and I had washed, hulled and crushed four pints of fresh strawberries, so it was okay to take my time. Even a small bite of toast made me gag. I couldn't eat a thing.

"When," I said, "will I learn that there's a price to pay for drinking. Shit."

I gulped my coffee and laid my head down. It felt like my brain would implode any minute. That whole episode should have warned me not to even leave the house, because the day got worse as it went along.

By the time I got back home to get ready for my stinking date, I was convinced that my last name should have been Murphy, 'cause Murphy's Law definitely applied to my day. The first cake I'd started for that god-awful wedding fell (a very bad sign), so I had to start all over again. Thank God I had an excess of ingredients. Luckily the second cake turned out beautifully. I didn't want to see another strawberry for a very long time.

When I had the second cake ready, I rushed out of the house at ten in hair curlers and yesterday's clothes so I could drop the cake off at the bride's house. No sooner did I whip around a corner after ridding myself of the cake, than I ran out of gas. I had forgotten to check the gauge. I was hot. I had to walk a half mile in my hair curlers and bedroom shoes just to get enough gas in my can to help me make it to the station.

Later, after I'd cleaned up, I got lost trying to get down to Whitman. No matter how long I drive in D.C., I don't think I'll ever get the hang of getting around without getting lost. The city is nothing but a maze. I had to ask four different people for directions before I was lucky enough to find a nice man who was on his way to the university. I followed him all the way, but wound up having to park about six blocks from the personnel office. When I sat down to fill out my application, I remembered I had left my damn resume in the car. I had to go get it. I finished the application and felt real good about turning it in.

I got ready for my date with some time to spare, but as soon as I snapped my tennis bracelet on my wrist, one of the links broke. I threw it on the dresser and put on my Pulsar watch that doesn't work because it needs a new battery. Hopefully nobody would ask me for the time.

After putting on my coat, I reached into my purse for my keys, but they weren't there. It took twenty minutes to locate them. They had been dangling in my front door lock all that time. Somebody could have walked right into my house and got me. Now I was running late. I had fifteen minutes left. It would take at least that long for me to get from Lanham to Greenbelt, so I drove like a madwoman. I ran two red lights and cut off a van trying to get there on time.

Jasper's is a great place for first meetings because the atmosphere is not exactly romantic, not exactly casual. It's somewhere in the middle. The lights are low enough to hide imperfections if needed and the decor is not plush, but extremely comfortable. There are large fireplaces and beautiful wood backgammon tables throughout. The fare is a mix of earthy to elegant American cuisine, and the crowd is mid-twenty to mid-thirty, for the most part.

I pulled into the parking lot adjacent to the Greenway shopping center, and scanned the area for a good space to put my baby, my Navajo Red '89 Honda Accord. I found a spot close to the restaurant, then parked and checked my makeup in the rearview mirror before I got out.

It was cold. Freezing actually. I walked as quickly as I could to get inside. Inside, I scanned the crowd at the bar, but not a man there looked anything like the description James had given me on the phone, so I asked the hostess if she knew whether someone was waiting for a Genie Gatlin. She knew. She led me toward a table on a platform near one of the cozy fireplaces where a gorgeous man was sitting.

James Caldwell was indeed everything Paulette had built him up to be, and more. Very tall with dark close-cut hair, deep-set dark eyes and a set of dimples grooving the cheeks of his chocolate brown face. He was so fine that every nerve ending in my body, especially those in the lower region, pulsated. But I was cool with mine. I didn't miss a beat in my strut as James stood, waiting for me to reach the table.

"You must be Genie."

I discarded my gloves and coat on the seat. He took my hand firmly and brushed a kiss across it with that mouth. Paulette definitely hadn't lied on that note, because a quick prayer was already in my throat that he was the type to taste forbidden fruit. I wanted to grab him right then and there, sprawl his fine ass across the table and have my way with that tasty body hidden beneath a gray silk shirt and charcoal wool slacks. Instead I took my seat across from him in the booth and set a smile on my lips that I hoped was sexy.

"And you're James."

He nodded that sexy head.

"I must say I'm pleased," he murmured.

His eyes moved slowly from my lightly made-up face to the end of what he could see of me above the table, which was just below my breasts. A shiver went up my spine. His gaze was so intense.

"Likewise," I breathed. This man was making me nervous.

"You're very beautiful."

"Thank you."

I decided then and there to leave everything I owned to Paulette in my will.

"I'm sorry I'm late, but things were a little hectic today."

"Oh, that's alright. You haven't kept me waiting that long. I just hope I can contribute to a more relaxing evening.

Mmmm! The brother was smooth, too.

I smiled to let him know that *I* hoped he could give me a more relaxing evening too.

"So what happened to make your day so hectic?"

"Everything. You know that wedding cake I was telling you about yesterday?"

He nodded.

"I beat the sun up this morning just to get started on it, but somehow it fell. I'm still trying to figure that one out. But anyway, I had to start again, and later on, after I dropped it off, I ran out of gas on the way back across town. Nothing big happened, it was just that a lot of little things that went wrong compounded into one big mess."

The waitress approached our table and we ordered drinks.

"You've been here before, right?" he asked.

"Once with Paulette. We had dinner here for her birthday last year."

"How's the food?"

"Great. Grilled chicken can't be touched. I assumed you'd been here before."

"Nah, I don't get out much," he said, perusing the menu. "Paulette suggested this place."

"Good ol' Paulette. So how'd your day go?"

"It was pretty okay. No major happenings. Just the usual stuff. I've got more than a couple roughnecks in my class this year who want to challenge me, but I can handle it."

"Where do you teach? Same school as Robert?"

"Not anymore. Robert's still at Northwestern. I transferred to Eleanor Roosevelt the beginning of this school term. It's right up the street from here."

"Mmm. You must really love teaching to have to put up with somebody else's kids all year round. Especially the ones that think they're so grown, and nowadays they all seem to carry guns. Look at that teacher over in Largo who was shot by a policeman's son, no less. Don't you ever get scared that might happen to you?"

"Sometimes. You can't help getting a little edgy when you hear about violence committed against other teachers. But for the most part I try not to think about it. Besides, there's no way I'll ever let some upstart kid intimidate me, gun or no gun."

"You say that now 'cause it hasn't happened to you.'

"No, I say it because I have a job to do and I enjoy doing it. Whatever obstacles arise, I'm willing to hurdle them. Any profession can be dangerous."

He looked so serious that I laughed.

"How is that possible?" I asked. "I cook for a living. What could be so dangerous about that?"

"You told me that cake you were baking this morning fell, didn't you?"

"So?"

"What if it had fallen on you? You could have lost a limb or something."

We both laughed good-naturedly at his corny ass joke. He was lucky he was fine, or I would have had to read him for that one. Our puzzled waitress set our drinks on the table.

"You all ready to order?"

Her hand was poised to write.

"Yes," I said, "I'll have grilled chicken."

"Baked potato or french fries?"

"Potato."

"Sour cream? Butter?"

"Both. And today's vegetable with a side of cinnamon applesauce."

She nodded and looked droolingly at James.

"Sir?"

"I'll have the steak, medium rare, with a baked potato and a garden salad with French dressing."

"What will you have on your baked potato, sir?"

The heifer's eyelashes were batting harder than Barry Bonds smacks a baseball.

"Sour cream."

"Okay, sir."

She sashayed away from the table.

"What's with that look?" he asked.

"What look? Oh. She was extremely obvious wasn't she?"

"What do you mean?"

"The way she was giving you the eye."

"The eye?"

"Come on, James. Don't tell me you didn't notice."

"To tell you the truth, I didn't."

"You noticed my look, but you didn't notice her eye?"

"No."

"And how is it that you missed that? She was so obvious."

"It may have to do with my not being able to take my eyes off you."

He put his drink to his lips and took my hand with his free hand. I lowered my eyes, hoping he hadn't read the lust written in them.

"Stop looking at me like that, James."

"Why?"

"Because."

"Because what?"

"Because it unsettles me."

"Why?"

I sipped my daiquiri. I was trying to be on my best behavior for Paulette's sake, but if this man kept baiting me, my sister act was going right out the window.

"I don't know," I said softly. "It just unsettles me."

He closed his eyes.

"Okay. How's this? I won't look at you the rest of the evening."

He looked so silly, all I could do was laugh and smack his hand playfully.

"Stop it."

"Stop what?"

"Open your eyes, James."

"You sure?"

I sucked my teeth.

"Open your eyes."

He did.

"Make up your mind, woman. First you want me to stop looking at you, then you want something else."

"You know what I meant."

I sipped at my daiquiri again and looked around the room, trying to calm my screaming libido. The conversations around us were quiet and relaxed. Except at the bar. Several suited men lined the bar, nursing their drinks. Three of them were engaged in a rowdy conversation that I was too far away to overhear. They were probably spouting off about the game on TV. The Bulls and the Bullets were playing.

I shifted my gaze to a couple sitting across the room. The man was very stocky, almost like a football player. His thick neck and square blunt face made me think of Mike Tyson. And the woman with him was all limbs. She was so thin she looked as if she had never tasted a meal before. But I watched her stuff a portion of cheesecake into her mouth with more gusto than a bulimic on a binge. People-watching in restaurants is one of my best bad habits.

James was steadily talking to me and I hadn't paid a drop of attention to him, so he waved his hand in front of my face.

"Huh?"

"I said, I thought you were going to fill me in on this theory you were telling me about earlier. And what are you looking at so intently?"

He looked over in the direction of my gaze.

"You see that woman over there in the blue sweater?"

"With the big guy?"

I nodded and giggled.

"She is tearing into her dessert like it is about to go out of style. Uh oh, here she goes again."

We watched the woman stuff the last huge bite into her mouth and laughed quietly. James's eyes were definitely talking to me. I imagined they were saying, "Just wait until I get you alone." Mmmm.

"Okay," he said, "Now."

He reached across and touched my chin with the tip of a finger.

"What is this theory you were going to tell me about."

"Well . . ." I remembered my promise to Paulette. I was glad to see the waitress coming our way.

She was juggling a tray of plates and had the nerve to flaunt her big booty in James's face when she turned to place my food in front of me.

"Will you be needing anything else?"

She looked like she wanted to devour the man. I guess if I had taken a peek at myself in the mirror moments before, I would have seen the same look on my own face. But hell, I'd been deprived for over a month and he was my date. I was entitled.

"No, that will be all, thank you," I said crisply.

"Alright. I'll be back to check on you a little later."

James flashed a silly grin at me, knowing the little hussy was pissing me off. I didn't say a word, though. I was too hungry for two things: sex and food. Unfortunately, at the moment I could only satisfy one of those hungers.

• • •

"Thank you for dinner, James. It's been a lot of fun. Call me and we'll get together again sometime."

We were standing out in the cold, shivering and huddling close to each other beside my car. James had just given me a chaste kiss on the cheek, which led me to the conclusion that he was one of those slow brothers who needed a few dates to build up some nerve. A picture of my big lonely bed and that awful toy flashed in my head, and I almost felt like crying when I gave James my keys and watched him open my car door

He glanced at his watch.

"It's still early, you know, Genie. Listen, I live close by. Would you like to come to my place for coffee? Maybe watch a video or something?"

Hell yeah. I liked that "or something." I wondered if he would think I was strange if I cut a few back flips across the parking lot.

"Oh. Well. That sounds kind of nice," I said. "Where d'you live?"

I hoped I didn't sound too eager.

"Townhouses 'bout a few blocks from here. I walked, so if you're interested we can take your car."

"You walked down here in this cold?"

"It's not that bad out here."

I clicked the auto lock.

"Says you. Come on, Jack Frost, get in."

I let the car heat up for a few minutes, then whipped out of the parking lot, bobbing my head to Earth, Wind and Fire's "Shining Star."

"Which way?"

"Straight. Then left at the light."

I sped up a quiet street.

"This is my school here on the right. When you get down to the stop sign, make a left."

I glanced in the direction James pointed and nodded as I maneuvered my car past a slow moving Grand Am.

"Must be nice to work so close to home."

I turned the corner and slowed.

"Yeah, it is. It's the one on the end here. With the porch light on."

I coasted through the lot and pulled into a parking space across from his impressive townhouse with an equally impressive BMW parked in front of it.

"Yours?" I asked, pointing at the sleek blue 525i.

"Yeah. Needs a new clutch, though."

We walked up the stairs and James fished his keys out of his pocket.

"This is lovely," I said, dancing from foot to foot. The wind was tearing me up. It was making me mad because I'd spent so much time on my hair, which was blowing all in my face. It was bad enough that I needed a new perm.

"Thanks," he said and opened the front door.

Inside was an immaculate foyer tiled in black and white marble with an elegant chandelier overhead. There was a dramatic spiral staircase leading to every kind of pleasure that my imagination could produce. I was so intent on what lay beyond those stairs that I almost ran into a fichus seated in a beautiful hand-painted vase.

"Watch yourself, baby."

Ooh, Lord. I had graduated to baby. I was in trouble now. Better yet, James was in trouble. He slipped an arm around my waist to steady me, and my blood seemed to run hot from his touch. He led me into a small den. It was tastefully decorated with fawn leather sofas and oak furnishings. A beautiful zebra skin rug was spread in the middle of the floor.

"This is beautiful. Where'd you get it?"

"Oh. Ronnie brought it back from Africa a couple years ago. It was one of the few items I got to keep."

"Ronnie?"

"Yeah. My ex-wife."

"Oh. How long have you two been divorced?"

"Almost a year now."

"Would I be prying if I were to ask why you divorced?"

"No. It's simple really. I want kids very much. She never did. She went out and got her tubes tied without discussing it with me and it was a problem, so we decided to go our separate ways."

I was admiring some of his artwork.

"I'm sorry to hear that. I can't understand why anybody who can afford to have them doesn't want them. Kids are a joy."

"You like kids then?"

"Oh, yeah. I have three godchildren—Paulette and Robert's little girl, Telaysia, and my other girlfriend Evelyn's twins, a boy and a girl. Hopefully one day I'll be able to have a few."

"I know what you mean. I enjoy other people's kids, but it seems to me there's nothing like having your own. You want that coffee now, Genie?"

He was touching my shoulder, and the last thing I needed was a hot cup of coffee. I was already much too warm inside.

"You have any ice tea or juice?"

"Here, let me hang your coat up for you. I think I might have ice tea in there. Take a look over there and see if there's a video you might want to look at. I'll be right back."

"Okay." I stuffed my gloves in my pocket and gave James my coat.

Come on, Genie, I told myself once he left the room. Get a grip girl. Get a grip. I did three sets of relax, relate, release and took a deep breath before examining the videotapes lining the shelves of an entertainment center. The man must have been a serious movie buff. He had a lot of films to choose from, but some of them weren't going to work. First of all, *Disclosure* had that hot desk scene. *Boomerang* had that thrill ride scene with Robin working Eddie overtime. It seemed like every movie I came across was either dumb as hell or had too much hot tamale in it.

"So what do you feel like tonight?"

Oh no. A loaded question. My back stiffened immediately. He was handing me a tall glass of tea with a wedge of lemon and staring at me with those midnight eyes. I felt like my breasts were torpedoes ready to be launched, and my panties might as well have combusted.

"Ah. Let's go with a comedy," I said, holding out a tape. "Can't go wrong with *Coming to America.*"

"Mmm. So you like Eddie Murphy?" He seemed disappointed by my choice.

"In this movie I do. Some of his other stuff is pretty lame."

James took the tape from my hand and put it in the VCR. He bent down in front of the console to hit the rewind button.

"You cold?"

"A little."

He moved near the fireplace.

"Well let's just fix that," he said, picking up some kind of remote. He pressed a button and the fireplace immediately flamed. The videotape wound down and I watched him walk back over to the television. He bent to start the video and check the tracking.

"You want anything else before we get comfortable, baby?"

Damn! Another loaded question. And why did his beautiful ass have to be in my face? I leaned back on the sofa, contemplating whether I should jump on his back or not. Six weeks without sex. People have committed homicides for less.

"No, I'm fine. Thanks."

"Hit that light for me, would you?"

"Sure."

Glad to have something to do, I reached up and flipped the switch on the wall. James sat beside me, placing an arm around my shoulder.

"Get comfortable, baby. You seem a little tense," he said, rubbing my shoulder and kicking off his shoes.

I took off my shoes, and had a sudden fear that maybe my feet would smell, because I had been in such a big hurry I had forgotten to spray my shoes. I sniffed the air on the sly. They were fine. I relaxed next to James and half watched the movie while I wondered what he was thinking.

Eddie had just gotten Shari to go out with him when James's bare foot lightly touched mine. It was so erotic I could hardly breathe. Just the soft cool of his toes barely resting on my arched foot like that. I had to close my eyes for a second. It was the best kind of foreplay. After a while he must have read in my mind or body language that I needed something more, because just at the right moment he cupped my face and turned me toward him.

"Are you really into this movie?"

I shook my head. I couldn't seem to speak or take my eyes from his. He stroked my face and kissed my brow.

"You're so beautiful, Genie. Especially now that you're so close to me."

His voice was so quiet and sensuous. I silently asked the Lord to help me, because if James's arm wasn't wrapped around my shoulder, I was sure to have slid down to the floor in a puddle.

"You know, I hope I'm not coming off too forward, Genie. It's just been a long time since I've met someone like you. You're so sweet and sexy. I just can't help myself. I know you feel it too. I think we both need to be close right now."

His lips were at my temple. He spoke so softly that I had to strain to hear him past the pounding in my ears. All I could do was whimper just a little. It'd been too long since I'd been held like this, and I was nervous.

When James finally kissed me, I felt like I was falling. Like how I imagine it must feel when you've jumped from an airplane and are waiting for the pull of the parachute time to come. Your arms and legs are just out there and you have no control over your own body. All you know is that you exist. Before I could really respond to him, his mouth was on my neck and we were both breathing hard. I fumbled with the buttons on his shirt.

"Let's go upstairs, baby."

I couldn't wait. I followed him down the hallway and up the stairs, into a dark room. James used a remote to open a set of vertical blinds at the window above his huge bed and the moonlight filtered in. He was so intense. God. His hands started touching me everywhere with so much passion that I thought I would die from the excitement of it. I was peeing ready. I had no shame. His touch drove me into such a frenzy that we started clawing each other's clothes away.

This brother was built. His chest was as wide as the Grand Canyon and full of soft, curling hair. His stomach was quarter-bouncing tight. His legs were long and well shaped. And he was mine for the taking.

The only thing in our way now was James's BVDs, and I was helping him get out of them fast. Oh yes. This brother was fine. This brother was downright baaaaad. Ronnie, or whatever her name was, was a fool because this brother had it going on. And then it happened. We finally got rid of the BVDs, and I saw that the brother was . . . not anatomically correct! Shit, he was no bigger than a toddler. I wasn't sure what to do. Scream? Laugh? Cry? If I had my clothes on I might have run.

Since I couldn't do any of those things without hurting his feelings, I simply froze. I felt like someone had just doused me with ice water. Why the hell didn't I pay closer attention to those little ass feet of his? He held that thing so proudly while he put a jimmy hat on it that I almost fell out.

"Oh, sweetheart," he was whispering, "You've got me so turned on. Look at how much I want you, girl."

Boyfriend had to be kidding. He fell with me on the bed, then moved on top of me. I didn't have the heart to tell him not to bring that thing anywhere near my pride and joy. I mean, this man was a close friend of my two best friends in the world. There was no way I could do anything but grin, bear it and think of some evil way to punish that damned Paulette.

James pushed my legs up above my head, I guess for better penetration, but Lord knows it didn't work. I didn't feel a thing. I closed my eyes so he wouldn't be able to tell whether I was enjoying it or not. All I felt was our skin bumping harder and harder and his sweat dripping onto my chin and chest. I was becoming as dry as a bone. I prayed he'd be a premature ejaculator, but no, Murphy's Law was striking again.

"Mmm. Do you like it, baby?"

I couldn't believe he had the nerve to ask me that. I swallowed an urge to shout "Fuck no!" and promptly shook my head. Then I went into a heavy panting that probably sounded more like asthma than pleasure. This boy (he was built like one, so I might as well call him that) was still pounding away at me, moaning and groaning harder than any black woman singing an old Negro hymn, after my second faked orgasm. I thought he'd never quit. Then finally, after at least twenty loooong minutes, he stiffened, grunted and was still.

Six whole weeks, almost seven, without, and now this. Damn.

Phase 5

"**H**ow was I to know?"

I was sitting in my stylist's chair next to Paulette, telling her off while Arleeta massaged conditioner into my hair.

"I knew I shouldn't have let you set me up. I knew it would be a mistake from the beginning."

"Genie, I'm sorry, girl. But you can't blame me. I ain't never seen the man without his pants. Serves you right for going so fast to begin with."

"Serves me right?"

I turned my head to look over at her. Arleeta turned it back and continued massaging.

"What d'you mean, serves me right?"

"The first date, Genie? You could've gotten to know him a little better first."

"Oh. That would've been great. Get to liking him and then boom! Bad sex. Yeah, Paulette, that would've really been terrific."

"You know what I mean, girl."

"Whatever. Anyway, how am I supposed to extricate myself from this situation now? He asked me to attend a seminar with him at Howard on Wednesday."

"Oh yeah, who's gonna be there?"

"Steve Cokely. But that isn't the point. How am I gonna get away from this man without hurting his feelings? I know Robert would never forgive me if I tell James the truth."

"Sure wouldn't. What you do is tell him you've made a mistake in sleeping with him so soon. Tell him your conscience is bothering you and that you've moved too fast."

"And then what? I can't very well let this man think he has a chance in the future. That wouldn't be fair to either of us. It's a shame, too, because we hit it off so well."

"That's terrible," Arleeta chimed in, flashing a gap-toothed grin. "But you could give him the 'I just want to be friends' bit. Lean back, girlfriend."

"You wanna know what I think? I think Miss Paulette here should tell him for me, since it was her idea in the first place."

"Me? No way. I am not getting involved in hurting that fine, sweet man because of your high expectations."

"High expectations? Chile, please. All I wanted was a good piece from the man and I couldn't even get that. If you call it high expectations for a woman to want the man she sleeps with to have at least an average dick, then you have got a problem. That little pencil he was working with was so lame."

Arleeta lifted my head and wrapped the towel around it to pat my hair dry.

"Both of y'all is crazy," Arleeta said, giggling.

I wiped the water out of my eyes with the towel.

"Come on, P, tell him for me."

"I said no."

"Why not? You're the one who did this, Paulette. It's your fault."

"I didn't sleep with him," she yelled over the noise of the blowdryer.

"I wouldn't have either if you had only kept your big mouth shut. I would've met somebody else sooner or later."

Paulette tossed her wet hair.

"Listen, girl, there's no reason to cry over spilt milk or small dicks or whatever. You need to just tell him that you've gone too fast and that the two of you should be friends. That will kill whatever plans he may have toward you."

"Mmhmm. Okay. But remember this incident next time you decide to try to help me change my lifestyle."

"Oh, I still think you need to change your lifestyle. I still contend that you should find your own man instead of messing around with these married men. But from now on, I'm staying out of it."

"Good girl. I've been wanting you to say that for the longest."

I left the salon with a fresh perm and a purpose. I was determined to get me some if it was the last thing I did. I got home and checked my messages. Two calls from Tess. That meant she needed advice. Both James and Robert had called. A missionary from church called asking me to add on five more pounds of potato salad and another three cakes for their church social.

I saved my messages, then dialed Nick's voice mail. He returned my call right away. Nick can be wonderful when he wants to be. I met him three years ago when I catered a birthday party for his wife, but have regretted accepting more than just monetary payment for services rendered ever since. The man can be a real bastard when he doesn't get his way.

Before I decided to spend some of my inheritance to buy my house, Nick set me up in an apartment in Rockville after we'd been seeing each other for about a month. Then all of a sudden, just because I wasn't available for dinner one night because of another commitment, he stopped paying the rent without telling me. He even went as far as retrieving the notices before I would see them, and one day I came home to find all my furniture sitting outside. I knew I would hate myself later.

"Hi, Gen. What's up, baby?"

"Not too much, Nick. I was just wondering what your plans are for tonight."

"Tonight? Why?"

"I thought maybe we could get together. You know, for old times' sake."

"Well, let's see. I've got a four o'clock meeting downtown, but I should be out of it by six. I can pick you up say about seven-thirty."

I was surprised he agreed to see me on such short notice. He never had when we were together. He must miss me or something.

"I have a better idea. Why don't I order Chinese when you get here."

"Alright, baby. Sounds fine to me."

Another surprise. Usually the only plans Nick agreed to were ones he made. Only because he couldn't stand not having the upper hand in any situation.

When he had me thrown out of my apartment I damn near begged him to get my place back for me, but he refused. He told me that he felt I was using him and that if all I wanted to do was sit around looking pretty all day and partying all night, I needed to find another benefactor. I moved in with Paulette and Robert for a few months, and finally bought my house. The trouble with Nick is that he's too shaky. One minute he's sweet as candy; the next, he's a snake. I swear, sometimes I think Paulette is right about these married men, because I have been through some stuff. Even with my theory. But what woman hasn't been through something when dealing with a man?

I promised myself and Paulette that I would never get romantically involve with Nick again, but after what happened with James last night, I was too horny to do the right thing.

The mood was set before Nick arrived. Brenda Russell spoke to my soul, her airy voice drifting through the speakers of my stereo. I had bathed and dusted a mist of powder all over my body, and my perfume filled my bedroom with its provocative, floral scent.

An array of vanilla creme–scented candles flooded soft light throughout the house. Staring at myself in my full-length mirror in the bedroom, I smiled at what I saw. Arleeta had curled my hair in flowing ringlets in front. The back was french rolled. I had on my Vermilion silk lounging pant outfit, with its loose sleeves and plunging neckline. I felt so sexy. I posed like I imagined a diva like Josephine Baker would have, and laughed at myself because my diva pose looked too ridiculous. Then I started clowning, making faces in the mirror.

When the doorbell sounded, I jumped. I tried to shake off the apprehension I felt about seeing Nick again before I opened the door. Brenda started singing about holding some man tight, if only for one night. I fixed a smile on my face. When I opened the door and saw Nick standing in my doorway holding a bottle of my favorite white wine and roses, I knew just what Brenda meant.

Phase 6

David

6

After three weeks of intense job hunting, I landed a tenure-track position at Whitman University, a school in downtown Washington with a solid reputation and one of the best creative writing programs on the east coast.

It's funny, but I've never wanted to teach. I never thought I was cut out for it. When I applied, a part of me felt like I was selling out. I felt, I don't know, like teaching would make me as complacent as editing had and I would never be able to recapture that pure streak of creativity that is the soul of true writers. But then, when I actually landed the job, I was just excited to be doing something—anything—again.

I spent the first week in a round of meetings with new colleagues, trying to learn all the new faces, and turning my office into a comfortable work atmosphere.

The office is pretty much a cubbyhole, but all in all, it's decent for my purpose there. I don't need a mausoleum in order to advise students, get some writing done and prepare for classes.

I have a long window that looks out onto what I'm sure will turn out to be a nice little park when spring comes. The walls are pale blue. The carpet is a darker blue, made of that thin cheap stuff.

I brought in a nice thick cerulean Persian rug from my office at home, and hung my framed black and whites of Baldwin, Hurston, Yerby and Hansberry on the wall above my desk. I also put up some wooden masks and a couple of family photo collages that Monica put together.

It's so good to wake up in the morning and have somewhere to go. I had forgotten what that's like. I like being able to get up to shower, shave and put on a tie in the mornings, and I hadn't realized just how much I'd missed it.

Monica's always long gone by the time I get up, but I'm used to that. She's very busy with her work. And now I'll be busy with my own. Since I won't be teaching until the summer, I'll have plenty of time to put together a skeleton of a novel and then review some books and materials for my course.

I'll be teaching Creative Writing to undergraduates. Unfortunately, it's a required course, which means I'm sure to get some knuckleheads who'll think they can hop a free ride through my course since their interests are far from writing. I'm not worried, though. They'll realize soon enough that I don't give free rides.

I want everybody who sits in my classroom to learn something. To take away some piece of knowledge about writing, or even themselves, that will stay with them the rest of their lives. It's a heavy goal, but I'm gung ho enough to try.

When I'm writing, I like to start early, so it was seven in the morning when I arrived at work the Monday of my second week. I snagged myself a cup of coffee and a carrot cake muffin from Roberto, the vendor who sits out in front of my building all day in a tight little cart.

Roberto flashed me a crooked tooth smile and handed me my change while I shifted from foot to foot, trying to keep warm.

"Take it easy," I managed to yell above the howling wind. It was so cold that my eyes were tearing up and my teeth chattered, so I felt like cheering when I cleared the stairs and felt the hard dry heat hitting me in the face when I opened the door and stepped into the building.

I pulled my ID from the breast pocket of my coat and flashed it at a fresh-faced kid at the front desk before sliding through the turnstile and waiting for one of the elevators to open. I noticed that one of them had an Out of Order sign in big bold letters taped over its steel doors. I looked up at the numbers above the good elevator to see what floor it was on. It said twelve, and that's where it seemed to want to stay.

"Always slow, aren't they? That, or broken like this puppy over here," a tall, slight, lemon-colored fella told me, pointing toward the broken elevator. His lips were drowned in a mass of thick curling black facial hair, and he wore a diamond stud in his nose and another in his ear.

"I think you're right," I mumbled. My eyes were glued to the 10 lit up above the good elevator and I was busy trying to pray the damn thing down. Out of the corner of my eye I saw a short, squat Korean woman walk up, hugging two large bags to her chest with mitted hands. Her blue wool cap was covered with a thick paisley scarf and she wore black army boots that were wet from tramping down the slick sidewalk.

The three of us stood watching the light above the elevator move slowly down until it disappeared altogether for a moment. Then the 1 lit up at the same time as a bell sounded, and we lumbered into the elevator.

"You press eight, please."

The Korean woman's voice was sweet and light like a long, clear note Miles Davis might have blown. Diamond-nose jabbed the 8 and the 2. I sipped my coffee and stared hard at his back, wondering how it is that a strong young SOB like him could be too lazy to walk up one damn flight of stairs. That kind of thing pisses me off in young people.

He whistled and unbuttoned his high collared coat before he stepped off the elevator and disappeared around a corner.

By the time I reached the tenth floor, my coffee was half gone and so was my urge to write. I walked down the quiet hall toward my office and unlocked the door and the smell of Christmas-tree car fresheners hit me. Mark had given them to me and I'd hung them on the doorknob.

I hung my overcoat and sport jacket on the coatrack in the corner and decided to call Monica, since we had missed each other for the past couple of days.

"Hey, babe."

"Well. What a nice surprise. What are you up to, working man?" she asked.

I put my feet up on the desk.

"Nothing, really. I just got in and I'm not much in the mood to put anything on paper right now, so I thought I'd phone my beautiful wife for a talk while I have my breakfast."

"I don't call a carrot-cake muffin breakfast, David. You know you should at least have some fresh fruit and bran, hon."

"And what makes you so sure that I'm eating a muffin?"

She laughed that rich, deep laugh of hers that reminds me of Eartha Kitt.

"Because I know my husband. And I know you don't watch what you eat."

Monica's laugh always makes me feel a little wicked.

"I know something that I could eat and not have to worry about counting calories."

I grinned, picturing in my head the blush that I knew was spreading across her face with that one.

"Oh David," she said, "don't be so gross."

Monica was so prim and proper sometimes. I cleared my throat and bit into my muffin.

"Anyway," I said, chewing, "it would be very nice if you could meet me at Nell's Grille for dinner tonight."

"Oh, honey, I'd love to but I can't."

Now how many times had I heard that? My heart fell. I thought about the last few nights I'd spent opening my famous can of mushroom soup and watching *Wheel of Fortune* all by myself. The boys were usually into their own thing.

"Why not?" I asked.

"Because, I'm meeting with some new clients tonight and I have to give them a grand tour of the city."

I almost wanted to ask if I could tag along, but I knew Monica wouldn't think that was a good idea. I could feel a twinge of anger tensing my jaw.

"Oh. Well," I said sarcastically, "do you think that I'll be able to spend some time with my wife one night this week?"

She sighed as if she were dealing with one of our sons.

"You're angry."

More like pissed off, I wanted to say, but I couldn't bring myself to admit it. I downed the last dash of coffee and pitched the cup at the wastebasket, but missed.

"I'm not angry."

"Yes you are, hon. I know that tone. But look, honey: When I accepted this job, I told you that at least for the first couple of years I'd have to work harder and smarter than the rest. There's a handful of people just waiting for me to fall on my face and I won't give them that satisfaction."

Another excuse I'd heard too many times. I was beginning to believe that I was married to Monica's job, not Monica. The thought made me tired. Tired of being pushed to the side by priorities that ranked higher on her list than I did. And I was tired of being damned lonely most every night.

"Look, babe, I—"

"Hon, I'm sorry, but my seven-thirty just arrived. I've really got to run. Love you."

Before I could respond, I heard a click and then a dial tone. I sat and listened to it a minute before I hung up the phone. There was nothing I could do but try to get some work done, so I pulled out some notes and went to work on the first few pages of my book. Before I knew it, I had worked through lunch. It was after two when I thought about getting something to eat from the deli on the first floor. I logged out of my computer and arranged my notes.

"Excuse me."

I turned around to find a very pretty, professional looking young woman standing in my doorway. She wore a yellow wool suit and held on to a smart briefcase. She seemed like she had a very easygoing personality. I liked her right away. But what I really liked were those legs of hers. She was a knockout.

"Yes. Can I help you?"

"I hope so." She was smiling at me with this warmth in her eyes that told me she was a sweet person.

"I'm looking for the English Department."

"Oh. The main office is just across the hall there."

She looked embarrassed. It was so cute the way she lowered her eyes.

"I'm sorry. My sense of direction must be off today. I'm sorry to have bothered you."

"That's okay. I've been here a few weeks and still get turned around sometimes."

"Well, thank you for your help."

She switched her briefcase to her other hand and turned to leave, but for some reason I didn't want her to go. I wanted to find out what had brought her. I wanted to be the one to have whatever answers she needed.

"Are you a new student?"

She turned in the doorway again, shaking her head in the negative and answering, "No. I've just been hired as a secretary in the English Department. I'm starting next week."

Something in me was smiling. I was glad I would see her again. I couldn't explain why.

"Welcome aboard, then." I stood from my chair and extended a hand to her. "I'm David Lewis. I'm a professor in this department. And you are? . . ."

Her fingers were small and gentle. I held onto them.

"I'm Genie. Genie Gatlin. It's good to meet you."

"Yes. It's good to meet you too."

She pulled her hand back and smiled.

"I guess I should go ahead in. I have to pick up some papers and things."

"Alright. I look forward to working with you."

"Me too. Have a nice day. Bye."

She shifted her briefcase again before she turned and walked away. She was so pretty. She didn't look like she should be a secretary in such a small department, trapped in this dank old building. She looked more like she should be modeling somewhere. Or at least working on the Hill for some high-powered bigwig. I was enchanted. Later, while I sat alone in front of the TV eating stale saltines and mushroom soup, I thought a little bit about Genie Gatlin's long legs and soft hands.

Genie

When I first learned that I'd gotten the position at Whitman University, I was psyched. It wasn't the position that excited me, of course. Being a secretary is nothing to celebrate over. What excited me was that I would be working in the English Department of a major university, meeting all types of people and exposing myself to all kinds of cultural differences. Plus, I knew I would be able to go to school practically free. I wouldn't have to touch another dime of my little inheritance.

But after a few weeks, any glamorized view that I had of university life was washed away by the constant ringing of the telephone, students trying to win the contest for who can ask the most stupid question, those good ol' boy Ph.D.'s (Prima hyphen Donna's) running

around with their self-important talk and their toddleresque temper
tantrums and worse, a bitch boss named Barbara Snowden. Hell,
drudgery stinks. But I prayed for a job, and I got this one.

I was in the middle of typing up 170 student names and addresses
for a merge document for a mailing when Barbara called my name.

"Genie."

I was so deep into what I was doing that I jumped at the sound of
her voice.

"Yes?" I rose from my seat and ducked my head inside the doorway
of her office.

Barbara was in her late forties. She looked like a shorter, much
thicker version of Tammy Faye Bakker with an extra pound of pancake
face makeup and less eye lashes. She wore these outrageous glasses that
were always falling off her nose. I was beginning to think that she was
a big gossip, too. As short a time as I'd been here, it seemed extraordi-
nary that I already knew a little dirt on several faculty and my co-
worker Justine. Aside from that shortcoming and her ever-growing
pettiness, she seemed to like me so far. I just hoped she didn't get any
dirt on me.

"Would you do me a favor?"

"What's that?"

She adjusted her crazy glasses. They slid down her nose again, so she
took them off and laid them on her desk.

"I know you're working on that big mailing, but would you mind
handing that off to Justine? Professor Lewis has a project he's working
on and he's asked if you wouldn't mind helping him with it."

"Sure." I put on my best kiss-up smile and the heifer ate it up.
"What's the project?"

"From what he explained to me, he's working on some material for
his course for the summer semester. You'll be helping him sift through
various books, old syllabi, exams. Organizing his notes. Things like
that. I think you'll enjoy it. He's a dream to deal with."

What she meant was that he wasn't your typical asshole professor.

"He has everything set up in his office and he's waiting for you."

"Okay."

I was glad. That mailing was about to be on my last nerve. I went in
to Justine's office and explained to her where I was with the mailing.
Then I walked across the hall to Dr. Lewis's office. He was on the telephone, so I stood halfway in his doorway, waiting for him to finish his

call. He looked up and smiled at me, gesturing for me to come in and sit down. I moved a pile of books that were scattered across a black leather armchair and placed them on the credenza behind it. Then I sat in the deep-cushioned chair and amused myself by watching the March wind blow leftover dead leaves along the sidewalk outside his window as people hurried by in their thick colorful hats and overcoats. Out of the corner of my eye, I saw Dr. Lewis put up a finger to let me know he would only be another minute. I nodded in response. He was such a nice man. Handsome, too. Dr. Lewis was very tall—I would say about six foot one. He had curly salt-and-pepper hair, cut close, and the nicest gray eyes. Those eyes were a strange and beautiful combination with his slightly lined, caramel skin, and he sort of reminded me of a black Marlboro Man because of his square jaw and dimples. He always wore well tailored suits in sedate colors, and I would bet anything he was something else when he was in his prime.

I realized I was staring at him, so to hide my embarrassment I looked up at some black and white photographs on the wall that looked like they were from a very long time ago and I wondered who those serious people were.

"I apologize for taking so long, Genie."

He replaced the receiver in the cradle, then turned to smile at me. He was the only professor on our faculty who seemed to really like people. All the other professors in the department treated me like a warm, replaceable body, but Dr. Lewis showed me the respect that all people should give each other in the workplace. From staff at the bottom of the totem pole to the highest-ranking positions, everybody in the workplace has an important contribution to make and should be treated accordingly.

"That's okay, I didn't mind," I said. "I was looking at your pictures up there."

He waved a hand toward the wall.

"Oh, those?"

"Mmhmm. Who are they?"

He gave me a strange look that made me feel stupid.

"You don't know who they are?"

"I don't think so. Should I?"

He shook his head and said, "Young people," like being young was the worst thing to be.

"How old are you, Genie?" he asked.

I gave him my "you're not supposed to ask a woman that question" look. "Why?"

He leaned back in his chair, looking at me like it didn't matter to him if I told him or not. "Just curious. You look about twenty, twenty-one."

I wondered where this was going and why he was getting all in my business.

"Add a few years. I'm twenty-five," I said.

He looked thoughtful for a moment. His brow creased. Then he looked at his watch. So I looked at mine. But then I remembered mine was broken. The clock on his wall said 1:20, which didn't mean a damn thing to me. Maybe he had a meeting to go to.

"Is something wrong, Dr. Lewis?"

"Hmm? No. Nothing's wrong."

"So who are they?"

"Who are . . . oh. A few of our esteemed authors. James Baldwin, Zora Neale Hurston, Frank Yerby, Lorraine Hansberry."

He pointed each of them out as he proudly said their names.

"Oh. I've read some of their stuff. Well, at least Zora Neale Hurston's, anyway. I had to read *Seraph on the Suwanee* in high school. Plus, I saw Hansberry's *A Raisin in the Sun* on video last summer."

I just knew that sounded pitiful. I was ashamed that I wasn't anywhere near as well read as he seemed to be. Thank God he didn't embarrass me about it. He just asked, "What did you think of *Raisin?*"

"It was good. I've wanted to read the play ever since, but I haven't gotten around to getting a copy."

Hadn't even thought about getting a copy was more like it, but Dr. Lewis didn't know that.

"Hold on a second," he said, shoving stacks of books and papers aside. He pulled a crinkled copy of the play from beneath several bound papers. It was a ratty paperback with bold orange letters printed across the front.

"Why don't you borrow it for a while, and after you read it we can sit down over lunch and discuss it."

"Okay. Thank you," I said, taking the paperback. "I'll be sure to read it."

I wasn't sure how. I was in the middle of reading three other books simultaneously as it was. He smiled at me and patted my hand the way my grandfather used to when I was a little girl. Then his face changed. The smile left and he reached for a yellow legal pad on his desk.

"Now then," he said, picking up a well-sharpened pencil. "Let me tell you what we're going to do with all this stuff. "What I want to do here"—his hand flourished over the boxes of books and stacks of papers—"is organize and catalogue all of this stuff I've brought from home that I've accumulated over the years. Now, the best way I see to go about this is for us to separate the books from the copied material, then divide the books into categories, such as poetry, plays, fiction, et cetera. After that, we can alphabetize by author and do a complete inventory. We'll deal with the copied material later, because that involves some other exciting work. So, what do you think?"

Exciting work? The man was nuts. He put his hands on his hips, reminding me of a sea captain, and his eyes were shining like he was having the time of his life. I could tell he wanted me to be as pleased as he was about going through a bunch of dusty old books and papers, so I said, "Sounds good."

I think that did the trick, because he patted my shoulder like I was his buddy. "Perfect. But before we get started," he checked his watch again, "I think we should eat first. You like pizza?"

"Of course," I said.

We ordered in a Domino's veggie pizza. I hadn't realized how hungry I was until the smell hit me. We cleared away most of the mess cluttering his desk and pulled our chairs close to it.

"So tell me, Genie, what brought you to Whitman?"

I took a sip from my soda.

"I needed a job. And I figure that maybe I'll take some classes here and there, decide what I want to do with the rest of my life while I'm here."

"What have you been doing up till now?"

"I had a catering business that I ran from home. I still do, but just on a small scale. I'll give you one of my cards."

"Why'd you stop doing it full-time?"

"After a while, I didn't quite like it."

"Why not?"

He was making a small pile on his plate with the onions he pulled off his pizza.

"I liked the cooking part. Actually, I love cooking. I enjoy the creativity of it, you know. The challenge of making something beautiful that's worth eating, the different colors and textures and flavors of food. It's very therapeutic for me."

"But?" he said expectantly.

I inhaled sharply. I turned toward the door when a rush of laughing students, released from a class down the hall, flew by the doorway trailing bookbags and jackets.

"But," I said, turning to face Dr. Lewis again, "the business end of catering has almost killed my creativity. I mean, cooking started to feel like hard, boring work instead of a labor of love, and I think after a while I stopped putting my passions into the food and started becoming a one-woman production operation, you know."

He nodded as if he did know. His beautiful gray eyes took on a reflective look, as if he was watching my words play out a movie of his own life. "I understand just what you mean," he said quietly. "I felt the same way for years as an editor down in Atlanta. Matter of fact, this is the first time in about twenty years that I feel like I'm being true to my art. When I started out after I earned my doctorate, I had so many dreams. I was going to write something brilliant that moved people. I was going to be the next Richard Wright."

"So what happened?"

"Trying to become the next Richard Wright didn't pay the bills. My wife was in school full-time, so the breadwinning was up to me. I had to do something to earn a steady buck, so I became a copyeditor and put my writing career on the back burner for a while. Little did I know then that I'd leave it on the back burner so long that I'd forget it was there and, more importantly, forget how to use it."

"Mmm. I believe it. The last few months I did catering, I barely cooked for myself. All I ate were microwave dinners and fast food, which is almost a sin for me, because I prefer fresh-grown foods. But here I am, a woman who grows her own herbs and vegetables, eating this kind of stuff."

I held up my half-eaten slice of pizza.

"So what's your best dish?"

"Uhm. I think I'd have to say, lasagna."

"Wow. My favorite."

"Oh, you like lasagna?"

"I love it."

"Well, I'll have to make you some one of these days."

"I might have to take you up on that. So how do you like Whitman so far, my friend?" The man seemed nice, but I swear he had more questions than Alex Trebek.

"It's fine," I said. "Okay, I guess."

"You guess?"

I wasn't about to spill my guts to somebody I didn't know from a can of paint, so I said, "Yeah. The students are nice and the atmosphere is great."

"Yeah, I think so too," he said, but he had that strange look on his face again.

"It sounds like we've both made some positive life changes by coming to Whitman." He picked up his can of Mountain Dew. "Tell you what," he said, "here's to the joys of cooking and writing. May we always remain true to our arts."

"I'll drink to that." I sucked the sauce off my thumb and lifted my can of Sprite.

We clinked cans, and I think he must have felt as silly as I did because we both began to laugh. Dr. Lewis had a very nice laugh. It didn't really sound like anything in particular, but it felt like something good I knew. Like the way the sun makes you feel when you come out of your house in a short-sleeve shirt the day that spring really arrives because the weatherman has told you that it will hit seventy five degrees. I knew I was going to like working with Dr. Lewis. He was pretty cool.

Phase 7

David

Monica and I don't make love anymore. We meet needs. I can't pinpoint exactly when our passion cooled. It happened without me really being aware the change was coming. See, over the years, we have put together this routine of work and kids and marriage. We both know our roles in each and have become so comfortable in those roles that everything we do now is second nature.

It's sad that our sex life has fallen in *so* well with our other routines, that sex is the same as going to the toilet now. I feel like I have to take a piss, so I head for the bathroom to relieve myself. My dick gets hard, so I roll over and reach for Monica to relieve my tension. And that doesn't happen too often anymore.

I remember what a pleasure it was a long time ago to kiss Monica and touch her body until she was begging me to get inside her. I felt like I had a power then that no other man could ever touch. Like I had some type of superhuman strength. Now it's the opposite with us. Monica tells me to hurry up and get it over with, like she doesn't really want me to touch her but she's doing me a favor because I'm her husband.

Sometimes I wonder if she realizes, as I do, that our sex life is only another part of our routine. If she does know, then what does she think has caused it? I'd really like to know, but I could never ask her that. I'm afraid she'll tell me that I'm just not giving it to her good anymore. Or worse, she may tell me that the little bulge around my middle or my thinning hair is a turnoff. Suppose she wants some punk with a tighter stomach than mine? Shit, Monica has changed too. Her waistline has stretched more than a little bit. I've noticed those, what she calls, crow's-feet and laugh-lines in her face. I know that she dyes her hair to keep it black, and I haven't complained. So she'd better not be judging all the changes in me. But she must be. She hasn't turned that career of hers into a lover for no reason at all. How the hell am I supposed to compete with her career? How the hell can I put the words together to tell Monica I am scared of getting old, that when I look in the mirror now I see an old man's face, and I'm afraid that life is moving on without me? She would never understand how I feel. Nobody can understand. Shit, I don't even understand why something inside me is calling out for a taste of my youth.

I think that's why I'm finding myself drawn to Genie. Her youth is a real refresher. She is a pleasure to work with. She's a bright, attractive, intuitive woman. I know she's fairly young, but when we talk, she makes me feel like I'm the kid. I've learned more about myself in working with her in the short time that I have, than I have in my seven months of self-analysis.

Truthfully, I came up with the inventory project so that Genie and I could spend some time together so I could get to know her better. I'm glad I did. There's definitely much more to her than a great pair of legs. It's a shame she's working in an office where she's clearly not appreciated.

The little project we had going only took us a week and a half to complete, and I wanted there to be some way for Genie and me to continue our personal interaction. I racked my brain about it. I didn't want to ask her to lunch again. We had eaten together much of the project, and it wouldn't look good for us to become lunch buddies.

An idea for how to keep our interaction going came to me on one of my early morning writing days when I bumped into her in the main office. It was seven in the morning and she was busy making coffee. I asked her why she was in the office so early. She told me that she was an early riser and liked the peace and quiet in the morning. For some reason I remembered that, and I buzzed the office yesterday around seven-thirty to ask her if she would check to see if I'd gotten a fax I'd been waiting for from a publisher in New York. She checked for me and told me it hadn't come. Naturally we fell into a pleasant conversation that lasted half an hour.

I figured there wouldn't be any harm in calling her again today to say hello, so I poured myself a cup of coffee and sat down at the kitchen table in front of a bowl of hot cereal with the telephone in my lap. It was quarter to eight. The house was as silent as a funeral home. Monica had dashed out over an hour ago, and Mark had caught the bus. Devin had hitched a ride from a friend with a new car who was a senior at his high school. I took a spoonful of oatmeal and checked out the headings on the front page of the *Post,* then dialed the office number.

"Good morning, English Department. Genie Gatlin speaking."

Her voice did something to me. I hadn't been this excited about talking to a woman in a long time.

"Good morning." I hoped she didn't notice my eagerness.

"Dr. Lewis, hi. How are you this morning?" She seemed happy to hear from me. Just the sound of her voice made my day.

"Fine. Just fine. I'm having some coffee and a little breakfast, looking through the paper a bit. How's everything with you this morning?"

"Good. I was just listening to some music and looking at the book of Nikki Giovanni poetry you gave me to read."

"Oh yeah?" I had wondered if she really was interested in all the books I'd loaded her up with. She had told me she liked to read, but she wasn't a fanatic like me. "What do you think of it so far?"

"It's good. Well, no, good is an understatement. She's phenomenal."

I laughed and told her she wasn't the first person to have said so and drank down some of my coffee. "She's one of my personal favorites, along with Lucille Clifton. Make sure you read some of her stuff. Listen," I said, "since you like Nikki so much, go ahead and keep that book as a gift from me."

She acted like I had told her she'd won the lottery.

"Dr. Lewis, I can't do that. This is an autographed copy."

"Sure you can. It's a gift."

"Really? You sure?"

I suddenly remembered that Monica had given me the book to celebrate our six-month anniversary when we were dating. I still remembered the feel of the blue velvet cloth she'd wrapped it in and the satiny pink ribbon she'd tied around it. Her eyes had needed me to like the gift and to love her then, and I had done both. But that was a long time ago. I hadn't opened that book in years, let alone thought about the damn thing, so it felt natural for me to say, "Of course, Genie. Keep it and enjoy it."

She thanked me so well that I wanted to give her more things. Beautiful clothes like those tight little skirts she wore, so I could watch those shapely legs move down the hall; tight sweaters and more of those sexy high-heeled shoes she liked to wear so much. I was getting a bit ahead of myself, though.

"So, Genie, anything going on there in the office this morning? By the way, what's your given name, I know it can't be Genie?"

"I'm not telling you."

"Come on. I'm sure it's not that bad. Tell me."

"Okay, fine. It's Eugenia. I was named after my paternal grand-mother. Happy now?"

I made a face that I was glad she couldn't see.

"Not really. I think I'll stick to calling you Genie."

"I wouldn't have it any other way, Doc. Look, let me ask you a question: What do you think of Barbara?"

A number of responses came to the fore of my mind, but none of them were appropriate.

"I haven't been with the department long enough to really form an opinion of her," I said. "Why do you ask?"

"Because I think—"

"Hold on just a minute, Genie."

I heard a noise. It sounded like someone was at the door. I thought maybe Monica had forgotten something. She was famous for that. I eased the telephone onto the table and tiptoed out into the hall and to the front window so that I could look out. I was relieved that the driveway was empty. I realized that the wind was probably disturbing the screen door, so I opened the front door and locked the screen. It was better if Monica didn't walk in on me chatting with Genie.

"Sorry about that, my friend." I adjusted my robe and sat back in my chair. "I thought I had a visitor at my door."

"That's fine. So anyhow, like I was saying, I'm really beginning to wonder about Barbara, you know."

My damn oatmeal had gotten cold, so I pushed it aside. Outside someone's dog started barking like a maniac.

"Why's that?"

"I mean, when I first came to Whitman, I thought she was this nice grandmotherly"—I winced at that word because Barbara was two years younger than I—"woman who wanted to take me under her wing and encourage me to grow. I mean, I really want to put my best foot forward in this job, Dr. Lewis."

"I know you do."

"Well, it seems to me that since I'm always on time, always helpful to professors and students alike and ready to do whatever is necessary to help the office run smoothly, Barbara should want me to do more and learn more."

"What's she doing that's bothering you so much?"

"It's . . . I don't know, Dr. Lewis. She's just so nitpicky, you know? It's like everything we do in this office is never good enough. I could break my neck making copies for this professor and typing up a quiz for that professor and running around answering calls and student questions, but all I get from Barbara is, 'Genie, didn't you notice the coffee was getting low,' or 'Genie, those plants need water just as much as we do.' I swear, Doc, that woman is enough to make me want to commit a crime."

All I could do was laugh. The woman was delightful. I got a kick out of listening to her get so worked up. I pictured her beautiful brown eyes full of fire, and it turned me on.

"And don't let me start on her gossiping. She dishes more dirt than anyone I've ever seen. I'm sorry, Dr. Lewis, I don't mean to go off like this, but that woman is getting on my last nerve. Working with you the past week and a half has been heaven. I wish there was some way I could work with you more often."

That caught my attention. I had to come up with some ways to make that happen.

"I'm sorry to hear that Barbara's on your case, my friend. I don't have to come in contact with her too often, as you know. All I can suggest is that you do like you've been doing, work hard, try to stay out of her way as much as possible. But I do hope you know how much I appreciate you, Genie. I really do, you know."

"Yes. I know. Thanks. I needed that reassurance to get me started this morning, Doc."

"Well, I'm glad I could do that for you. Listen, I'd better run if I want to get some work done this morning. I've got a couple of meetings this afternoon, but I'll be in around two o'clock, so if anyone's looking for me, could you let them know?"

"Sure I will."

"Good. See you later this afternoon, then."

"Okay. See you then. Bye."

"Bye-bye."

I felt so good after talking to Genie, I zipped through stacking the dishwasher and taking a shower. Then I wrote a full seventeen pages into Chapter Two of my book. Already I was feeling like I had dropped ten years off my age.

Genie

Paulette and I have gone kite flying every March. What made us more excited this time, though, was that it was Telaysia's first time out, so we brought along my 35 millimeter Kodak to capture the moment on film.

Before Telaysia was born, Paulette used to bring her bad-ass little cousin Nathaniel. Nathaniel is six. He had a terrible habit of kicking the back of my seat while we were in the car. Every time I see him I want to snatch a knot in his behind. My tag-alongs are always my two godchildren, Sasha and Simeon, my friend Evelyn's children. The twins are well-behaved seven-year-olds. Now that Telaysia's of age, thank God Nathaniel didn't come along with us this time.

Kite flying is a ritual for me and Paulette that started in middle school. In eighth grade we entered our school's kite-flying contest. The prize was twenty-five dollars. I had never flown a kite before. I went out and bought this cheap glossy pink plastic kite with a picture of Penelope Pitstop in her aviation gear on it. It had a long tail of pink and yellow ribbon ties. I was so proud of it. Both me and Paulette lost the contest. My kite barely made it off the ground. Paulette's line tangled in a telephone wire. But we were hooked. We've gone to the park to fly kites every year ever since.

We hit the uncrowded parkway early, heading for Buddy Attick Park. Since we had three kids and three kites, we drove Paulette's big blue Voyager. Telaysia sat in her little carseat making all kinds of squeals because Sasha kept waving colorful toys in her face to amuse her. Simeon stared out the window with a finger in his mouth and the other hand fiddling with his ear.

"Girl, pop in that Prince CD for me."

"Paulette, I'm not listening to all that whooping and hollering this early in the morning. Let's listen to something soft, like Luther."

I removed one of my red leather gloves and rifled through a stack of CDs.

"Mmmm. Better yet: Aretha. Paulette, slow this big boat down, girl. You're going to hit one of those barriers or something." I slid Aretha Franklin's *Best of* . . . CD into the CD player.

"Honey, I know how to drive. It isn't my fault that there's always construction going on on this stupid parkway. My baby will probably be finished with college before they finish messing with this road. Ooh, girl, 'Natural Woman.' Turn that up a little." Paulette popped her fingers and did a "waoo" with Aretha's background girls.

I turned up the volume. "Y'all alright back there?" The twins replied with a sing-song "Yes." I turned around to get a quick look at them. All three kids were bundled up like little brown Eskimos in their hats and scarves and jackets. Still, I hoped they would be warm enough while we were in the park. It was a crisp day with a steady wind. Prime for kite flying. But bad for giving little ones the sniffles.

When we reached the park, we filed out of the van. Paulette and the children waited beside the van while I handed out the kites. Buddy Attick was my favorite park. It had a lake and children's playgrounds, and lots of clear open space for kite flying.

A line of evergreens edged the parking lot, hiding the sloping grassy park from our view until we moved between them into the open area and saw a web of snow-white seagulls circling the air above the wide lake as gracefully as ice skaters. The lake was still half frozen. People were walking their dogs, just feeling the fresh air or gazing up at their kites. The sky was a soft, sunless gray, making the day seem colder than it was. But I still felt alive and rejuvenated, in spite of the numbness of my face in the biting wind.

"How about over there, guys?" I pointed toward a stretch of clear space where the kids wouldn't have to worry about running into anyone or tangling their kites.

"That'll work. Genie, hold this a minute, would you?" Paulette handed me Telaysia's fluttering plastic Power Ranger's kite we bought at Kmart and hefted Telaysia onto her hip, then we all tramped across the field.

"Alright Simeon," I said, bending, "let me get you started first."

He turned kite and body away from my outstretched hand.

"I could do it myself, Aunt Genie."

"Fine, little man." I turned toward Sasha and reached for her kite. "Okay, sweet pea. Now you go over there and start running."

Sasha jogged off, her little head bobbing and her pink and white scarf flying out behind her, Red Baron style. She kept turning back to see her kite. I watched it sail out above me, riding on a crest of wind as easily as those seagulls.

"Look at me, Aunt Genie. Look. I told you I could do it myself!" Simeon's kite was so high up it looked like a dot in the wind. The boy was truly amazing for his age. He was grinning at me, showing the empty space his two front baby teeth had deserted.

"Go ahead, Simmy!" I shouted.

"Mines is going high too, Aunt Genie. Look!" Sasha said. I gave her the thumbs up.

"Yes it is, Miss Thing. I'll tell you. You guys are pros."

I put my hands deep into the pockets of my red quilted coat and stood back watching the children. Paulette and Telaysia were trying to make her kite fly. It kept nose-diving into the ground like an airplane. Every time it did, Telaysia pointed at it and burst out laughing. Then she'd run to it on her chubby little legs and fall over. I whipped out my camera and started snapping. Maybe one day I'll be able to bring my own kids out to the park to fly kites.

・　・　・

On Sunday evening I went over to Paulette and Robert's for dinner with a wok full of shrimp stir-fry, a pot of rice and a pan of sushi and egg rolls. Paulette had gone to Blockbuster and rented two of our favorite blaxploitation movies, *Dolemite* and *Coffy*. Every now and then when me and Paulette got into our hip mode, we would drink a lot and watch those badass movies from the seventies. They were so corny that we would sit back and laugh our asses off. But we loved them just the same.

Robert carried my bags into the house and Paulette helped me set up the food in the kitchen.

"Mmmmm, girl. This looks some kind of good."

She picked a California roll out of the pan and bit into it.

"Paulette, stay out of the food long enough to help me put some of this on the tray."

I paused. I heard male laughter float up to the kitchen from the basement.

"Who's that with Robert? You invited somebody else over? Girl, I'm glad I made a whole lot of this stuff." I proceeded to put the rice into an attractive porcelain dish.

Paulette started twisting her ponytail around her finger.

"Now, Genie," she said, "promise me you won't get upset, okay?"

"What?"

She backed away from me.

"Promise you won't leave, G. It wasn't my idea in the first place. I didn't even know, girl. I swear."

"Paulette what are you talking about? Know about what?" I tested an eggroll wrapper to see if it was still warm enough to serve.

"Uhm. James is here," she whispered.

I blinked twice. I felt heat gathering in my face and an overwhelming calm.

"What did you just say?" I was totally in control of myself, but didn't realize I was shaking my head.

Paulette got that Lucy Ricardo look in her eyes that she always got when she was up to something. "Come on, Genie, it's only one evening. Just black folk getting together for some good food and stuff, girl. Come on."

"I don't believe this. Paulette, how could you let this happen? And why didn't I see his car out front?"

"Girl, he got rid of that Beamer. That's his black Cirrus out there. But I had no idea that Robert invited him. My eyes almost fell out when I opened the door and saw him 'cause I knew you'd be pissed. You know I wouldn't do anything like this to you on purpose."

"Well, I'm going home. You guys enjoy the meal."

Paulette grabbed my arm.

"No, Genie. Robert told him you were coming and he knows you're here now."

"Why the hell didn't you call me and tell me not to come then, Paulette? How the hell am I supposed to walk downstairs and act like everything is everything when I've been avoiding him like the plague? He's bound to ask me why I haven't been calling him about another date. Shit, Paulette, I can't embarrass myself like this. How could Robert do this?"

"Genie, get a grip, now. You swore me to secrecy, remember? Robert has no idea that you don't want to be bothered with James. He thinks he's still playing matchmaker. And poor James doesn't know you were a dissatisfied customer."

I rolled my eyes.

"I'm up here freaking out and here you are making stupid jokes. Why did I ever let you get me into this mess?"

"Come on, Genie. There's nothing you can really do now except go down there with a nice smile and a friendly hello. Come on. I've got your back." She thrust a tray at me. I sucked my teeth and took it like the fool I am. I pulled away when she tried to put a hand on my shoulder to squeeze it. She smiled at me just like Lucy does when she knows she has Ethel by the jugular.

"I'll go first," Paulette said excitedly. I wanted to kick her down the stairs. I pictured what she would look like sprawled at the bottom with shrimp and vegetables stuck in her hair. I settled for pulling her ponytail, and she giggled under her breath as we walked down the stairs. I had to do five relax, relate, releases in my head just to feel like I could turn on some sort of phony smile. I swear, I hate being fake.

Soon as I hit the last step. I mean, I didn't even get my foot sunk into the carpet good before the man was up and out of his seat from in front of the TV to greet me with his grinning self. What got me was that he still thought I liked him.

"Heeeey. There you are. It's been too long, girl." Shit, it had only been two months, and that wasn't near long enough. My stomach tightened. James took the tray from me. He set it on Paulette's cocktail table and pulled me into a deep, tight embrace. I breathed in the Nautica cologne that clung to the curve of his neck.

"Let me look at you, baby." He stepped back away from me and smiled like he was satisfied. I had forgotten how fine he was. His Tommy shirt fit him to a T and the jeans he wore molded his thighs like only paint could. He had let his hair grow out on top in thick curls, and damn if he wasn't sporting an earring.

When I realized I was smiling too and feeling a little nervous, I forced my eyes to drop briefly to zipper level. "Mmhmm," I told myself silently, "get a grip, girl. You know the deal."

"You look beautiful," James said. He strip searched me with his eyes and I felt like crossing my arms over my tight, chocolate velour sweater. I could see Robert smiling so hard in our direction that his big head was probably hurting. I wanted to bop him on it. Him and his big-legged wife.

"Thank you," I said to James, and I touched his shoulder like I meant it.

"How have you been these past couple months?"

I knew it. He wasted no time in bringing up the subject of our not having seen each other since that terrible night.

"Just fine. And you?"

"Ah, everything is cool. You know, work, work and more work. I joined Bally's a few weeks ago, so I work out every night now after school. And I'm still doing the tutoring for the kids over in Anacostia."

Hunh. Trying to impress me. He should have thought about that before he dropped his pants.

"How do you like your new job?" he asked. I guess he'd heard about that from Robert.

"It's okay. It's not my dream job, but I think it's a start in the right direction. They keep me hopping over there, and there's one professor I work with who's really a nice guy. I think I can learn a lot from him."

"What do you do over at the university?"

So far so good. As long as we kept the subject light I could handle dealing with Mr. Caldwell.

"A little bit of everything. I work in the English Department. I could be doing anything from light research to proctoring exams to ordering books to arranging lectures to preparing presentations. It's a mixed bag, really. I spend a lot of time running around."

"Don't you think it's kind of funny that you were down on teachers when we first met, and now here you are working in higher education?"

"You know, I thought about that. It is sort of funny. But what I'm finding is that a lot of the professors are pretty interesting people. I mean, the kinds of things they've done. We have one guy who came to us from *Newsweek,* and another guy worked as head writer of a CBS soap opera years ago. And they all seem to know a lot of fascinating people too. And I see exactly what you mean about the students. It can be pretty fulfilling to make a difference in someone's life. Even if it's a small difference."

"Sounds like you think your job is more than okay, Genie."

"Actually, there's good and bad points about the job. The management style stinks. There seems to be a lot of bureaucracy around there.

My boss is a micro manager, and it's difficult sometimes to deal with so many personalities at once because most all of the professors are demanding types. But the people I'm meeting and the things I'm learning—that's well worth the crap I have to put up with. And as long as I'm satisfied with my growth progress, I'm happy enough."

"Well, I'm glad you have a plus. My job's the same way. I could do without some of the idiotic bureaucracy too, but the kids outweigh the negatives."

"I hear you."

"So, Genie, tell me, baby, when are we going to see each other again? I thought we really hit it off. I know we hit off. So what happened with you?"

"Uhm. Well, see, James . . ." I ran a hand through my curls and licked my lips, hoping Paulette would notice. That was our signal from her single days that one of us needed to be rescued immediately. I hoped she remembered.

"Well would you look at all this beautiful food Genie was kind enough to make for us. You like Chinese don't you, James?" She laid a hand on his back.

Robert glanced at her, confused. I thanked God that He was in His heaven, and I could tell from her face that Miss Paulette was about to go off on one of her tangents.

"And you know, Genie makes these egg rolls and sushi herself. But then you already know she cooks, but the thing is, you must try this stuff. She cooks like an angel, honey. Let me tell you—"

"Uhm, babe," Robert interrupted, "he already knows that Genie is a good cook."

"But Robert, Genie doesn't just cook. Homegirl throws down. Excuse me, James," She looked up at him apologetically. "I'm sure you know how capable Robert is of being modest about the accomplishments of others. But, well, I like to give credit where credit is due."

"I see," James told her.

"Now," she began again, leading him toward the sushi, "these are called—what are these called again, Genie?"

"California rolls," I offered and leaned back against the wall to watch her work.

"That's right. California rolls. Have you tasted these before, chile? See, these don't have that nasty raw fish in them. They have crabmeat in them."

"I know, Paulette. I love sushi."

"Oh. Then you'll love these." She jabbed a fork into one. "Taste this. Go ahead, taste it."

"Paulette," Robert warned. She tossed her head and waved him off. There was no stopping her now. I thought I would die from holding in my laughter.

James took the fork and bit into the roll.

"What do you think?"

"It's good."

"Good? Honey, it is divine. But look, why don't you"—she led him by the arm to the sofa—"sit right here. Robert will pop *Dolemite* in so we can all trip out off Rudy Ray Moore, and Genie and I will fix you gentlemen a hefty drink and a plate of eats. Mmkay?"

The brother gave up and did as he was told.

Paulette sidled up to me and whispered, "Girl, I'm going to ply him with so much booze he'll forget who you are."

Then she rubbed her hands together and reached for the Remy.

•　•　•

"Dr. Lewis, answer me a question: What's the best way for a woman to let a man know she's not interested without really letting him know?"

He was quiet for a long time. I was sitting in my office twirling the telephone cord and staring up at my wall calendar, making a mental note to change it to the correct month when I got off the phone.

Dr. Lewis and I had, I guess, become friends. At first I was a little reserved with him when he started calling. I'm so used to people, especially men, having an angle that for weeks I wondered what his was because this telephone thing of ours started right out of the blue. And lately he was too nice to me. Paid too much attention to me. He was so patient during my first awkward days, that every time he came around I braced myself, waiting for him to reveal his true self. But he stayed the same and that confused me.

So then I started watching him when he wasn't looking. I noticed how people spoke so well of him. Students and staff. Everybody he came into contact with seemed to really respect the man. He was so knowledgeable. Not just about writing, but everything. I noticed how other professors went to him and asked him these obscure questions that he amazingly knew the answers to—or if he didn't, he knew who had the answers. I watched him for two whole weeks and was too impressed. And I realized something. One of the most beautiful things to see in motion is a confident black man who accepts nothing less than the respect that he earns.

During our project is when I truly understood that Dr. Lewis is genuinely a nice guy. I finally opened up and let myself reciprocate the admiration and respect he made me feel he had for me. In fact, I felt somewhat honored that he would think I have something important to offer. I mean, the man is superintelligent. Went to all the right schools. He let me read one of his short stories, and I see now that his talents are fierce too. He's warm, sensitive, funny, creative. What really hooked me into letting the man see a piece of the real me is that he really listens to me. I mean, I can tell by his eyes that he really wants to know about me. Hear about my bad days with Barbara and whoever else. And he isn't one of those stinking shrinks that watch you spill your guts while they rob you blind. He's just somebody who makes me feel like he's interested in what I have to say. That simple.

As long as I can remember, I've never had a male friend in my life. But Dr. Lewis is different. Like a real dad would be. Protective almost. Somehow, my instincts told me I could trust him.

I was glad when he continued calling in the mornings. His voice brought some life to the office, and every word of encouragement that he gave me somehow made me feel grounded.

He still hadn't said a word. "Dr. Lewis?"

"Why would you ask me that?"

"There's this guy I went out—"

"Oh. A guy you've dated. Oh, I see."

"Yeah. Well, anyway, his name is James, and we went out one time and he really likes me, but I don't ever want to see him again."

He was quiet again. I drummed my fingers on the desk and noticed that some of my nails sported chipped polish. I pulled my fuchsia polish out of my desk drawer and went to work.

"Why don't you like the guy? What's the matter with him?"

I stopped filling in the chipped spots for a minute and thought about how to respond. I couldn't just come out and tell another man that James has a little dick. I mean, suppose Dr. Lewis was ill-equipped too? Then that would hurt his feelings.

"Nothing's wrong with him. Well . . ." I was glad he couldn't see me blushing.

"What?"

"Nothing, really. I mean he's nice, he's handsome, he really has a lot going for him but he's . . . he's just . . . not right for me."

Even if Dr. Lewis was built like a stallion, I couldn't bring myself to tell him about my sex life. I only wanted him to have good thoughts about me.

"No sparks, huh?"

"Yes. Exactly. No sparks. But he's really nice though, and I don't want to hurt his feelings. So come on, fix my life. What should I do?"

"You know, Genie, I always find honesty really is the best policy in most cases. Tell him you think he's a great guy but you aren't interested in getting involved with someone you know you can't love."

"I couldn't say that, Dr. Lewis. That's too mean. Besides, that wouldn't be at all honest of me."

"How so?"

"I don't believe in love. It doesn't exist for me."

"How can you say that? Love is the most beautiful emotion of human nature. It's been written about the world over. People have killed and died for it."

"When's your birthday?"

"In August. August 18."

"So that makes you a . . . What sign are you?"

"Leo. Why?"

"Leo. I should have known."

"Should have known what?"

"That you're a Leo. Now I understand why we get along so well. I'm a Libra, and Leos and Libras are supposed to be highly compatible. Only thing is, Leos always spout that romantic crap about love. I don't buy into all that pretty b.s. Anyway, love doesn't have anything to do with my situation. I just have to figure out how to get this kid off my back."

"You're too goddamn cynical."

"Yeah, yeah. Stop giving me compliments."

He laughed like I had said the most hilarious thing. I wondered sometimes if he was senile. He'd kill me if I told him that.

"But look, Doc, I've done everything I could to let him know I don't want his attentions. I haven't returned his calls, I've blown him off when he has gotten ahold of me. But still, when I went to my girl-friend's last night he had the nerve to show up, and now he's wanting to know when we can see each other again. I can't take it. But the last thing I want to be is an asshole about it."

"What about having his buddy tell him?"

"Robert doesn't know. I couldn't bring myself to tell him either."

"Okay. Why don't you have your friend, what's her name?"

"Who? Paulette?"

"Yeah. Have Paulette tell her husband then."

"I guess I could do that. She's the one who got me into this mess in the first place, you know. She's the one who fixed me up with this nitwit. But look, I don't want to make Robert upset either."

"Woman, stop shooting down my ideas. I'm a man, so I understand this kind of thing. Trust me. It would probably be better coming from Robert rather than you, since you have that choice. I know I would prefer it that way. In fact, I had that experience in college. I was stuck on this girl, Julie Templeton." He drew out her name like he was remembering what she looked like. Then he gave a short laugh. I got the feeling he was telling himself the story, more so than me.

"This girl was something else. Face like a movie star. Big, pretty legs. What the Commodores called a brick house. Mmm. Had every guy in school running after her, including me, which was saying something because I wasn't a bad looking cat."

"Oh really. So you were real smooth, huh? Big man on campus. Had all the ladies in an uproar."

"I won't say that, but I had my share. I was pretty athletic. Ran track for two years. There weren't too many girls I wanted to date that I couldn't get next to."

It was my turn to laugh. Dr. Lewis killed me with his conceit. The way he swaggered into the office every day all perfectly groomed and together, you could tell he thought he looked good. So did a lot of the female students, and that only seemed to further swell his head. I felt like it was up to me to bring him back to earth, so I always teased him whenever he showed his conceit.

"And what year was this that you were in college, Dr. Lewis? Was this in the early or late 1940s?"

Boyfriend didn't think that was funny. But I laughed my head off.

"Has anybody ever told you that you talk entirely too much, Genie? Try to listen to the story without interrupting, would you."

I could hear the lightness in his tone, so I knew he wasn't upset.

"Okay, professor. Go ahead. Entertain me."

"That's better. So as I was saying—oh damn! Hold on a minute— another call is trying to come through."

While I waited I pulled my phone bill out of my carryall. It was late as usual. I had lied and told some rude woman at Ma Bell that I had sent the payment already when I realized my damn cut-off date was just around the corner. I grudgingly wrote out a check and sealed it in the envelope.

"Sorry about that."

"That's okay. You have to go?"

"No. So, anyway, this Julie Templeton. She let me take her out one night. Everything went wrong on that date, I'll tell you. First, we got lost trying to find the movie theater I wanted to take her to. When we finally made it there, we found out that the theater was closed down, so I went to plan B which was to take her to dinner. Well when we got back in the car, my car wouldn't start."

"Oh no." I was laughing so hard I almost knocked over my half-open bottle of nail polish.

"Oh yes. I was driving this old VW that was on its last leg. It was one of those cars that you pretty much had to pray for wherever you wanted it to go. Man, I'm telling you, it was one step away from the junk heap. Anyway, I got this guy in the parking lot to give me a jump."

"And what was Julie doing? I'll bet she was cursing you out."

"No, no. Julie was real understanding. I kept apologizing and she kept saying, 'That's okay, David. These things happen.' I drove her back to the dorm and told her I'd make it up to her. I was convinced she would let me take her out again, see because she had let me kiss her. I went to my dorm whistling, confident that I'd get another date with her. The next day I met up with a buddy of mine on the track who Julie knew pretty well. He told me that Julie had called me everything but a child of God and swore she'd never go out with me again."

"Aw, poor baby. You must have been crushed."

"Not really. I was a little upset, but not crushed. I had lots of girl-friends who didn't care whether I had a car or not. So you see, if this James is as great as you say he is, he'll bounce back soon enough."

"Thank you, professor, for that lovely stroke of my ego."

"Anytime. Take down this number, Genie. You have a pen?"

I reached for a blue papermate. The ink had dried out. I reached for another one.

"Now I do. What number?"

"212-555-5134. You can reach me at that number tomorrow if you want. I'm going up to New York this afternoon for a writers' conference. I'm on the first panel. I might need you to wake me up in the morning so I don't miss the first session at eight o'clock."

"Take me with you." I envied the professors their flexible schedules.

It made me almost miss trading in catering for a nine to five gig.

"Wish I could. But listen, try to enjoy your day. I'd better go throw some things into a bag and run some errands. My flight leaves at noon."

"Okay. You try to enjoy your conference without me."

"That'll be difficult. Believe me, if I could take you along I would." He sounded like he really did wish he could take me along.

"Mmmhmm. How long will you be away?"

"I'll be back in the office Thursday."

For some reason that bothered me. I was disappointed that I wouldn't see him for a few days. He was the only person in that office who ever really had time for me.

"You'll be gone that long?"

"That's not long. Only a couple days."

"Well, remember to bring me something back."

"I'd better run. Onward and upward."

"Bye. Have a safe trip. Oh, good morning." I waved at Professor Stevens when he walked into the main office to get his mail. I hung up the phone. I changed my calendar and picked up my bill, then hurried out of my space. It was almost nine o'clock. Way past time for me to make the damn coffee.

•   •   •

It seems like each year that passes I forget a little something about what Mama was really like. I mean, some nights I stare up at the portrait of her hanging over my fireplace and look deep into her eyes for a long time, trying to remember who she was before her breakdown. I mean, I know that she was funny, but I can't ever seem to come up with a single joke she might have told. I remember she loved to cook like I do, but can't remember what her favorite dish was. I think it was jambalaya, but sometimes I want to think it's paella, my favorite dish. I don't know. Marilyn and Tess never really talk about her.

I never really knew Mama anyway, so I don't know why I'm afraid I'll forget her. For a long time when I was a little girl, she was just this presence in the house that was on the same level as God. She was somebody I said "no ma'am" and "yes ma'am" to, and she pressed out my hair for church on Saturday afternoons and let me lick the cake batter from the mixing beaters, and she always smelled so good because she owned more Avon than she ever sold. I was in total awe of her. That's how I knew her when I was little.

When I got older, she never became my friend. I thought of her only in connection with my father. Those roses she hated. That stuff she wore just to please him. Her move to the basement. Her tears. I just wish I could have gotten to know her better. How she felt. What she thought about, what she was like as a girl. Instead I only see her in my nightmares.

The dreams about Mama are the same:

I am sitting at the baby grand piano playing "Brian's Song," in the house where I grew up. All the piano keys are black and the sun is shining on my back through the big window at the front of the house, making me feel hot. When I get halfway through the song, I feel this cool hand on the back of my neck, so I turn around to see who it is without taking my fingers off the keys. It's Mama, and she's crying without making any noise. I try to remove her hand from my neck, but her grip is too tight. It's hurting me, so I ask her to stop but she stands there with tears coming down her face, and then with her free hand she starts digging a finger into her left eye. Blood starts spurting out of it onto my face and I am screaming hard and wanting to fight her off but I can't because my fingers won't leave the piano keys. They're frozen there.

Mama throws her eye on the floor and I can see blood and all kinds of filth in her hollow socket. I want to close my eyes because I'm sure she is going to kill me, but my eyes refuse to close. I am still trying to move my legs or my hands, but I'm paralyzed and I cannot turn away from her. When she reaches into her right eye, blood and some type of weird fluid that must be embalming stuff splashes all over me, and I am screaming and crying for her to go ahead and kill me. But all she does is try to speak to me. She groans almost like Linda Blair did in The Exorcist, *but no words come out. She just groans, and it's horrible.*

When I woke up that night I was screaming and sweating real hard. My brand new peach baby doll pajamas and my bedsheets were soaked with my sweat. I was shaking uncontrollably, my throat was raw and my mouth was totally dry. I could feel my heart booming inside me, and up by my right wrist a knot was forming, because in my struggle to come out of the dream, I had knocked over the crystal touch lamp and alarm clock that sat on the night table beside my bed. Thankfully nothing had broken. The lampshade had a small indentation and the clock's plug was half pulled out of the wall, so I plugged it back in and the large red numbers blinked off and on like a car turn signal.

I cried a little while I put the lamp and clock back into place and called time so that I could reset the clock. I think I was crying because I was grateful that I was safe. When I tried to stand up, I almost fell over. My legs felt like rubber weights. I forced myself to calm down a little and turned on the television real loud for company. Some old black and white musical was playing on AMC. I turned the channel so I wouldn't have to think about "Brian's Song." *In the Heat of the Night* was on, so I left it on that station.

I was so scared that I turned on every light I passed when I went down the hall to the kitchen. I turned my head away from the living room so I wouldn't have to look up at Mama's eyes over the fireplace. I pulled a big plastic cup down from one of the cabinets, then reached into another cabinet for my bottle of Sambuca. On the way back to my room, I left the lights on, not caring a bit about conserving energy. I threw off my damp pajamas and changed the sheets, then I put on the black and white Snoopy gown that Evelyn had given me for Christmas and took a long drink that made me cough like I had TB, so I set my cup on the night table and watched Tibbs chase down some bad guy. Outside, the wind was howling like crazy. A slow rain fell and droplets were tapping at my windows. Now and then I heard a car sluicing up the street. I wondered where anyone could be going so late at night. But I was glad too because it made me feel less lonely. Somebody else was up besides me.

I looked over at the clock. It was a little after three. I was too jittery to go right back to sleep, so I opened my night table drawer and pulled out my dream dictionary. I don't know why I did that. I had looked up mother and piano and eyes and blood and tears and screaming so many times that I knew what the signs meant by heart. I already knew what the dream was about anyway. What I really wanted to know was what Mama was trying to say to me, and the book couldn't tell me that. I got mad at the book like I always did when I wanted it to tell me more than it could, so I tossed it back into the drawer and pulled out this book of Sandra Cisneros poetry called *Loose Woman,* which Dr. Lewis had loaned to me.

Dr. Lewis seemed like he was addicted to giving me books. He made me read, it felt like, every author ever published. Some of the stuff he gave me wasn't so great. Like Wallace Thurman's *The Blacker the Berry.* . . . I hated that so much, I read it in three nights because I couldn't bear to spend more time on it than that. Dr. Lewis and I got into a debate about the book's contribution to black literature. I only finished the book out of respect for the classics. I may not know a lot about what the literary world considers good literature, but I know what I like and what I don't like. And I didn't like that one. That's what I told Dr. Lewis, but he didn't get it. He always thought he was right about everything. But how many men don't?

I kept sipping from my cup, and I guess the Sambuca was really doing its job, because out of nowhere that mellow feeling started creeping up on me, making me feel like I could hardly hold my head up. I was already sleepy; now I was getting drunk, too. I set the cup on the night table and pulled the covers up over my head. The last thing I remember is hearing the intro for *The Jerry Springer Show.*

David

Why should I be pissed off with her because the whole time I was in New York Genie didn't once call me? It wasn't like it was a big deal. I woke up Tuesday morning at seven on the nose, waiting for the phone to ring. When it didn't ring, I showered and shaved, then dressed and ordered up some coffee and a blueberry muffin from room service. I knew she couldn't have forgotten to call me. I thought it was more likely that she'd lost the number. Since she probably *had* lost the number, I called into the office, only to get Justine's stale voice on the answering machine.

The city was alive and kicking. I listened to the news while I watched the traffic out of my window until my breakfast came. I consumed it as slowly as I could because I tried the office one more time twenty or so minutes later. It was 7:49. No Genie. I sat there wondering if she'd changed her mind about that character she'd wanted to get rid of. I thought maybe she had spent the night with him. All sorts of things ran through my mind that morning. I couldn't even enjoy the goddamn paper, thinking about her lying in the arms of some chump who probably didn't deserve her in the first place.

I put my watch on and looked over at my empty bed, thinking about how tempting she would look asleep, naked and tangled up in those white sheets with her brown skin gleaming and her hair all wild. But then I told myself I shouldn't be thinking about her like that.

I thought about trying the office number again, but decided against it. I had a busy day ahead and I needed to focus. But damn, I missed her. Her soft little voice. Her laugh. She never let me take myself too seriously. She had this way of making an old man like me feel brand new.

When I realized I was being stupid, I gathered up my things and made for the door. I couldn't figure out what the fuck I was thinking anyway. I reminded myself that I have a family and that my marriage is twenty-six years old, which is a miracle in today's society. I thought about how I was just beginning a new career that makes me feel alive again. I reminded myself of something else too. That I'm too old for that young girl. That's what I kept telling myself all that day so I could perhaps shake some sense into myself. But it didn't work.

Matter of fact, I tried to put Genie out of my mind the whole time I was in New York, but she kept slyly finding her way back into my head. My second day in the city, I got it in my mind to walk Genie out of my thoughts. I thought maybe seeing the sights might divert my attention. My walks through town led me to the UN. To the Empire State. Then I hopped a cab to go back in the opposite direction, up to Radio City; then to Harlem, to the Apollo. All I wished was that Genie was there with me. I felt like the loneliest man alive in a sea full of people. That, more than the silence of my telephone those two mornings I was in that hotel room, really is what set me off. So I stayed away from the office an extra day to get my head together.

When Friday came, I still wasn't in the best of moods. I walked into the main office to get my mail with a chip on my shoulder the size of Gibraltar. It was early. Nobody else was around yet, except some guys outside the office down the hall, moving some big furniture.

I smelled the coffee brewing in the main office and walked down the hall toward it. My heart lurched a bit. Genie was at the coffee machine pouring herself a cup. Damn—I wanted her. She was wearing another one of those sexy two-piece outfits with an easy access skirt that showed just enough to make a man like me almost desperate to see more of her. Her face lit up like a Christmas tree when she saw me. That made me feel kind of good. But I frowned at her. I was still angry. She didn't seem to notice. I wished she wouldn't put on outfits like that one. Lately, we've eased into the habit of giving each other a friendly hug, so she walked toward me with her arms at half-mast.

"Heeeeey, Dr. Lewis." I wanted to side-step her, but my body wouldn't let me. Not with the way her firm little hips were moving and the imprint of her nipples against the fabric of that top she had on. She smelled good, too. Compared to Monica, Genie was so slim with her tiny little waist. I could have wrapped my arms around her twice. I held her as tight as I could without breaking her, a moment longer than I should have, just because it thrilled me to have her so close. Of course, she pulled away first.

"I missed you. I thought you said you were coming back on Thursday, you jerk. You know, it's not the same around here without you."

She was smiling up at me. I wanted to ask her, if she missed me so damn much, then why did she let me sit up in that funky little hotel room two mornings straight without calling me? I wanted to ask her in what way had she missed me. Like a friend, or like a woman misses her man. I knew too well in what way I'd missed her, but I couldn't allow my wishful thinking to get the best of me.

I have to admit I felt strange having missed Genie more than I had missed my own wife. Hell, I'm sure Monica hadn't craved my company too much either. She was so busy preparing for her precious upcoming board meeting, I don't think she even realized that I hadn't called her while I was away. Well, I did call the boys when I checked into the hotel, so I guess it was enough for Monica to know my plane hadn't crashed. Damn. I must be a lucky man. A wife at home who barely gives me the time of day, and a pretty woman at work who hadn't thought enough about me to call.

I walked past Genie and made a big display of pouring myself a cup of coffee.

"I'm sure the office was just fine without me," I told her. I hoped I sounded like I didn't care that she'd said she missed me.

"But not me. It was too quiet for me without you around. Hey, I like that tie. It's beautiful." She walked up beside me and fingered my tie. I wanted to take that hand and put it on the part of my body where it belonged. When I was a private in the army and scared to death that the drill sergeant would single me out for some form of mental torture, my body would find a life of its own and tense up taut as a damn straight pin. That's how Genie made me feel now.

"Thanks. I picked it up while I was in New York," I said.

I was hoping she wouldn't notice my hard-on, and I was glad when she turned away from me to stir cream and sugar into her coffee cup. Clumsy me spilled some of my coffee on the table.

"Shit." I grabbed a few napkins and cleaned up my mess, then poured more coffee into my cup.

"Well, Doc. Tell me all about your trip. I want to hear about the conference. I want to hear about New York."

"Maybe later, Genie. I really need to get caught up first. By the way," I said, walking back up toward the worktable where I'd left my mail, "I brought these in for the office." I held up a box of chocolate-covered marzipan Statue of Liberty impressions. "Why don't you set them out on the coffee table."

She hesitated. I couldn't tell whether what I'd said bothered her or not. I'd really bought the damn things for her after hunting what felt like every store in the city, trying to figure out what she'd like. I had no clue what she liked. I tried to remember what kinds of things I had bought for Monica when we were courting, but young women these days are different. I have no idea what really makes them happy.

I finally gave up and figured I couldn't go wrong with candy. Just about every woman in the world loves that. Then, on the drive in, I thought that maybe it might be inappropriate for me to give just her something like that. Firstly, I wasn't at all sure how she'd take it, and second, I thought she might feel like it was okay to let somebody else in the office know that I had bought her candy. That wouldn't look good. I have three years ahead of me before I'm up for tenure, so I have to be on top of my game. Halfway wanting an affair with the young office secretary is not the way to be on top of my game.

She took the box out of my hand. She didn't look so happy to see me any longer, but she still said, "Thanks. That was very nice of you," and went to set the box up on the table.

I had only been away a few days, but I had a lot of snail mail and E-mail to sift through, so I went into my office to start my day before the kids interested in working in our writing center started showing up for interviews. I was almost through with my mail when I heard a knock on my open door.

"Hi."

I turned around and Genie was standing in my doorway like she was afraid to come in.

"You can come on in."

She walked in and avoided the empty chair beside my desk and looked out of my window. I was enjoying a view of her.

"I'm not here to disturb you," she said, crossing her arms over her chest. "I just wanted to see if it was still raining out. It's been raining all week, you know. I wish there were windows in the main office. I feel so isolated in there because I can't see what's going on in the world."

She wanted to talk. I put down a letter from *Emerge* approving an article I'd written for "The Last Word" column about how black male faculty fare in academia.

"I don't see how anyone functions without a window. I think I'm a bit claustrophobic," I told her.

"Yeah?"

"Yep. I once had an enclosed office when I started out. Couldn't figure out why I was always so depressed. Turned out it was the suffocating feeling from being in a room without a window."

"Mmm. Maybe that's what's wrong with me."

"Excuse me. Professor Lewis?"

We both turned to see a stocky redheaded kid with bad acne and a crewcut.

"Yes. What can I do for you?"

His body took up the entire doorway, so he turned sideways to get into the room.

"Hi, I'm Mac Bishop." His powerful hand was pumping mine so hard I felt it all the way up to my shoulder.

"I'm here about a job in the Writing Center."

With every word he spoke, one of the buttons on his plaid shirt threatened to pop off. I glanced at my watch.

"Oh great. Good to meet you. Have a seat."

Genie fanned me a wave of her fingers and left the room while I rearranged my desk a bit to prepare for the first of several interviews.

•   •   •

It continued to rain steadily, so I decided to close up shop after the last student interview and take some work home with me. After fighting the heavy traffic on Route 50, and finally hitting my street, I was more than a little surprised to see Monica's Mercedes sitting in the driveway. I wondered if something was wrong or if she had stopped in to grab something she'd forgotten. I was even more surprised when I opened the front door, and was greeted by the smell of steak.

"Monnie?" I called out, dropping my coat and hat on the stairs. The exhaust fan and the light in the kitchen were on, so I put my briefcase by the banister and headed for the kitchen. I pushed through the kitchen doors and my eyes almost popped out. There was Monica, wearing some kind of kimono thing with her hair up, grilling steaks. I was so flabbergasted that I couldn't say a word.

"Oh hi, sweetie." She put up a cheek for a kiss like this was an everyday scene for us. When I leaned to kiss her I sniffed, trying to see if I could smell any liquor on her breath. I couldn't. But I did wonder if maybe my wife had been cloned and the real one was still at the office.

"Monica?"

She gestured toward the counter behind me. "David, hand me one of those long knives, honey. I want to make us a nice salad."

"What's all this?" I asked her. I dropped the knife because I poked myself with the damn blade tip. She picked it up and rinsed it.

"Just a little spontaneous romance." I watched her slice up the tomatoes and cucumbers.

"Spontaneous romance, huh? Where'd this idea come from? And where are the boys? They should be home by now."

"To answer your second question," she said without looking up from her chopping, "the boys have gone camping."

"Camping? With who?"

"You remember my friend Ida, don't you? Well she and her husband and their two boys have a place up at Shenandoah, so she invited our boys for the weekend. Apparently her husband, John, is one of those serious outdoorsmen, so they'll be fishing and hiking and all since the rain's supposed to clear up late tonight. The idea that we'd have the house to ourselves for the weekend made me think about how we could use the time wisely. So, I rushed back here and saw the boys off, did a little shopping, and here we are." She put down the knife and put her arms around my neck. All the anger that I'd felt toward her was melting away. I loved looking into those brown eyes of hers.

"David, don't think I haven't been hearing you when you tell me we don't spend enough quality time together. I know I have the tendency to get caught up sometimes, but I love you very much. I want to make you happy always."

I didn't realize before she said it that I had wanted to hear her say those things to me for a long time. I smiled down at her. I'm sure I looked just like a satisfied cat. I touched her face, almost like I thought she wasn't real.

"So we have all weekend alone, huh?" I was starting to feel kind of hot, so I started kissing her ear and her neck the way she liked for me to.

"Mmhmm. All weekend. I turned off the phone and put the machine on. I turned off the fax and left my laptop at work. So David, if you've brought any work home, I want you to start a fire in the fireplace and burn all of it, because you and I are only going to be into each other this weekend."

"Oh babe, I can start a fire without the fireplace," I told her and let her know it by opening that robe of hers and doing some exploring. In the back of my mind, I remembered my thoughts about Genie, and I felt a little guilty about ever having thought about another woman when I had all I needed right in my arms.

"David, not yet." She pulled her robe closed. "You'll ruin dinner, and I worked hard on it."

I put my hands behind my back, smiling.

"Okay. Hands off for now."

She sampled some type of noodle dish sitting on top of the stove.

"Good. Why don't you go change into something comfortable, sweetie, and pour yourself a drink. I have a bottle of chilled wine in the dining room, and in a few minutes I'll have everything set up on the table."

"Great." I loosened my tie and almost ran to the bedroom to change.

By Saturday evening I was beginning to feel like I'd won the lottery and Monica was the prize. We had just enjoyed a nice round of lovemaking, and my body was well relaxed. Monica was down in the kitchen putting together a little snack for us, so I stretched out on the bed and flipped channels, hoping to find us a good movie to watch.

"Leave it there, honey."

Monica came into the room carrying a small tray of cheese, crackers and fruit.

"That looks like *Terms of Endearment*. I like Shirley MacLaine."

I made a face.

"Monnie, come on, do we have to watch this? I was hoping we could look at something less sap—"

There was a faint ringing coming from the dresser.

"Monica, what's that?" I asked. I knew it was her cell phone, and felt a little betrayed. Monica looked guilty when she set the tray on the bed and scooped up her cell phone from the dresser. She answered hurriedly, then held a brief and quiet conversation that I couldn't really make out, so I picked up the remote and hit the mute button for the TV, but I was too late.

"David, honey." She leaned across the bed to kiss my chest. "I need to run to the office for just a minute."

I almost felt violent. I cursed myself for having been so stupid.

"I thought you said," I managed to tell her, "that this was our week-end, Monica. You told me nothing was going to distract you from me this weekend."

"I know what I said, honey." She moved away from me to search the closet and already I felt that wall between us again.

"But honey, that was Mr. Derwood. There's a small crisis that I have to handle. I'll be back before you can even remember I've gone. I promise."

How many times had I heard that? I wanted to tell her to go to hell, but I refused to let my temper show. I kept enough of my cool to get out of bed calmly and put on some underwear.

"If it's only a small crisis, why can't you let someone else handle it? I was able to put my work aside for you."

"David, you don't understand," she told me.

I understood perfectly. She couldn't even focus on me for one week-end without letting her job come first. I watched her put on her clothes as fast as she could and pick up her briefcase. I guess I looked as disappointed as I felt, because she suddenly remembered I was still in the room and came over to kiss me, but I turned away from her.

"Honey, I'm sorry," she said. "I'll be back as soon as I can."

To me, that wasn't good enough, and my glare told her so. She obviously didn't care whether I was hurt and angry or not. She grabbed her raincoat and rushed out. When I heard her car start up and speed off like she was rushing off to something far more exciting, I found myself a shirt in my drawer. I had to get the hell out of the house. I refused to sit around waiting for Monica to remember I was alive. I figured I could at least go for a little drive to clear my head, so I reached for a pair of pants lying on top of the clothes hamper and started to put them on, but something fell out of one of the pockets. I picked it up and put on my glasses so I could get a better look at it, and then I thought about how Monica had lied to me, making me believe that she was for once putting me ahead of her job. I put my wedding band on the dresser before I left.

Genie

I decided to learn how to meditate. One of the professors, Professor Kemp, kept telling me I should give it a try. He said that meditation, finding your center, is what makes a person feel true spiritual completeness, and that it helps you relax and feel better when your body is maxed out on stress. Dr. Kemp is such a strange man, wearing his little hippie attire, and always running around talking about saving the planet, and pushing vegetarianism. At first, I chalked him up to be one of those pathetic sons of the sixties who aged externally but inside couldn't get past eighteen. But when those dreams about Mama kept coming, I began to wonder if the nut might have a point, so I asked him how a person goes about this meditation crap.

Dr. Kemp told me that the first key to beginning the exercise is atmosphere. He said that my meditation environment should be a place where I feel comfortable and that I should add any nuances I feel good about, like candles, soft music or incense. So I bought all three. I got white candles, a tape that played the sounds of the ocean waves and some incense called Calming Mist, and I chose the living room as my comfortable place because the *feng shui* here is perfect.

Dr. Kemp said that the second step to meditating is breathing. He said that I had to become conscious of my own breathing. He demonstrated how I should close my eyes and inhale deeply, hold it for several seconds, then exhale until I felt my body was fully relaxed and I became able to link thoughts of my breathing to control over my body. Then, he said, I could begin to focus on what he called my invisible third eye. He told me it is in the center of my head, right between my eyes, and that it's sort of like the eye to my soul. He said that once I was able to tune everything out by focusing on that eye, I would begin a spiritual journey that's scary at first, but that I could commune with my inner guide, other spiritual beings and maybe, I thought, my mother.

I was too scared to try meditation by myself, so I talked Paulette and Evelyn into trying it with me. They both thought I was nuts. I didn't care what they thought, though. I figured that if meditation was the solution to stopping my dreams about Mama, then I would be able to get a good night's sleep without having to take a drink to get the courage to go to bed at night.

"Okay, ladies," I said, coming out of the kitchen with a tray, "first, we'll drink our herbal tea to help us shake off any strange humor we might feel about what we're going to do here." I looked pointedly from Paulette to Evelyn.

"Yes, oh spiritual one." Paulette elbowed Evelyn and they started to laugh, but I ignored them and set down the tray to pour hot water into our mugs, then I placed a Celestial Seasonings blackberry teabag in each mug and offered them spoons and sugar.

"Okay ladies, let's drink." I sat with them, Indian style, on the floor and took a sip of my tea, then looked around the room, making a last check to see if everything was in place. The candles glowed and the incense gave the room a fresh floral smell. I had turned the music just high enough for us to know it was on, but low enough so that it wouldn't disturb our concentration.

"Genie is it okay if we talk while we drink our tea, girl?" I liked that Evelyn was whispering. Already I could feel myself relaxing. The shot of Sambuca I had put in my mug hadn't been a bad idea after all.

"Of course we can talk."

"Good," Paulette chimed in, "because I have to tell y'all the latest about Sheila. Now this is going to really curl your hair."

"What happened?" I asked her.

"She finally left him for good."

"Ooh, girl, you mean Marcus?" Evelyn was always so dramatic.

Paulette looked at Evelyn like she'd lost her mind and said, "No, I mean Martin Lawrence. Of course I'm talking about Marcus."

"How did that happen? Last you told me, they were in couples counseling and Marcus was trying to work out his anger problem."

"But Genie, what Sheila didn't know is that Marcus has a drug problem too."

"What?" I almost spilled my tea. Evelyn and I both tripped off of that.

"Yes, y'all. Did not girlfriend tell me that she was on her way to work but her car went out on her, so she got a tow truck to tow it to her father's shop. He's a mechanic for Buick and he said he would take a look at it when he got off work. Honeys, Sheila got herself a cab home, thinking her man was way out in Virginia at work. Well," she paused to take a sip of tea, "she got a little surprised when she saw his Legend sitting in front of the apartment, but she said she didn't really think much of it, because she thought maybe he was running late or had gotten sick or whatever, right?" She looked at us both like she wanted us to answer her, but we knew she only wanted to make sure we found her story interesting, which we did.

"Well, y'all, the woman went upstairs to the apartment and unlocked the door, and lo and behold who was laid out on the couch butterball naked, taking a hit from a crack pipe, but Marcus, and some skanky little chick who lives across the hall from them."

"Ain't that a bitch." Evelyn said.

"So what'd Sheila do, Paulette? Did she finally get a backbone and go off, or what?"

"Girl, no. You know Sheila isn't the type to take a stand, poor thing. Not even in her own house. All she did was leave like she hadn't seen a thing and went down to the corner to the Shoppers to call her sister to pick her up."

"And Marcus didn't even try to go after her?"

"He was probably too high, Genie. He probably didn't care what went on around him at that point. The man is rotten to the core."

"I've said it once, and I'll say it again—that Sheila is a disgrace to the female race," Evelyn said.

I put on my serious face again. "She sure is. Okay ladies," I said, "that's enough chitchat. I think we should begin now."

I took their mugs and put them back on the tray. I had already explained our meditation process when they'd arrived, so when I took my place on the floor in our circle, we all closed our eyes and began our breathing. I was a little excited about trying something that could solve my nightmares. I focused only on the sound of my breathing until I felt this sort of inner tingle, or energy, the kind of exhilaration you feel when you've completed a major workout. When I felt all floaty like that, I turned my attention to my invisible eye just like Dr. Kemp had told me to do. For a minute I wondered if I was being ridiculous. I peeked to see if Paulette and Evelyn were screwing around, but they weren't. I could tell they were really getting into it, and it made me want to try harder. I shut my eyes tighter so that maybe I could focus better on that third eye, but just when I thought I was getting somewhere, the damn doorbell rang.

"Shit," Paulette said, "I told Robert not to come over here bugging us again. I'll get it." She turned on the lamp and swung open the front door, all attitude.

"I—oh." Paulette stepped back and looked over at me. I was shocked as hell to see Dr. Lewis standing in my doorway with rain dripping off the brim of his brown hat.

"Dr. Lewis? What are you doing here?" He shook out his umbrella and set it on the porch and said, "Hi, Genie," like he was a regular guest in my house. I was speechless. I got up and just stared at him like a dummy.

"So you're the Dr. Lewis I've heard so much about. Please come in. This is Evelyn Pierce, and I'm Paulette Beardsley." Evelyn smiled and put up a hand. Paulette shook his hand then closed the door.

"Nice to meet you both. Please, call me David." He walked in like he owned the place, in tight jeans and a brown leather coat. It was the first time I'd seen him in casual clothes, and the man was looking good.

He had too much nerve, though. Friday he'd treated me worse than a stepchild, and I still don't know why. I probably should have told him I accidentally threw the number away when I was cleaning out my purse Tuesday night, but I didn't think he would make such a big deal out of it. There wasn't a reason to get an attitude about that. But he definitely had one when he came back to the office a day later than he said he would.

Then the Negro had enough nerve to show up at my house? Why was he here? I couldn't for the life of me figure it out.

"Let me take your coat and hat for you," Paulette said.

Nodding his thanks, he handed them to her, and I noticed that he had a little muscle going on under his shirt.

"Genie, how are you this evening?" He had the nerve to hug me. I let him for a second, then I pulled away. How could he stand there acting like this wasn't strange? I ignored his question and asked, "How'd you know where I live?"

"I found this," he said. He reached into his pocket and held up the little salmon-colored catering card I'd given him more than a month before.

"I had no idea you live so close to me. I thought I would just stop by and see how you were. It wasn't too difficult to get here," he said, "but I went a bit too far up 202 and had to turn around."

He made himself comfortable on the sofa next to Evelyn without being asked.

"Oh," was all I said.

What I wanted to do was ask him why the hell he thought he could just pop in on me like that. I could have had a man over. If he had been anyone else, I'd have read his butt up and down my living room. Paulette and Evelyn were wondering what my problem was. They both kept sort of looking at me, waiting for me to say something else. I was too surprised by this whole thing to even come up with casual conversation. Finally Evelyn said, "So you're a professor?"

Dr. Lewis shook his head. "Genie and I work together at the university," he said.

"So you live in this area too, huh?" This was from Paulette. She sat down beside him. Those two were like flies on honey.

"Cheverly."

"Oh. You are close by. Well, it's good to finally meet you. Genie's mentioned you. I hear you're writing a book, too. What's it about?"

"It's a fictional slave narrative. I'm researching various archive and county records, and taking some of the actual historical accounts like those by Olaudah Equiano, Linda Brent, Frederick Douglass, some others, and I'm formulating a fictional picture from them."

"That sounds interesting. Will it be something like *Roots?*"

"Uhm, in some ways. As far as the subject matter and research are concerned, it's similar. The difference is that my project is fiction, not a genealogical unearthing."

Paulette smiled.

"I like that idea. Let me know when it's published and I'll make sure I buy a copy. And of course you have to sign it for me."

"Same here," Evelyn said.

Dr. Lewis patted Paulette's leg.

"I'd be happy to."

"You know," he said," in my haste to escape the downpour, I forgot to ask if I was interrupting anything here. I hope I haven't intruded."

Now he remembered his manners. Where were his manners before he decided to get behind the wheel and point his car toward my house? Paulette quickly said, "Of course, not, David. Right, Genie? We were just sitting around doing the girl thing and all. We're glad you stopped by."

He seemed relieved and it made me feel kind of bad. I wondered if he was just lonely and wanted to talk, like I sometimes did.

"Yeah, Dr. Lewis," I said, "it's good to have you." I tried to sound like I meant it. That's when my hostess personality clicked in on autopilot.

"Can I get you anything to drink?" I asked him.

He rubbed his hands together.

"Sounds good. You have wine? And please, Genie, we're not in the office. Why don't you call me David."

"Okay, uhm, David." I don't know why I felt embarrassed saying his name. I guess I was too used to calling him Dr. Lewis.

"Sutter Home okay?"

"That's fine. Thanks," he said. I moved toward the kitchen like a zombie and poured some Chardonnay into one of my best goblets.

"Here you go," I said, handing him the glass when I returned. I noticed that something was different about the living room, and realized someone had blown out the candles and turned off the music while I was in the kitchen.

"So Genie," he was sipping at his wine, "you have a very nice home here. How long you been living here?"

"About two years." I couldn't figure out why my voice was cracking.

"Do you like it?"

I cleared my throat.

"Very much. It's a pretty quiet neighborhood. Paulette and Evelyn are close by."

"That's nice. That's one of the things I miss about Atlanta."

"What's that?"

"Friends."

"Oh. Yeah."

That had to be why he was here. He didn't know anybody else in town. But then again, where the heck was his family on a Saturday night?

I tried to think of something more to say, because I hate uncomfortable silence. My legs were beginning to feel a little wooden, so I sat in the chair across from the three of them and put my feet up on the ottoman.

"Who's that in the portrait?" Dr. Lewis asked.

"My mother," I said. The only thing I had told him about her was that she had passed away, and that was only after he'd told me his parents were dead.

"She was very beautiful. Reminds me of you." Was I dreaming or was he flirting? He was swirling his glass of wine and it seemed like his eyes were sparkling.

I smiled and thanked him. I wasn't quite sure, but I think Paulette and Evelyn were giving me the eye. My face was getting hot, so I fiddled with the tassels hanging from the multi-colored afghan that was folded across the back of the chair. I figured maybe that damn Sambuca was probably just kicking me in the butt, making me a little punchy. And here we were silent again.

"David, do you play cards?" Evelyn to the rescue.

"Yeah I do. I love cards. You?"

"Mmhmm. I like to play."

What game do you play?"

"Tonk. Genie thinks it's too complicated even though she plays a fair enough hand, but Paulette and I get some real competition going when we start playing."

"Is that so? Well, I happen to be somewhat of a pro at cards. That's how I financed my last year of college, although the real game then was poker."

I rolled my eyes toward the ceiling on that one. He looked just like a peacock.

"So you wanna play?" Evelyn asked.

"Sure. Why not."

Paulette pushed up the sleeves of her sweater and said, "Great. I'll get the cards."

Dr. Lewis and Evelyn moved over to the dining room table while Paulette got the playing cards from a drawer in the kitchen. I got the feeling they were all glad to have something to do.

"Genie, you coming?"

"No, Ev, I think I'll sit this one out. I'll just watch you guys play." The only thing I wanted was to know why Dr. Lewis was at my house on a Saturday night like this. This was kind of weird. I found Jeff Loerber's *West Side Stories* CD and popped it in, and flipped open my latest copy of *Bon Appetit.*

The three of them played cards for an hour. By that time everybody had given me hints that they were hungry, so I threw some barbecued wings, macaroni salad and fresh fruit together in the kitchen. I was kind of proud of Dr. Lewis. Paulette and Evelyn are very good players, but he beat the pants off both of them. I felt a little more relaxed with him in my house by then. I guess it didn't hurt that I'd taken the liberty of downing a few shots of Sambuca while I was cooking. After preparing the food, I joined them at the table.

"Now what is this about this theory you have about men, Genie? You've never mentioned anything like that to me."

"I'm surprised you didn't tell David about that, Genie." I could have killed Paulette, with her big mouth.

"No, I haven't told him about it. Who brought that up anyway?" I crunched a slice of apple.

"Oh, I was just asking the ladies here why a girl like you doesn't have a steady. Evelyn told me it has something to do with some theory of yours. So what's this theory?"

This man was proving to be every bit as nosy as an old woman.

"It's complicated, Dr. Lewis."

"Oh, no it isn't. Actually it's pretty simple." Paulette was talking to the man like they knew each other from way back.

"Come on, tell him Genie," she said.

She was *that* close to making me whip her behind. I took a bite of chicken and kicked her under the table. She had the nerve to smile at me like it was funny. Meanwhile, Dr. Lewis was looking dead at me, waiting for me to explain.

"It's just that I don't believe that men are trustworthy. So when I meet a man I'm interested in, I tell him upfront that I'm not interested in a relationship, I don't believe in love, I only want a . . . a . . . companion of sorts." Shit. I wasn't about to tell this man what really comes out of my mouth.

"So, you don't trust me?" His gray eyes were dead on me. Paulette and Evelyn were definitely enjoying the show. They were going to get royally cursed out when Dr. Lewis left.

"In a sense I don't."

"What do you mean by that? Just because I'm a man?"

"Yes."

"But I also thought that we were friends."

"Dr. Lewis, we've known each other a few months. I wouldn't call that—"

"Are we friends, Genie?"

"Of course."

"Well, trusting is a part of friendship."

I was ready for his ass to go home. The last place I wanted to be put was on the spot. He was looking at me like he wasn't sure if he really knew me, and I hated that.

"I know that. And I do feel that way, Dr. Lewis."

"Then what are you saying?"

"Dr. Lewis, my theory doesn't apply to you. It only applies to men who interest me. I mean . . ." Shit. That didn't come out quite right. I could tell I hurt his feelings, but I wasn't sure *why* his feelings would be hurt. Paulette must have picked it up then too, because she changed the subject.

"So, David how long have you lived in this area?"

"Close to a year now."

"You like it? Or do you miss Atlanta?"

"I'm liking it here more now, but I've lived in Atlanta for thirteen years, so I do miss it. It took me a while to get used to the people here."

"You know, everybody says that. I'm from here, so I don't really notice the difference. But lemme tell you, when my parents retired to North Carolina and I visited last summer, it was a trip how nice the people are down south. I mean, they speak to you on the street and the store clerks are helpful. I was shocked. 'Cause up here, you can get into a lot of trouble talking to someone on the street."

"That's too true," Evelyn said. I was mute. I was too scared that I'd say the wrong thing again.

"Yeah, I remember when I first moved here, I kept speaking to people and some would speak back, but some would look at me kind of funny. It's a strange world we live in. Well, ladies," Dr. Lewis said, looking down at his watch, "I think I'd better get going. It's been nice meeting you two. I've really enjoyed my evening."

I think he was just upset about what I'd said. I could tell he was ready to escape.

"Oh, David, the pleasure was ours," Paulette said. The three of them shook hands. I was up and out of my chair getting his coat and hat.

"I'll walk you out." I told him. I wanted to make things right. I'd acted like a serious "b" the whole time, and I hadn't made him feel all that welcome.

I took our jackets out of the closet and got my boots out from under the sofa.

"Here you go." I said. He took his coat and hat from me and put them on while I opened the door.

"Okay ladies, you have a good one."

"G'night."

It had stopped raining altogether, but it was cold, very dark out and the sky was starless and clear. Across the street a boy was walking this massive black Rottweiler. I turned on my porch light and walked with Dr. Lewis over to his car.

"Dr. Lewis, I hope I didn't . . . I mean, I'm sorry about what I said. You know I think the world of you."

"No, no. I understand how you feel. Listen, I apologize for acting like such an asshole yesterday. I wasn't in the best mood and I took it out on you. Then I show up over here like I have a right to. I just . . . wanted to say hello. Excuse my lack of manners."

"Come on, now." I grabbed his hand. It was so big and soft. I remembered thinking so the day we'd met.

"I'm glad you came. I hope you'll come again. I'd like to think that if we're friends, then you should be welcome in my home. Right?"

We both chuckled. Glad, I think, that the tension was gone.

"Okay," he said smiling. He took hold of my upper arm to pull me toward him and squeezed me. For some reason I wished he didn't have to let go.

"You're a wonderful woman, Genie. You know that?"

He looked down at me with those powerful eyes. I think they were having some kind of effect on me, but I told myself not to read anything into the look he was giving me. I couldn't help but smile, though. He was the only man who ever made me feel like he meant the things he said.

"And you're a wonderful man, Dr. Lewis. Thanks for being my friend."

"Thank *you*."

He kissed my hand, then turned and opened his car door.

"I'll see you on Monday," he said.

"Enjoy the remainder of your weekend."

"You too." I waved goodbye and watched him speed up the street like a bat out of hell before going back inside.

"Girl, why didn't you tell me how fine he is? I should have known. All this time you've been talking about, 'Dr. Lewis did this, Dr. Lewis said that.' You never once said he looked like that!" Paulette fell out on the couch, howling like she was hurting.

I was not in the mood for this shit.

"But girl, did you see those dimples when he smiled?" Evelyn said to Paulette.

"Dimples, honey—what about those unusual eyes. And that walk."

"Oh, I know." Evelyn said. "For the first time since grade school, I do believe I have a crush."

"Just imagine, Evelyn. Genie gets to work with him every day. I don't think I'd ever get any work done with him around."

"Will you two stop. I mean, really. He's just a man. And on top of that, he's old enough to be any of our fathers, I'm sure."

"Well, honey, he looks a damn sight better than my old man," Paulette said.

"Heck yeah. My daddy doesn't look anything near like that." They gave each other a high five.

I rolled my eyes.

"Will you two hush. I swear. Dr. Lewis is just a nice older man. You would think Denzel just busted in here, the way you two are carrying on."

"What's wrong with Miss Thing over here?" Paulette asked Evelyn.

"Honey, I don't know, but my guess would be she's mad because a good-looking man broke up our little seance."

That pissed me off.

"For the last time, Evelyn, it was not a seance. It was meditation, and you're damn right I'm mad because that man had no right to just show up here like we have that kind of understanding."

I wasn't sure why I was reacting like this.

"Excuse the hell out of me, then Genie. But it was obvious that the good professor has the hots for you."

"What? He does not." I turned away so they wouldn't see me blushing.

Paulette spoke up then. "Mmhmm," she said, "the whole time he was here he was checking you out. Even when he carried on conversations with me and Evelyn, he kept looking at you. Girl, he wants you, trust me. But wait a minute. First things first. Is Dr. Lewis married?"

"I didn't see a wedding ring," Evelyn said.

"He's married," I told them. "But even if he wasn't, I don't want him."

"Bump that, Genie. My question is, why is he sniffing around you on a Saturday night? Have you been giving him a vibe? 'Cause now that I know he's married, I'm not liking this one bit."

"Paulette, don't go there," I told her, "he's my friend, and that's it. Plus, like I said, he's married."

Paulette and Evelyn stared at me.

"I'm glad you noticed his married state as a stop sign, but when has that ever stopped you before?" Evelyn said.

"Look, guys, Dr. Lewis is my friend. He's the first man I've ever known who I respect and admire. I care about him. I care about what he thinks of me, and that's all."

"That may be all it is to you, Genie, but he definitely sees you in a different light," Paulette said.

"No he doesn't," I said.

"Listen, I just want you to be aware. You saw his face when we were talking about that theory stuff. And let me tell you something else. I have yet to see a man that will show up at a woman's house for the first time, unannounced, and in a storm like he did tonight, and be thinking of friendship. I don't like it, girl."

"That's because you don't know him, Paulette. Dr. Lewis is different. He's not like these other men out here."

"Genie, you have only known the man for two months and a handful of days, and you're telling me he's different from other men? Negro, please."

"Okay. Well, what about those phone calls every morning?" Evelyn added.

"What about 'em? All we do is sit up and talk about nothing. He's never said anything out of the way to me."

"Fine, Genie. Then how about those little hugs, like the one we witnessed in here earlier. If he'd have squeezed you any tighter he'd have broke you."

"Yeah," Paulette said, "what about those hugs? You call that proper business etiquette to be pulling your secretary into your arms every time you see her? Something's not right."

"Paulette, stop it, okay? He's just friendly. He's one of those touchy feely kind of people. I will admit that at first I thought it was strange, but he's always putting his hand on someone's shoulder when he talks to them and stuff. There's nothing to that."

"Are you attracted to him, Genie?" Paulette asked. I couldn't tell a lie because she knew me too well.

"I think he's handsome, if that's what you mean."

"You know what I mean. I mean, would you sleep with him if he wanted you to? I'm getting tired of you with this married man business. On top of that, those office romances are explosive situations, girl. I don't want that to happen to you."

"You don't have to worry about that, Miss Paulette. I am not interested in him like that and he's not interested in me like that. We are friends. I am not looking for anything more with him. The last thing I would ever do is sleep with my friend. So stop tripping you two and go home."

I tried to act nonchalant about the whole thing while Paulette and Evelyn were there. But after they left, I was so on edge about whether Dr. Lewis was attracted to me or not that I didn't dream all night. For that matter, I didn't get any sleep either.

Phase 8

Genie

I got to the office at 7:15. There's something about the quiet of morning here that I love. Maybe it's because I like having that extra slice of relaxation after the morning rush. Or maybe it's just my awe at how such a noisy, boisterous place, full of students and panicked professors, can so thoroughly cool down.

I clicked on all the lights, checked my mail and unlocked the door to my office. My office isn't really an office. It's more like part of a labyrinth. None of the walls are built up to the ceiling, and every room is connected by doors. So because of a lack of privacy, I call my office my space. I love my space. I put all these colorful pictures and quotes on my bulletin board. The students are so sweet sometimes. They're always giving me things from their homelands that I put on my desk. We have students from all over the world. Thai, Egyptian, Saudi, Greek. My desk is full of unusual items.

I hung my raincoat on the hook on the back of the door and set my carryall and purse down under the desk. Then I went down the hall to turn on the coffee machine to give it a chance to warm up while I listened to a few cuts from my Anita Baker tape.

I sat in my swivel chair and pulled the newspaper out of my carryall so that I could check my horoscope for the day. It told me a lot of junk about it being my day and that people would notice my style and flair. There was nothing stylish about me today. I had thrown on the first thing I had come to in my closet, which was a pair of tan and blue print pants with a blue pullover top and a cream-colored crocheted vest. I especially didn't feel like this was my day. There were dark circles under my eyes from worrying myself sick over what's happening between me and Dr. Lewis. Something was definitely happening.

Over the past few weeks, Dr. Lewis hasn't once mentioned a word about having shown up at my door. Not even during our morning phone conversations. And I wasn't bringing it up because I didn't want him to think I was thinking about it. But I did notice how he started watching me when he thought I wasn't paying attention.

Justine and I share front desk coverage. When it's my turn to staff the front desk, and Dr. Lewis is in his office across the hall, I sometimes see him staring at me out of the corner of my eye. He has started giving me compliments like crazy, too. I thought that maybe it was his way of flirting, and I wasn't sure how to handle it at first. His intentions confused me. Oddly enough, it hasn't made me feel uncomfortable. Truth be told, I've kind of started to like it. What's been bugging me is that I've found myself noticing him too. I mean, it's like whenever Dr. Lewis walks into the office these days, I'm so aware of him that I can barely concentrate on my work. I'm aware of how he smells and how sexy he looks in his suits. Mmm. I swear. The man is looking more and more appealing all the time. But I'm getting scared. I don't want to think about Dr. Lewis like this. The man is the closest thing I have to a real dad. And, I guess, kind of a mentor too. But the tension between us has really escalated.

I was pissed with myself because I couldn't wait for my phone to ring this morning. Seven-thirty came and he still hadn't called. I got so restless that I started pacing the floor, but at about quarter of, I heard somebody's keys jingling at the front door and I remembered it was Wednesday. Dr. Lewis always came in early on Wednesdays to write. I checked my makeup, fluffed my hair and rushed behind my desk so I could strike one of those lazy "I ain't trying to impress" Naomi Campbell poses. I guess it worked because he said, "Hi, beautiful," and leaned against the doorframe looking fine as all outdoors in a thick fabric dark blue shirt with red pinstripes and some tight, dark blue slacks.

He was smiling at me and making me feel like my horoscope hadn't lied after all. Sometimes Sydney Omarr really does know what's up with my life.

"Hey, cutie. What's going on?" I tried to sound casual, but my body was so tense not even a masseur could work out the knots in my muscles. I wished I could run to the ladies' room a minute to relax, relate, release a few times. I settled for doing it in my head.

"Nothing's going on," he said.

He sniffed the air.

"So where's my coffee, lady?" he said. "You know us addle-brained professors can't figure out how to operate that machine back there."

It was an inside joke. Some of the professors said that Barbara would rather have me and Justine make coffee than help a student get registered for classes.

"Shut up."

We both laughed like we had never felt so good. I couldn't understand why Dr. Lewis's laughter gave me this much pleasure, until his face changed and he started looking all serious.

"I'm just kidding. Come here."

Damn him for being sexy. Damn me for thinking so. I was out of my chair before he could blink, and when he put his arms around me he sighed just like he did whenever we walked up to the Au Bon Pain some mornings and he bit into one of his favorite carrot cake muffins.

We stood in my doorway with our bodies linked together like two puzzle pieces for a long time and I listened to his heart, wondering what he was thinking about but too afraid to ask him. I finally tried to pull away, because I knew by the way he rubbed his palms slowly up and down my spine that he wanted to kiss me. I needed him to kiss me, but I was afraid of this thing between us.

Dr. Lewis held me tighter, and I swear I felt like I could barely breathe. Like a vise grip was wrapped around my chest. The telephone started to ring and he still wouldn't let me go. But when I felt his lips brushing my throat like a feather, I didn't care about the damn phone. I suddenly knew that I'd been waiting for this moment with him for quite a while. And I didn't care that we work together, or that what we were about to do could destroy our friendship. The only things that mattered were the pressure of his thighs pushing me against my desk, the soft feel of his shirt against my fingers, and the fact that when I raised my head for his kiss and saw his eyes, I felt an earthquake break loose inside me that wiped out all my thoughts.

Somehow my body knew what to do. I closed my eyes and found his lips. He tasted like strong black coffee. But, oh God, that kiss was so sweet that the fact that I was kissing Dr. Lewis meant nothing to me. Nothing at all. We were both a little clumsy and it was okay. I was so caught up in the moment I don't know when or how the kiss ended. I just know I felt fuzzy. We were both breathing like we had run a marathon, and my whole body was slightly trembling from the after- shock. We held each other for a long time like we were afraid to let go, not saying a word. When I finally opened my eyes, the first thing I saw past his shoulder was the printer. I remembered where I was. So I pulled away from him.

"What did we just do?"

My voice was a squeak in the quiet room. Dr. Lewis didn't seem to notice. He looked so pleased with himself that I wanted to shake him back to reality. He took my face in his hands and said, "I think I just kissed you and you just liked it."

He was too right. I had liked it. Matter of fact, some perverse part of me wanted him to do it again. I shook that feeling off. I had to think realistically. An affair with a friend was a major no-no. An office ro- mance was an even bigger negative, and no amount of shouting from my angry libido would make me feel differently. Would it?

"Dr. Lewis, listen—"

"Don't call me that," he said. "I want you to call me David."

He started rubbing my hair and slouched a little to look me closer in the eye. "Call me David, alright?"

He was on my last nerve; and furthermore, he was messing up my hairdo. I wanted so bad to run and hide from my feelings, which were really beginning to confuse me.

Okay. David," I sighed, "we're friends. Remember?"

He just leaned against the door frame with his arms folded across his chest and looked at me with the silliest grin in the world.

"Come here." He tried to pull me close again.

"No, Dr.—David. I can't. You're not hearing me. This isn't a good idea. This can't happen, 'cause you're a married man."

Did that just come out of my mouth? Paulette was right. I *am* a hypocrite.

"I think we just made a mistake," I continued, "and I don't think we should let this happen again. Do you?"

He didn't answer. He leaned over and kissed my forehead. The phone started to ring again and we both looked at it, then back at each other. I think we both felt kind of awkward.

"Aren't you going to say anything?"

"Yeah. You are such a beautiful woman that I can't think straight when I'm around you. But that was pretty stupid, wasn't it?"

"Yeah, it was," I said, but I didn't feel like I was telling the truth. My mouth was still tingling. I could still taste him and I liked that very much. I didn't move away when he reached out to touch my cheek.

"I find you attractive, Genie. I can't say that I don't think about making love to you. What we would be like together. What you would feel like beneath me."

Oh God. His voice was so soft that he could have been kissing and caressing me all over again. My pride and joy was ready to stage a revolt against any rational thoughts I had about this whole situation. I pictured him between my sheets, his body wrapped around mine. I wondered what his skin would feel like against my lips. I wondered if he knew how to please a woman. But I checked out those long hands and feet and knew he wouldn't disappoint me. This man was no James Caldwell. So I thought, why shouldn't I go for it? I wasn't really seeing anybody right now anyway. Why should I hesitate just because we're friends? Hell, maybe that might make the friendship better. We were still Genie and David, no matter what. We still had the same things in common. We still genuinely liked each other. No roll in the hay would change that.

Just when I was convinced that I should invite David to my place tonight, he switched gears on me.

"Shit." He hit the door with the side of his fist and gave a short laugh. "What am I saying? As if this were possible. I can't do that to my wife. She doesn't deserve that. It wouldn't be right."

I or my libido one was thinking, Who said anything about hurting your wife? She doesn't need to know. Before I got a chance to respond, the front door opened and David and I moved apart. He put on his "Dr. Lewis" face and I settled into my chair at my desk.

"Ah-hah. Professor Lewis. How are you sir? Good day for a meeting, eh? And today's meeting is going to be most fascinating I assure you." It was Dr. Winthrop, the only other black English professor in the department. He taught basic American Lit.

Dr. Winthrop was a lighter-skinned Yaphet Kotto with a neat appearance and a dry sense of humor. He was very cool, too. Minded his own business and was never as difficult as some of the others. He always made me laugh. He and Dr. Lewis seemed to really like each other, which was a good thing, since they were the minority on our faculty.

"I am not enthused about going to today's faculty meeting."

"I'm sure. I'm sure. It's going to be a battle, I can tell you."

"You're right. And we have to sit through two hours of it. You know, the Zulu warriors had a saying before they went into battle: Today is a good day to die."

I didn't get it. But they were laughing their heads off. Then David moved closer to Dr. Winthrop.

"I'll tell you, my friend," he said, lowering his voice like I don't have perfect hearing, "our good Professor Lloyd is going to go out kicking and screaming, hoping he can kick one of us on his way out, you know."

Dr. Winthrop nodded solemnly as if his life depended on his agreement. He stood in front of the mailboxes opening his mail, leaving several pieces lying there while he and David discussed Dr. Lloyd. I wondered what the discussion was all about, but I was learning that professors are damn near as sneaky and secretive as the CIA.

I liked Dr. Lloyd very much. At first I thought he was cold and distant. The students thought so too and complained loudly about it. He definitely thought he was golden boy, but one night I stayed late so I could look some stuff up on the Net. He came in before his class started and we had a nice talk. He struck me as a decent enough man, I think. Just a little misunderstood is all. Not everybody fits in.

When Justine came into the office I let those thoughts go for a while. I started some coffee and sat down at the front desk with some work, but couldn't seem to do anything but think about Dr. Lewis. I watched him kick back in his chair, make phone calls and look over his mail until it was time for him to go to the faculty meeting where they planned to crucify poor Dr. Lloyd.

David

The faculty meeting lasted much longer than I expected. I wasn't very vocal. All I could think about was Genie. What happened between us had had a chance to sink in. I realized I was scared of Genie

and what she made me feel whenever I got near her. But more importantly, I'm scared to death of me.

I don't know what I'm capable of these days, and I don't understand
why. There seem to be so many emotions churning around inside my
head and my heart that I feel like a teenager all over again. What the
hell is this? I'm a good man. I'm a good Christian. I've always done the
right things. I've always tried to make my family proud of me. I was
the first in my family ever to go to college. I'm still the only one ever to
earn a doctorate. I married a good Christian woman. We have our
house. We have our two children. More money than I ever thought
we'd make. This is what I worked so hard for all these years.

I'll never forget that I grew up in the projects. All those growing up
years, all I dreamed about is what I have now. But what exactly do I
have? A wife who's little more than a stranger. A house that's always
empty. Two kids who grew up too damn fast and don't need me anymore unless it's to open my wallet. What am I supposed to do now? I
don't know where my place in my own family is anymore.

But, damn, that kiss. Genie really laid it on me. I was surprised as
hell. I had hoped, but I never really thought she'd respond like that. I
never thought in a million years that I, myself, would act on what I've
been dreaming about doing since I met her. I kept reviewing what happened in my head, but I couldn't figure out exactly what drove me to
kiss her today out of all the other days I've felt like doing it. Maybe because Monica and I had another major blowout last night. Monica re-
fuses to see that she's taking me for granted. Then I come to the office
and see Genie.

We've been flirting for weeks now and it's made me feel so alive. It's
gotten to the point where I can barely sleep at night because I'm thinking about Genie so much. Sometimes I just want to hold her so bad. I
mean really hold her so I can show her how I feel because it's hard to
hold these pent-up emotions inside.

This morning I had to at least kiss her. So I walked in there and I
put my arms around her the same way I would do if we were about to
make it together. I just held her like that and massaged her back. I was
so turned on I started breathing heavily. I backed her up against her
desk a bit so that she could feel me. Feel how rock-hard I was. Know
how much I wanted her right then because I didn't know how to say it.
I was afraid she might be upset with me and think I was too old.

When she didn't try to pull away from me and I felt her arms
tighten around me, I had the greatest urge I've ever known to just

stroke that long, curved, cinnamon throat of hers with my mouth. So I went for it. Damn, she was sweet there. She smelled so good. She was so soft there that I just held my lips against her skin. I was itching to kiss her. I wanted her mouth to open like a hot cave and swallow me. At least that's what I was thinking, and she must have read me, because she looked at me. I saw a thousand degrees of need in those eyes. I wanted to fulfill it, and mine.

Thank God she stopped me from going too far. I'm glad she had sense enough to remind me that I'm a married man, because I wasn't thinking clearly at all. I couldn't think about anything but Genie. What she smelled like, what she might taste like and most of all what she probably felt like, all warm and moist. Winthrop most certainly would have come in and caught me making love to her. I don't know where my common sense was today. Worse than that, I must have been crazy to think I could do what I did this morning and not feel any guilt about it. Marriage is serious business. What I did with Genie was wrong. How can I face Monica, knowing what I've done?

I decided to go home after my meeting. I felt a surging need to be there to remind myself of who and what I am. I escaped the tiny, airless conference room as soon as the meeting adjourned. I heard Winthrop calling after me, but I didn't feel like talking about what had just happened with Lloyd. I maneuvered my way through a group of students and took the stairs instead of the elevator. I jogged down three flights and burst out of the building. I didn't even stop off at my office for my overcoat and the book chapters I wanted to edit tonight. Instead I went straight to the faculty parking lot. I shut off the alarm and hit the ignition when I got inside the car, then made for Penn Avenue. As I drove, I felt even worse. I started remembering things that I haven't thought about in years. Like the day I asked Monica to marry me. The way she looked when she walked down that aisle toward me. I made her promises that day that I never thought I would break. Damn. And the day she gave birth to Devin. Happiest day of my life. And then Mark. What's happening to me? To us? I wanted to ask Monica so bad. I picked up my cell phone and dialed her office.

Yvonne, her assistant answered.

"Derwood-Covington, Monica Lewis's office."

She sounded like the Bell Atlantic recording when you dial information.

"Yvonne, is she in? It's David." I maneuvered my Mazda around a green, broken-down Fiat.

"Hi, Dr. Lewis. Hold on a minute and I'll see if I can catch her between meetings."

That would be a real trick. I stopped at a red light while holding and put on the oldies station. They were playing one of my favorites: "Stubborn Kind of Fellow." A few raindrops hit my windshield and I turned on the wipers.

"Dr. Lewis, Mrs. Lewis wants to know if she can reach you at your office in about an hour or so."

Now how did I know I'd be put off? Nothing I'd said to Monica last night had made any difference. I had the urge to tell Yvonne to tell Monica that she and her meetings could go to hell, but I swallowed that urge.

"That won't be necessary, Yvonne," I said. "Tell her I'll catch her at home later. Thanks." I clicked off.

So much for that. Monica just didn't quit. If I truly wanted some attention I wouldn't get it from her. That's why I was in this predicament.

I sped up New York Avenue onto Route 50 in a hurry. The traffic was sweet. There were hardly any cars. I zipped along and took the Cheverly exit, then stopped off for some gas before heading home. By now it was pouring again like it was this morning. As much as I love spring, I hate April rain. I ran for the front door and went inside. Going upstairs I noticed I was tracking wet grass through the house, but I was beyond caring whether Monica was going to bitch about it when she saw it. Maybe she'd think the boys did it.

I took off everything but my underwear and T-shirt and lay on the bed. I was feeling too many different emotions for one man. It made me weak. Genie was so young and beautiful. So full of life. Being with her made me feel like floating. Her kiss this morning had sent me spinning. The way she looked into my eyes like that. Her hands going up around my neck, pulling me closer. Her tits full against my chest. That neat little waist of hers. How could any man not want to be with her?

I'm the one who's supposed to know better, but she's the one who made all the sense. When she told me that we shouldn't have let it happen, she was right. There are too many strikes against us. I'm married. She's young. We work together. We're friends. I could jeopardize my marriage, my family, my career—hell, everything that's important to me. What's more, what would my boys think of me if they knew this about me? If they knew their dad was lusting after some hot young thing in a short skirt. That kind of man goes against everything I've ever said I stand for. It isn't right.

What I must do is leave that girl alone. I need to stay away from the office a while and give things a chance to cool down. I have to find a way to talk to Monica about how I feel. Maybe we can see if we can restore the communication to our marriage, maybe take a vacation and get away from it all once classes end. Maybe then everything will work out. I love my wife. I love my wife. Oh, God. Why can't I get that girl out of my head?

Genie

I don't know what's wrong with Dr. Lewis, but the hell with him. He's been out of the office for two whole weeks, and hasn't contacted me once. Not even a "Hi, dog, this is cat. They have Alpo on sale at Safeway" phone call. I made the mistake of being worried about the damn man, so I sent him an E-mail asking him if everything was okay. Then I left a message on his voice mail telling him to call me, and still I got no response. Well, David Lewis can kiss my brown butt.

I know he doesn't think I'm tripping over that tired little kiss. I hope he isn't tripping over it. For God sake, it was only a kiss. Dr. Lewis is too old for me for one thing. He's going gray. He's got wrinkles. He has to be at least fifty. That makes me half his age. I'm a baby compared to him. When I was born, he was already a grown married man. So what, he's handsome. Some old guys got it like that. But I don't care about that. I don't need his lust. Sex is fleeting.

What I need from Dr. Lewis is his friendship and his advice. I miss my buddy. I need my friend so much. I need to talk to him about things like that damn Barbara. She's been in one of her moods again, raising Cain over the dumbest shit. I wish she would just get herself some professional help like regular white people and stop taking her pain out on me and Justine just because she can. Bitch. The way that woman manipulates people, she's sure to die one miserable old bat one day.

And then Robert's not speaking to me since Paulette told him that I don't want to see James anymore because he's ill-equipped. I asked Paulette not to tell Robert that part, but she claims she never lies to him. It was getting hectic giving James so many stupid excuses, so

Paulette had to tell Robert something. I just wish she hadn't told him the truth. Robert told Paulette that this just proves to him what a shallow woman I am. I felt like telling Paulette to tell her husband to take the first train to hell.

Then Eric is still calling me like crazy. Leaving me these sorry punk-ass messages that make me wanna scream. If he keeps it up, I'ma threaten to tell Debbie on him. And meanwhile, I've let myself fall back in step with that fool Nick. Anyway, all of this stuff has gone on in my life and Dr. Lewis is nowhere to be found. "He's working at home" is all Barbara would tell me.

I swear, I don't know what to do. But I would like to have the chance to explain to Dr. Lewis that he doesn't have to feel guilty about what happened between us. All I really want to know is that he's still my friend. That wasn't too much to ask for.

It was getting close to lunchtime, so I ran across the street and whipped out my Most card so I could get some cash. I punched in my code and asked the machine for a twenty. It complied, so I ran around the corner to the deli for a chicken salad sandwich and a Fruitopia, then I started walking fast back up the street. *The Young and Restless* was about to come on and I wanted to get back to the conference room TV so I could see what my baby Victor was going to do about that damn Brad Carlton.

When I got upstairs in front of the TV, Cricket was telling Danny where to get off. I knew how she felt. 'Cause if Dr. Lewis's overreacting behind was around I'd have told him the same shit too.

David

I decided to go back. I couldn't stay holed up in the house forever. I had to face Genie again to see how I felt about the situation. But I was still dead scared. Things weren't any better with Monica, and I knew in my heart that I still wanted to ask Genie to let me take her to bed.

When I got a phone message from Genie the other day asking me why I was avoiding her, I picked up the phone to call her right away so I could explain to her that it's not her I'm avoiding, but the situation itself. But I stopped myself. Same thing with an E-mail note she sent me. I started a reply seven times before I forced myself to move away from my computer. What was I going to say to make Genie understand my end of things? I'm old and married and we work together. The last thing I want is to be labeled a dirty old man who's running around screwing his secretary. End of story. It's best if I keep my pants zipped and do my work.

Man, my work. I haven't written one sentence since I kissed Genie. Not one. Every time I've tried, I start thinking about her. Every time I've thought about her, it's made me want her so much it's all I can do not to run out that door and go to her. Why didn't I agree to Monica's suggestion of a commuting marriage and just keep my black ass in Atlanta? Life was simple then. I was normal then. But as the days went on I knew I had to face reality. I was here in Maryland now. I had a job to do. Besides, Monica and the kids were beginning to suspect that something was wrong with me. I couldn't hide forever.

I woke up early Friday and spent the morning having breakfast and reading the paper. I went for a run to get my blood circulating, and after I returned I showered and shaved and had a little talk with my dick. When I dressed for work, I put on the most unattractive clothes I could find. An old short-sleeved shirt, a thin green sweater. One of my oldest ties. That was green too. My most unflattering color. If Genie was still attracted to me like this, then she was crazy. I even parted my hair on the side. I looked at myself in the mirror. I definitely look fatherly, if not grandfatherly.

All was quiet by the time I walked into the office around eleven. Genie was at the front desk working on something. She looked up with the most beautiful smile in the world. It made me ache to see it. I turned away.

"How're you doing?" I said. I breezed by her without really looking at her, picked up my mail. On my way to my office I heard her say hello like she was puzzled. So far so good. Now all I had to do was make it through the rest of the day. I had a shitload of mail to go through. Two weeks is a long time to be away. I had calls to return. Students to see. I took care of the mail first. I had dealt with the E-mail from home, so that wasn't a problem, but my voicemail was full. I hadn't retrieved my messages because I didn't want to hear Genie's voice again. It was just another temptation. For the rest of the morning I refused to look in

Genie's direction. I was grateful for every interruption. Even Barbara's. She waddled her big ass in and took up a half hour of my time complaining about the demands of the students. Then she tried to get my sympathy by giving me the latest update on her heart attack scare. Hell, didn't she know she was one donut away from the grave?

By the time Barbara finished her speech I was hungry. It was around one. Genie was gone from the front desk and I was glad. I logged out of my computer, turned out my light and locked my door. I wondered where Genie was. Probably lunch.

I went down to the deli for a tuna sandwich and some Fig Newtons, and on my way back to my office, I ran into Genie walking down the hall in front of me as soon as I got off the elevator. What she had on hurt my feelings. There was barely nothing left to the imagination with the skirt she wore. It was some variation of pink and about as tight as the glove that O. J. couldn't fit. The blouse she was wearing was hugging her tits better than I could. I was straining to see more while I cursed her under my breath. She knew what she was doing. The way she moved, too. Oh Jesus, I just wanted to reach out and lift that skirt up and . . . Uh. I refused to think about that. She turned the corner and finally acknowledged that she saw me. Little tease.

"Hi, Dr. Lewis. So you finally came back."

"Yep." I barely got out a response. Her tits were talking to me. I couldn't keep my eyes off them.

"How was your time off?"

"Fine."

"Dr. Lewis, can we talk a minute?"

"Genie, I'd really like to chat but I've gotta run. I have a lot of work to do now that I'm back."

The look on Genie's face really bothered me. I should have explained to her why it was important for me to keep my distance, but what good would that do? It was best if she just stayed away for a while. For the first time ever I closed my office door. I felt strange with my door shut, but I didn't want Genie to think she could come near me today. Sometimes misery doesn't love company.

Genie

He was so cold today that I wondered if he was angry with me or something. Bastard. The whole time he was out of the office, I kept thinking that we would talk. I kept thinking we would straighten things out. Whatever "things" are. I guess he's not my friend after all, because all I saw today was a selfish son of a bitch. I didn't kiss you, Dr. Lewis. You kissed me. That's what I kept saying to myself. I said it when he walked into the office this morning wearing that foolish getup. What was he trying to prove with that? I said it again when he acted like I don't exist. And he was so rude with me in the hall. I kept wondering what I did.

All I did was try to talk to him, and he acted like I'd committed a murder or something. I had two weeks worth of my life to talk to him about, and all he did was brush me off like I was nobody. I hate him.

Then when he slammed his door the way he did, that was the last straw for me. I went into the bathroom and cried so hard, I had to keep flushing the toilet so nobody would hear me. The world must be ending or something. I shed tears over a man for the first time in ages. What is wrong with me? Whatever it is, I'm not putting up with his shit. I should have known better than to believe any man could be my friend. So screw him. No-good piece of shit. Does he know how many men I turn away? And I had the nerve to think he would teach me something about life and maybe rub some of his culture off on me. He was only being nice to me because he wants sex just like every other no-good asshole out here and now he feels guilty about it, so he's blaming me. I was too through. I went home early because of that man.

I picked up a bottle of mimosa on the way home. When I got in, I talked to Paulette about what happened and was so upset I wound up polishing off the whole bottle. The mimosa made me sleepy. I collapsed in the bed and stayed there until about six, then got up because I was hungry. I tossed a salad and heated up the rest of my pork chops.

I refused to stay in the house. I needed some sisterhood too, though. I had planned to see Nick, but I blew him off and called Paulette and Evelyn on three-way to see if they wanted to go to the movies. *Crimson*

Tide was playing at nine and Denzel was just what I needed to make me feel better about things.

"Sure I'll go. I could use a good movie," Evelyn said. "What theater is it playing at?"

"New Carrollton."

"Who's driving?"

"I'll drive," I offered. "I can pick you guys up at twenty of. How's that?"

"Fine." Paulette said.

"Well okay girls, I'm about to hang up. I have to see if Simon can sit for Sasha and Simeon."

"Alright. Bye," I said.

I heard Evelyn hang up.

"Paulette you still there?"

"Course. So are you alright now?"

"No, Paulette. I don't get it. I'm not the one who crossed that line between us, so why is he acting out?"

"That's how men are, Genie. You know that. He's probably scared because of what happened. If you had listened to me in the first place, your little feelings wouldn't be hurt right now and the friendship would be intact."

"Forget you, Paulette. Anyway, what does fear have to do with this situation? We know it won't happen again. So why can't we just pick up and move on? Why all the drama over one little kiss?"

"Genie, it's easy for you to feel that way. You're young, you're pretty, you don't have any responsibilities. Whereas David has the world on his shoulders. I know you didn't ask him to kiss you or for him to react the way he has, but emotions are a bitch. You know what I'm talking about."

"Not really, Paulette. I feel like if you say you don't want to do something, then don't do it. But I need my friend. I kind of got used to the idea that there was a man out here who had my best interest at heart. But you know what? If he wants to be petty and act like a child about this, then so be it. Meanwhile, I have a life to live and some goals that I need to get on top of. Namely, what classes I'm going to take over the summer. I went through the catalogue this morning and I've narrowed it down to three choices. You know my tuition benefits are about to kick in, girl."

"Yeah, you told me. Telaysia! Get off of my skirt. Stop it girl. You'd betta!" I heard Telaysia put up a hell of a fuss.

"Hey, you want me to let you go, P?"

"Yeah, Genie. But look. I have got to get out of this house. Dealing with those screaming kids all day then coming home to this little monster has got me scatterbrained. You mind if I come over and hang out with you until the movie starts? It's Robert's turn now. I said stop, Telaysia! I'ma get in the shower and put on some going-out clothes. I'll be over there in about twenty or so."

"Okay. Check you in a little while."

I clicked off the cordless and turned on the TV to watch Carol Burnett while I greased my hair to the scalp. It was really growing out of that hairstyle that I had rushed to the shop to get, but was now tired of. I brushed it up into a ponytail. Then I went out to the kitchen for a Klondike. I love those things, but I try not to indulge in ice cream too often. I was polishing off my second Klondike when I heard Paulette come to the door. I turned off the porch light and unlocked the door.

"Hey girl," I said as I opened the door, and I almost fell out on the damn floor.

David

I had to go to Genie. That's all there was to it. I felt awful all day about the way I'd treated her. She didn't deserve that from me. Genie has never been anything but a good person to me.

I left the office later than normal because I had convinced myself I was on a roll. But after my coffee break, I came back to my desk and read what I'd been writing all day, and, well, it was crap. The dialogue was weak and the scene I had been working on hadn't taken any real shape. So I scrapped it, figuring I'd have to start again some other time.

I was so mad at myself for the way I'd acted for the last couple of weeks that I just grabbed my coat and went out to the car. I forgot to turn off my computer. I jumped off Route 50 too soon and realized that the exit I took was the way to Genie's house. By the time I pulled up in front of her house, I'd convinced myself that all I wanted to do was tell her I was sorry and give her a big hug. Tell her I still wanted us to re-main friends.

Genie looked ready to faint when she opened the door. She had her hair different from the way she normally wears it. It was up on top of her head and all shiny. She wasn't wearing that little skirt either. She had on the same blouse, but she had on some jeans and some type of embroidered vest, like she was about to go out. I wanted to take her in my arms and show her how sorry I was, but the look on her face stopped me.

"Can I come in?" I said, after standing in the doorway a minute too long.

She was staring at me like I'd been resurrected.

"Whatever," she said.

She stepped aside. Man, a black woman with an attitude is some-thing else. The tension was pretty thick. I walked in feeling a little ridiculous in those clothes.

"What are you doing here, David?" She closed the door. Her arms were folded across her chest and she looked ready to do battle. I'd brought it on myself. I just wanted to hold her and make her under-stand why I was tripping off the line like that. If I could explain it.

I put my coat on the arm of the sofa and sat down.

"Genie, I know you're probably angry with me. You have every right to be. I acted like a jerk and I wanted to tell you I'm sorry." I looked up at her to see how she was taking that. She looked as confused as I felt.

"You're damn right you acted like a jerk. A major first-class jerk. You hurt my feelings."

"Sweetheart, I apologize. I wouldn't hurt you for anything. I hope you know that."

"Well, you did hurt me."

She turned away and sighed like she wasn't sure if she should accept my apology or not. But I could tell the cold front was warming up.

"What's wrong with you, David? I don't get it. One minute you're kissing me, then the next minute you're running away like I've done something wrong. I haven't done anything wrong."

"I know that. Come sit beside me." I patted the sofa cushion. She sat down next to me and I wanted to touch her so bad. From the looks of her eyes I could see that she'd been crying, and I felt like shit about it. I could also tell that she wanted to believe me. I wanted to show her I was truly sorry, so I took her hand and held it tight.

"Genie, this is hard for me. I want you so much, but . . ." I couldn't find the right words to let her know how I felt.

"David, I've missed you. I've missed you so much. There's just some things that only you understand and I . . . I needed to talk. Oh, David, you just don't know . . ."

"Genie, I wish I did know," I said.

I thought about how Monica and I seemed to be doing worse and worse every day. Monica didn't want to talk. She didn't want to spend time with me. She didn't care how I felt anymore. I thought about how this woman sitting right next to me actually cared about me and wanted to spend time with me. Talk to me. It was so good to feel like somebody wants you. I looked at Genie, but didn't say anything. I was just paralyzed with fear and need.

"Please tell me you're still my friend," she said.

"You know I am. That won't ever change," I told her.

She kissed my cheek. Her free hand was rubbing my neck. Then my hair. The only light she had on was the overhead one in the kitchen, and the TV was going. I put my hand on her shoulder and finally the thing that I knew I'd really come for happened. I pulled Genie toward me and kissed her the way I had thought about kissing her for the past two weeks. This time it was different. I can't put my finger on what was so different. But it was. Maybe because I knew what was coming next. I wanted to get the hell out of here. But at the same time, I knew I wasn't going any damn where but to Genie's bed. The woman was seducing me and I was helping her do it.

She stood up suddenly and turned off the TV. She took my hand and I stood up and followed her to her bedroom. I knew I wanted to run then. What if she didn't like it? Hell, what if she thought I was out of shape? I sucked in my gut. I hadn't been with anybody but Monica for thirty years. Even that was the quick missionary job for the past several years, except for rare moments. I was totally out of practice with this thing. How could she look at this old body and want it when I didn't even want it?

I was grateful that Genie was aggressive, because I honestly didn't know what to do next. I felt awkward standing in front of the bed. Hell, she was downright good at this. She lit two candles. She put on some soft music. Jazz or something, I think. I don't know. I was too afraid to pay much attention. Then she came to me. While I was kissing her neck, she started taking my clothes off. The woman didn't seem to have any inhibitions.

"David, are you okay with this?" My pants were down around my ankles, and she was asking me if I was okay. I wasn't going to answer that. I was nervous as anything. But they say it's like riding a bike. So I started doing what I thought was natural. Together, we peeled off her clothes and lay down on top of the bedcovers side by side, facing each other. My thoughts were running a mile a minute, but my heart was beating quicker than that. I caught a cramp in my side, so I had to let my gut go. Genie didn't seem to mind. She just moved closer to me. Put her arms around my neck and sighed my name into my mouth.

Everything she did to me, I loved. Enjoyed giving back to her. She smelled and tasted the way I had imagined she would. Like sweet salted chocolate. I couldn't get enough of her. The newness of her. The feel of her was firm and tight. In some small way I felt like I was reaching back through the years and touching a part of myself I'd never hoped to find again.

Afterward she lay in my arms stroking my jaw. Our legs were tangled together like grapevines and the bed sheets were saturated and warm against me. I felt like the woman had squeezed every drop of energy out of my body. It was a good goddamn feeling.

"David?" Genie said quietly. Her voice was hoarse from screaming like a banshee.

"Yeah," I said, wanting a cigarette for the first time in over a year.

"Where in hell did you learn to do all that?"

I was embarrassed. The woman never minced words. I laughed then I said, "This old dog still has a few tricks in him, Genie."

She looked up at me with those big brown eyes and said, "That's for sure."

I started kissing her fingertips. I think that's the only part of her I hadn't tasted.

"It's amazing that I see you all the time and think how beautiful you are," I said, "but right now, like this, you look more beautiful than I ever thought possible."

Pussy has a way of making you talk in sonnets. Especially when it's new to you. It's like a drug that way. I'd forgotten about that. I guess she thought I was pretty corny, because she made a face and said, "I take it you've never done this kind of thing before, huh?"

I said, "I haven't been with anyone but Monica in a very long time."

"How long?"

"A long time."

I was too embarrassed to say. I didn't want her to think I was some inexperienced old guy. Although I am. I've only had two others before Monica. Both were serious I thought at the time. I never was the Don Juan type even though I could have been. My grandmother didn't raise me to be that way. So I was more of a talker than anything. I wondered how many lovers she'd had, but didn't really want to know. With those Diahann Carroll eyes, that amber skin and sultry little voice? She was probably just killing some time with an old fella like me.

She must have felt my defeat in the slackening of my arms around her, because those fingers started tracing circles on my thigh. She was looking at me like she didn't want anything else but this closeness between us. When she turned her face up and kissed me, I felt like I could do anything. Hell, I felt like I could whip Holyfield. Well, maybe at least get in a few body shots. Genie slowly ended the kiss and we stared at each other in the candlelight. Looking at her like that was all I wanted to do.

"Where'd you get those pretty eyes?" she asked.

"My mother."

"Really?" She ran a finger lightly across my lashes.

"Yeah. She was part Irish. My grandmother, her mother, was an Irishwoman. I have a picture of my mother in my wallet. Remind me to show it to you. People tell me I look just like her. She's the one who cursed me with this hair." I reached up and ruffled my hair a bit.

"Nothing's wrong with your hair." She ran her fingers through it. "I love your hair. It's so soft."

I liked that she found me attractive. For so long, I had missed this kind of attention. I didn't know how much until she came along.

"Thanks," I said, "but while everyone else was walking around yelling Black Power and making a statement with their 'fros, I felt like I was the only one who couldn't have one. I was never sure where I fit in during the Movement. Some people never let me forget it."

"There's worse things, David. Believe me. I'll bet you were very close to your mother. What was she like?"

"I don't know, babe. When they died, I was only five."

"Oh. That's awful. You don't remember anything about them at all?"

"Vague things that I'm not sure even happened. A hypnotist friend of mine down in Atlanta keeps trying to convince me to let her put me under, but I'm not interested. If I don't remember, I don't remember. That's just how it is."

She looked away from me. Past me. Over at the wall. I wondered what was wrong.

"And I thought I was bad off being separated from my mother so young. David, I want to ask you a question I've never asked anybody in my life." She looked alive again.

"What's that?"

"Was it good for you?" She looked like she was afraid I would say no.

I laughed. I wasn't about to tell her that I'd never had it so good. So passionate. I hugged her closer.

"Yeah. It was," I said.

She kissed my chest.

"For me too. Do you have to go home?"

She sounded so hopeful that I would stay all night.

"Afraid so," I told her.

"Oh." She rolled away from me. I rolled over after her. She had to know that the last thing I wanted to do was go home. No one was there yet anyway. It was only eight o'clock. Monica was working late. The boys had basketball practice on Friday nights.

"I'm not going anywhere yet, babe. We still have a while." She rose on one elbow and started running her fingers through my hair. I made good use of those breasts in my face.

"Good," she said. "That means we can have a talk. I'm scared, David. I don't know what this is we're doing. Will you stop doing that so I can think straight?" I pulled her back down on my chest and kissed her forehead.

"You know David, you're the first person I've been with who I've cared about. How are we going to fit this into our friendship?" I felt strange seeing her like this. The hard edges were gone. How was I supposed to know what we should do next? Sometimes age can be a real burden. You're expected to know so many things that you have no clue about.

"I don't know, Genie. I'm all mixed up right now. I feel completely exhilarated, yet I feel terrible about having to go home and face my wife, knowing that I've been unfaithful."

"So you're sorry that we've made love? I need to know, David, 'cause I don't think I can take your avoidance. If you think you're going to be all freaked out about this tomorrow, let me know right now."

I rolled her onto her back. I wanted to be inside her again. To show her that . . . I don't know. I guess I wanted to show her that we were still connected to each other even though this night was a one-time affair. This was another thing I had forgotten about. I hadn't made love three times in one night since I don't know when.

"That's not going to happen, babe," I said. "I promise you that." We made love slow this time and fell asleep in each other's arms.

Genie

"Alright, Genie, no holds barred."

"What do you mean?" I hoped I looked innocent.

I was sitting in a booth at the Silver Diner with Paulette and Evelyn, drinking some good hot coffee and feeling like crap because David had worn me out good. I was also very, very concerned about my behavior. David is the only man I've slept with who I actually worried about pleasing in bed, and that freaked me out a little. I was attracted to him, I needed his friendship, and now I was losing track of myself somehow. In some small way I was losing control. But that was something I wasn't about to try to analyze.

"Don't give me that mess," Paulette said, "I was born at night, Genie, but not last night. Although something major was happening at somebody's house last night because I saw somebody's red car parked out in front of somebody's house and all the lights were out. So what gives, Genie? We missed our movie because of your behind."

"First of all, Paulette, will you please stop talking in code. Second, last night is none of y'alls' beeswax."

"Oho. Defensive and tired. Mmmhmm. I see those dark circles, Genie. So, did Dr. Feelgood make you feel real good, girl?" Evelyn said.

"Why is sex all you guys talk about?"

"Aw come on, Genie," Paulette said, forking honeydew melon into her mouth, "it's not like you're going around doing much else, now."

"I won't take that as an insult."

"Okay. Just don't take it as a compliment either." Paulette laughed her head off.

"Okay. See. That's why I'ma call Evelyn tonight and tell her everything, but you won't hear it from me, Paulette."

She grabbed my wrist.

"Aw, Genie. Come on. I was just playing, girl. I'll pay for breakfast. How's that?"

"I guess that's a start." I put syrup on my french toast.

"Well?"

"Alright, okay. Yes, David was over last night. Yes, he took me to the moon. Yes, it was wonderful and passionate and terrific. But. We have decided to remain friends and not let last night happen again, because I don't want him to feel guilty about it, and I seriously don't want him out of my life."

"I don't believe your fast butt. "

"See, that's why I didn't want to tell you. And anyway, it wasn't my fault. It just happened. I didn't even know he was coming over."

She was shaking her head at me and said, "You just couldn't rest until you got some, could you? Genie, you've made a big mistake with this."

"I agree," Evelyn said.

"It's different now, y'all. We talked things out and it's not happening again. David's fine about it. We both are."

"You really believe you can be . . . what am I saying, I know you can pull back and still be friends with him but the question is, will it work vice versa?"

"I hope so, Paulette, because I care about the man. You know that. I can't imagine things not being the way they are with us. I hate to say it, but I've kind of come to depend on him like I depend on you guys. So I hope he'll be able to put last night behind him."

"Well, I hope so too. Last night should not have happened. The man freaked the heck out when you two kissed. How's he gonna stay in control now that he's had a piece of the pie? He probably has some less-than-sexy wife at home, and here you are with your hot self just handing him a freebie. Girl, I don't think he's gonna be able to handle it. I don't mean to sound like a broken record, but this whole thing is dangerous."

Paulette was getting on my nerves. She was always talking without knowing all of the facts. David and I had already agreed that last night would be our one-time thing. It was special for both of us, but it was just sex. Now it would be out of our systems and we could be the way we were before.

"Paulette, David and I are chilled out. Trust me." I drank some more coffee.

"Alright. Just watch yourself, girl. This could turn into a volatile situation."

"Mmm," I said, drinking more coffee, "it won't."

"Well, good for you. Is he hung?"

"I'm not going to answer that, Evelyn."

"Since when don't you give us details?"

"Since it's none of your business. David is different. He's not one of my little conquests, and you know it."

"Fine then, Miss Touchy. Keep your little scandalous affair to yourself. So what do you ladies have planned for today?"

Paulette licked syrup off her fingers and said, "Me and Robert are going to buy a few things for the house and take Telaysia to Chuck E. Cheese. Hey, why don't you bring Sasha and Simmy along to see the big mouse? We're going at about noon."

"That sounds good. I'm sure Sasha and Simeon would definitely be up for that. What about you, Genie?"

"Who, me?" My mind had wandered back to last night for the hundredth time. I couldn't get over how great it was. I took another swig of my coffee and set the mug down. How the hell was I supposed to keep my hands off this man when I still didn't feel like I'd had enough of him yet?

"Yes, you. What are your plans for today?"

"Oh. Nothing major. I'ma mail off my taxes finally, and wash my car."

"You sign up for classes yet?"

"Not yet. Monday. That's when touch-tone registration opens."

"You gonna get into a particular program?"

"Not just yet. I'ma take a few classes as a nondegree student first, see how I do."

"What are you taking?"

"A basic English course and a math. I was going to take David's class too, but now that we've been together, I don't think that's such a good idea."

"I hear you," Evelyn said, then, "Well you guys. I've gotta go. Simon's coming over to fix my garbage disposal."

"Oh really," I said. "Evelyn, correct me if I'm wrong, but it seems like all of a sudden lots of stuff is breaking in your house that Simon has to come fix. What's up? You trying to get back together with him?"

Evelyn blushed, so I knew something was going on.

"I'm not going to say that I'm trying to get back with him, but we've been seeing eye to eye lately."

"Well I'm glad, girl." Paulette said. "If you want my opinion, you two should never have broken up in the first place."

"Mmm. Well we still have some issues, Paulette. If something rekindles for me and Simon, then that would be wonderful. But I'm not dropping my panties for him just yet. He still has very backward ideas about women. And I need my independence. But on that note, my sisters, I'm outta here. Paulette, I'll be at your house at noon."

I half waved at Evelyn and stared out the window, still thinking about David. Before he left he did the sweetest thing while I was sleeping last night. He took my *Erotique Noire* book and placed it on the pillow next to me with one page bent. It was Kalamu Ya Salaam's Haiku #107. David is too much. But he's right about what he told me last night just before we fell asleep with him inside me. Playing with fire is scary as hell. But oh, the thrill.

David

The woman is utterly consuming me. Completely. I can feel myself being sucked in and I'm totally powerless. Why does it feel this good? I took two long showers at Genie's before I left, but I could still smell her on my fingers. I was almost paranoid that Monica would smell it too. On the drive home I felt pretty bad about what I'd done. I even shed a few tears. It's hard to face that the things you believe aren't as black and white as you expect them to be. But then I asked myself, If I hadn't been with Genie, what would I have been doing? I'd have been at home, alone, in front of the TV as usual. Probably would have ordered Chinese from the delivery joint around the corner from my house. Or I would have done some more research on the Internet. There wouldn't have been anybody to hold me the way Genie had. Nobody to make me feel like I could climb Mount Everest in a day. I'd tried with

Monica, but she just wasn't biting. I figured maybe the marriage was over and I just didn't want to face it yet.

I got home at eleven and Monica greeted me in the kitchen. I had made sure that my clothes and hair were as neat as when I'd left this morning. Monica had just gotten in herself. Surprise, surprise. She was making herself a fruit salad and talking on and on about how she was going off to Dallas first thing on Monday for a round of meetings to discuss the possibility of Derwood-Covington opening an office there. She said she'd be gone a few days, if not a whole week. She sounded like she'd known about this trip for a while, the way she carried on. It was news to me. She probably had been afraid to tell me, because normally I would have put up a fuss and demanded that we spend some time together over the weekend. All I felt this time was relieved. I think she knew something was wrong, but she didn't say anything. I wished I could just turn back around, jump back in the car and go where I knew I was wanted. It was comforting to know that somebody's arms were open just for me.

I nodded like I gave a damn about what Monica was saying, chucked one of her sliced bananas in my mouth and went upstairs to shower again. By the time I collapsed in the bed, I couldn't sleep. My body was at home, but my mind was still in bed with Genie. Reminded me of that song. I couldn't stop thinking about her. The softness of her skin. The way she curled her body around me like a hot little snake. If only I could have stayed with her. I never knew that a woman could make me feel so good. So wanted. That's all I kept thinking about while I lay on my side, as close to the edge as I could get. I just wanted to make myself disappear altogether when Monica finally came into the bedroom, wearing that damned yellow nightgown that makes her look like a target, and plopped in the bed next to me. I felt angry with myself for getting old, angry with Monica for treating me like an inanimate object and angry with life itself. Genie was my only bright spot.

Somehow I got through the night. I dozed off and on until the sun came up. Monica and the boys were still asleep when I got up. It was eight when I went downstairs to my office and dialed Genie's number. I was disappointed when her answering machine came on. Where the hell was she anyway? Asleep? Maybe in the shower. I hung up without leaving a message. I didn't want to talk to her machine. I wanted to talk to her. I wanted to tell her I was thinking about her and that I still felt good about last night. But I reminded myself again that she and I agreed that it couldn't happen again. Genie and I made a memory last night that we'd always be able to hold on to, but that was all it was. From now on, we'd be strictly hands-off. Provided that my hands would listen to me.

I made a pot of coffee, put on some pants that were in the laundry room and brought the newspaper inside.

"David?" Monica yelled from upstairs. I wished she would just hurry up and go to Dallas.

"Yeah?"

"Honey, would you put on a pot of tea, please. I don't have time to make us breakfast this morning. I have some loose ends to tie up at the office this weekend before I leave on Monday!"

Figured. I hooked up the brewer and measured out an amount of tea and spices. I fixed myself some instant grits and toast and sat down to read the paper.

"Hey, Dad." Devin walked in, sleepy-eyed and wobbly.

"Hey, son. What's going on in your world? I haven't seen much of you lately."

"I know, I been busy, man" he said. "I've been trying to crack on this girl in my astronomy class. She hangs out at the rec after school, so that's where I hang out too."

I grinned at him. The boy reminded me too much of myself. He had his mother's delicate features, but he had my eyes and smile.

"Oh?" I put the newspaper aside. "What girl is this we're talking about?"

"This girl named Kelli. She's bad, Dad. Every dude in school is trying to get with her."

"Yeah?"

"Yeah. Man, I'm trying to take her to the prom." He took a gigantic bowl out of the cabinet and poured probably half a box of Lucky Charms into it.

"Well, have you asked her yet? You know the prom'll be here before you know it."

"I know, I know. I'm just working up my nerve. See, she's famous for breaking a brotha down for being weak. So when I step to her, I have to come correct. So, I've been networking with some of her girls. Trying to find out what she likes, you know, how she likes to be approached. Soon as I get my confidence together, I'ma step to her and hit her with my smooth rap. And shoot. That'll be all she wrote."

"Boy, are you still talking about Kelli Patterson?" Mark came in bouncing around like he was in the ring. I'd thought about getting the boy some boxing lessons because he loved the sport so much.

"You know it, man." Devin said, stuffing his mouth with cereal.

"Boy, that girl is not going to let you take her to no prom. Big-head self." Mark had my personality. Always starting trouble. Just like I did with my brother Aaron when we were growing up.

"Dad, tell this fool to shut up before I have to knock 'im out."

"Alright guys. That's enough. Mark, you leave your brother alone about the girl, and Devin, don't call your brother a fool. There aren't any fools living in this house, because I'm not raising any. Okay?"

"Okay, Dad," Mark said, "but I still think Romeo here is gonna strike out." He dodged the punch Devin threw and ran upstairs laughing.

"Dad, how did you ask a girl out when you were in school?" Devin looked worried.

"Son, it's not easy to face possible rejection. But let me tell you this: It's alright to want to feel like you're cool and all, but what girls like most is if you just be yourself. So try that. But don't act too eager. You're already a good-looking kid. You're smart. That was a good idea you had about finding out what she likes, because that gives you an edge."

"You think so, Dad?"

"I know so."

We finished breakfast in silence. Monica came down, drank her tea and after she left for work, I went up to the bedroom and called Genie again. I needed to hear her.

Genie picked up on the first ring.

Hello?" she said.

I laid on my pillow and closed my eyes. I was picturing her the way she was last night.

"I still smell you, Genie." I hoped I sounded sexy.

"David?"

"Who else." I hoped she wouldn't try to give me an answer to that. Pretty girl like that probably had fellas coming out of the woodwork like termites. I was relieved when she said, "Hi. What're you doing?"

I put my hand up to my nose and inhaled.

"Smelling you."

"What?"

"Nothing. I was just thinking about you, that's all. I called you earlier but I got your machine."

"I know. I saw your name on my caller ID. I went out for breakfast earlier."

"You did?"

I wanted to ask her who with. I couldn't believe she would sleep with me, then meet some other man bright and early, like last night didn't mean anything.

"You still okay about last night?"

The hell with that. I was still on whether she'd gone to breakfast with another man or not.

"Yeah. So where'd you go for breakfast?"

"The Silver Diner. I meet Paulette and Evelyn there for breakfast a couple times a month."

I felt much better.

"Oh. How are those two?" I wondered if she'd told them about last night. I wasn't asking. I know how women talk. I've walked in on too many of Monica's telephone conversations where she was telling her friends things about me that I would have rather she'd kept to herself.

"They're both fine. Paulette is as crazy as a loon, but what else is new. Evelyn may be trying to get back together with her ex-husband, Simon."

"Mmm. So what are you doing right now?"

"Nuthin'. Laying across my bed watching TV. I'm so tired." She was yawning. I patted my zipper, smiling.

"Wonder why."

She started giggling like a little girl. I wished I was there to kiss her smiling face.

"Well. Somebody was insatiable last night," she said.

I was enjoying the hell out of this conversation. My whole body was tingling.

"If I seem to remember correctly, somebody else wasn't putting up a fight to stop me, now, were you?"

She laughed again.

"David, you are crazy. Oh, you know that was sweet about the haiku. Thanks. I liked that."

"I'm glad. I flipped through it last night after I watched you sleep awhile. You know you snore?" I felt like messing with her. It had been a long time since I'd felt this playful.

She gasped. "I do not!"

"Softly, Genie. But you do snore."

"Liar. If you were here right now, I'd show you who snores."

"Mmm. What else would you show me?" I whispered it. The boys were watching wrestling just in the next room. I glanced over at my doorknob to make sure I'd locked the door. I was glad that Monica had given them their own line when girls started calling the house like crazy. I didn't have to worry about one of them picking up.

"What else would you like to see, baby?" She was turning me on and she knew it. I unbuttoned my pants and put my hand in my briefs.

"Whatever you've got," I told her. She was getting turned on too. I heard her shifting and she was breathing kind of hard into the phone.

"I miss lying next to you, Genie."

"I know," she said. It wasn't what I wanted to hear.

"David, are we having phone sex? Because you're making me hot." I felt like I was doing something bad and I liked it.

"That's what I'm supposed to do, babe. Why don't you put your hand where you want me to be right now." I was breathing hard too and getting frustrated. The knock on my door scared the hell out of me.

"Dad?" It was Mark.

"Hold on a minute, Genie." I adjusted myself. "Yeah, son?"

"Dad, I need snaps for the carnival today. Could I get twenty dollars out of your wallet? It's in the bathroom." Shit, I would have signed over the house to him if he would just go away.

"Go ahead, son."

"Okay. Dev needs some money too."

"Fine, son. Twenty apiece." He was satisfied with that. I heard his footsteps retreating.

"Sorry about that, babe. My son."

"That's alright. How old's he anyway? He sounds grown."

I felt embarrassed to tell her because he was only nine years younger than she, but I mumbled, "Sixteen."

"Oh. And the other one's older, right? By a year?"

I didn't want to talk about that. "Yep," I said.

She was silent for a minute. I scrambled to find another subject. I guessed the mood was shot.

"Hey, what are you doing Monday evening?" The weather had finally broken, I think, for good. I thought it would be nice if Genie and I could get to know each other in surroundings outside of work.

"Oh, David, I have plans Monday night. Why, what'd you have in mind?"

Now I knew how my son felt about that girl he wanted to ask to the prom. I felt rejected. I cleared my throat.

"Never mind. It's not important. It's just that Monica's gonna be away for a few days and the boys aren't around much. I wondered if you wanted to catch a film. No big deal."

"That sounds good. How about Tuesday? I'm free Tuesday night if you wanna go."

"Can't. Winthrop's hosting a reading Tuesday for the Black Student Union. I promised to show my face there."

"Okay. So Tuesday's out too. And I can't Wednesday, 'cause Evelyn's having a Mary Kay party. Well, what are you doing today?"

"Today?"

"Yeah. I'm stuck with nothing to do today but wash my car."

I knew Monica would be safely tucked away in her office all day. What else did I have to do besides putter around the house and do a bit of yard work? So I said, "Why not?"

"Great," she said. "You like crabs?"

"Love 'em. I don't get a chance to eat them as much as I'd like, though. Monica and the kids hate the smell and complain about picking them."

"You know how to cook 'em?"

"Yeah, of course."

"Wanna get some?"

"Okay. We can do that."

"Good. I'm going up to Trak Auto to get some wax for my car. I'll be here after that, so come on over anytime you're ready."

"I'll be there." I hung up the phone feeling revitalized. I felt like going with the flow. Guilt hadn't gotten me anything but time alone. I was ready to let whatever was going to happen between Genie and me just happen. Why did I always have to be the responsible one? For once, I was going to do something that felt good to me.

I got over to Genie's house around eleven. She was just finishing up her car. I parked mine in her garage because she motioned for me to. The sky was clear as a bell. The Dogwoods were on the bloom. Pollen was out with a vengeance and I could feel my sinuses protesting a bit. It was about seventy-five degrees already, so I wore a burgundy short-sleeved shirt and a pair of khaki shorts. I liked the way Genie checked my legs out when I walked toward her. She had on a pair of tight jean shorts and some low-cut top. Her eyes were hidden behind a pair of blue eyeshades and beneath her Yankees ballcap was a long ponytail. I was confused. I know she hadn't grown that much hair overnight. But damn, she looked good enough to eat in more ways than one. She lowered her head and checked me out above the top of her shades.

"Hey, you," she said. She smiled at me bright enough to stop my heart.

"Hey." I smiled back and rubbed my hand down her bare arm. My body was betraying me already. I hoped she couldn't tell. She waved at some kids out in the yard next door to hers.

"I'm just about ready." She walked up the middle of her yard through the thick green grass and wound up the long garden hose on a base situated between the pink and white peonies and azaleas.

"The irises are nice." Patches of purple and gold ones had bloomed outside her living room window. She definitely had a green thumb.

"Thanks." She turned, swinging that ponytail and walked back toward the car. Then she blessed me with a full view of her sweet upturned ass when she bent to get the bucket so she could pour out the soapy water. She ran up the steps with her bucket and towels, calling over her shoulder, "You can get in the car. I'ma grab my purse and car keys."

I felt strange getting into the passenger seat of her car. I worried about whether someone I knew might see us together. I was glad I hadn't made any friends except at work. But then, that would be another situation if we saw anybody from work. I was on the lookout. She came back wearing this bright red lipstick that I wanted to drown in. I reached over and rubbed her smooth brown thigh like it was mine and forgot all about whether we'd see someone we knew.

We sped down Route 50 with the windows down. Her ponytail was swinging and these gold bracelets she wore kept clinking when she changed lanes. She was playing some kind of jazz tape. It was the same kind of stuff she'd played when we'd made love. It didn't sound bad at all. I had thought girls her age listened to all that rap music that my sons were so hung up on.

"Who's this on the tape?" I asked

"That's Boney James."

"Boney who?"

She reached into some kind of cassette compartment and pulled out a cassette cover.

"That's him."

I looked at the cover a minute like I gave a damn, then handed it back. I guess she couldn't tell when someone was trying to make idle conversation. So I shut up and looked out the window a while because

I was nervous. If I let myself get too comfortable, I knew I could really fall for this woman.

My nervousness was replaced by honest to goodness fear when I realized that Genie was trying to kill us. Genie's one of those aggressive, screaming drivers. She cut people off. Glared at people who moved too slow in the fast lane as she passed them. I didn't even drive my Mazda the way she drove her car. By the time we parked down by the wharf, I was sweating and holding onto the sissy bar that most people hang their dry cleaning from. Genie has so many sides to her that I wasn't sure what I was getting myself into.

Genie

Things started off kind of shaky, but once David relaxed we began to have a really good time. We talked, we laughed and we fought about my driving. The Negro had the nerve to tell me that I was a maniac behind the wheel. I told him he could get out and walk if he didn't like it. He batted my fake ponytail and laughed at me. Jerk. Spending time with him like this was kind of nice. For a minute I wondered what we were doing. Here we were spending more time together, when we knew that we should be playing it safe.

When we got back to my house with the crabs, I made him put on an apron so he wouldn't get his clothes dirty. He looked so cute chasing crabs around the kitchen floor, wearing my apron, that I forgot about my promise to behave myself. He put the lid on the pot and I walked up behind him. I wrapped my arms around him and stood on my tiptoes to kiss his neck. He turned around and we kissed for a long time, then he held me like he was trying to squeeze the blood out of me.

"D, I can't breathe," I said.

"Oh," he said. Like he didn't know his own strength. Big six-foot, nearly two hundred–pound man, and here I am five foot four and all of one hundred twenty-five pounds, being squashed to death.

He let go and I spread yesterday's newspaper out on the kitchen table.

"Wanna beer?" I asked.

He nodded and I opened some Michelobs for us.

"When I was a little girl, my uncle, Uncle Eugene—he was named after grandma too—well, in a way he was. Well, Uncle Eugene would come to our house every Fourth of July with a bushel of crabs and a box of fireworks. He would grab one of the crabs out of the bag and scare me with it. I'd be running through the house screaming and laughing." I laughed, remembering that.

"He still around?"

"No. He died when I was eleven. He had throat cancer and it spread to his lungs."

I didn't add that Uncle Eugene's death was a year before Mama's breakdown. I wasn't ready to tell David about that. We sat down next to each other at the table and David held my hand.

"I'm sorry," he said. He didn't have anything to be sorry for. It's funny how people say that when they hear that someone's dead, just because they don't know what else to say. David said that same thing when I told him Mama was dead, too.

"Tell me about the rest of your family. What are your sisters like? Are they like you?"

The fan was going and so was Rose Royce's "I Wanna Get Next To You."

"Nothing like me. I'm the odd one. They're both older than me. Marilyn's the oldest. She's thirty-one. She's married for the second time to this really great guy and she has a son, Keith. He's eight. They live in Miami. We don't talk much. Tess is thirty. She's in North Carolina. She's got kind of a weight problem of sorts. Last time we talked she'd broken off with her boyfriend, but wouldn't tell me why. What about you? You have any brothers or sisters?"

"A brother. Aaron. We don't talk, though. He lives in Van Nuys. I haven't seen him since Monica dragged me to one of my family reunions five years ago. He's got a wife and a daughter. He's a computer programmer."

"Why don't you two talk?"

"It's complicated, Genie. We just aren't compatible. I better check those crabs."

Sometimes David struck me as very secretive. He could talk me to death about almost anything, but he never said much about himself. It was hard to get a sense of who he is.

I watched him pull up the lid on the crab pot, smiling. The steam rushed out to touch his face and he breathed it in.

"Oh yeah. These babies are done now. Look at that, would you." The crabs were bright orange now. They were jumbos. He took the tongs and pulled one up by the claw to show me.

"Looks good. Bring 'em on over."

I rubbed my hands together. He put several on the lid and dumped them on to the table in front of me. They were too hot to pick with, so I sipped my beer and watched David wipe up some crab spice he'd spilled all over the counter. I swear, the man was clumsy as all get-out. But not in bed.

He started talking to me about something. I don't know what he was saying because I was too busy looking at his long, hairy legs and remembering last night. My mouth watered. I wanted him again. The way his hair curled at the back of his neck. Good Lord. His wide back that I'd held onto and pressed my nails into last night. Before I even knew what I was doing, I walked over to him and planted another kiss right on him. He liked it too. He grabbed me, pressing me against the counter, and kissed me so deeply I felt it in my toes. But then he moved away from me and I almost fell on the floor.

"Come on, babe. Let's eat," he said. He started fumbling with the apron strings and took the apron off.

"Alright," I said. On our way to the table I pinched his butt before he sat down. I don't know what had gotten into me.

David

After we ate our crabs, Genie decided she wanted to rent a movie from Blockbuster, so I told her to go ahead and I'd clean up the mess. I put the few crabs that were left in a paper bag and set them in the refrigerator. I dumped the trash and tidied up the kitchen and opened another beer for myself.

Genie had told me to make myself at home, so I looked around the place a bit. The two other times I'd been here were at night. I talked to her fish for a while, then wandered down the hall. I wanted to see what her bedroom looked like in the daylight. It was small, but pretty. Feminine. Kind of crowded, but well done. She seemed to have an eye for where things should go. That, or she'd really been reading all those *Better Homes and Gardens* magazines stacked up in her magazine rack.

I nosed around in her closet, which I shouldn't have been doing, but that was where she kept her bigger hardcover books. I wanted to see what else she'd been reading. I was impressed. She had a few books on African cultures, which I was going to ask her to let me borrow, something on great women in black history, some interesting-looking books on the Roman empire and Henry the VIII, and something on the Holocaust. I saw something sticking out of a box behind the Holocaust book, so I took a look inside. I put it back quick, but I was smiling. Genie was a bit freakier than I thought. I decided that I would try to bring this up in some way later on.

I went back down the hall to sit in the dining room so I could look out across her backyard while I drank my beer and listened to the oldies station. That's when the telephone rang. It only rang once. Then her answering machine picked up. She hadn't turned the machine down, though. Some guy started talking, and he left an explicit message on the machine. He began telling her what he wanted to do to her if he could get a hold of her. It took everything in me not to pick up the telephone and cuss the son of a bitch out. I mean, I had a serious itch to clean his goddamn clock. But it wasn't my place to do so. So I did the only thing any other man in my position would have done. I erased the goddamn message.

Then I got angry at Genie. I mean, she just screwed the bejesus out of me last night. Would she really turn around and screw some other guy? Hell. I felt like jumping in my car and taking off. But it was my own stupidity, thinking I was something special. Genie was a single woman. How can I expect her to play the virgin just because I came into the picture? I felt like a failure all over again. Monica didn't want me. And now Genie didn't want me either. I was probably just another man to add to her collection. I put the beer on the table and sat down in the chair. That girl didn't a bit more want an old cat like me than a man in the moon. I heard the front door. She walked in looking fresh and beautiful with her warm brown eyes and the thighs of life in those tight shorts. I felt like I had something to prove. I walked over to her before she could even put the bag on the table, and I grabbed her and started kissing her like no tomorrow.

"David?" she said, trying to dodge me. I knew she was confused.

"I need you, babe. I have to have you right now." I was kissing that spot on her neck that she told me makes her lose control. She shouldn't have told me about that.

We made it right in the middle of the living room floor like two wildcats, with the radio going and half our clothes still on. But I must say that I performed like a superstar. That bragging SOB on the telephone can't touch me.

Genie

Registration week is the week that professors and staff think of with horror. It's a time of students jam-packing the front office to the hilt, thrusting out their forms for signatures, wanting to get into closed classes, wanting to meet and greet their advisors because they're brand spanking new to Whitman. They want a walk-thru on how to get their student ID, what they needed to do to take the Test of English as a Foreign Language, how to get around the campus and, in essence, how to start their new lives because some don't read the intimidating student handbook and bulletin with all the information in it they need.

Registration week is bedlam. A time when the staff hopes that all the professors will show up. At least, that's what I'd heard. I had been lucky to have missed that week for the spring registration. My baptism was going to be a milder case. Summer registration.

I made sure I got plenty of rest the night before. David came over again. But this time we just kicked back and watched some Sidney Sheldon movie on cable and argued over the popcorn. I still wasn't sure what was happening with us. All I know is what I believe about God always sending you somebody. I feel like David was sent to me to watch over me. I had prayed for him, and he appeared in my life just when I needed him to come. Plus, we've been having fun just being to-gether. I never had that with any man, so I know he's my godsend.

David told me last night that he wanted us to get to know each other better. He asked me if we could spend more time together while his wife is away since he'll be free to come and go. Like a softie, I told him that would be fine with me. My big thing is that I want him to spend the night with me. All night. I was beginning to wonder if David was turning me into some totally other woman. David said he would cancel out on the poetry reading so that Tuesday would be free and clear. He's just so wonderful to be with. He's the best person in the world to talk to, and I feel like I'm learning so much. Our friendship, or whatever it was, had grown by leaps and bounds in such a short time that my brain was having a hard time digesting it all.

I thought about all of this while I stared out of the window at the tunnel wall, riding the subway in to work Monday morning. I had dropped my car off at the dealer so they could cop a look at my muffler. A rental car would cost, so I scrounged together my chump change and got on the train. The train was full but quiet. WMATA trains are pretty clean and safe. Nowhere near like the movies I've seen of the ones in New York. I was a little squished because some really big lady with an obvious upper respiratory condition sat down next to me. It was all I could do to stay alive in the tiny space I had. I was grateful when the train reached my stop.

I elbowed my way through the crowd and took the escalator up to the street level. The air was so warm it felt damp. It was eight in the morning but already everything around Whitman was teeming with life. A chic Chinese woman was handing out little red and white restaurant menus to everyone as they got off the escalator. A coal-colored man with long reddish dreds had set up his portable keyboard and was belting out "This Little Light of Mine" in a light, mellow tone. He was pretty good. I reached into my black leather babydoll purse and tossed a dollar into his cup. He nodded at me, smiling while he played on.

Most people were in a big hurry. They waited in groups for the walk signal. Traffic was thick and cars zoomed by with horns beeping every minute. I took a look at some hammered silver bracelets at a table set up to the side of a hot dog cart near the man singing gospel. The table was draped with colorful silk scarves in reds and blues and golds. The owner, an Arab-looking man with curling jet-black hair and perfect white teeth, had spread the bracelets artistically across the scarves. The bracelets were too expensive for my taste, so I moved across the street with the flow of people when the signal turned.

No matter how I feel about my job, I was starting to love Whitman. Walking around the campus is like stepping into another world. The brick buildings are mostly old and ornate. Most of them have a comfortable sixties feel. Everything is easily accessible. But what makes me feel most at home are the people. You can walk down any street, any hallway here, and hear maybe three different languages at once. Everybody is so different at Whitman. The smells, the different shades of skin, the different styles of dress. As I've gotten to know some of the students, I realize that for all our differences we're all unfailingly alike. Too bad racists can't see that.

I walked up a block from my building to the Au Bon Pain with its bricked sidewalk and ivy-filled outdoor seating. The chairs and tables were a jade green wrought iron with pastel umbrellas to block out the sun. I was meeting David there for coffee, a habit we'd grown into ever since we became friends. I saw him sitting at our favorite table, reading the paper. He had on his glasses and he was eating his favorite carrot-cake muffin. The place was deserted except for us and one woman in a corner flipping through a magazine.

"Hey, you." I touched his arm when I reached him. He looked up from his paper and smiled at me like he was glad to see me. It made me feel special.

"Good morning, sunshine. Have a seat and I'll get us some cappuccinos."

"Make mine a mocha blast."

"One mocha blast coming up." He folded his newspaper and stood up. I unbuttoned the jacket of my lavender pantsuit and took my seat.

"You been waiting long?"

"Just ten minutes or so. You look beautiful today."

"So do you," I said.

The man *was* looking good too and knew it. He was wearing a tailored pinstriped dark blue suit with a pastel shirt and a nice silk tie. His shoes were black and had tassels on them. His hair was smoothed back the way I like it. I would have to mess it up later. He was just so damn tall and sexy he made me want to grab him. He had a meeting later this afternoon with a Ghanaian doctoral student he thought might help him with some site research for his book. I watched him walk into the Au Bon Pain. *Glide,* actually, because the man didn't just walk.

I fought with a bee while David was gone. After I won, I sat back and relaxed with *Sula.* I was reading it again for the second time. David came out of the building toward me with his usual regular cappuccino and my mocha blast.

"What are you reading?" he asked me.

I held the book up so that he could see the cover. He nodded and took a sip of my mocha.

"Very good. I keep saying I should get some of this mocha every time we come here. You want any of my muffin?" I shook my head. All of a sudden I felt kind of moody. I figured it was probably PMS.

David looked at his watch. "Monica's probably halfway to Dallas by now. We still on for dinner tonight, babe?"

"Yeah. Where're we going?"

"I thought we'd go down to Susquehanna's. Eat outside if it's a nice night, and water-watch. Maybe take a nice walk. How's that?"

"That sounds good, sweetie. I'm game."

"You okay, Genie?" His gray eyes were on me hard. I never got tired of looking into them.

"Yeah. I'm fine," I said. But I wasn't fine. Something was very wrong with me. I wondered if maybe I was coming down with something, but I chalked it up to PMS and turned the page of my book.

When we got to the office, Justine told me that I really was lucky to have my first registration period be during the summer. Most of the professors were gone or leaving, and a lot of our regular students and new enrollees wouldn't be coming until fall. I was grateful for the reprieve.

I touch-tone registered for my classes, then computed the rest of the evaluation totals from our spring classes and typed up the student responses from their forms. The phone rang off the hook as usual, but only a trickle of students at a time came in the door. My mechanic called and confirmed that I did need a new muffler. He told me the car would be ready by Wednesday. David was in his office most of the day. He looked busy as heck, so I didn't bother him. But now and again we caught each other's eye and smiled or waved like we were teenagers.

Barbara was out again for her monthly heart attack. I found out from Justine, who'd been there five years, that Barbara was a hypochondriac. She claimed every ailment from Lyme disease to bone cancer. She'd apparently, according to her own stories, survived Legionnaire's disease twice. David said she was delusional. As much as I couldn't stand her ass, I felt sorry for the woman. All she had in the world was a cat and some goldfish that she kept having to replace because, unlike her, they did die.

I met David at his car after work, and by that time I was sure that my period was coming soon. Why else would I be this fidgety? And clumsy? I dropped everything that wasn't attached to me. It was like David was rubbing off on me big-time. I'd read my horoscope on the Net and although I could tell it was some kind of cryptic warning, it was too difficult for me to decipher. It said something about rising tides. I looked for signs all day, but all I felt was sick in my stomach. I had checked the calendar in my purse and my period was due to arrive within the next five days. At least me and David would have this time together, even if I was evil. PMS is a mutha.

I put on my seatbelt and we headed down the street.

"You sure you're okay, Genie?"

"Yeah. I'm fine, Doc. Just PMS, I think. How'd your meeting go?"

"Not bad. It was very promising. Winthrop's doctoral student Michael Kemeh's going to go over to Ghana sometime around the end of May to make some arrangements for me. Apparently he has quite a few connections at the university. Depending on how things pan out, I'll probably have to go over myself around the end of June."

"That does sound promising. You know, I've always wanted to go there."

He reached over for my hand like always and squeezed my fingers.

"So have I. I think it's about the only place I haven't been. I'm pretty excited about it. So how'd your day go? I didn't see you much today."

"Fine. I got registered and went over at lunchtime for my books. Six of them, David. For one basic English course. I think our new part-timer, Professor Haden, is intent on killing me with this class. Probably because he's all buddy-buddy with Barbara. Reminds me of your method of torture."

"I don't think encouraging students to read is a method of torture, babe." He stopped at a light.

"Yeah, but trust me. Any professor who chooses a book like Burroughs's *The Naked Lunch* is some kind of sadist."

David laughed and I wanted to kiss those laugh lines around his eyes. The light turned and he took off behind a New Yorker with a cardboard sign in its back window that said Stolen Tag, with a license plate number beneath it.

"Oh yeah. According to my mechanic," I said, "my car needs a new muffler. He said it'll be ready sometime Wednesday."

"You wanna hitch a ride with me tomorrow, then?" We were getting close to the restaurant and David started perusing the street, looking for a place to park.

"Yeah. That sounds like a plan. Better than riding the subway. Pick me up about seven. David, what are you going to tell your kids about where you are tonight?"

"I have that covered. Don't worry about it." He beeped at a stopped cabby. The driver let someone out and we moved on. David found a space and we took off our seatbelts and got out of the car. It got on my nerves when he wouldn't tell me what was going on. He dropped his keys trying to get them into his pocket. He reached down and picked them up.

"Well, what if your wife calls you tonight and you aren't home?"

"Honey, calm down. Come on, I'm starved." He looked annoyed and put his hands in his pockets. Screw it. His wife wasn't my problem. We walked down the stairs through a maze of restaurants and shops past some beautiful, lighted water fountains that reminded me of Rome.

Susquehanna's is an elegant two-story, old-world restaurant situated along the Potomac. Their biggest attraction is not the food, but the atmosphere. I'd been there for drinks for my twenty-first birthday.

"It's a little breezy out here tonight, babe," he said. I linked my arm through his, not caring if anybody saw us. I guess he didn't care either, because he didn't resist.

"I know, but it's so warm and beautiful. Come on, let's sit over here." I pointed to a table with an unhampered view of the water. There were already several people out. The sun was setting, and it was a devastating orange backdrop for the small white boats that were on the water in the distance. The wind was whipping my hair every which way, so as soon as David pulled out my chair and helped me settle, I pinned up the back of my hair, but left my bangs out.

David went to the bar and got our drinks. He handed me the Seabreeze I'd requested in a glass with a straw and a slice of lime and sat down with his beer.

"This is so beautiful." I said. He smiled over at me like he thought so too and brushed my bangs out of my eyes.

"So are you." His hand moved to my thigh. He was so handsome. The waiter came and took our order, and for a while we just sat back people watching without saying anything, while the water rolled in front of us.

"Genie?"

"Yes?"

"I want to ask you a question."

"What, baby?"

"Have you been with anybody since we were together the past weekend?"

Now where did that come from? I looked over at David, but he wasn't looking at me. He was looking everywhere but at me. He seemed nervous. He started biting his lip and twisting the neck of his Corona bottle.

"No, David. I haven't. Why?"

He was silent as a monk who had just taken vows. I leaned my head to the side and kind of got in his face to make him look at me.

"Why?" I asked again.

His eyes were on the table.

"I just wanted to know," he said, "because we haven't talked about . . . I wondered if you have other lovers. And if, well . . . I know you haven't asked me about wearing a condom, and we've not discussed birth control."

I understood where he was coming from. We did need to have this conversation. I hadn't brought it up because, at first, we were supposed to have just had that one-time fling. But even that was irresponsible of me. I wasn't usually so stupid, but somehow with David, I didn't think things through.

"David, I guess you know I'm no saint. But I don't have unprotected sex. Believe it or not, I've never had unprotected sex with any man but you. I don't know if I felt it was okay to do it because I felt you were a safe bet or not. I don't know. It was careless of both of us to have done it. But I haven't been with anybody since you, and I don't want to be. I would like to know what this is we're doing, though. You haven't said anything. Oh, and incidentally, I'm on the pill." I looked up to see what he thought about that, but as usual, his face didn't reveal a thing.

"I feel so ignorant about all of this, really. I've never had to worry about AIDS or any other STDs. It's been a while since I've had to even worry about getting Monica pregnant, so this is new to me."

"I understand," I said. "I've been tested for HIV twice in the past few years, and both times it came back negative. Plus I get regular pap once a year, and everything turns up clear. Normally I'm super responsible about this kind of thing. I don't know why you've come along and ruined my good sense, David."

"Sorry," he said. "Look, I guess I'm not so sure what we're doing either. What do you think we're doing?"

"Having a good time together. Getting to know each other. I'm a little confused because you did say you didn't want us to sleep together anymore after that first time."

"I know what I said," he told me. He sounded a little defensive, so I left it alone and concentrated on my drink while I looked out at the water.

"Genie, how do you feel about me?"

I cleared my throat on that one and looked over at him. He was acting like he was oh so interested in the cyclists going by. I wondered why he was asking me that question, because I hoped he wasn't falling for me or anything. I didn't want to hurt his feelings, so I took the safe road on that answer.

I shrugged and said, "I think you're a good person. You're caring, you're sensitive, you're warm. You're one of the best people I know." He looked at me like he could see right through me or something. Like he wanted to say something deep and meaningful but wasn't ready to, and it gave me the creeps. This was getting too real for me.

"I didn't ask you what you think of me, I asked you how you feel about me."

"David," I said, "let's not get heavy with this thing okay? I like you a lot and I care, but . . . ."

"I get the point." He drank down half of his beer. I could tell he was pissed at me by the way his jaw was set. I wanted us to have a nice dinner together, not this anger. Didn't he understand that no woman in her right mind would fall for a married man? Especially a woman like me.

"David, what do you want me to say?" I put my hand on his arm.

"Nothing. I asked you a question and you answered me."

"But you seem like you wanted to hear something else."

"Don't worry about it, okay." I knew this man couldn't be in love with me this quick. We had only just started sleeping together. I don't understand why body sharing sends people off the deep end. This was my friend and I didn't want our lust to change that. I wanted him to know exactly where I stand so there would be no doubts. He was a friend with special privileges. That's all.

"David, remember when we discussed my theory that time you came to my house?"

"Yeah, I remember. Of course I remember. You said you only talked about it with men who interest you."

Shit. The man would remember how I put my foot in my mouth and make this conversation more difficult than necessary. I sipped my Seabreeze.

"I wasn't completely open with you about it."

"I know that. You didn't even want me to know about it."

"There's a reason for that. I didn't want you to think I was some kind of low woman, just because I feel the way I feel."

He looked at me again. Finally.

"What do you mean?"

"Okay, how do I explain this." I took a long breath. "Uhm, I don't fall in love. I've never fallen in love. Usually when I meet a man and we're going to start something, I just tell him that I know he wants my pussy and I want him to know that he can have it without playing games as long as he's willing to treat me with respect and isn't cheap."

David looked completely appalled by my bluntness. I knew he would be, and that was what I'd been trying to avoid.

"And they go for that shit?" he asked. I figured I might as well keep going.

"Yeah. They're married," I said, "why wouldn't they go for it?" I could see the storm brewing in his eyes, but we needed to get this out in the open.

"Let me get this straight," he said. "You exchange sex for money? Is that it?"

"No, David, you've got it all wrong. I'm just protecting myself is all. I really don't see many men."

"But the ones you do see. They're all married."

"Yes."

"Why?"

"Because that's extra protection."

"In what way, Genie?"

I couldn't really explain it, because the whole thing was starting to sound immature and stupid to me and I didn't know why. I was beginning to feel like I had to defend the way I chose to lead my life.

"David, it just is."

"Is that what we're about? You plan to give me sex as long as I take you to nice places and wine and dine you?"

"David, you know it's not like that between us."

"How should I know what's happening here?"

"Because you're different and you know that." He was definitely angry now.

"I don't know shit about what this is to you. You don't know how hard it was for me to take that step with you, Genie. I went through emotional hell over this." He was whispering to me, but his eyes were hard.

"I know that," I said. Why was I feeling like I was about to start crying?

"In what way am I different, Genie?"

My chest felt tight so I couldn't say anything. I just swallowed hard and took another long drink of my Seabreeze, hoping it would mellow me out just a little at least.

"I wanna know why it's different with me, Genie," he said.

"Because, David, I need . . . I need you." I looked away then. I couldn't believe I had admitted that to him. This whole thing was getting way out of hand here. "Listen," I said, "I'm gonna run to the ladies and then freshen my drink. You want another?"

"Sure," he said, and he sounded so damn satisfied with himself. I jumped up from the table and got out of there fast. I didn't like this feeling, and I had to put a little distance between us for a minute.

I walked into the restaurant trying to profile and almost fell and broke my neck in my slippery lavender slingbacks. The inside of the restaurant was softly lit and quiet. I walked up the stairs hoping not too many people had seen me slide across the marble floor like James Brown. Thank God the stairs and the top floor of the restaurant were carpeted.

When I left the ladies room, I walked back down the stairs and went out to the bar for our drinks. I prayed that David would get a hold of himself. He was a married man, for goodness sake. The last thing he needed was to get strung out on me. The last thing I needed was to play around with that love shit. Ever. I just couldn't have it. I've worked too hard to keep my cool to let it slip on a married professor who was twice my age, with kids. Oh, no. I leaned across the bar to get the bartender's attention.

"Excuse me, can I get . . ." The words died in my throat. I felt sick all of a sudden. My stomach was churning so hard I thought I was going to choke or something. I was so cold all of a sudden that I shivered and felt kind of faint, so I reached out for the person closest to me. It was some big white guy.

"You okay, Miss?" He steadied me. I backed away from the bar and turned so fast that I almost slid down the walkway. When I got back to the table I was still shaking.

"Babe, is everything alright?"

I was beyond thinking. I shook my head no. "David, take me home, please."

He looked at me like I'd turned into an alien right before his eyes. "Genie, what is it? What's wrong?"

"Nothing. I just have to go. Please David, just take me home."

"But our food hasn't even—"

"David, please!" I whispered it, but he knew I meant business. I was clutching my stomach and I could feel the bile rising up my throat.

"Alright, honey. Lemme settle the bill. Here, sit down," he pulled out my chair. "I'll be right back."

"Hurry back," I said. My voice was so shaky. I sat down and laid my head on the table. I felt so weak. So sick in my stomach. My head started hurting and I got scared. David came back and laid his hand on my back.

"Can you walk, honey? Do you need me to take you to see a doctor?"

"No. Help me get up. I think I'm coming down with something." He pulled me up and I leaned on him. I closed my eyes and tears started streaming down my face. I was still cold, so he stopped and took his jacket off and put it on me, then he kissed my forehead and asked me if I was sure I could make it to the car. I wasn't so sure, but I shuffled along, leaning on him for support. When we got to the car he settled me in on the passenger's side, and I swear he must have driven ninety all the way to my house. My eyes were closed, but it felt like the car was moving on air.

"Where's your keys, babe? Lemme have 'em so I can open the door and get you inside."

I reached into my purse and handed them to him. My stomach and head were still hurting and I was crying softly. He ran up the stairs and unlocked the door, then he helped me out of the car and took me in the bedroom. I was so glad I was home. David undressed me and put the trash can by the bed in case I threw up. He put a warm compress on my head and covered me up with an extra comforter.

"You want some tea, honey?" He asked me. He sounded kind of scared. Just like I felt. I shook my head no and asked him for some aspirin. He brought me two and some water. I took them and asked him if he would come lie down with me and hold me. David took off his shoes and got in the bed next to me with his suit on and his arms around my waist. We slept like that all night.

David

I don't know what's wrong with Genie. She won't talk to me. She won't do anything. All week she's sat in that bed of hers, sick to her stomach. She isn't pregnant. She got her period the other day. But she won't go see a doctor. I stayed with her most of the week, because she didn't want me to leave her. She just kept asking me to hold her. She wouldn't eat anything, hardly, and kept getting these terrible headaches. I was glad I had forwarded my line at home to my cell phone, because otherwise Monica would have known something was fishy.

I went in to the office on Thursday to check my mail and my class enrollments, and when I came back Genie was sitting in a corner in the kitchen sobbing and holding her stomach. She wouldn't even let me take her back to the bedroom. That was the end for me. I wasn't sitting around worrying like hell another day. I searched her purse for her phone book and called Paulette at work.

"Yes, may I speak with Paulette Beardsley, please." I know I sounded tired. I looked at myself in the bedroom mirror and my eyes were bloodshot. I needed some rest and a decent meal.

"Hold on a moment."

I waited a few minutes, then Paulette came on the line.

"Paulette speaking. May I help you?"

"Paulette, this is David. Something's wrong with Genie and she won't let me take her to the doctor. Can you come over to her house?"

"Well, David, what's going on? I haven't bothered her because she told me not to. She called me Sunday night and told me that the two of you were spending the week together."

I ran my hand through my hair. These two didn't seem to have any secrets.

"I don't know. She keeps telling me her stomach and her head hurts, and I think it must hurt pretty bad, because she keeps crying. I went to my office today for a bit, and when I got back, she was in the kitchen floor in pain. She won't even let me move her."

"She's still there now?"

"Yeah. Can you come?"

"I'll be right over." She hung up and I felt relieved. I went back down the hall to see if I could get Genie up.

"Babe, come on. Lemme get you back to bed." She jerked away from me. She was really trying my patience.

"Stop acting like a child, Genie, and get up from there, now." I sounded so damn fatherly. I grabbed her arm and made her stand up. She resisted at first, but then she let me lead her to her room. I sat her in the chair and changed her sheets. Then she let me put her under the covers.

"David, lie down with me." I was wiping her face. I put the Kleenex to her nose and she blew. Why was I babying the woman like this? I figured it must be love. I got into the bed and went through the routine. I felt so good being this close to her, but I was so worried about her. I wished she would let me take her to a doctor.

When I heard the door, I almost leapt off the bed.

"Who's that?" She was half asleep. Tired as I was, so was I.

"I'll be back. Just stay in bed."

I've never been so glad to see someone in my life. When I saw Paulette I almost pulled her arm off getting her inside. She looked different from the last time I'd seen her. More put together. I guessed she had to dress a certain way for work, because she was in a nice suit and her hair wasn't in that ponytail.

"I finally got her to bed," I said, leading Paulette down the hall as if she didn't already know where the room was.

"Good. I'm glad you called me, David."

"Okay, ladybug, what's wrong with your behind?" Paulette said. She walked over and put her arms around Genie. Genie started to cry. I didn't know what the hell to do. I just sat in the chair and hoped I was inconspicuous.

"Oh, Paulette," Genie said, "I can't handle it. I can't. I don't have anybody, Paulette. Nobody." I was confused as anything. What the hell was she talking about? Paulette was rubbing her hair and shushing her like a baby. Then you know what they did? They threw me out. Paulette closed the door right in my face and said she wanted to talk to

Genie alone. They were in there so long that I gave up and went on home. I'd been home so little during the week that I hadn't noticed what a mess the house was. I was pissed off with Genie. She wouldn't tell me what was wrong with her, but she'd talk to Paulette about it. Maybe it was some female thing with her tubes or her ovaries or something. I didn't think Genie was the type to be embarrassed to discuss that kind of thing with me, but who knows why women do the things they do.

I dumped all the trash and did a shitload of laundry. I picked up and straightened up a bit in every room. If Monica had come home to this mess, she'd have had a cow right on the floor. I noticed that there wasn't much in the fridge, so I made a run to Giant and picked up a few items. When I got everything like I knew Monica would want it, I called Genie. Paulette answered.

"Hey, how's everything?"

"Not so great, David. I think maybe you should stay away for a while."

"Stay a—why?" This was crazy. All I wanted to know was why Genie was tripping off the line like she was.

"She has her reasons. Please, just trust me on this. It's better if you don't come by." I was numb. I wanted some damn answers.

"Where is she, Paulette? Put her on."

"I can't. She doesn't want to talk right now." I wanted a cigarette like no tomorrow.

"You aren't going to tell me why? I've been over there for three days with her. I've worried myself sick and you won't even give me a clue as to what's going on. Is she really sick? If it's a female thing, then just tell me that, but tell me something."

"It's not any female thing. David, do you feel like I would lie to you?"

I didn't know the woman from Eve, but I did know she loved Genie like I did. I could count on that.

I didn't say anything.

"I want you to know that, my personal feelings about your relationship with Genie aside, I think you're a good man. Let Genie have a few days to get herself together and then she'll call you, okay? I promise."

I was too tired to argue anymore.

"Okay," I said and just hung up the damn phone. I was a little hurt, but I left it alone. I went in and took a shower and shaved. Then I fell across the bed naked and slept for four hours. By the time I woke up, Monica was home, bringing in her suitcases and the smell of honeysuckles. I was so glad to see her. With her, I knew where things stood. Even if I didn't like where things stood. I pulled her into my arms and kissed her like I hadn't really admitted to myself that I was in love with another woman.

●　●　●

I taught my first class early Wednesday morning. It went well. I have fifteen kids. I'm sure it's going to be a pretty good group. Two of them work on the school paper. They groaned when they saw the reading list on the syllabus, but they cheered when I told them they would only be responsible for writing two short stories and two poems. Genie still hadn't come back to work and she still hadn't called me either. I missed her so bad. Every now and then over the weekend, I pulled out the picture she'd let me have. It was a shot she'd taken at the beach last summer. She had on a blue and white bathing suit with a skirt thing that matched it. The suit was sexy as hell. But what I liked most about the picture was the way she was smiling. That was the same way she'd looked the first time we made love. Satisfied and tired.

I briefly talked with Michael Kemeh about his plans for Africa, went to my doctor for the first of my vaccinations, then I lunched with Winthrop at the Faculty Club and went back to my office to polish another article I'd sold. This one was for a writers magazine on ways to handle writer's block. I'm not an expert on the subject, but I'd read a bunch of articles and talked with several other writers about how they dealt with it. I was proud that my work was getting this small recognition. I'd applied for a grant from the NEA and hoped it would come through so I could finance my trip to Ghana and stay a little longer than originally planned.

My telephone rang while I was doing a spell check. I picked up. It was Genie.

"Hi, baby," she said, melting me with just those two words.

I felt like we were strangers. I didn't know what to say. I put her on hold and closed my door. There were some people milling around in the hallway.

"Hi. How are you?"

"Okay," she said. But she didn't sound quite like herself.

"I miss you, babe. What happened with you?"

"I'd rather not talk about it on the phone."

"When can I see you, then?" I was hoping she would tell me right now.

"Uhm, tonight. Can you come at seven? I'll make you dinner."

Why'd I have to wait?

"That sounds good. I'll be there at seven."

I stopped off at Caruso's and bought her some peach roses on my way. Her favorite color. She looked so normal when she opened the door. She looked well rested and she had on some kind of loose gown thing. She looked pretty. Her face lit up when she saw the flowers, but she didn't have time to admire them, because I put them on the coffee table and grabbed her and hugged her tight. She had me so afraid.

"David, you're going to break my ribs."

"Shut up, woman, and kiss me." I could smell booze on her, but I didn't say anything about it. I gave her my whole tongue. I didn't want to let her go when the kiss ended, so I sat down with her in my lap and just held her. She started kissing the side of my neck.

"I'm sorry about last week." She looked up at me like she was scared.

"It's okay." I was rubbing her thigh. I was in seventh heaven.

"No, it wasn't okay. You were looking forward to being with me and I had to trip out like that."

"Tell me what this is all about."

"I saw Edward, my father, at the restaurant we went to. I haven't seen him since my mother's funeral. That was eight years ago." Now things were making a little sense.

"Did he see you?"

She shook her head. "No. But David, seeing him just brought it all back, you know. I never told you this, but my mother killed herself because of him. I was the one who found her."

"Oh, baby. My poor baby. I'm so sorry." I didn't know what else to say. "What happened to make her do such a thing?" I asked.

Genie moved off my lap and started pacing. She stopped after a minute. She plucked a glass of something or other off the dining room table and then sat across from me while she sipped it. Then she started talking very slow.

"My father—Edward—was a big ladies man. My mother couldn't deal with it. She tried. But she couldn't. And when I was eleven she had a nervous breakdown."

"Oh, sweetheart." I stood up to go to her, but she waved for me to stay in my chair.

She took a deep breath and let it out and said, "Anyway, she was really sick. She moved down into the bedroom in our basement and stopped going to work. Stopped doing everything. Then it was a lot of crying spells. A lot. And then she started doing strange things. She wouldn't say anything much to you. She forgot things. There were tantrums sometimes. It was horrible."

"Wasn't she getting any help?" I took off my suit jacket.

She shook her head and took another drink. She had stopped looking at me. She was looking over at the fishtank beside her like I wasn't even in the room. I understood. I had seen people I loved suffer too.

"Nope. Edward didn't believe too much in that stuff. He shipped her off to a cousin's for a month or so. When she came back, she seemed alright. For a few days. Then she started crying again and tore up the basement. Edward finally took her to a doctor, but all the doctor did was give her a bunch of medicine. Mama was on so much stuff, David, she was just in a dream world." She sighed again and paused for a minute, bowing her head like she was so tired of remembering it.

"We acted like everything was okay. We acted like . . . We didn't pay her a lot of attention. Edward had this woman come in and take care of her. She should have been in an institution, but Edward wouldn't admit that she was sick. He just couldn't admit that. Nobody would challenge him. Then one night I went out on a date. I got home. Went to check on her like I always did before going to bed. She was . . . She was . . ."

Genie stood up then with tears in her eyes and I couldn't stand it. I went to her.

"It's alright, babe. Don't. You don't have to talk about it anymore. I'm here, babe," I said.

I held her tight, hoping I was letting her know that I would take care of her. I hoped she knew she could trust me. I couldn't believe she had lived through something so terrible. No wonder she was so cynical about life. She'd been through more in her young life than others experience in an entire lifetime. Devin was the same age now as Genie had been when she'd lost her mother. I thought about how protected my sons are. I wanted to be close to her and I wanted her to let me protect her too. I don't know how we started kissing, but we did somehow, and I picked her up in my arms and took her to the bedroom. She was very passionate with me, as if she'd missed being with me. I think it was what we both needed.

After we made love, I continued to hold her. She was so quiet. I was lying there thinking about what she had come to mean to me in this short time we had been together. No woman had ever made me feel so wanted. She was making me feel things again that I thought were dead a long time ago, and I wanted to hold on to these feelings. I wanted to hold on to her.

"Genie, do you love me?" It came out of my mouth it seemed before I'd even had a chance to think it.

She turned to look up at me in the dimming light slipping through the bedroom window.

"David, I . . . David, why are you asking me this?"

"Because I think I love you, and it scares me." I felt like a weight had been lifted off my chest. No matter what her response was, I was glad I had the balls to finally say it. She was quiet again. It was a few minutes before I realized she was crying. I turned to face her.

"Why are you crying?" I don't know what I expected, but I didn't expect this.

"I don't deserve your love, David. I don't." She turned away. I wasn't having that.

"With the way I've acted ever since we've become involved, I'm the one who doesn't deserve to be loved, Genie. I've been grappling with my feelings for days now. I just can't stop falling in love with you. I don't want to stop. That's why I really need to know how you feel."

She put her head on my chest again and sobbed a bit this time, but she finally calmed down after a few seconds and said, "I can't stop falling in love with you either, David. I think it's too late for me to try not to anymore too." I patted her on her shoulder, feeling like I'd won the lottery. It was all I'd wanted to hear.

Genie

I don't know how I got myself into this mess. I don't know how I let that damn love sneak up on my black ass and make me want this man the way I do, but I've had a lot of time to think since our night at Susquehanna's and I know this has got to be what love feels like. It is so scary. I'm so torn about the whole thing because on one hand, I like the way this feels to me. When I'm with David I feel so good inside. So complete. On the other hand, I know that this is just plain crazy, but I don't know how to stop it. I've tried to apply my theory in some ways, but David is much more to me than an open wallet and zipper. So damn much more. I can't believe this is happening to me. I've been so careful for so long. I thought I was strong enough to handle this sex thing with David. What I should have done was stayed as far away from him as humanly possible after that first time we were together. Damn. I still should just tell the man to get out of my life, so I can go back to the way I was before. I can't, though, because my heart is in it now.

If I'm truthful with myself, I have to admit that I still want to be in love with this man, even knowing all the damn odds against us. I want to go down to every radio station in the city and announce it on the air. I want to come down center court during half time at a Bullets game at the Arena and tell everybody there. I want to do talk shows, bragging about it. Maybe put it out on the AP wire, even. I'm in love with David Lewis. Yeah. My heart is in it now and I couldn't run from these feelings even if my name was Flo Jo.

But at the same time, I keep thinking, so now what? Like, now do we carry on like we have been, me giving up the stuff and him going home every night to some other woman when I want him in my bed? Now do I become one of those idiot women running after him with my tail between my legs, begging him for a commitment?

The man has two kids at home he's still in the process of raising. He has a twenty-six-year marriage to think about. So what if she isn't all that attractive and sounds like a career-happy control freak. She's still his wife, and the man may be spouting off all this love shit to me, but he's not saying a word about what this all means to him.

And then there's the other thing too. The big thing I'm not strong enough to ever tell him about. How do you just blurt out to somebody that the real reason you've avoided loving someone so long is because your father sexually abused you? How can I tell him that my own mother was home when he raped me? That she heard me screaming and saw it happen and decided to kill herself rather than the son of a bitch who hurt me? David would never be able to handle it. He would look at me and always remember what Edward did. It's bad enough that I have to live with this shame for the rest of my life. I don't want David to be ashamed of me too.

At least seeing Edward again gave me the strength to tell Paulette about it. It's so crazy, but I thought she would stop being my friend if she knew. I just knew I would lose her once I told her, but I had to tell somebody close to me or I was going to go crazy. Her only reaction was that she wanted to run out right then and put a bullet in him. I told her Edward was getting his. I found out from Tess that he's been diagnosed with the same cancer that killed his brother, Uncle Eugene, so his days are numbered. Paulette felt bad that she had been trying to get me to see him again. I told her it was my fault for not telling her sooner.

Seeing him was the worst. As the years have passed, I've been able to make myself believe that he doesn't exist. That none of that stuff ever happened to me. Most of the time I feel almost normal, but seeing him brought back all the fear I had when I was a girl. He looked sick. He was all gaunt and shrunken and his hair was mostly gone. His skin was sallow and wrinkled now, but I knew it was him. I would know those horrible eyes anywhere.

I hate that I flipped out the way I did, but when I saw Edward sitting at the bar like that, I wasn't a grown woman enjoying a night out with my man. I was that same girl who was so scared of him at night that I sometimes wet the bed, hoping that would keep him away. But I don't want to think about that whole thing anymore. It's just too painful right now. I couldn't tell David any of that. That's why it was so hard for me to admit to the man that I love him, because admitting it meant so many things. It meant trusting a man with my heart. It meant trying to figure out what's next. And then if what *is* next has anything to do with longevity, it meant figuring out if I should tell him about my past.

David held me while I cried a little more. I had to cry. I was scared of this whole thing. Poor thing, he didn't know what to do. I got up and went into the bathroom to get cleaned up, and he came with me and turned on the shower.

"You alright, now, sweetheart?" He put his hand on my back. It was wet from testing the shower water.

"Yes. I think so," I said. How could my heart feel heavy and wonderful at the same time.

"You wanna tell me why you're this upset about it?"

I blew my nose and said, "David, this wasn't supposed to happen." I looked at him standing behind me in the bathroom mirror.

"I know, Genie," he said, "but I love you." He looked at the floor like he was ashamed of himself and it was all his fault, which it was. If he wasn't so damn good to me I wouldn't be having this problem. I turned around to face him.

"But what now, Doc?" I asked him. I was holding his hand.

"To tell you the truth, I haven't thought this far ahead, Genie. I don't know. Maybe we should . . . What do you think about us getting away from here for a while? Just to take a break from the pressure."

He tested the water in the shower again and got in, pulling me in with him.

"I'd like that," I said. "Where would we go, and when would we go?"

"Well, I think we should go soon, and I have an idea of where to go." He started washing my back for me and scrubbing it with my back brush. It felt so good I just closed my eyes.

"Where?" I asked and turned around.

"How does a rental house on Roanoke Sound in North Carolina sound to you?"

"Like a dream come true. North Carolina?"

"Yep."

"Where in North Carolina?" I took the bar of Coast from him and started soaping him up.

"Outer Banks. It's about . . . five hours from here."

"Hmm. That means I can see my sister Tess. I'll give her a buzz tomorrow. I haven't seen her in too long. But David, I don't have any leave saved up—and plus, I can't afford it."

"Don't worry about any of that, babe. I'll take care of it."

"Oh, David, what the hell are we doing?" I asked. But I didn't want him to answer me, because I didn't want to know. I just put my arms around the man as soon as he opened his mouth to speak, and I kissed him.

David

I was really going out on a limb now. I told Barbara I was going out of state to do some research for a paper I was presenting at a conference, and I needed Genie to act as my assistant. I told her that Mac, the young man working in the Writing Center who graded papers for me, was going to take over my class while I would be gone. As luck would have it, I had documentation. A Call for Papers mailer had come to me from the Education Department about a conference focusing on the effects of ebonics on written English. Barbara bought that transparent lie, I hope. Even if she didn't really buy it, she wouldn't have said no to me, no matter what I told her. The only thing she was interested in was the birthday card I gave her. Anyway, when I left her office, Genie had a week off with pay with no leave time lost.

I just told Monica I was going to a conference. She would never have believed what I told Barbara. Monica had good sense. That night Monica was working late again, so I called Genie to see what she was doing.

"Hi, babe," I said.

"Hey," she replied, sounding somewhat drained. I was worried about her. She didn't seem to feel too great about loving me. I can't lie—it was making me feel magnificent that she did love me. For a long time now, I'd wanted somebody to really love me.

"You alright?"

She let out a sigh and said, "Yeah, I guess," at the same time.

"What are you doing tonight?"

"I have a date with McGarrett," she said. Did I hear her right? Who the hell was that? My heart went double-time and I swallowed hard, not knowing quite what to say until she started to laugh.

"*Hawaii Five-O,* honey. It comes on cable in a little while," she said. Meanwhile, I was still feeling lightheaded.

"Don't kid with me like that," I said.

"Aw, baby, lighten up," she told me, still laughing at my expense. "You have got to be the most serious man I've ever known." She was pissing me off.

"You're not funny, Genie," I said, and she stopped laughing.

"You mad?" she asked. I ignored her.

"Listen, I'm on my own tonight, you want to catch a film with me or something?"

"No, not really. You remember, I catered that dinner party tonight. I'm just too pooped to go sit in a theater for two hours. But if you want to come over, I'd love to see you."

That made me feel good and I said, "I'll be there," and hung up.

When I got there, she was on the phone giving advice. She opened the front door smiling, with the cordless phone tucked between her ear and shoulder. When I came in she put an arm around me and kissed me softly on the lips, then closed the door behind me. She looked good. She looked like she was going to bust right out of her tight red half top and the short shorts she had on. Damn, the woman was a sight for my sore eyes, and I patted her butt when I walked by her to set the wine I'd brought on the dining table. I wondered why Monica had just let her shape go the way she had.

"Mmhmm," Genie was saying, "I know exactly what you mean, girl." Then she sat on the sofa and said, "He said what? Oh no, I can't believe him. Well, Marilyn, if I were you, I would find the nearest exit and get out of there. You are much too smart and talented to be putting up with crap like that. And now that you're certified too? Girl, you had better find another job. You don't have to be in this situation. I didn't have the chance you and Tess had, so be thankful and make the most of your education. But look, I have to run because that gorgeous man I was telling you about just walked in."

I ran a hand through her hair and smiled at her, and she took my hand and kissed my palm.

"Okay," she said, "tell my Keith that I love him and he had better not get any new girlfriends to replace his Auntie Genie, okay? Love you, bye."

"Your sister?" I asked.

"Yeah. Her boss is giving her grief and she wants to get out."

"What does she do?"

"She's a CPA."

"Mmm. So"—I pulled her onto my lap—"you've told her about me, huh?"

"I had to. She asked me if I was seeing anybody. I didn't want to lie."

"What'd you tell her about me? You told her you've been getting naked with some silly old guy?" She laughed, but I was half serious.

"No," she said, messing in my hair, "I told her that you're handsome as hell and intelligent and gentle. That you are a beautiful person and that I finally met someone who knows how to make me feel like a woman."

The woman knew just how to get to me. I squeezed her and started kissing her.

"David, wait," she said.

"What?"

"Nothing. It's just that I know where it's going to lead if we start kissing." I knew too. It was exactly where my dick was wanting to go, but I kept that to myself.

"Let's just relax for a little while tonight. Is that okay?" Not exactly, I thought, but I let go of her and nodded anyway.

"You've got your week's vacation from the office," I said, and smiled because she looked at me like I'd performed a miracle.

"How'd you manage that?"

"Don't worry about it. Just pack tomorrow night and we'll leave after breakfast on Saturday."

"Damn, Doc, thank you. I don't know how you pulled that off, but I appreciate you for sure. You eat yet?" she asked.

"A sandwich earlier."

"You just refuse to eat right, don't you?" I rolled my eyes on that one. She sounded like Monica, and I didn't want to hear it. I assume she could tell because she let it go.

"Guess what," she said. "I have a little surprise for you."

"Oh?"

She got off my lap and said, "stay right there," and went out to the kitchen. I was pretty curious. She yelled for me to close my eyes, so I did, and I heard her walk by me and open a door.

"Genie, what are you doing?"

"Don't look, David." This wasn't what I was in the mood for. I'd had a long-ass day at work, whereas she'd left early to get to that gathering.

After about ten minutes or so she came over and took my hand and led me down the steps. I smelled oil, and the air there was cooler and a little damp. A radio or a tape was playing some Four Tops.

"Okay, open." We were standing in the garage and she was buck naked. She had the comforter from her smaller bedroom spread out on the hood of her car. On top of that was a tray with some kind of delicious looking hot hors d'oeuvres and dessert. The wine and two glasses were there too. This shit was turning me on. It was something about the smell of the garage and the car and the food and this naked, insane woman that made me so hard I was hurting. Damn. Genie was giving me butterflies in my stomach at my age.

"What is this?" I asked her. I started taking off my clothes, though, and I threw my tie and sport jacket inside the house.

"Just something fun and different. You like?" She looked proud of herself. I threw my pants inside and smiled and said, "Hell yes." I looked down and my dick was giving a stiff salute, but when I reached for Genie, she dodged me.

"Stop, honey. Come on," she said. We got up on the car carefully and started feeding each other while I tried my best to impress her by reciting a little Neruda to her about "her feet," and then a poem I'd written myself about her that I called "Afterglow." She loved it.

"This must be the strangest thing I've ever done, Genie," I said to her, looking around me. I was eating the last of the shrimp she'd fed me.

"Good. Sometimes it feels good to loosen up and do something different sometimes, doesn't it?"

I looked around the garage again. The Tops started singing "Bernadette," and the Merlot was making me warm inside. I was sitting up beside the tray. Genie was lying on her stomach, across my lap, with those chocolate titties pressing right into my thigh. Monica wouldn't have even done something like this in her day.

"Yeah," I said, "it does feel good. I love you, babe." I caressed her back and she leaned her head against my stomach and said, "I love you too. I have something else for you." Her eyes were sparkling when she looked up at me.

"What?" I thought I knew what she meant, but apparently I was wrong because she pulled a small blue box from beneath the comforter and gave it to me saying, "This."

I opened the box. Inside was a gold heart shaped key chain that had *#1* on it and a key on its ring. I held it up and looked at her with a question in my eyes.

"It's the key to my house. I wanted you to have it." I was touched. I wanted like hell to be the only man in her life, and this was her way of telling me I was.

"Thanks, baby," I said. I didn't know what else to say, I was so moved by the damn thing. She slid off the car to put the box on the tray and put the tray on the ground. Then she climbed up on me and put her hand to the middle of my chest to push me back, and I leaned back gladly while she positioned herself on top of me. Now who'd have thought you could have the most exciting sex imaginable on the hood of a damn car?

Genie

I was so excited about this whole trip thing. I felt this was a big step for me and David. Like maybe we had a future together. Plus, I wanted to see my sister Tess and have her meet David. It had been at least five years since we'd seen each other. That was the year she, Marilyn and I had taken a cruise to the Bahamas.

Me and David checked in at the rental office and got to our cottage around five. I was tripping because the woman who had given me the key had called me Mrs. Lewis. David had just smiled and told her thank you for the key, since my tongue was tied.

"Oh, this is nice, Doc. Look." I was pointing out the hot tub in a glass-enclosed room.

"Yeah, it's nice alright. Babe, you wanna help me take this stuff up to the bedroom?" I turned around to see him struggling with the bags. If he hadn't brought so much fishing gear, he wouldn't have had this problem. But I didn't say anything. I picked up my bags and followed him upstairs.

Our bedroom was even more beautiful than the rest of what I'd seen. It was huge. It looked like something straight out of *Interior Design.* It was done up in varying shades of melon and blue. The walls were a deep melon with white crown molding. There was a sitting room with a chaise and a beautiful Ethan Allen sofa. Our bed was enormous. The windows were floor-to-ceiling, with lovely cornflower blue valances, and walking on that pale blue carpet was like walking in a field of lush, high grass.

In our bathroom there were his and her sinks and a serious Jacuzzi that looked like it could fit me, David and a few other people in it. Everything was gleaming white. I turned the light on and peeked in, then rushed over to the bed and threw everything on it. I kicked off my shoes. I was home.

"David, I'll be back."

"Where you going?" He was fiddling with his tackle box that looked more like a mechanic's tool box.

"To check out the rest of the place," I called out as I ran down the stairs two at a time.

• • •

This vacation was just what we needed. We unpacked everything, finished off the lobster tails that we ordered in, and cracked open a bottle of Champagne that I mixed with juice for Mimosas. We chilled out in the hot tub with our Mimosas and looked out over the Sound. The moon was full and a few stars were out and the moonlight on the water made it look like black glass. David leaned his head on my shoulder and kissed me.

"This is more perfect than I imagined. You know that?"

"Uh huh. I'm glad you suggested it. I love you so much, David." I still felt disoriented hearing myself say it. But it was the truth. He just made me feel so overwhelmed and strange inside. I wasn't going to fight it anymore. I knew he loved me just as much.

"I love you, too," he said. "You don't know how it feels to me to feel your love at this time in my life, Genie." For some reason he thought that was a good reason to start feeling me up.

"Honey, let's just sit here a while and enjoy the atmosphere."

He looked determined to have his way.

"We can do that all day tomorrow, babe. Come here to me."

I was beginning to wonder who had the upper hand here. He was definitely time enough for my stubborn, evil behind. He pulled me on top of him. It was the first time I'd done something like this in a hot tub. Especially feeling like I was in full view of the world in front of the long windows. But who would see us in this secluded place?

"Oh God, David. Yes." It was all I could say when he entered me. I felt like my blood had turned to lava and my skin was going to split wide open. His arrogant ass was completely calm. He was talking to me and making me feel like I wanted to get violent.

"That's right, baby," he was saying to me softly, "tell me you love it. Tell me you want it just like this. We both know this is what you needed. Just let go, babe. Just let go."

I was whimpering and losing my mind. I swear I understood now what Paulette and Evelyn meant about how you feel when you make love with someone you love. It was good to my body, but there was a space somewhere inside me that was spilling over with something unique and exquisite. I felt like my soul was completely sated with

David inside me. I almost wanted to burst into tears, it felt so right to have him love me like this, but all I could do was feed the ache growing in the center of my belly. I took his head in my hands and kissed him with everything I had in me.

"Oh, God. It's so sweet, David. It's so sweet I'm gonna die!" I didn't mean to scream that in his ear, but I was reaching my breaking point. He was starting to lose control too. We watched each other with a mixture of awe and satisfaction.

"Is it good to you, babe?" he asked, straining to keep his composure.

"It's good, baby," I told him. My hips worked faster, making the water slosh against our bodies.

Some kind of way our movements fell in perfect sync, and our bodies hit a smooth rhythm that was something like Jimi Hendrix's fingers working that guitar of his. That's the only way I can explain the sweet agony of that shit. I think we both saw stars when it was all over.

In the morning after David's run, I fixed us omelets, turkey sausage and blueberry muffins with fresh squeezed tangerine juice. He looked so pleased. I was pleased with myself. This was our first real breakfast together and I let myself pretend that I really was Mrs. Lewis and that we were on our honeymoon and would be going back to *our* house next week. Was this really me getting all squishy and strung out? Paulette and Evelyn would have paid cash money to see me like this. I sat across from David, and the look in his beautiful eyes told me he knew just what I was thinking. He was grinning at me like an idiot.

"What d'you wanna do today?" he asked. He folded his newspaper and put it beside his plate.

"You mean you're not going fishing?"

"That's tomorrow. I have to go out real early for that on a head boat. You wanna come? We can find you a rod today." His hand found my knee under my silky black robe. His feet were massaging my ankles and I made a mental note to give my baby a mini pedicure later on.

"I'll pass. I don't like fishing, and you know I don't eat fish. I think it's completely inhumane. What would Porgy and Bess think of me?"

He looked at me like I was insane. The same man who wanted to get hair plugs over a few strands of missing hair that nobody noticed but him.

"Genie, calm down. You make too much of things. Your kissing fish have nothing to do with it."

"Whatever. I ain't going. Why don't we take our bikes out and ride into town today. Then we can come back later for a swim and have some lunch." There was a kidney-shaped pool at the side of the house. This was indeed the life.

"Long as you don't think you'll wanna do any shopping. I don't want to get stuck carrying bags in one arm and walking my bike back here with another." He sounded like he'd had that experience with *her*. I really didn't want to be reminded that there was a *her*. Of course I moved my legs. I didn't want him to touch me anymore. I was ready to tell him to kiss my brown butt.

"I'm going to do my shopping when my sister gets here and you're off fishing. I'm not totally insensitive, Dr. Lewis." He hated when I called him that. That's why I said it. He had the nerve to cut those pretty eyes at me. Cute SOB. I decided to pull out before we started bickering over nothing like we had the whole drive down.

"Look, I'm going to put these in the dishwasher. Are you done with yours?" I asked.

He moved his arm off the table so I took his plate and said, "I'm ready to take a shower." I went off to the kitchen. When I came out he was sitting in front of the TV, channel surfing, which I dearly hate. I think he was pretty mad at me, but I ignored him. I went upstairs to get cleaned up. I knew just how to deal with David's little attitude.

I put on my new hot-mama yellow cotton skorts that were probably illegal to wear in some states, a tight white V-neck T-shirt and some yellow Keds. David copped one look at me and started acting like he knew. He watched me walk all the way down the steps and I knew what he was thinking. Of course I had to get him to fasten my money pouch around my waist. The man was practically salivating by the time he got it on me.

"You gonna get dressed, honey?" I asked him, laying a hand on his chest.

He patted me on the rear and said, "Yeah. Give me about fifteen minutes."

I okayed that and gave him a quick kiss, then sat down to look at a yachting magazine sitting on the coffee table. David came back in record time. He looked nice and I told him so. He had on jean shorts and a white DKNY pullover. I don't know why he always complained about his body. He was very fit and sexy. He had on his sunshades and I could smell the Tommy cologne I'd bought him.

We hit the bike trail with our rented purple twelve-speeds, and thankfully no one else was out. I wanted to feel like the two of us were the last man and woman left on earth. That changed quick once we got out on the main road though. Quite a few other people had gotten my same idea.

David did much better than I did making it into town. We had to stop twice just so I could catch my breath. He laughed at me the whole way, because it wasn't much more than a mile. But when did I really get this kind of exercise? He ran two miles every day. All I did was leg crunches and push-ups before bed to keep my stomach right and tight.

The people were so friendly in town. They spoke to us like they knew us. We locked our bikes up and walked around to all the quaint little shops and novelty stores. David bought a blue Duckhead baseball cap and had the nerve to put it on backward. I didn't know what he was trying to prove, but he still looked good, though.

The town was crowded but calm and very modern. From what David told me, they had just really started to develop the place over the past ten years. Before that, there were still a lot of wild horses roaming the beach and mostly the area was only populated with small fishing villages. I found that hard to believe. The houses were fairly on top of each other, big massive constructions built up on stilts to avoid water damage. And the shopping centers looked just like back home, with movie theaters and outlets and a million restaurants. David told me that one of the main attractions was the prime golf courses. But he didn't golf and neither did I, so we didn't pay much attention when we passed the club.

We found a video store and rented *The Five Heartbeats* because he'd never seen it before. Then we shared a vanilla cone at the ice cream shop. I was having the time of my life. What was really great was that here, so far away from home, we didn't have to hide how we felt. He pulled me close to him whenever he felt like giving me a kiss. He kept his arm around me or held my hand while we walked. And I ate it up. The thing I love most about David is that he's so affectionate.

"You're okay to ride back, aren't you?" He was teasing me again. I was trying to look brave even though my legs felt like they were filled with bricks.

"I think I can manage, Doc." I put my hands on my hips to show him I didn't think it was funny.

We started riding back to the house. I was already breathing hard from all that stinking walking. I didn't know how was I going to make it back to the house in one piece.

David

I hadn't had this much fun in decades. Not since before the boys came and Monica was a normal woman in love. I started feeling like Genie was my wife. It scared the piss out of me at first, but to compare Genie's love to all the things Monica never did, never gave anymore, was no comparison.

When we got back to the house after riding, poor Genie was so tired that I suggested she shower and take a nap. It made me feel like Hercules to know that this woman is half my age and has none of my stamina. I told her not to worry about lunch. I'd take care of it. I seasoned a couple of boneless chicken breasts, some eggplant and some steaks, and threw them on the gas grill. She had shown me her gourmet style this morning. I wanted to give her a taste of mine.

I made a fresh fruit salad, because I know how much she loves fruit. I sliced up the chicken breasts and eggplant when they were done and wrapped the steaks in foil for our dinner later. I made a salad with the different types of lettuce she'd brought. Why anybody needed three different kinds of lettuce, I don't know. But I put in all three, added some chopped egg, green and yellow pepper, cherry tomatoes and the chicken and eggplant. Then I seasoned the salad with the Caesar dressing she'd bought. By that time she came downstairs, rubbing her eyes and yawning like one of my kids. I guess the smell woke her up.

"Mmm. What's this?" she asked.

I had set the table with her linen napkins and everything. I felt like patting myself on the back.

"It's lunch. You feeling better now?"

"I feel fine." She stretched. "This looks good, Doc. I'm about to faint I'm so hungry. You want something to drink?" she asked.

I nodded. She brought back two glasses of apple juice and we ate every drop of food while we talked and gazed out at the calm waters. After lunch we decided to watch the movie, so we cuddled up in front of the big-screen TV beneath a blanket. I really got into the movie.

Mostly because it took me back to when I was a kid. When the phone rang in the middle of a good part, I paused the video. Genie and I had agreed that I would be the one to answer the phone since Monica or my kids could call at any time.

"Hello?"

I was hoping it was Genie's sister. It was Monica. I looked over at Genie. I guess she could sense who it was because she turned off the TV and made her exit. There were rocks in my chest that were growing into boulders.

"David, hi, honey. I miss you already. I got your message on the machine and just wanted to touch base. Everything alright?" Missed me already. Yeah, right. She didn't even know I was alive when I was there.

"Yeah, I had a safe trip," I said. "I was really tired when I got here, so I went right to sleep after I left you the number. I would have called you this morning, but after my run I had to get over to the center for the conference." When had I become this adept at lying?

"How're the boys doing?" I asked.

"Fine. Devin finally asked that Kelli to the prom. David, you should see him. He's on cloud nine around here. And she's the cutest little thing too. Looks like a doll baby. Mannerly, too. And smart as a whip, David. In the Honor Society, and she's got a scholarship to Princeton."

"Sounds like our son made a perfect pick."

"He certainly did. He can't wait for you to meet her. When you get back, he wants you to take him to find a tuxedo. I told him the three of us would talk about renting the stretch Mercedes he has his heart set on. What do you think?"

I was thinking I was feeling guilty about missing out on a milestone in Devin's life just because of something I wanted. I had to be the most selfish bastard in all of creation.

"Devin's a good boy, Monnie. I think we should let him go all-out for his prom. I mean, he is an honor student himself, and he's on his way to Morehouse in the fall. He's shown himself to be responsible enough to get some rewards. Tell him I said it's okay with me, and that we'll find the best tux in Maryland. What's Mark up to?"

"Same as usual. Him I had to punish for a few days, because he skipped school yesterday with some fast little girl and her father came home and found them kissing."

"What?" The guilt piled higher.

"Mmhmm. I told Mark he was lucky her daddy didn't knock him into next week. We had a long talk about girls and sex and what happens when boys don't keep their zippers up." I felt like she was talking about me. "Anyway," she said, "I had better get back to business. It looks like I might have to go back to Dallas for a couple of days when you get back here. Love you, bye."

It was just like Monica to give me that news in a hurry so she could make a quick getaway, and that snatched me back to reality. I could be a good father to my boys and still make Genie my wife.

I went upstairs to find her after I hung up. She was lying on the bed, probably feeling vulnerable.

"You wanna come back down and finish watching the tape, babe?" She didn't even look my way.

"No. I don't feel like it."

"Why?" I started running my hand down her leg.

"I just don't, David. I can't take this. What are we doing here anyway?"

"What are you talking about, honey? We're here to spend some time together."

She laughed and said, "Yeah. But what is that gonna do? I'm in love with you, David, but you have a wife and responsibilities. I don't have anything tying me down. We shouldn't have even come here."

I was nervous about having this discussion just yet. I was sure I wanted Genie, but I wasn't so sure about ending things with Monica. I didn't want to hurt Monica like that. But at the same time, I wanted to be with Genie. It was confusing as hell.

"Babe, don't do this," I said. "A few minutes ago we were having a good time together."

She turned toward me.

"David, do you still love your wife? Because I don't know how to feel about us. Things are just out of control and I'm very scared about this. The last thing I need is to be hurt by you."

Hell, I was scared too. I wanted to take the next step, but I didn't want anybody to get hurt because of me. I lay next to her on the bed and put my arms around her.

"I would never let that happen, Genie. You don't ever have to worry about me hurting you. As far as Monica's concerned, I just need you to trust me and give me some time to deal with that. Okay? Can you do that?"

"I trust you, David," she said. "That's a big deal for me."

"I know," I told her. "I hope you know I don't take it lightly. Guess what?" I got off the bed.

"What?" She sounded completely uninterested. I know she was still hot under the collar about the phone call.

"I noticed that these folks have a CD player and a whole stack of CDs in the family room. You wanna go take a look at them? I could use a dance partner." She looked at me then.

"Baby, I can't believe you. Why are you trying to make light of the situation?"

"I'm not, Genie. I'm just trying to get back to the mood we were in a few minutes ago. Can't we please do that?"

She sighed and said, "Maybe you're right. What do they have?"

"That's my girl. I think I saw Marvin Gaye, the Temptations. Stuff you like. Come on. Let's go see."

She followed me downstairs and lit the candles she'd brought with her. We wound up dancing to Teddy Pendergrass and, after that, Barry White. She was a good dancer. She found some jazz CD by a group she liked called Fourplay and put that on. Since we were both getting a little tired, we just kind of held each other close and rocked to the music. For me, it just didn't get any better than this. Monica would never have danced with me like this. She didn't want to do anything but work. I knew there was nothing left between Monica and me to salvage. It hit me that I didn't want to lose Genie because I was being hesitant in taking a next step.

"Babe?" I said.

Genie lifted her head from my shoulder and I tasted those lips.

"What, sweetie?" She whispered it like she was turned on. I could see in her eyes how she felt about me. The way she looked at me made me know I wanted to make this woman happy, so why was I waiting? I took a deep breath and plunged in.

"You know, maybe we *should* discuss what's happening between us, since we have this time all to ourselves. I know that we haven't known each other that long, Genie. But I know when it's right. I know when it's real." Hell, I was sounding like Teddy Pendergrass. "I guess I'm trying to say that for me, our coming here together was . . . I love the way you make me feel, Genie. I think I want to find out just how far we can take this thing that's growing between us. I think we should try to work toward something permanent."

I didn't think I articulated my feelings well enough. But I figured she got the picture. I just hoped she wouldn't cry again. This was the most emotional woman I've ever seen. But she surprised me. This time she pulled away from me and walked out onto the balcony like I hadn't just bared my goddamn soul. I stood there for a second wondering what I should do. Wondering what she was thinking and feeling. Maybe she didn't want the same things I did. But how would I know for sure if I didn't find out? I went out there on the balcony and put my arms around her waist. She leaned her head back against my chest.

"David, maybe we should just give it some time. I need to know that you aren't running away from something that's part of you just because I make you feel good right now."

This was a switch.

"Wait, am I missing something? I thought you wanted a commitment between us," I said. "That's how you made it sound upstairs."

"I do. I mean . . . I don't know. I don't want to be some little homewrecker. But at the same time I'm jealous of what she is to you, David."

"Genie, I had reasons to turn to another woman a long time ago. I never have because I've never wanted to. You came along and now a lot of things I used to believe in don't make sense anymore. I'm in love with you. I don't understand exactly how this happened between us, but I know I need you in my life, babe. You obviously aren't aware of what you are to me. I idolize you, babe."

Damn. I closed my eyes and called myself an idiot on that one. I hadn't meant to say that to her. Sometimes love makes you open your mouth and let out things that shouldn't be said. I hoped she didn't think I was a fool, but I think she did. She turned around and looked at me like I'd slapped her, and I could have kicked myself for it.

"Idolize me?" she said. "David, you don't even know me. You don't know who and what I really am."

She stepped past me and went inside. I couldn't figure the woman out no matter how hard I tried. I couldn't go after her. I stayed out there on the balcony, staring at the water for a while longer, feeling disappointed. The conversation had been a bust and I thought that maybe she needed to be alone a while. I knew I did. One minute she was asking me to tell her how I felt. The next minute she was throwing my feelings back in my face. I didn't get it. A few minutes later I heard a splash, so I went around to the side of the house to see what it was. It was Genie. She was in the pool. And she was cutting the water so fast I could barely see her.

Genie

All I can say is that I must have really put some kind of whipping on the man for him to tell me he idolizes me. He obviously didn't know what he was saying. I feel like telling him to be careful what he wishes for 'cause he just might get it. He may think he's getting a diamond in the rough, but if he decides to look closer he'll see I'm just a cubic zirconia with a passable pair of legs.

It's so much easier to live shit out in your head than it is to actually experience it, you know. In my head I can be a woman who's good enough for a man like David. In truth, I'm just me. I've never done anything great. Never been anywhere special. How can he possibly idolize me?

If anyone should be idolized, it should be him. I mean, look at him. He's gorgeous. He's a professor. He's beyond intelligent. People look up to David. They look to him for leadership, and this is something he takes in stride. Idolize me? Hmm. He's widely published. He's writing a book, for goodness sake. This is a man who's traveled the world. He's done most of the things that other people only dream about. And where have I been? Sitting in my living room and dreaming, like everybody else.

I didn't know what to say when he told me that stuff. I felt so . . . humble. All I wanted to do was to get as far away from David as I could, so I made a break for it. I was glad that he didn't come after me, and I hoped he understood that I just needed some space for a while. This rollercoaster was going much too fast. Was I the same chick who pretended like I was his wife just this morning?

I felt so anxious that I had to do something. So I went upstairs and dug out my blue one-piece bathing suit and put it on. Then I went around the side of the house to the swimming pool and climbed the pinewood stairs. The pool sat deep in an elevated deck overlooking Roanoke Sound, and the view of all that calm blue water with the backdrop of sun and those tall trees was so beautiful that I wished I'd remembered my camera so I could capture it for Paulette and Evelyn.

I put on my swimming cap and did a couple of stretches, then geronimoed right into the water and started doing some laps. It felt good to scuttle through that cool water like one of my fish. I could feel the tension easing out of my muscles and I didn't want to stop. I don't know where David was. Maybe he was still on the balcony kicking himself for telling me some mess like that. I swam hard until I got tired, then I turned on my back and did a dead man's float while the water tickled my neck. All of a sudden the water splashed in my face and almost choked me.

I came up out of the water, coughing.

"What the—?" It was David. He had jumped in, I guess, to get my attention. Didn't he know he already had it?

The chlorine started burning my eyes, so I reached for my towel up on the deck and wiped them. When it was safe to open my eyes, I saw that David was standing in the water in his black trunks, looking edible as all get-out and staring at me like I'd hurt his feelings. I didn't want my baby's feelings to be hurt like that. I swear, I was a ball of confusion. I wanted to tell him I couldn't live without him either, but at the same time I didn't want to hear another word about relationships or love or anything close to it. The whole thing just felt bigger than me. Stronger. Bit by bit I was losing my control, and I couldn't stop it. Lord knows I wanted to make a life with David. But we'd only been in this thing a hot minute. A cool head and some objective reasoning was what was called for. Where in the world is Dr. Joyce Brothers when you need her?

David was still looking at me like I had just destroyed him, so of course I went all softie.

"Baby, I'm sorry," I said. I was surprised he let me put my arms around his neck. He pulled me close to him and didn't say anything. I kissed the drops of water on his brow.

"Just excuse me, David. I'm a little crazy right now. It's . . . Things are moving sort of fast, don't you think? I mean, I've never had to deal with anything like this before. I don't know how this whole thing works."

"And you think I do, Genie? Look, I'm only going on impulse here. Don't think I'm not just as confused as you. Good God, just look at me. I'm standing here with you in a goddamn pool talking about this, for Christ's sake. If that's not confused, I don't know what is. I've been lonely and depressed for some years now and I'm sick of it. I'm sick of feeling sorry for myself. You've"—he put his hand beneath my chin and lifted my head—"you've made me feel alive again, Genie. That matters to me. You matter to me. I've spent a better part of my life in a dead marriage, and now I'm learning that life's too important not to take the risk of grabbing the things that make us feel alive."

All I could say was, "Oh, David." And we started kissing like no tomorrow.

The man had worked a root on me or something because I was definitely falling for this shit. In true fricking Hollywood fashion I got all tearful and dramatic, just like that doggone Meryl Streep in *Bridges of Madison County* when she knew she wanted a life with Clint so bad she could taste it. Except me and David were in a pool in North Carolina, with Roanoke Sound in the distance. And knowing that he wanted only me, I was determined to follow the man to the damn moon if I had to. I swear. This love thing is kicking my brown butt hard.

•   •   •

David had already gone out fishing by the time I woke up in the early afternoon to a knock on the door. For a minute I was confused about where the heck I was, until I remembered what had happened last night on that kitchen floor, where I was lying on a bed of pillows with a comforter. I started grinning so hard my cheeks hurt. I jumped up and wrapped the comforter around me because I was naked as a jaybird. The kitchen was a disaster. According to my standards anyway. Fruit peels and melted puddles of cool whip and chocolate syrup spills were all over the counter. David and I had done a little too much experimenting with foods last night.

I peeked out the front window to see who was bugging me and saw this pencil-thin, coffee-brown woman with long, reddish hair in that Holly Robinson style. She had on a flowing yellow dress with a pair of Espadrilles. Now I knew the Jehovah's Witnesses couldn't possibly have caught up with me down here. Did they go on vacation too?

"Just a minute," I called out. Maybe it was one of the ladies from the rental office. I ran upstairs slipping and sliding on the hardwood steps and cut the corner into the bedroom. The first thing I saw was David's silk bathrobe on the bed, so I put it on and went running back downstairs, half tripping over the bottom of the robe and trying to finger-comb my crazy hairdo into something less scary. I opened the door.

"Genie! Girl!" The woman grabbed me and squeezed the blood out of me. What tripped me out was that I saw Tess's car parked in the driveway. I pulled back.

"Tess?" She was downright hot to trot gorgeous.

"Surprise!" She posed a second. "Killed me not to tell you I've lost so much weight, girl, but I wanted you to see me like this for yourself. Not hear about it."

I was still trying to process all this.

"Tess?"

"Mmhmm," she said. Some things didn't change. She walked in with her model body and closed the door. I was completely stunned and amazed.

"Girl, you look beautiful. Look at you with your bad self." I touched her on the hip where there used to be a pillow of fat. "I forgot you were coming today. Come on in to the living room and have a seat."

"This place is truly beautiful," she said, looking around.

"Yeah, it's nice, isn't it? I'll show you around in a little while. Can I get you anything?"

"Some ice water'd be nice." I obliged, then sat down on the sofa with my legs tucked under me. I kept staring at her like I couldn't believe she was real. It was so good to see her.

"How're you doing, girl?" I said. "But wait. First off, I want to hear all about how you lost the weight. And something else is different about you too, but I don't know what." She took a sip from her glass.

"I had liposuction done, Genie. Three years ago. Then I had my eyes done. Had the excess skin around my eyes tucked."

"Whoa," I said. "You made some major changes. What made you do all this?" I gestured a hand in her direction.

She exhaled loudly. "Couldn't take it anymore. Darryl's shit. My low self-esteem. I been wanting to talk to you about all this for a long time, Genie. Every time I called, matter of fact. Things had gotten so bad I was ready to kill myself, girl. But then I did something else that I'll never regret."

"What's that?" This was all news to me. I would not have guessed that Tess was going through so much pain and didn't let on. No wonder she never said very much.

"I went into intensive therapy, Genie. I mean, I really worked hard on turning me into somebody I could love. And when I was strong enough, I confronted Edward about what he did to us. That's how I found out about the cancer, Genie."

My stomach started doing flip-flops. Something welled up inside me that was akin to fear, but I knew there was nothing for me to be afraid of. I wasn't a young girl anymore. I wasn't defenseless anymore.

"I thought you found that out from Aunt Doreen. How the hell did you get the courage for that, Tess?" The tears started rolling. I grabbed her hand and held it because I needed to remind myself that there are loving touches. Not just dirty filthy touches. I needed my skin to stop crawling.

"I had to, Genie. It was all part of my healing process. To stand up as an empowered grown woman and say all the things I couldn't say when I was a little girl. That's when I really felt like I had gained control, and could really lose the weight. All that time I never realized that I made food my protection. Whenever I was feeling like I deserved what Edward was doing, I ate. I took my mental picture of myself and put it in physical terms so I could look at myself in the mirror and see the person I thought I was. A nasty, sloppy pig."

"Oh, Tess. No."

I put my arms around her and we held on for dear life. I thought about how we'd all found out that Edward had hurt all three of us when we'd stopped Marilyn from sticking him with a butcher knife after Mama's funeral. Marilyn still can't talk about any of it. That was a turning point in my life, though, when she jumped him. Before then I just thought it was me. I thought I was the one with the problem. I was only thirteen when he started touching me. Started making me lie down and watch television with him at night is what he called it. The TV was on, but his hands would be under my nightgown. I thought it was my fault for being too pretty or too flirty with boys. I suffered in silence, when all the time Marilyn and Tess had suffered too. The night he came in drunk and raped me when I was seventeen? Snatched me up off the piano bench while I was practicing the scales. I thought that was my fault too, so I didn't think about it.

I had gotten real good at acting like everything was normal and that I was happy, running around and joining every school activity, trying my damnedest to make sure everybody liked me. I just acted like it didn't happen. Acted like I hadn't seen Mama standing at the top of the steps, crying because she was too damn out of her head to help me. I begged her to help me. But she couldn't. I could tell that she wanted to, though. I got up that next morning like nothing had happened and went off to school as usual. That evening I was able to put on the new sundress Edward had bought me as an apology and go out on a date with Tommy. I was such a good actress. Still am.

I got up from the couch and went in the bathroom for some tissue and poured myself a glass of Sambuca.

"So where's this David you wanted me to meet, girl?" She blew her nose and drank some more water.

I smiled, thinking about my sweetie pie. I don't know why the man was having this effect on me.

"Fishing," I said. "He'll probably get back in here around two. I told him I hope he doesn't catch anything. It's inhumane to eat those poor things."

"What a hypocrite, Genie. You eat meat."

"That's different," I said. Me and David had had the same argument last night.

"How's it different?" she asked me.

"It just is. I don't have a pet cow or a pet pig or pet chicken. But I do have pet fish, and I can't bring myself to offend my darlings just because of David's macho b.s. He only does it because he wants to get in on the caveman scenario of man killing his food, and I think it's stupid."

"Well, speak for yourself, 'cause I do love to eat me some grilled cat fish twice a week. It seems like this thing between you and David is pretty serious, though. It's a trip to see your face light up when you start talking about him. What's he about?"

"Tess, you won't believe it, but I'm in love. I'm scared to my toenails, but I really think David's the one."

She hit me on the leg.

"*The* one? You sure?"

I shook my head like I really was sure and knew what the hell it all means.

"Yep. I can't believe that God is playing this joke on me, but I've been bitten by the bug and I've got the bump on my heart to prove it, girl."

"Well, go girl. Go on then. So what's he like?"

"He's double every good thing in a man, but then he's irritating as all get-out too. A regular control freak. I think he believes he's going to run my life, but he'll understand sooner or later that us women of the nineties wear pants too. I'm still trying to understand why I like his bad points too, though."

"Screw that, Genie. Is he fine?"

I broke into a smile and leaned my head back on the sofa.

"The bomb, girl. He's older. Tall, dark and suave. And he knows it too. He is a mess, girl. But, you'll see for yourself when he gets in here.

I'm telling you Tess, this man has me singing love songs like a fool."

"You, singing love songs?" She couldn't believe it. I couldn't believe it myself. And I had the nerve to be telling somebody my shame.

"Honey, was I not in the shower yesterday morning singing 'Betcha By Golly Wow' at the top of my lungs?"

She leaned closer to me.

"I thought I saw the words 'dick-whipped' written across your fore-head."

"I don't know what you're talking about, Tess," I said, laughing.

"He's married though, isn't he." She knew me well enough to know that much.

"Well, we had a serious, long talk last night and he's decided that he's getting his own place as soon as we get back. He said for his kids sake we need to be discreet for another year, but once he files for divorce, we can date out in the open. Then when his divorce is final, we'll find us a house and get married."

"Wow, Genie. That's a lot to deal with. You just met him not too long ago, didn't you?"

"Three months. But we both know it's right," I said, using David's line. "He's been unhappy in his marriage for a long, long time; and me, well, you know I've done enough dirt. I'm scared though, Tess. You know this is all new for me, and I'm just . . . Anyway, maybe now I can settle down. Have some kids. Enough about me and David, though. Just tell me what you think of him after you meet him. But what about you? How'd you go about kicking Darryl out of your life, and are you seeing something tall and fine now, Miss Skinny Minnie?"

She looked a little embarrassed.

"I met this doctor at the hospital, girl." Tess was a radiologist.

"Does this doctor have a name?"

She almost looked shy about it.

"Alex," she said. "He's a pediatrician. We've been out on three dates and I think the sparks are starting to turn into a bonfire."

"Ooh. Sounds righteous."

"It is, Genie. It is. He is so fine, inside and out. Anyway, I cut Darryl loose when I started making the other changes in my life. We just couldn't find a way to grow together, that's all. He was happy the way he is, putting all that junk into his body. Well, I was on a mission to eat healthy and exercise and surround myself with positivity. He wasn't for it. He started trying to tear down my esteem all over again just to make me want to give up."

"I'm glad you were smart enough not to let that happen."

"No way. I'd gotten too far. I know how you feel about therapy, Genie. I felt that way too. But I'm living proof that it does work, and I think you should give it a shot." I rolled my eyes. I had already heard this crap from Paulette and now I was hearing it from my sister.

"You sound like the poster girl for those shrinks."

"No. I sound like I know what I'm talking about. You don't think the things you do tell your past on you, but girl, they tell the story. Everything we bury has a way of coming to the surface in one form or another, Genie. I'm not trying to push you. All I'm saying is, just think about it. I guess you haven't told David anything, have you?"

If my teeth weren't attached I'd have spit them out. I did almost choke on a sip of my drink.

"Are you nuts? Tell David for what? It would only cause problems for us. I want to be a woman who David can respect. Not some tainted package."

"See there. That's something you need to work out right there. You aren't a tainted anything. You're a beautiful, vibrant, intelligent woman. If David loves you the way you say he does, then you owe it to him to tell him everything and he owes it to you to understand and help you work through it."

"Tess, we've just started out. We're too new for me to lay all of that on him. I've known Paulette forever, and you know I just told her. It's bad enough that I saw Edward at that restaurant we went to a couple weeks ago and freaked out. David would shit bricks if he knew somebody had hurt me. But mostly I think he'd look at me different from the way he does now. I mean, Tess: Last night he told me he idolizes me."

She had the nerve to laugh when I was sitting there looking like a worrywart.

"Girl, please. That was just his dick talking to you. He idolizes what you've thrown on him. He'll calm down after a little while."

"Well just bust my little ego bubble, why don't you." I was mad because she was sitting there looking like a million dollars, so I couldn't call her a fat-ass anymore.

"I'm sorry, dear heart. But my point, is if you and David are going to have a future together, you have to tell him everything."

I thought about sitting down with him and trying to do just that. It would be impossible. I couldn't even deal with our future without first doing laps in the pool. How would I ever be able to air my dirty laundry to the man? I said the only thing I could say to Tess.

"I can't."

That's when David decided to make his appearance, looking like God's gift and smiling at me.

"Hey babe," he said. "Look what I've got."

He was wearing the cap he'd bought and a blue and white sweatsuit with a T-shirt underneath. The sweatjacket was zipped halfway. He was carrying a cooler. He opened it and showed us five big fish on ice.

I yelled, "No, I can't look," and covered up my eyes.

"Those are beauties," Tess said.

"David, close that thing and get it out of my face. Oh—David, wait a minute, this is my sister Tess. Tess, this is David Lewis."

"Nice to meet you," he said. I saw them shake hands through the peep hole between my fingers.

"It's good to meet you too. I've heard such good things about you."

"Same here. I'm going to clean a couple of these babies and grill 'em a little later. Tess, you're staying for dinner I hope?"

"Sure, I am. Genie and I have a lot to catch up on. What are these anyway?"

"Rock."

"Yum."

I jumped up off the couch.

"For the record, I am very offended by this entire display. I'm going to take a shower and make myself some soup and a salad."

David grabbed me by the waist with his fishy hands and gave me a sloppy kiss. For some reason I didn't mind at all. I just went upstairs, whistling "Betcha By Golly Wow" like a true fool.

Phase 10

Genie

I drove out to the Silver Diner to meet Paulette and Evelyn early on a Saturday a week after my return from North Carolina. I was agitated for two reasons. I hadn't had my coffee yet and trying to sleep at night without David beside me was near impossible. I didn't like being apart from him. Our week together had spoiled me to his holding me at night. His presence had become part of my norm. I was used to his habits now. Being without him was like living without part of myself. It felt strange to be in my house alone when I returned. Like my house was big enough to swallow me. What made it worse was that David had decided that we couldn't see each other again outside of work or even discuss our future until he asked his wife for the divorce. It had been a lonesome week.

I walked into the diner, taking off my shades, and spotted Paulette already sitting in our favorite corner booth sipping coffee and reading a portion of the paper.

"Hey, miss."

Paulette looked up smiling.

"Hey now," she said. Then taking a closer look at my face, "Ooo. Who beat you up last night?"

She got the finger for that one.

"You don't look like Tyra Banks this morning yourself," I told her.

She licked her tongue out at me. Our regular waitress, Janet, came over just as Evelyn made her way toward us.

"Two more coffees?" she asked and Evelyn and I nodded.

"Hey divas." Evelyn placed her purse on the floor and slid into the booth beside me.

"Good morning, Ev. So how's everything, Genie? All recovered from your trip?" Paulette asked sarcastically.

Why was she starting already? I hadn't even gotten comfortable yet. My eyes were glued to the menu and I was nodding my head to the music playing on the jukebox. Someone at another table had chosen "Why Do Fools Fall in Love."

"There *you* go," I said.

"There I go what? I was just asking a question."

"Mmmhmm," I said. "In that case the answer is yes. I've recuperated just fine. Let me have the Metro section please."

"I still don't see what the point of it was, G., for you and David to go down there. You're just getting yourself further involved in this mess. It's not wise, girl."

She passed over the entire paper minus Style.

"You've said that before, and I didn't come here this morning to listen to you preach to me. I don't have time for it," I snapped. I found the part of the paper I wanted and put my menu aside. My appetite wasn't all that keen today. A bowl of Rice Krispies and some bacon were good enough.

"Oh, but you have time to waste on somebody else's man."

"Paulette, don't start with me," I warned.

"I just don't want to see you hurt. Is that wrong?"

"The state I'm in right now, I need my friends to be here for me."

"What's wrong with you this morning?" Evelyn asked.

The coffee hit the spot. It was piping hot, but I managed to drink down a good bit of it. I hadn't told the girls a thing about what I'd been going through, and I swear I was ready to burst. This was something I didn't think I could handle alone. I desperately needed their support.

"Okay. Here's the deal. I've been holding out."

"Holding out on what," Evelyn wanted to know.

"Uhm. Damn. I hadn't even planned to go into all of this with you guys, but it's driving me crazy not to talk about it."

"About what, Genie? What is it?" Paulette had stopped checking out the movie listing and was giving me her full attention now.

"Well. When David and I were in North Carolina . . . How can I say this? Uhm, well, David and I decided that we want to be together, and he's supposed to be telling his wife he wants out."

"What?" They were both caught off guard with this latest revelation. I knew it wasn't what either of them wanted to hear, but it was my life and I intended to live it the way I saw fit.

"Yeah," I said, running my hands through my hair. I needed a glass of Sambuca for real. "I was under the impression that he was going to do it sooner rather than later, but it looks like he's going to take his time doing it. I don't know what to do. He won't talk about it at all. At the office he acts like there's nothing going on between us but the work, and he won't call me. I'm trying to respect his request for space, but damn."

I'd said all that and got nothing but silence. They were looking at me as if I'd just said I was joining the damn circus.

"Are you two going to just sit here gaping at me?" I asked.

"What are we supposed to say, Genie? I'm so thrilled you're breaking up the man's marriage? Is that what you wanna hear? I don't know about Evelyn, but if you expect me to support you with this, then you're asking too much of me. I can't believe you would sink this damn low."

Paulette turned to look out of the window and I felt like I'd been slapped. I had expected a negative reaction, but not this kind of opposition. I didn't know how to respond to this, but it was evident that no amount of argument from me would do any good.

"You feel the same way?" I asked Evelyn.

She looked uneasy, as if she were trying to come up with something diplomatic.

"Just spit it out, Evelyn. I'm interested to know if you share Paulette's view on this."

"Genie, the man's been married a long time and he has kids. This kind of thing can be hard on kids. You know how it affected the twins when Simon and I broke up. And then you haven't known him long—"

"Excuse me, Evelyn."

I'd had enough. She stood up to let me slide out of the booth.

"This is for my coffee," I said, tossing a few dollars onto the table.

"Genie, wait a minute. Don't go like this," Paulette said, holding my arm.

"No. I need to. I'm too stressed out right now. I'll see you guys later."

"Genie . . ."

"Bye."

I don't know why I had hoped for a better response. It was too much to ask for, I guess, that your friends be in your corner no matter what. I wanted so bad to talk to somebody about how I was feeling. This waiting game was taking its toll on me already, and it had barely been two days since the last time I'd seen David. Hell, it had been a whole week since we'd even talked about it. Not a second had passed that I didn't wonder if he'd changed his mind since he dropped me off in front of my house coming back from N.C. Maybe he had gotten back to his real life and decided that everything that had happened between us in the Outer Banks was some silly fantasy. How could he possibly leave his security for me?

There was hardly any traffic, but I was careful not to speed too much. Getting a ticket would only compound my stress. I was a little hungry, so I stopped off at McDonald's for an Egg McMuffin, then headed home. When I pulled up in front of my house, to my surprise, David's car was parked out front. I was so happy I could hardly stand it. I pulled into the garage and almost forgot to put my car in park.

"David?" I called out, coming into the house through the garage door.

He appeared from the living room with fish food in his hand. He looked so good to me. Even though his face looked strained and tired, he still had a tan from last week and he'd gotten a good haircut probably this morning.

"Babe," he said. "Where've you been?"

"Silver Diner," I said. "What are you doing in here overfeeding my fish?"

He set the canister on the table and put his arms around me.

"Mmm. Damn, I missed you."

"Me too, David. It's been hard, baby."

"I know," he told me.

I eased back so I could look at him.

"Did you . . ."

"Not yet," he answered and I was so disappointed I wanted to cry. I lay my head against his chest, but he lifted my face and kissed me on the nose.

"Don't, Genie. I'll talk to Monica soon, babe," he said. "I promise."

"You haven't changed your mind?" I asked.

"Genie, I love you. You know I do."

His eyes were so sincere that some of my fears seemed to be put to rest.

"I know."

"Well, then. Just know that this is going to take a little time, honey. This whole thing is killing me in more ways than you could ever know. But just be patient a little longer. Think you can?"

"Yes. It's difficult, but yes."

"Good," he said, leading me to my bedroom. "Because I've been thinking about it so much that I want to be able to put it out of my mind right now. I just need to be close to you today. I need to make love to you, babe. I need to make us both feel good."

"David, it's been so lonely without you," I told him as he unbuttoned my blouse and let it slip to the floor. I closed my eyes and accepted the firm kisses he placed on my shoulder and breast.

"I know," he said, "but sooner than you think, I'll belong to you for good."

Phase 11

David

Yesterday, I did the hardest thing I've ever had to do. I moved out of my house and into the apartment I found in Greenbelt. We all took it very hard. Me, Monica, the kids. Devin and Mark were so hurt they couldn't even watch me go. Just stayed holed up in their room. Monica didn't watch me go either. She hasn't come home since I told her a week ago that I wanted us to separate. She's been staying with her friend Ida in Arlington, and she can't even talk to me without crying on the phone. "I know it's another woman," she keeps saying. "I know it, David. Just tell me the truth." I would rather admit to being a serial killer than tell her that I'm in love with someone else. The part of me that still loves Monica won't let me tell her the truth.

There are some things about life that I know. I know that people come and go in your life. I know that the "keepers" who touch your life do not come a dime a dozen. I know that you should put your family first. But I know that because we all have the power within us to make whatever changes that are necessary to make us whole, we should do so. But how do you do it all? How do you keep all the "keepers" and put your family first so that they can be happy, but then also put yourself first so that you can give the people you love the best of yourself?

I was no good walking around that house miserable as hell, trying to hold onto air inside that marriage. I was no good to my sons. I didn't make a hard try at getting to know them better because I was so focused on why shit wasn't working inside me. So I made the decision to go and here I am hurting them anyway. But which decision causes the long-run pain?

I asked myself that last week before I had "the talk" with Monica. See, everything we do in life is measured through pain and pleasure. Sometimes we have decisions to make that will cause pain no matter what we do. I want to think I chose a lesser pain. That's why I knew I had to go. I sat back and visualized what it would be like for me to stay miserable, burrowing deeper into my shell while my sons go out and experience life, then realize they never really knew me. But then, I thought, what would it be like if I gave myself what I need, which is this change and a new life with Genie? Well, then I saw myself being able to focus on my kids, focus on being a better father to them. A more accessible father. Once they get over the shock of Monica and me splitting, they'll see the change in me was for the better. Making that decision was the easy part. Ending my marriage was devastating.

I kept wondering if there was any proper way to close the door on my marriage. I wondered what would be the proper thing to say to Monica. I knew it wouldn't be easy for either of us. For so long it's been a third of our personal definers. We got jobs. We became married. We became parents. Everything we've done since our early twenties has worked into those three categories. So when, I wondered, did we ever get the chance to become people? What I was doing was something totally out of the realm of those definers. It was foreign to me. Frightening to me. I racked my brain about how and when to tell her I was leaving, but as the week after my return from North Carolina aged into a month, I realized there would be no right time or place to end the marriage. The gut-wrenching anguish of facing the fact that something I've invested my heart and soul into has failed transcended the boundaries of a gentle breaking away.

Once I understood that, I was able to say it aloud. Although the full magnitude of what I was saying didn't hit me until my first night alone in my two-bedroom apartment last night. I was not just saying no to the years of neglect and what I felt was Monica's mistreatment of me. I was giving up everything familiar to me that I took for granted. I hadn't even been aware before this that I'd taken her for granted on a lesser level. Seeing her clothes in the closet and the smell of her. Coming home to a livable house. Her voice. The tap of her fingers on her laptop in bed most nights. Seeing the silly romance novels she read lying on her pillow. Her very presence has been so overpowering as to have been invisible to me. How could that be?

But I knew I made the right decision when Monica and I sat down together on that rare Friday night when we were both at home early. It was storming outside and the lights kept flickering. We were in the family room drinking the cinnamon hot cocoa she made and I said, "Monica. We need to talk." She didn't want to talk, she said. She wanted to finish reviewing the budget projections for the next fiscal year. It made me angry that she'd said that. I had wanted to be human about telling her I wanted a divorce, but in that moment my anger outweighed my fear and carefulness and I said, "I'm leaving you, Monica," without even blinking. I think a lifetime passed before she said anything, but when she did speak, it was, "Why?"

I laid out my reasons to her. More than wanting her to understand, I think I wanted for her to make it easy for me, and she did that. She got up quietly and packed two suitcases and drove in all that rain to Ida's house. I think it was her way of beating me to the punch. She wanted to leave me before I had the chance to leave her. All that did was give me relief. I lay down on that sofa and cried twenty six years of tears.

Telling the kids was even harder, if that can be believed. Neither of them understood. Both of them cried. They don't know yet what I mean when I say that the marriage is dead. That Monica and I don't love each other in a married sense anymore. That I've reached a point in my life where I need to add some definition to it that I can be proud of. They only understand that things won't be the same. That I'm going to be twenty minutes away and not a few steps down the hall. And that their mother is hurting right now. It half killed me the way they clung to me and asked me to stay. Half killed me. I didn't think I could physically live through it. I wanted some hole to open up in the floor to swallow me. But I wanted most to show them that my leaving is for the greater good. They'll get used to the idea and realize that if I didn't do this thing for me, I would be living a perpetual lie.

I came into my quiet apartment building at about seven from my morning run with the newspaper and a half gallon of Sunny Delight. It was Sunday. Everybody was still probably dead asleep. I'm on the third floor, because the last thing I want to hear is somebody's kids running above my head, so I climbed the three flights of carpeted stairs and unlocked my apartment door. The apartment is simple. Stark, right now, since all I've got are boxes piled upon the floor. The carpet, the walls, the appliances—everything is neutral. Fresh and new, too, since the complex is only four years old. I put a sheet up over the sliding door leading to the balcony and that's my only decoration. I don't have a stick of furniture yet. Just my clothes, my books, my computer, fax machine and a thirteen-inch black and white television from the garage. I plan to use the second bedroom as my office, of course.

The place has a foyer when you come in the door. Two steps lead to the living room to the right, where the balcony is, and the dining room to the left. The eat-in kitchen just off the dining room has those double beveled doors like my kitchen at home. I mean, my old home. Back up the steps and down the hall are a bathroom, a mini laundry room and the first, small, bedroom. Then farther back is my bedroom, with another bathroom. Genie gave the place a thumbs up when she saw it yesterday. That made me feel like I really had done the right thing.

I pulled off my sweaty shirt and put it on a box in the living room. I put my keys and the newspaper on the counter in the kitchen. Put the juice in the empty fridge and made myself a bowl of cream of wheat and some instant coffee that I put in a paper cup. I don't have dishes yet, even. I let my breakfast sit while I hooked up my computer in my new office. I wanted to see if Michael had left me any E-mail messages. He was most likely on his way to Africa by now. I checked the E-mail but didn't see a thing except a few notes from colleagues and some of my students. I left those unopened. They'd keep until tomorrow.

Someone knocked on my door and I eyed the peephole. I was shocked as shit because it was Devin. I swung the door open. I was so glad to see him.

"Son," I said.

"Hey, Dad," he said, sounding like his usual self.

He wouldn't look at me, though. He had his hands in his pockets and his head was down. I grabbed him and pulled him into a hug.

"Come on in, son." He seemed kind of shy about it, but looking around a bit he went ahead and walked down the steps into the living room.

"Come on. Pull up a box," I said, gesturing for him to sit down. I was a bit ashamed. If he'd waited a few days, I'd at least have had some furniture for the place

"Thanks, Dad." He didn't seem like he minded. It's hard to tell with teenagers. He was staring at the sheet on the sliding glass door. It bothered me that he wouldn't really look at me.

"Dad," he said, "I couldn't just let you go like that, man. I'm still not happy about all this, but I talked to Kelli about it last night and she helped me see that you've got your own life to live. I mean, dag, you ain't out there trying to stop me from going to college out of state just because I'ma be leaving here. You always encourage me to do the best thing for myself. No matter what. And well, uhm, you're a person too. I trust your judgment and I know you're probably doing the best thing for you right now, just like you said."

I needed to hear that so bad I almost broke down. I put my hand on his shoulder and squeezed it.

"Thanks, son." I was smiling. "Like I said before, sometimes we have to make the hard decisions in life. You'll make some too. But what you have to do is face whatever the situation is like a man. Stand by your decision. And if you ever find that you made the wrong decision, be man enough to admit that you were wrong. I guess Mark doesn't share your opinion, huh?"

Devin fidgeted in his pockets. He jingled his change and looked at me for the first time since he got there.

"He's hurt, Dad. You know how close he is to Mom. He's been calling her over at Aunt Ida's every day. Talking to her and stuff. She's real upset about what you doing. She's coming back home today. I think Mark just needs some time to get used to the idea and stuff."

Mark would take it hardest. He was the one who kept all his feelings harnessed inside of him. He was so like me it was amazing. The whole thing made me feel so old and tired, I wanted to die.

"Yeah. I'll give him time to let it all sink in then I'll try to talk to him again. Devin, I want you to know that I'm still your Dad, okay? I hope both of you know that I love you more than anything else in the world. What happened between your mother and me is a whole separate issue. There are no sides to take. We both want the best for you and Mark. I want you two to be strong, productive men one day soon. I know your days are numbered before you go off to college, but if you'll let me, I want to spend as much time with you as possible. Mark too, if he'll give me a chance."

"I'd kind of like that, Dad. We haven't spent any real time together in a long time. I'll work on Mark and see what he has to say."

My son was giving me his support. That felt like gold to me. I hoped Monica wouldn't try to influence Mark against me. I wasn't sure what she'd said about me. But that was something I couldn't control. All I could do was make sure that both boys know I'm one hundred percent part of their lives.

"Listen, you want anything? I don't have much, because I haven't gone to the grocery store yet, but I can fix you some hot cereal. Maybe some orange juice?"

"No thanks," he said, standing. He started cracking his knuckles. "I've gotta go. I wanna be there when Mom gets home."

"Oh, alright," I said. "Well, you want to see the rest of the place first?"

"Some other time, Dad. I just wanted to tell you I was in your corner if you need me to be."

We hugged again at the door and he was gone. I went in my bedroom to look out the window overlooking the parking lot. I saw Devin get into Kelli's car. One down, I thought, and one to go.

●   ●   ●

I sat in my office at work on Monday with my mail and I reread the letter from the NEA, because I almost couldn't believe it. I'd been accepted to receive the grant. I could use the money to pay for my trip to Ghana when summer classes ended. I felt good. Things were good. I looked up from the pile on my desk and saw Genie sitting there looking at me with those big baby browns. She blew me a kiss and I reached out and caught it, feeling like the luckiest bastard in the world. We were so good for each other.

Genie was being very patient with me, and I love her for that. She told me she'd give me all the space I need in order to get adjusted to my new lifestyle whenever I say the word. But at the same time she let me know that she was there for me. Like yesterday. She came over with lunch, a few pictures, curtains for the bedrooms and some vertical blinds, and hung them up for me while I ate. She said she'd gotten the curtains for me from the woman who'd redone the chair in her bedroom. I'm no expert, but they looked expensive to me. She told me not to worry about the cost, but I slipped the hundred I had in my wallet into her purse when she wasn't looking. I'll give her more later. She got the blinds for the sliding glass door from Montgomery Ward on sale, she said. They were very nice. I planned to buy the very black leather furniture that Monica hates. Genie hung the pictures up on a short wall opposite where I planned to put my sofa. I'd seen the pictures on her bedroom wall. She told me they didn't match her room anyway, so I was okay with it.

I felt like King of the Hill buying stuff for my place. Normally Monica did all of that. All she liked was that Queen Anne shit. My creative input was never welcomed. I liked having the freedom to choose without having to make a compromise. Genie was helpful too. I was amazed that our tastes are so similar. We practically zoomed through picking out the living room and dining room furniture, and a table and chairs for the kitchen. I bought a CD player because Genie insisted I get one, and then two tall black bookcases. I decided to continue sleeping in Devin's sleeping bag until I got the bed I wanted. I'd seen one in a Danker ad in the Sunday paper that I'd set my heart on. But I did find an oak desk and a chair for my office.

Then Genie took me to some frilly place called Bed, Bath and Beyond and made me spend almost a grand on bedding and towels and bathroom items. All kinds of crap. She even made me get linen napkins and napkin rings. Women go too far, I think. And it wasn't over. We hit Hecht's and bought two sets of everyday dishes, pots and pans and crystal glasses and silverware and shit. Then she had me buy everything known to man at the grocery store. But I give it to the woman. She still had the energy to line my shelves with paper and help me put everything away. Had my place looking almost like home, with the plants and pictures and all. The furniture arrives today; she told me she would come over tonight and help me with that too. How can women shop like that, and still like putting junk all around the house? I guess it isn't for me to know.

I spent a few hours on a chapter for Winthrop's anthology on the work of Langston Hughes. My contribution was my assessment of the Simple character. I had already done my research and outline, so all I had to do was thicken the stew, like Stevens always says. I worked on my chapter until I thought my eyes would cross from looking at the computer screen, and by the time I looked over at the clock I realized I had to get home to meet the delivery guys. They were bringing my furniture in a couple of hours.

I looked over at Genie. She was busy talking to a student. She was so good at that. You could tell she cared about the students tremendously, and that made me proud. When she finished and the student left, I picked up my telephone and called her.

"You think you can get out of here early with me, babe?" She was smiling from ear to ear.

"Yeah. It shouldn't be a problem. I think I feel myself coming down with a fever or something."

"So you're hot, huh?" I asked her.

She didn't want to play along with me. She said, "Be good, baby."

"Fine," I said. "Meet you at the car in ten minutes?" She looked over at me and nodded yes, so I hung up and tidied up my office a bit. I stopped by the men's room on my way out. When I got to the car I waited a few minutes before she showed up.

"Hey," she said.

"Hey, hey."

She had put a straw hat on her head. She looked great. Had on a long tight white dress with no sleeves. She was wearing some of that big Caribbean looking jewelry, a necklace and a bracelet.

I turned up the radio and headed on home.

•   •   •

"David, where'd you put those magnets I gave you?" I wasn't interested in any damn magnets. I was too busy kissing her shoulder and pulling her back against me.

"That drawer."

"Oh." She was moving around the kitchen with me attached to her like a leech.

She started sticking these fruit magnets on the fridge door like I couldn't live without that junk.

"Mmm. David, quit it."

"Give me a kiss." I turned her around in my arms. I was feeling more than amorous and was mad at myself for not skipping work this morning and going over to Danker for that bed. She struggled a second but gave in. By the time she started trying to push me off again, I had her dress half off and her bra loose.

"Come on, babe. We've got at least another hour."

"I can see you won't take no for an answer," she said. My answer was in my smile.

We stumbled out into the living room and threw our clothes every which way. Then I was inside her. I groaned because it felt so good and lay there just for a moment to hold on to the distinct pleasure of reacquainting myself to her body. It had been a few weeks. When I'd been going through the mental difficulty over how to leave Monica, I hadn't been able to get romantic. My mind had been too affected. The space of time between my coming to a decision to end my marriage and my actually doing so left me so useless that I couldn't work and barely ate or slept. All I could think about was what I was going to do to Monica and the kids and dread it. It was so hard on me. Hard on Genie too. But all that's changing now. Each step I take now is a step toward our future.

Genie's eyes were closed. We kissed like we were starving for one another, and I got so excited that I picked up speed. Her fingers were kneading the small of my back and she was so into it that it made me go nuts. It was over kind of quick.

"David, get up off me, sweetie. You're killing me." I *was* smothering her. I wanted to stay that way for the rest of the day, I was so tired from all the moving and shopping and doing. It was catching up to me.

"Give me a minute, babe," I said. Then I rolled off her. She jumped up and beelined for the bathroom with her clothes under her arm and closed the door. When she came back out she looked like I'd never touched her.

"I'm tired as shit, Genie." I was laid out on my back in the floor with my pants halfway up.

"I figured you would be. You've been pushing yourself nonstop for over a week now. You need your rest. Did you sleep any better last night?"

"Not really."

"Did you try what I told you to?"

"Genie, that's silly."

"Honey, it works. If you can't sleep, it's a good way to help you relax."

"I'm not into that meditation shit."

"Well, you refuse to take anything to help you sleep—"

"How about I just wait a few days, let's see if I can get used to the place. It takes time."

She shrugged. "You're right. It does take time. I'm just worried about you, David. You look so out of place."

"What do you mean by out of place?"

"I don't know. Like a fish out of water. It's okay to be afraid of all this. I feel like you're trying to be stronger than necessary about this. It's okay with me if you show that you're upset over having left home. It's natural, sweetie. I think that's why you can't sleep."

"It's been two nights and I'm in a sleeping bag, for Christ's sake, woman. This has nothing to do with fear or depression or anything else."

"David—first of all, I didn't say a word about fear or depression.

Now, I'm not going to get into an argument with you over it. I was just voicing my opinion."

I realized I was being so defensive about it because she was right. As good as I felt about being out on my own, I still missed the life I'd left behind. I missed the surety of it, the comfort.

"Come here." I got up and straightened out my pants and held her. We jumped when the knock on the door came. I went over and checked the peephole.

"Shit. Genie, go back in the bedroom and close the door. It's Monica." I felt like scum asking her to hide like that. But Monica was technically still my wife. I didn't want to hurt her any further. I surveyed the living room to make sure Genie hadn't left anything out. I didn't see anything, so I went ahead and opened the door after I fixed my clothes.

"Monica." She looked like she'd had as much rest as I'd had. Her eyes were a bit swollen, but she was put together in a beige suit. Her hair was up. I noticed she was still wearing her wedding ring, so I put my hands behind my back because I didn't want her to see I'd taken my band off.

"Hello, David. I'm sorry I'm here unannounced but I tried to reach you at work and in your car. I tried your cellular phone, too. Devin told me he called you at work this morning and that you said your phone here doesn't come on until tomorrow."

"Yeah. That's right. Monica what's this about? I have furniture coming in a few shakes."

She walked in past me, inspecting the apartment.

"Nice place. Devin said it was nice," she said. "You have a decorator help you or something?"

I knew where this was going, so I said, "Yes. As a matter of fact, Ben Winthrop recommended the woman who did his townhouse." Did that sound like the truth? She didn't look like she bought it.

"Oh. Well. Everything's working out just swell, huh? I mean, you up and walk out on our marriage like it meant nothing to you. Now you've got your fancy little apartment and your fancy decorations, and meanwhile I—"

"Monica, stop it!"

She burst into tears and leaned against the wall. "Oh, David," she said, "David, I don't understand you with this. I know I wasn't the wife you wanted me to be. I know I haven't tried hard enough and I didn't listen when you tried so hard to get close to me. But I'm human,

David. I'm human! I have feelings and this is tearing me apart. I can't stand that you have someone else in your life!" She broke down completely. This wasn't happening. My girlfriend was in my bedroom and my wife was standing in front of me making me feel like jumping right off the balcony. I didn't know what I should say. I just brought her close to me and held her until she got herself together.

"I'm sorry, David. I'm sorry. I'm just . . . I didn't come over here for this." She pulled a wad of tissues out of her purse like this was something she did a few times a day. She cleaned her face up a bit and looked at me with sad, wet eyes. I still didn't say anything, because I was afraid I'd say the wrong thing.

"I came because I guess we need to sit down at some point and discuss a few things. You know, Devin's graduation is coming up next month. I need to know if you still want to be part of the celebration."

"Of course I do. That hasn't changed."

"And then, we were going to rent that Caravan and drive him down to Morehouse in August. And we were planning to take Mark and his friends to Phillip's for his birthday. I haven't even told my family, David, and I'm not sure what to tell people who call the house for you. Leonard called last night and I told him you were out. I didn't know what else to say. That's why I came."

I wanted to be anywhere but standing here watching my wife cry because of me. I wished she would just go home and leave me alone, because I needed to think. I hadn't really thought about all those things she mentioned until now, and it made me feel like crying too. I hated myself for this shit.

"Listen," she said, "why don't you call me and we'll have dinner or something when you're ready to talk, huh?"

I nodded. I couldn't find my voice anywhere. I just wanted her to go. I opened the front door for her and when I closed it, Genie came back down the hall looking so distraught. I just knew she was angry that I was putting her through this shit. But she surprised me again, like always. She just walked up to me, looking like an angel in all that white and she said, "Come here, sweetie. I understand." We sat on the floor together and she let me lean on her shoulder until the furniture guys came.

Genie

"**A**lright ladies, now let's put on our refresher, shall we?"

I groaned. I had been lucky enough to miss Evelyn's Mary Kay party, but somehow this woman, DeeDee, who was tenaciously recruiting salespeople, had roped Paulette into giving one. There were five of us sitting around two card tables in folding chairs in Paulette's basement. We all had towels around our shoulders and little cosmetic mirrors in front of us. We had used our hot, wet cloths and had dabbed our faces with creams and astringent and mess it seemed like a hundred times. I never understood who would want to wake up and do that junk every single morning.

Of course I couldn't seem to do any of the stuff right. DeeDee, the happiest, most godawful excited woman I have ever seen, kept singling me out to show everybody else how *not* to cleanse your face. Her assistant, or should I say partner in crime, was a short attractive dark-skinned girl named Melanie. Melanie was handing the stuff out to us that we needed with an everlasting smile on her face. Either she'd taken a toke of something, or her man was in a good mood this week.

I wasn't buying a thing. I was determined not to. But DeeDee looked like she was the type not to take no for an answer. The only reasons I agreed to attend were because it was Paulette's party, David had agreed to teach Dr. Kemp's evening class, and DeeDee had promised all of us a free gift. I don't know about the other ladies, but I had my eye on the A Capella gel sitting on the cocktail table with a big gold bow on it, and I was ready to do battle with any heifer in here to get it.

We put on our makeup and everybody remarked that their faces felt clean, clean. Then the moment of truth arrived. Paulette's coworkers, Sheila and Bernice, both agreed to hostess parties next month and they bought the entire two-hundred-and-some-odd-dollar face kit. Evelyn, of course, had already done a party and was selling the stuff. Paulette was the hostess of this party and had bought a kit from Evelyn already. All eyes were on me. I felt like the main course at a cannibal dinner.

"Well, Genie?" DeeDee's big Elizabeth Taylor eyes were burning a hole in my face.

"You know, DeeDee, this has been a wonderful experience"—I'd been to two before—"but I think I'll pass on the kit and everything. But thank you for giving me a refresher course on putting on makeup. I really needed it."

She cheerleadered her way over to me and said, "Oh Genie, come on. Here you have two dear friends showing all this positive spirit. Don't you want to join in on the fun?"

No, I didn't. I wanted to go home, eat a big salad and spend some quality time with my man if he had gotten there yet.

"Oh, DeeDee, I'm really glad that you all want to share your fun with me, but I think what I'll do is buy a few things from Evelyn at a later date. I'm having a small cash flow problem right now, so I'll just have to let my fun begin when I can."

Why was I sounding like I needed to make an excuse to this lady?

"You sure, hon?"

I nodded like being left out of "the fun" was the hardest thing in the world to cope with. I looked over at Paulette and Evelyn just bursting, trying not to laugh at me. I would deal with them later.

"Alright. But how about a party, then? Won't cost you a cent, and as hostess, you get to pick any one item out of the catalog, depending on how many sales come in."

I was tired from working all day and this white woman was working a groove in my last nerve.

"DeeDee," I said, "I have five vicious pit bulls at home. The county won't allow me to put them outside because they can jump the fence, they know how to open unlocked doors, they bark all the time, they know how to attack and they won't let me bathe them. Sorry." Paulette and Evelyn both snickered, then coughed.

DeeDee's face got pale beneath that Mary Kay makeup. She didn't say another word in my direction. She backed up and clapped her hands together with a smile and said, "Well, ladies. Melanie and I are pleased as punch that you could all make it. You ladies look stunning. As you see, we have some gifts here on the coffee table." I was ready. This was my moment. "And we ask that you take one on your way out. Thank you and good night." They started packing up while they held a conversation with Paulette and Evelyn.

I went over to the coffee table. Bernice was already fingering my gift. I was on the verge of telling her to drop it or she was going to pull back a nub, but she spotted two bottles of Pure Bliss body lotion and put my A Capella down. It disappeared into my carryall.

After everyone left, Evelyn and I stuck around to help Paulette clean up. There wasn't too much to do, so we finished fast and then sat back on the couch with some herbal tea.

"Ah. I'm too through, you guys," Evelyn said.

"It's the truth, girl," I agreed. "I'm glad I did my homework during my lunch hour today."

Paulette started to giggle.

"Genie," she said, "I know I'm crazy, but you are crazy. Telling that woman you had pit bulls."

"It was all I could think to say. Sometimes you have to act like a nut to get people to leave you alone."

Evelyn started laughing too.

"Yeah, but the look on your face, girl. You looked like you didn't know what to do with all those dogs. For a minute there I thought we'd have to get some smelling salts for my girl DeeDee."

"Come on, it wasn't all that bad. Hey, I got my jar of A Capella, so it was a prosperous night. I'ma get in the shower and try some of it out on David's cute behind when I get home. See if he likes it."

"So things with you two are coming right along then, yes?" Paulette said.

"Yep."

"I can't believe it myself, Genie," Evelyn said. "The one you finally fall in love with is the one who leaves his wife. How'd you manage that?"

"E, the marriage was over with long before I arrived on the scene. I swear, y'all, he is really something special to me." I started staring off into space again, thinking about my honey.

"I'm pissed as hell that he's married, Genie, and that you refuse to transfer out of that department. You know how I feel about that shit, but now that he's made that move, at least, and I see you looking like you have a spotlight shining on your face, I can tell he makes you happy, and that makes me happy."

"God, Paulette stop making me feel all sentimental." They both hugged me.

"How'd the wife take all this, Genie?" I wasn't about to go into the ugly details of yesterday at David's apartment.

"Not well. I feel for her because she still loves him, but David gave her chance after chance to work on the marriage before it totally collapsed. There was nothing else he could do. One of his kids seems to be handling it okay, but it sounds like the other one has issues with it.

David swears he'll come around, but I'm not so sure. I can tell it's really affecting David a lot, even though he tries not to show it. I wish there was something I could do to make him feel better."

"There's nothing you can do, Genie. They have to work it out between them," Paulette said.

"I guess. But when I see him in pain like that, I feel like a homewrecker for real. Evelyn, you and Simon still headed toward the bedroom?"

"Genie, where have you been? We crossed that threshold a few weeks back."

I almost spit my tea out.

"What? Nobody told me." I glared at her.

"Well, you were dealing with the will he/won't he leave thing with David, so I gave you your space. But yeah, we got down finally because the sexual tension was too much for us both. And girl, it was good. I mean, brother pulled out all the stops. But the best part was the next morning. You should have seen Sasha and Simmy when they saw their daddy at breakfast. They were so thrilled."

"Well go, girl. You two talking at all about him moving back in?"

"We made the decision to take things slow. Not everybody's Speedy Gonzalez like you, Genie."

Paulette cracked her sides on that one.

"My baby said that we are not moving too fast. It's just that everybody else is moving too slow and can't keep up, Ev. So just kiss my brown butt." I licked my tongue at her and glanced at my watch. "Speaking of, let me get my butt home, 'cause David should be there by now," I said.

"Aw, look at her run out of here, will you, Evelyn." Paulette said. I waved at them and walked slowly up the steps, but then when I got out the door, I jumped in my car and rode on up the street in a hurry. I missed my David.

· · ·

We were just relaxing in bed tonight. We read to each other from Walter Moseley's *Black Betty* and fed each other strawberries. It was hot in the house because I refused to turn on the air until June, so we had taken off all our clothes and turned on the fan that sat on my dresser. When we got to a good place to stop in the book, I turned off the light, opened the window and lit a candle. We lay on our backs holding hands. The radio was on low. We started acting silly, singing Luther's

version of "If This World Were Mine" with the record, and I was surprised he knew all the words, because usually he just made some up.
Knowing the words didn't help much, because neither of us could sing
a lick. I think we were upsetting the dog next door, because it kept
howling and making us both laugh. When the song was over, David
put his face against my shoulder and inhaled that A Capella and sighed
like he was content. I just knew I was the woman.

"Kemp's class is the most unorganized crap I've ever seen, Genie.
He's completely veered from his syllabus. The class hasn't learned a
thing about Shakespeare's work this entire session."

Didn't he know he was supposed to be thinking about how good I
smelled? "David, let's not talk about work tonight, okay? Let's just be
together and enjoy each other. Talk to me about something else."

I think he got a little miffed. He let my hand go.

"And that would be?" He sounded all professor-like now. He was a
trip.

"I don't know. Anything. How about what it was like for you growing up. You never talk about that."

"'Cause there's nothing to say, really. It's damn depressing. What do
you want to know?"

"Everything about you." I was rubbing the soft hair on his tummy.

"Okay. I'll start from birth. I was born on a cold, cold night in January in 1892. It was—ow!"

I had hit him on the head and he started laughing at me like a fool.

"What'd you do that for?" He was really getting a kick out of himself.

"The real story, David. I want to hear about you. I'm serious."

I could see him smiling at me in the dim candlelight.

"It was a joke, babe. Come here. I'll tell you what you want to hear."

"No more playing around?"

"No. No more playing. Besides, I don't want a head injury."

He pulled me close to him and told me such an interesting story
that I wondered if it was true. He sounded kind of sad, so I guessed it
was. He told me how his parents died in a fire when he was five and
that he and his brother, Aaron, went to live with their grandparents in
Chicago. He told me how poor they were. How he would go to bed
hungry some nights. He told me that he, his uncle, and his brother
stole food sometimes.

The things he told me made me feel so close to him. I didn't pity
him. I felt like I had a kindred spirit lying beside me. He had seen

some hard times just like me and had made it through to the other side. I really wanted to tell him about me. I would have liked to let him know that I understood what it was like to keep going in spite of everything. I thought about what Tess said, and I knew she was right. But I still couldn't find the words to tell him, so I started kissing him to show him what was inside of me. "Genie, come on and cut on the air, babe. I'll pay the bill when it comes in."

That was his fourth time asking.

"David, the bill isn't the point. I can pay my own bills. This is a matter of discipline. I never turn my air on until June, and I told you that."

"No, this is a matter of your trying to give me a heat stroke." He moved away from me and turned on his side, facing the wall.

I kissed his back. The man was fricking impossible to handle. I didn't know how I was going to deal with him on a daily basis once we got married.

"David, you do have the option of going home." I knew I didn't mean that. I couldn't help myself from turning into one of those women. I just wanted to be right up under him every minute.

"I told you I don't feel like driving, woman."

"Fine."

"Hey, babe."

"What?"

"You think I look old?"

"No. I think you're getting on my nerves, David. I wish you would stop asking me that. Getting older is really not a big deal."

"That's because you're young enough to say that. You won't say that when you get to be my age. It's damn hot in here, Genie."

"Whatever, David. You like peach ice cream?"

He turned and looked at me like I was stupid.

"I don't go out of my way to have it, why?"

"That's all I've got in the freezer and it'll cool you off."

"So will the a/c."

I nudged him hard and he laughed at me. I jumped off the bed.

"Where you going?" he asked, reaching for me. I dodged him.

"I have an idea."

I went to the kitchen for some ice. I put it in a small plastic bowl and took it in the bedroom. David was laid out on his tummy, so I put the bowl on the bed and straddled him like a jockey, and he grunted.

"Woman, what are you doing?"

"You ever seen *Do the Right Thing?*"

"No. I don't care for Spike Lee's films."

"Spike's alright. Anyway, I'ma show you what Mookie and Tina did when they got too hot."

He lifted his head and turned to look back at me. "What the hell is a Mookie?"

"David, shut up and put your head down. I know what I'm doing."

"Yeah, and it's always something crazy."

"Just be quiet."

I picked up an ice cube and rubbed it down the back of his neck. He shivered. I ran it down his spine and followed it with warm kisses.

"Mmm. That's nice, babe."

"I know," I said.

I slid the ice across his shoulders, then massaged them and started icing and kneading the muscles in his upper back. I knew he was loving every minute of it. I could tell by the way he kept so still while I rubbed the ice on him again and went into those quick little karate chops like I was a real masseuse or something.

My fingers were working fast. I stopped to run my tongue partway down his spine, then I started with the deep kneading again. By the time I reached the middle of his back, he was moaning and groaning like we were making love. It was starting to turn me on, but I kept my attention on relaxing my man. I worked my fingers to the bone until my upper arms felt like I'd been working out. I guess he realized I was getting tired when I started to slow down a little. Somehow he flipped me, and I found myself on my back and he was over me with a piece of ice in his hand. He slid the ice up my thigh and started moving it toward my pride and joy.

"What are you doing?" I asked. I clamped my legs together tight. David didn't care. He just laughed like he was the bogeyman coming to get me. I squealed and escaped him. I ran down the hall at top speed, laughing at the top of my lungs, and David chased me all through the house. I hoped the neighbors wouldn't be alarmed by all my screaming. When I nearly broke my toe on the leg of the dining room table trying to dodge him I figured that was enough playing. I ran back down the hall and he finally caught me when I hid where I knew he would find me. Right in our bed.

We woke up bright and early Saturday morning and played two heavy games of tennis. David beat the skin off my butt. The man had no mercy on me at all. To cool down after our last game we went on one of our walks by the lake down the street from the courts. The place was totally deserted, except for the birds we heard high up in the trees surrounding the lake. It was crisp out. A kind of blue-tinged gray morning, like David's eyes. I was glad I had worn sweatclothes instead of my cute little Steffi Graff tennis skirt after all.

"You want me to come with you to your mother's grave, Genie?" David asked.

"Why do you ask that?"

He tapped me on the butt with his racket. Some ducks waddled into the water and swam together in a perfect line. We put our tennis rackets down so we could sit on the little bench near the lake for a while.

"Mother's Day passed and you didn't mention going out to visit. Now Memorial Day's coming up and I was thinking about the last time I visited my parents' grave. They're buried in Austin in my father's family plot. I thought you might like to go visit your mother's grave."

"I haven't been out to my mother's grave since she was buried, David."

"Why? It's not far, is it?" He wiped sweat off his forehead with the white handtowel he had swung around his neck.

"No. She's buried here in Maryland. I just don't think I can handle it, David. I don't know. I try not to think about things like that."

"I think it's important for you to take some flowers there. Spend some time reminiscing. Maybe that's why you keep having that dream. You might be subconsciously feeling bad about not going."

Reminiscing was the last thing I wanted to do.

"I don't know, David. I want to go, but I'm scared to. It might bring up a whole new set of emotions for me."

He started rubbing my hair the way I liked for him to.

"I know it's scary. But you know that in order to become healthy you're going to have to make some kind of peace with your past, right?"

I wasn't so sure that was possible. My past was too overwhelming to do that, but David didn't know that. It made me uncomfortable, the way he was looking at me. I almost felt like he could see my past in my eyes. I looked away toward where the bike trail began and spotted a man I'd seen many times before, doing Tai Chi.

"I don't know, baby," I said, still watching the man's slow, fluid movements. "Aren't there some things that happen in life that you can't ever reconcile yourself with? I mean, sometimes people who you love hurt you and you never get the chance to ask them why. Or they never explain to you why. How in the world do you get over that, David?"

I know David thought I was talking about Mama, but I was talking about Edward. I mean, I was his kid. I loved him. I trusted him implicitly. All he did was use that against me. Against all of us. It's hard having questions that you have no answers for. Like, I've always wondered if he was abused too. From information I've read on the Net, that's the case a lot of times. Maybe if I understood what made him mentally sick, then I could try to work some of the pain out of my own head, but the thought of ever confronting him like Tess did made me cringe up inside. I laid my head against David's chest because I needed his strength.

"Lemme put it to you like this," he said, rubbing my shoulder. "There are people who we love who hurt us, yes. Don't think I haven't been devastated in my lifetime. But what you have to learn is that it's not your job to understand or analyze why other people do what they do. That's on them."

He tightened his arm around me and I'd never felt so protected in my life.

"What you have to do for your own sanity is deal with what's within your own power to deal with. No, you can't dialogue with your mother to find out what you want to know. Hell, it's a possibility that she couldn't have explained her actions to you anyway. But it is within your power, Genie, to say, 'Hey. Something awful's happened to me. But I'm not going to let it take over my life. I'm not going to let it affect my relationships, or my physical health or my ability to love.' That's how you take control of your own life, Genie. You're a stronger woman than you think you are, you know."

It's crazy, but I wished I'd had a father like David. His sons don't know how lucky they are. I think what makes me love him so much in the first place is that he already sees in me the woman I'm so desperate to be. It just seems like his love and his caring automatically bring the positive things out in me.

I put my arms around him and hugged him and kissed him all over his face like he was leaving for war in the morning, and he just sat there and took it like a man. Some guy rode by on his bike and looked at us like we were the biggest idiots in the world. But who cared? I was in love.

"I'll go, David, if you come with me," I said, wanting him to be proud of me and wanting him to think I was brave, too. We picked up our rackets and starting walking toward the car so we could go for our usual breakfast at IHOP.

"I told you I will." He put his hand out and I took it. I squeezed it tight, though. I was frightened to death of taking this step.

•   •   •

"You ready, honey?" It was early on Memorial Day and David poked his head into the bedroom. I nodded and straightened the collar of my blue Ann Taylor dress. I had just gotten off the phone with Tess. She was so proud of me for doing this. She told me that going to visit Mama's grave was a good first step for me even though I'm not in therapy. I was scared for myself for doing this, but at least my David was going with me.

I did a few relax, relate, releases to get myself together, and I forced myself to get up off my unmade bed and follow David out to the car. I wasn't sure what kind of Pandora's box I might be opening by going out there. I only knew that I needed to try this thing to see if I could find some semblance of peace within myself about Mama's suicide. Maybe it could even give me the strength to tell David everything. That was something that weighed on my heart ever since North Carolina, and even more after hearing about his own childhood.

It was so warm and sunny out. Good barbecue weather. A nice cooling breeze was blowing, but my hands were still sweating. My mouth was so dry I kept swallowing and I felt like my bones were brittle, I was so stiff when I got in the car. David opened the sunroof and turned on the radio as we sped up 450. He started singing "Sitting on the Dock of the Bay" along with Otis Redding, even though he didn't even know all the words. I was quiet as a mouse, but real calm. I just looked out of my window and thought about how strange life can be sometimes. I never would have thought I'd be going back to that place.

When we got near the cemetery, David pulled off to the side of the road, where a man sat in a chair with a bunch of wreaths and bouquets of flowers he was selling. David bought a heart-shaped wreath of pink flowers and gave it to me for Mama's grave. Then we rode up the street a little further to the cemetery and parked the car. My stomach felt like it had a weight in it or something. It was almost like I was having an out-of-body experience, and I was reminded of what it was like riding in that black Lincoln Town Car on the day of Mama's funeral.

"You want me to come, babe?" David squeezed my hand.

I shook my head no. "I have to do this part by myself. I'll be back in a little while." I marched on up the hill like I was going off to my first day of school, wishing Tess and Marilyn were with me.

It was a small site across the street from Mama's church. I searched Mama out and found her headstone in the expanse of bright green grass, and I noticed there were other solemn people paying respects to their loved ones, either by themselves or in tight little groups. Yet I've never felt so alone. So set apart. So this is Mama, I thought. This is what she is now. This is her home. I thought about the portrait in my living room and smiled a little, because part of her lived there too. And in me. The grave marker was plain gray slate with her name on it. Maxine Annabella Gatlin. It said the year she was born. The year she died. What hurt was knowing that when a person dies, their grave cannot communicate all the in-between. It can't tell you how that person might have touched someone else's life. Or their dreams. Or their pain. It's almost like the only important things people accomplish are being born and dying.

I reached out and put my stiff fingers on the cool, smooth headstone and started to cry. My heart was so full. I felt so small and unimportant. So useless. My thoughts rushed back to things that the headstone could not tell. Things I thought I'd forgotten. Back to me saying, "Mama. Why is the sky blue?" And her answering, "Because when you were born, you came down from the sky like an angel. Now the sky just misses you, that's all."

I went back to her playing hopscotch with me in the driveway in her bare feet. She could never make it all the way without losing her balance and laughing. I went back to her teaching me how to make pancakes with Bisquick. Her giving me my very first Vigorol perm. Her whipping my butt for taking scissors to her azaleas the time I tried to make leis for my classmates. The last time she was normal was the summer before my twelfth birthday, when she took us three girls out shopping for Tess and Marilyn's college clothes. She bought herself a new blouse from Raleigh's that she never got to wear.

The ugly memories came back too. The three months she spent at Fitzgerald's house in St. Louis because Edward didn't want her to go to a sanitarium. She only needed a good rest, he said. Edward telling me that he would put Mama away out of state if I didn't be nice to him. He started coming in my room, watching me undress. He would get into bed with me at night, and then I wasn't Genie anymore. I wasn't me. It hurt too much to be me. I was a jaguar or a fast moving gazelle in the depths of the Serengeti and he couldn't catch the real me for nothing. I could escape. I needed my Mama so bad, I didn't know what to do. But she couldn't help me. She couldn't help me.

I fell to my knees in front of her headstone, weak and shaking, and I opened my mouth, but no sound came out. I was so tired that I squeezed my eyes shut, remembering her eyes that ugly night. Remembering how I cried out. Screamed for her, trying to shake her out of whatever stupor she'd slipped deeper into over those five years. Mama was already dead even before she killed herself. But before then I'd had hope. Before I found her like that, I always thought that someday she'd be free of the pain that made her separate herself from reality. I guess that's what she was trying to do when she killed herself. Give herself some freedom.

I put the wreath beside the headstone and touched her name etched into it. Maxine Annabella Gatlin.

"I forgive you Mama. I forgive you and me both," I said. I pulled my flask out of my purse and took a long swallow of Sambuca. Then I turned away and started walking back to the car. Back to David. I wiped my eyes and stopped crying, because I didn't need to. Mama was free. And I had found me somebody to love.

Genie

"Genie, for the last time, you cannot give these students free rein. If we don't keep supplies locked up, if we just let these students run willy nilly around the office using whatever computer they want, when they want, then we might as well forget about having any control around here. They'll steal everything right out from under us and we won't get any respect at all."

Barbara had called me into her office for one of her paranoid Hitler speeches about student dishonesty because I'd let one of the GTAs teaching a Summer II course have a red marker to grade some papers. I was so sick of her and her Kabuki theater makeup, I was ready to spit. The only thing that made her lard butt tolerable on a daily basis was David. I was in love and didn't give a damn about what this lonely bitch was griping about. All she really needed was a good, stiff one anyway. But I didn't know who'd be dumb enough or lonely enough to slip her one. I thought maybe I should order up a brown box in her name and have it sent to her address. She must have known what I was thinking by the look on my face, because she stopped suddenly, remembering I was still in the room. I swear, the woman loved to hear herself talk.

"Genie," she said, "I'm only telling you this, hon, for your own good. One day you'll work in another office somewhere and you'll remember all the important things I'm teaching you now."

"Thank you, Barbara. I'll remember that." While I'm choking you to death, I thought. I left her office and went into David's for a love refill.

"Hey, sweetie," I whispered. He looked up from his computer.

"Hi. Come on in. Just let me finish this one last part." He started typing away. I sat at his desk and crossed my legs.

"What are you working on?" I asked.

"Article."

"Mmm." I sat there watching him until he finished up.

"Now then." He swiveled his chair toward me. "What can I do for the sexiest woman in the world?"

That got him a big smile.

"Gimme a minute, Doc, and I'm sure I can think of several things. You talk to Michael?"

"Yeah. That's what I wanted to tell you earlier, but you were with some students. I'm going over in a few weeks."

"That soon, honey? Wow. I wish I could go too."

"We've been through this, Genie. You can't come with me. It's impossible. I'm going to be running around the whole time I'm there, and it looks like I'll be gone for a month."

"What? A month? You never said you'd be away that long."

"I know, babe. But now that I've gotten this grant I can do more thorough researching. Michael's made arrangements through the university over there for me. He's arranged places for me to stay as well."

"That was good looking-out on his part. A whole month, though, David? That's not gonna work for me."

"It'll fly by, babe. You'll see. Just tell me you're excited for me."

I rolled my eyes at him. "I'm excited for you." He had the nerve to grin at me.

"You sound like you want my head on a platter."

"I do, but not the one you think. So what are we going to do while you're gone, have long-distance phone sex?"

"I think we can go a month without, sweetheart. That's not so long."

"Says you. Make sure you leave me those hot-to-trot blue BVDs of yours so I can put them under my pillow and have sweet dreams at night."

He made a face at me and leaned closer to me.

"You are so bad, woman. I see now I'm going to have to teach you a lesson you won't soon forget."

I uncrossed my legs. His eyes were like magnets, the way they stuck to my every move.

"Ooh. That's just what I'm in the mood for, Professor. A lesson only you can teach. Are you coming over tonight?"

"I can't, Genie. Devin just called me. You know he's graduating tomorrow. His girlfriend's parents are having a pregraduation celebration for the kids and I promised him I'd be there."

All of a sudden I felt kind of possessive. I felt uneasy knowing that David and Monica would have to come into contact with each other.

"Oh. So I guess Monica will be there too," I said, like a true jealous woman. It's a wonder my face didn't turn green.

"Genie, you know I can't help that. My sons are a priority. I promised them both I'd be around as much as possible and I meant it. I know you know this isn't about Monica."

"I know that she wants you back too, David." Lord. I was acting like that simple heifer Phyllis on *The Young and the Restless*.

"And I want you," he said. "I think I've already proven that, and I shouldn't have to tell you that every time this kind of thing comes up." He looked pissed, but so was I. How could he not understand where I was coming from. I didn't have any security with this man. Only a promise.

"Professor Lewis, can I see you a moment?" As usual we were interrupted by a student. He had stuck his head in the doorway, and that shit pissed me off too. We couldn't even have a disagreement in peace.

"Sure, give me just a second and I'll be right with you."

He turned back toward me.

"David, I don't want you to go," I said.

He threw some papers up on his desk and sighed like I was bugging him to death.

"Stop whining, Genie. I'm not going to fight about this."

"Well, come over to my house after the party." I was pitiful and knew it, but I didn't care.

"Baby, I have to get some work done too. We've been spending so much time together that I'm behind in my work."

Now that really pissed me off. I understood that his kids had to come first, but work too? So that meant I was third on his list, unless he put Monica above me, too.

"Well excuse me for interfering with your precious work, Dr. Lewis," I said and jumped up out of my chair all big and bad. I said it loud enough for the student in the hallway to hear me and I think my neck was working. David tried to grab my arm, but I flounced myself out of there and went and got my purse and my carryall from my space. It was time to go, anyway. Who did he think he was? And why was I wasting my time hotfooting behind the Negro like I'm Edith Bunker or something? I had better things to do than to be put off with a lame excuse from some old man. He could just kiss my brown butt. Twice.

When I got home I did something stupid. I let my alligator mouth write a check my ass couldn't cash. I let Eric come over to my place for a drink, thinking I was going to sleep with him to prove to myself that David could be taken or left alone. Eric was as gorgeous as ever in a tan Armani suit and sunshades. He'd lost a little bit of weight, but he was still buffed. I don't know what he was trying to prove with the shades. It was dark outside. He sat down on the sofa and looked around like he was trying to figure out if anything had changed since he'd last been here. Then he looked satisfied with what he had surveyed and loosened his tie.

"What would you like to drink?" I asked him. I had enough nerve to be playing David's and my favorite lovemaking CD. Pieces of a Dream's "Goodbye Manhattan." I knew I was wrong.

"Come on, Genie, stop frontin', baby. You know what I drink."

Now how presumptuous was that? I was two seconds from reading his behind. I took a deep breath and tried again.

"What can I get for you, D—Eric?" Oh Lord. I was flubbing my lines already and hadn't even taken one leg out of my panties yet.

"Come on, Genie. Remy's my drink. On the rocks." He looked upset that I'd forgotten. But with all that's been going on with me, who had time to remember something like that?

I went into the kitchen and fixed the drinks. I made mine a double of Sambuca and went back out to the living room and set both our drinks on coasters.

"So what have you been up to pretty?" He started massaging my leg.

"Working and living." I shrugged and took a sip of my drink.

"You been seeing anybody?" Like it was any of his business. I took another sip. And another.

"Eric, I think you know I'm not the loner type." I had an attitude, but I didn't understand why. I was the one who had initiated this.

"Then why'd you call me, Genie?" 'Cause I'm stupid, I felt like saying. 'Cause David has my nose open wider than Dionne Warwick's and it scares me to death that I can't do without him.

"I wanted to see you. Was that alright?" I hoped I sounded sincere.

"I'm glad. I've missed you, baby." He leaned over and kissed me with his Remy breath and I hated every second of it. First of all, he wasn't holding me the way David does. He didn't taste like David, and David would never grab me by the hair to pull me closer. David's techniques were more conservative and tender. I couldn't believe I could tell the difference between the touch of a man who loved me and the touch of just any old man. I was highly offended and couldn't get what I'd seen in Eric in the first place. My robe was wide open. His hands were on me and I wanted to run out of the room.

"I can't!" I stood up and closed my robe. I was almost ready to cry, guilt was beating me up so bad.

"What's wrong?" He looked so concerned that I felt kind of sorry for him.

"This isn't right, Eric. I'm sorry. You have to go."

"I don't understand." I picked up his sport jacket and handed it to him.

"I know you don't. Please just go."

"Woman, I swear, you are off your rocker or something," he said.

"I think you may have a point there. But you have to go. Bye."

I walked over and opened the door. I just wanted him to step.

I was so glad when he left. How could I have done something as childish as this? Who was I trying to fool? David is my best friend and the only man I need. I sat in the middle of the floor listening to the rest of the CD and remembering what David had done to me the last time we listened to it together. After it played all the way through, I put on some Norman Brown and just sat there on the floor, crying my eyes out because I was afraid that David would see Monica and change his mind about us. I imagined all sorts of terrible things. There she was, out with my man, probably making champagne toasts to their graduating son, while I was at home with puffy eyes, feeling sorry for myself. My pity party was interrupted by the telephone.

"Hello?" I said.

"You know I love you, don't you?" It was my baby. It was so good to hear his voice that I just melted. I was so ashamed of myself for doubting him, and I wanted to give myself a black eye for thinking another man could ever take his place. That could never happen.

"Hey," I said.

"You missing me the way I'm missing you?" He sounded all sleepy, like he does when he wakes up in the morning.

"More." I wasn't holding back.

"You wanna see me?"

"I thought you had some work to catch up on." I sounded like the baby he always made me feel like.

"The work will be here whenever I get to it. So do you wanna see me or not?"

"You know the answer to that, Doc. I'm about to get off this phone and find me something illegal to put on. Maybe light some candles."

"Maybe pull that box down from your closet?" I blushed. It still embarrassed me that he'd been snooping and had found that crazy thing. He told me he was going to blackmail me because of it one day.

"David, shut up. You know I don't need that thing."

"Mmm. Well what is it that you need?" The Negro was feeling playful tonight. I was not in the mood. All I wanted was for him to hightail it over here and give me my propers. But I played along.

"I need something only you can give me. You on your way, Doc?"

"I'm on my way, sexy." He hung up and I hurried up and got rid of any evidence that Eric had been here.

•   •   •

Me and Paulette decided to spend some chick time together on Saturday, since Robert was taking Telaysia to visit his mother and David was elbow deep in his work. Sometimes just the two of us needed to bond. Although Evelyn is a close friend too, there were some things me and Paulette kept between us.

We spent the morning shopping, and wound up getting a bunch of stuff for Telaysia and our men. Then we went over to the hairdresser's to get our nails done and Arleeta plucked our eyebrows. We were both suffering from PMS, so we bought a box of Brach's chocolate cherries and a bag of Almond Joys and rented *Steel Magnolias* and *The Way We Were*. We were definitely in weep mode. We took the movies to Paulette's house and cried our little hearts out over *The Way We Were*.

"Girl, girl, girl that was sad. Mmm. She loved that man." Paulette turned the movie off.

"I'm telling you," I said, putting another bite-sized Almond Joy in my mouth.

"Could you do it, Genie? You think you would be able to let David go like that? Just watch him walk away?"

"I don't know about that. That would be like taking a part of me away. I wouldn't be whole anymore. What about you?"

"And see Robert with some other woman? No way. I'd send him to hell first."

"I know you would. I don't understand how two people can love each other that much, and it not be enough. I don't get it."

"It happens."

"Yeah, it does. I just hope it never happens with us, you know. I swear, Paulette, it's like I'm on a constant watch just waiting for David to change his mind. I don't know how to relax into this relationship."

"After all you've been through? It's going to take some time for that and you know it. I just wish you would tell him everything." I was on my umpteenth piece of candy.

"I wish you and Tess would stop badgering me. I've made some progress, Paulette. I went to see Mama and I haven't had the dream since. I just want to feel normal, P, you know. I want to be like every other woman in love. When you fell in love with Robert, the only thing you had to tell him about your past was that you lied about your weight and you never learned to cook. That's a big jump from me telling David about things I'd rather forget. I won't risk losing him over that."

"David loves you, Genie. I see it every time I see the two of you together. That man adores the hell out of you. Now what if he was hiding something about his past, then decided to share it with you. Would you drop him for something he had no control over?"

"That's me, though, Paulette. I know how I would react. I can't say how David would react."

Paulette hit the rewind key for the tape and looked over at me.

"That's my point. You told me you thought I wouldn't be your friend anymore. That was the most ludicrous thing I've ever heard. You know you my girl and I'ma stick by you through whatever. I think you aren't giving him enough credit."

I put the rest of the candy on the table. I just wasn't ready to tell David something like this.

"Paulette, I don't want him to look at me and see me as some kind of victim. I won't have that."

"I don't see you as any victim, Genie, and neither will he. We both happen to be people who love you and care about you."

"Just put the second movie on, please. I really don't want to discuss it. I have enough to worry about, what with David's obsession with his age, and school and Monica's hang-up calls."

"Hang-up calls?"

"Yeah. For the past week I've been getting these hang-up calls at work and at home. Two and three a day."

"You tell David?"

"No. He's got enough on his mind. Hopefully she'll get tired of it sooner or later."

"It could be one of your old boyfriends. Eric or Nick."

I shook my head.

"Nope. David's old home phone number is what shows up on my caller ID. I waited a minute and star-six-nined her the other day, and her answering machine picked up."

"You leave a message?"

"No. You know me better than that. I'm not going to play those games. I just hope that eventually she'll stop. If not, I'll change my home phone number to an unlisted one, although there's nothing I can do about work."

"I say you do yourself a favor and transfer the hell out of that office, but who am I?"

"That's the same thing I've been wondering about you for years. Now will you put on the other movie, please. I'm ready to boohoo again."

I was so mixed up. It was so much easier when I could hide behind my theory and just not feel anything for anybody. There's something to be said for that lifestyle. Trying to love a man may feel like sunshine in your veins most days. But sometimes it just makes you feel bone-tired.

David

"**S**orry I'm a bit late. Have you ordered yet?" I sat in the chair across from Monica at Nell's Grille in Annapolis. We had decided to meet here for lunch. It was a small, quiet spot that we'd stumbled upon when Monica had asked me to take her to some outlet mall or other once. I hated lying to Genie about having to catch up on work, but I knew that telling her the truth meant another fight. I wasn't going to fight with her about seeing my own wife just to clear up some things.

Monica looked good in a red and white dress I'd bought her for our last anniversary. Red was a good color for her. She looked calm and well rested. Like she was getting herself together. She was even laughing like her old self at Devin's graduation celebration the other night. It felt good to see her like this.

"No, I only arrived a few minutes ago, myself," she said.

I signaled for a waiter and we ordered drinks.

"How's things?" I asked. She shrugged, like things could go either way. Then she reached out and covered my hand. Rubbed the back of it with her fingers and looked at me like she missed me. It made me feel sad.

"How are things with you, David? You getting along alright without us?" She was smiling slightly as if she was trying too hard.

"I'm making it. I'm supposed to be spending some time with Devin next weekend. I wish Mark would come around."

"You have to give him time, David. He's having a hard time with all of this. I think he never realized how much he counted on you." She sounded like she was talking about herself more than Mark. This was so hard. I felt like in saving my life I'd ruined three others. I couldn't work it out in my head how to go about living with that.

"I know, Monnie. I understand." The drinks came and I took a long sip of my Coke after we ordered.

"So how are we going to deal with Devin's departure?"

"I think what I'll do is meet you guys down there. And then about Mark's birthday, I'll be in Africa then. I asked him if he'd celebrate with me beforehand, but he didn't go for that idea. I just wish I knew how to reach him."

"I'm working on it. He's become so withdrawn lately. I try not to let him see me upset, if that helps."

"Thanks, Monnie." I touched her cheek. I felt like a real bastard for thinking that she didn't care about me. Here I'd walked out, and she was still making sure the kids saw me in a positive light.

After my grilled lobster salad and her chicken breast arrived, we did our taste tests and dug in.

"How's work?" I asked, surprised that she hadn't brought it up.

"Same. Busy," was all she had to say.

"I told you I got the grant, didn't I?" I was groping for some sort of real conversation. Not the glossed up crap we'd been tossing at each other just trying to be polite.

"Yeah. You told me at the party the other day. David, what's she like?"

I think my heart stopped beating, because I didn't feel alive. I couldn't say anything. The lobster in my throat felt like it was expanding. Monica was looking at her food as if she was having a conversation with it.

"You can't tell me anymore that she doesn't exist, because I've seen you two together. Don't be angry with me for doing some detective work. I couldn't stand not knowing for sure. She's very pretty. Very young, David. I can see now why you left. I wondered what she's like, though, because she doesn't really look like the type you'd be interested in. Is she good to you?" She was looking as if she wanted to die, and I knew I did.

I was speechless for a minute. I took in some more soda.

"Monica, I don't want to have this conversation."

"David, come on," she said, "we're adults here. You didn't think I would be so stupid as to believe that there was no motivating factor to get you to walk out on our marriage, did you?"

"Monica, don't." I could see she was close to tears, and I didn't want a scene. More than that, I didn't want to see that pained look in her eyes.

"I mean, the two of you were walking along, holding hands. You looked so happy with her, David. I know it was all me. I take responsibility for what's happened to us. I haven't made you feel that way in a hell of a long time. I know I made some very dear mistakes that I wish to God I could take back." The tears came now and I had to look away. I felt a throbbing in my heart.

"But, she's nothing more than a girl. She's got to be half your age if a day. Do you love her, David?" Everything in me wanted to lie to Monica. But I couldn't anymore. I'd done enough lying to her. It was time to put all my cards on the table, and maybe then we could both make our fresh starts without any lingering skeletons.

"Yes." I said finally, hoping she wouldn't make a scene. She took it well, though. I guess she already knew what I'd say.

"You planning to marry this girl?"

"Our failed marriage has nothing to do with her, Monica. You know that."

"And you don't feel anything for me anymore?" She knew how to push my buttons.

"I'll always feel something for you, Monica. Always."

"I want us to try again." She wiped her eyes with her napkin." I want to make things right between us."

"I don't think that can happen, babe."

"David, don't say that."

"It's the truth, Monnie."

"Why are you throwing twenty-six years of our lives away on a girl who's nothing more than an old man's folly. Do you know how ridiculous you look driving around in that red sexmobile of yours with her? I can't believe you have succumbed to a case of mid-life crisis. Soon as someone her own age catches her eye she'll be gone. And then who will you turn to? You'll turn to me, David, that's who. I've always been there and I'll be there picking up the pieces when this thing is over."

She was pissing me off royally. Mainly because she was sitting there speaking my thoughts as if I'd given her cue cards. I had to say something. I had to fight my way out of her attack.

"You were never there, Monnie. I was always alone. Waiting for you. Now you want to make it work, but I can't do that. Genie loves me," I said. Monica looked a bit afraid.

"Oh. Yeah. Well, so do I. And a lot longer than that little girl playing dress-up. We have a history together, and you know it." She calmed down a little and gave me a look I'm sure she's used during a multitude of presentations.

"Look, David. I'm not going to beg you to come back. I have enough pride left not to. But think about it. Think about what we meant to each other. I know now that I need to make changes in my life, and I know that I don't want to face the rest of my life without you. We have children together, David. A home."

I couldn't listen to any more of this. She was making me confused as hell. I hated feeling suffocated like this, so I said, "Okay, Monica. I've had enough of this," and threw my napkin down next to my plate.

I stood up, flipped open my wallet and tossed several bills on the table. Then I walked out of there feeling like shit. If I didn't know anything else in the world, I knew Genie loved me and we were going to make it. I got into my car and went to find Genie to prove to Monica that she was dead wrong.

•   •   •

I got to Genie's house in a panic, but she wasn't at home. I remembered she told me she was going shopping. I stopped by the mall and picked up a few things, then drove back to my place and got started on some work. After a few hours of that I left Genie a message, then turned on the TV and listened to the campaign updates. It looked to me like

Clinton was going to get the job done again. He had a pretty good lead over Dole. I ate a can of mushroom soup and some wheat toast and listened to the neighbors across the hall have another of their knock-down, drag-out fights. Those were the angriest two people I've ever come across. The man was a big, blustery fella from the Bronx. His wife was a big-haired woman who reminded me of one of those Mafia wives.

I was lonely. I lay in my bed, listening to all that racket next door, thinking about all the changes in my life. It was such a big gamble to take for a woman I'd only known five months. How did Monica know me so well? How could she tell that I was scared to death of this new love and that I felt like I didn't know my elbow from my asshole anymore? How the hell did she find out about Genie, anyway? But then again, I guess it would have been easy enough. Outside of the office, Genie and I had been pretty careless with our relationship. But it felt good being out in the open. Thank God Monica's not a petty woman. She could burn my ass at the stake if she wanted to.

The racket across the hall stopped and I wished it hadn't. Sometimes the loneliness seemed to cover me like a shroud and made me miss having my family. I missed knowing that at some point there would be noise in my own house. I had a serious need to make sure Genie really felt the way I did, because there was no way I could live my life alone. I reached over to the night table for the telephone, but heard somebody at my door, so I got up and put on a shirt and answered it.

"Hi. I got your message." My lips met Genie's like mine were the desert and hers were a steady rain. I hugged her until she tried to move away. It was like what happened with Monica earlier had been erased.

"Where've you been, babe?"

"I told you where I'd be. With Paulette. We had a time. And of course I had to get something for my favorite person in the world." She had a big white Penney's bag. Her hair was windblown and she looked happy to be with me. I noticed something about her was different.

"You cut your hair?"

"No. I got Arleeta to pluck my brows. You like?"

"Yeah, I guess."

How was I supposed to know? I shrugged and went in the kitchen to get me some water. She followed behind me. She loved me, alright.

"Doc, you didn't even act like you want to see what's in the bag."

"I'm sure it's nice, babe. Everything you get me is nice. What is it?" I sat on the stool at the breakfast bar.

She opened the bag and pulled out some trousers that I didn't like the color of, but the shorts and two shirts were nice. I was smart enough to know not to comment on the pants.

"These look good, babe. Thanks."

"I'm trying to give you a hint."

"I missed it. What was it?"

"Well, I was thinking . . ."

"About?"

"Well. You'll be gone the rest of June and part of July. I know when you get back you'll be doing some heavy writing. Then you'll be gone for a week in August to take your son to Atlanta."

"Yeah. I'm following you so far." I crunched a piece of ice.

"I thought somewhere in between we could take another mini vacation. Nowhere far. Just maybe somewhere like Luray Caverns. That's what I was trying to get at. So what do you think?"

"Whatever you want to do is fine, babe. Listen, come down the hall a minute."

"Why?"

"Just come on. I have something I want to show you," I said.

I took a small box out from under the pillow and tossed it. The smile I received was priceless.

"What is this?" she asked. But she had already reached for it on the bed and was opening the box. Her eyes got big as saucers.

"David?"

"You like it?"

She got a funny look on her face when she put it on.

"You don't like it," I said.

She shook her head and said, "No, it's not that. It's beautiful." She was holding the ring up to the sunlight coming through the window. Then she took it off her finger again.

"So what's wrong?" I sat up then. I didn't know what to think, from the way she was looking. She came over to where I was sitting on the bed.

"What's this mean?"

"What do you mean?"

"I mean, what's the ring mean, baby? Or does it not mean anything?"

I pulled her down on my lap.

"It means," I said, "that I love you. That I want to be the only man in your life for the rest of my life. Is that what you want?" I almost wanted to hold my breath waiting for her to answer me.

"You know that's what I want."

I'm sure I looked relieved.

"Good. Then this ring is my promise to you. That I'll always love you. I'll always be here for you. I'll never hurt you, Genie, and I wanted you to know that."

She didn't say a word, but she kissed me. We both slipped the ring on her finger. It was her favorite. A garnet. Two carats. Surrounded by diamonds. Cost me a hell of a lot, but her reaction was so worth it. We didn't even make love. That's what I genuinely liked about the woman. Sometimes me and Genie could just enjoy each other's company. We just held each other and talked until we fell asleep. It was really special. Monica had it all wrong. Genie would never leave me for another man. Neither of us could ever walk away from a love so deep.

Genie

"**D**amn y'all!" I had enough nerve to be standing right in front of the Jesus bookstore with my bad mouth.

"What?" Paulette and Evelyn both wondered what my problem was. I was so frustrated with those two. We had done champagne brunch at the Market Inn and then come to the mall to buy our books for the book club we had started with some other women from the neighborhood.

"I've been hanging out with you guys all morning, talking with my hands so much you could swear I know sign language, and neither one of you have noticed my ring!"

Paulette screwed her face up at me. Her new short haircut made her look a lot like Toni Braxton. "Your what?" she said. I flung out my hand.

"Girl, that's beautiful. Look, Ev." She bumped Evelyn's arm. "Where'd this come from?"

"I got it from Elvis. Paulette, you know good and well David gave it to me."

"Excuse the hell out of me," Paulette said.

Evelyn pulled my hand closer like she wanted to take my arm off.

"David? This thing is bad, girl. That man loves him some Genie," Evelyn said to Paulette.

"Now, I know the Negro did not propose when he isn't even divorced yet, G. That is tacky." Paulette looked like she had an attitude.

"No, dummy. This ring is a promise, not a proposal. It just means that when he is completely unhitched, we will be taking that next step, which is to get engaged." She could tell she had made me mad, and she put a hand on my arm.

"Don't get me wrong, Genie," she said, "I like David a lot. I think he's really been good for you. Matter of fact, I think you're good for each other. Does this ring make you feel any more relaxed about him?"

We walked on until we got to B. Dalton.

"Much more now, I think. I know it's brought us even closer, if you can believe that. Look, I'm going over to check out the New Age section first," I said, walking away from them. "I want to see if they have Linda Goodman's *Love Signs,* so I can see what she says about me and David. Grab me a copy of the book too, Ev."

"Okay."

"Thanks."

I walked off and perused the shelves of books but couldn't find what I was looking for. So I went to find Paulette and Evelyn, but stopped dead in my tracks, because right in my path was none other than Monica, and she was headed right for me. I was sure it was her from the pictures I'd seen in David's office. Ever since the calls started I figured she might try to approach me sooner or later. Part of me wanted to make a break for it, because being anywhere near the woman scared the shit out of me. I was okay when I didn't have to think of her as a real person. I preferred that. But another part of me was secure with my relationship now and wouldn't have walked away for anything. I had wondered a lot what kind of woman she was, because David didn't like to discuss her.

We sized each other up. I was glad my hair was done and so was my makeup. I had on a short mint-green button-up sundress and some low-heeled green sandals. Even though I looked good enough for a confrontation like this, so did she. Her hair was cut short in front, but long in back, and looked dyed, it was so ebony. She was made up and wore several beautiful rings. Tasteful gold jewelry was around her neck. She was heavy, but wore it well in a slimming black pant outfit. The woman definitely had an air about her. That graceful, aged elegance that reminded me of a woman who knew who she was and how to take care of her business. Shit. She was the kind of woman I wanted to be, and for a minute, I wondered if David was crazy to have traded her in for me. It was like trading in a Q45 for a damn Nova. But then I remembered that she hadn't treated him well when she'd had him. That was her fault, not mine.

"Genie? Am I right?" Her voice was like silk against skin, it was so smooth. She knew damn well she was right.

I nodded my head yes like a child and wanted to pinch myself for not speaking up.

"And you must be Monica," I said, after I remembered I could talk and had been doing so for years.

"Yes, I am." She had the nerve to reach out and shake my hand. Then she put a manicured finger to her cheek and said, "You're even younger than I imagined. You must be, what, nineteen, twenty?"

"Neither," I said, feeling uncomfortable. I didn't know what to do with my hands, so I kind of awkwardly held them together and fiddled with my ring. She gave me a smile that told me she thought I was ridiculous.

"Doesn't matter. David must really be feeling his oats running around with a hot little number like you."

I just looked at her, not knowing what to say.

"I guess you know we have two children," she continued. "Two sons."

"Yes, I know that." I wished Paulette and her big mouth would appear to help me out here.

"I've been wanting to have a chat with you," Monica said. "I know this isn't the most convenient place, but I noticed you from the next aisle and couldn't resist." That sounded farfetched to me. It was more like she'd followed me from David's apartment this morning and had waited for an opportunity to catch me alone.

"What do we have to talk about, Monica?" I know I sounded like I wanted her out of my face, because I did. This woman was for David to deal with, not me. She gave a quick laugh and said, "My husband, of course. Listen, is it possible that we can take a walk to the coffee shop and sit for a minute?"

I wasn't going anywhere with her. How could she be so proper about this thing?

"That's not a good idea. I think you should talk to David if there's anything you need to discuss."

"Oh, sweetie," she said, "this involves David, but it's about me and you. Two women. You see, I think we understand each other, Genie, at least I understand your type. A woman like you sees a man like David, a man of stature, some security, and you latch onto him because you want somebody to take care of you. And it's easy, since you're so fresh and new. You have a pretty face and some young leg to give up. But I just wanted to tell you that it won't last. You've confused him, yes. But you don't have him, Genie. He's just living out his second childhood for a brief time because he's afraid of getting older. That's it. Once he remembers how important family is, how important the investment he's made in our marriage is, he's going to leave you high and dry in a heartbeat without looking back. Now let me tell you who I am, in case you don't know."

She put a finger to her chest and said, "I'm fifty-two years old, darling, and I've been a married woman longer than you've been alive. I've loved that man and put up with that man and had babies for that man, so I hope you don't think I'll just sit idly by and watch you destroy what David and I have built, because I won't. I won't."

That scared me. I didn't want David to have to go through some ugly fight with this woman. His kids wouldn't survive it and neither would he. I would walk away from him before I would allow him to suffer that.

"You told David you wouldn't contest a divorce," I said.

"And I wouldn't. If things went that far. But this won't go that far. Like I said, I have a history with that man. You have no idea what it means to commit to someone. To love someone. It means much more than laying on your back for an evening. You mark my words, little one. He'll remember what's important."

As I listened to Monica talk, I thought about the things David had told me. I thought about his surety about us. I could see the desperation in Monica's eyes and I knew I didn't need to defend myself to her. Her marriage was over before David ever knew me. Looking at her, I realized she wasn't really a Q45 at all. She was just someone who hadn't known what she had until it was gone. And so I looked at her and said, cool as a cucumber, "Monica, you're the one who drove him out of your life. Don't try to make me live with your mistakes. They're your problem." Then I walked away like Alexis fucking Carrington would have done, and went to find Paulette and Evelyn. I caught up with them checking out the children's books two aisles away. Although Monica's words bothered me, I was determined not to let that scene overpower me. David was definitely teaching me some shit. And I was proving myself to be a pretty apt pupil.

• • •

Those moody blues stuck to me like Krazy Glue the rest of the afternoon. David was leaving in two days. We had to say our goodbyes tonight, though, because in the morning he was picking up his sons to spend some quality time with them before he had to go. They were going to see him off at the airport, too, and I bet anything that Monica would be there with bells on. Not so long ago I believed that the only things you could constantly trust are change and God. But then, here comes David, and I've had to reevaluate that. We've built up a trust between us that makes me know that he is committed to what we share. It was best for me to stay out of it and let David deal with Monica in his own way. No matter how I felt about it.

While I was driving back from the mall it started to rain steadily, but the sun was still out. The devil was beating his wife. I felt like he'd beaten me up a little, too, because I was still recuperating from my run-in with Monica. What's more, I didn't know how I was going to let David go off to Africa without making an ass of myself. I stopped off at the post office to drop off some letters and ran over to Bath and Bodyworks to get some more cherry vanilla scented candles, mango body cream and some bath salts. I had already gotten something delicious from Vicki's Secret while I was at the mall. David was the kind of man who truly appreciated all my little extra touches.

I wanted tonight to be special so I had reserved a suite at Loew's at L'enfant Plaza. David didn't know a thing about it. He thought he was meeting me at my house and we were going to dinner. But Simon had a manager friend down at Loew's who got me a discount rate for the suite. What I had done was left a keycard for our suite in David's glovebox when I left his apartment this morning. There was a card taped just inside my front door at home for him, giving him step-by-step directions on how to find me and where to find the keycard.

I drove downtown in light traffic and almost got a ticket because I was speeding and whipping around cars, trying to make sure Monica wasn't following me. I was relieved I didn't see her anywhere. When I got to the hotel I checked in and went up to the suite. It was so lovely. It reminded me of the decor in the beach house we'd rented in North Carolina, with its large oak furnishings and high ceilings. The sitting room was the size of a double bedroom with a wet bar and a television hidden inside one of those cabinets. I looked at my watch. It was almost six.

I took off my sandals, and my bare feet hit the most beautiful carpet imaginable. It was like walking on clouds going down the little hallway to the bedroom, where a huge four-poster bed was draped with cream panels. I opened the set of heavy drapes at the window to look out a second and let the sun in. Then I went to work on preparing for this night that would give me and David both something to hold onto when we lay in our empty beds missing each other, thousands of miles apart.

I unpacked my bags first, then laid David's midnight-blue silk pajamas out in the bathroom along with my Vicki Secret gown, and I set the candles in long crystal stems shaped like wings, along the edge of the Jacuzzi tub. When I pulled back the covers on our bed after stripping the six red roses I'd bought, I sprinkled petals on the sheets. The rest I set in the bathroom so I could sprinkle them in our bath. There was a knock at the door. That would be dinner. I grabbed my purse and found my wallet inside and opened the door.

A gentleman wheeled in the tray of duck l'orange, wild rice salad, rosemary potatoes, asparagus tips, assorted breads, Brie and Melba toast I'd ordered, and set everything up to the side of the intimate table in the sitting room that had already been set for dinner. He set a silver bowl of ripe strawberries on the table and put the wine to chill on ice. I tipped him, and when he left I put the remaining candle in the middle of the table. Then I changed out of my sundress and took a quick shower. I put on a silk, champagne-colored lounging gown with Elizabethan sleeves and touched up my makeup. I figured David would be here any minute, so I lit the candle and put some Michael Franks on in my portable CD player, which I'd set up in a corner of the room.

When I heard the door about ten minutes later I was sitting on the sofa trying my best to watch a dirty movie. I clicked it off and jumped up, trying to look innocent.

"Babe, what's all this?" David came in looking around and smiling.

I threw back my arms and said, "Surprise."

"You did all this for me?"

"I did all this for us." I walked into his embrace and planted chocolate spice lipstick kisses down the side of his face.

"You are the sweetest woman. Nobody's ever done anything like this for me."

I planned on keeping him. Monica told me I didn't know what

commitment is. I don't think she knows that you have to work at a relationship in order to keep it alive. That includes romance. I decided that little episode between us this afternoon wasn't worth telling David about.

We kissed for a long time, and when it looked like it was going to turn into something more, I pulled away.

"Baby," I said. "Come on. I have all this beautiful food here. Why don't we eat before it gets cold."

That didn't seem to register. He pulled me close again and started kissing my nipples. His hands were cupping my ass to pull me against him and I was starting to feel like I couldn't keep my balance.

"No, David," I said. It was a weak protest.

"Oh, Genie. I want you. Just a quickie, babe. The food isn't going anywhere."

"No, David. Come on. Not like this. I have everything planned out." I felt like he had several hands, the way I had to keep pushing him off me. He relented. Somehow I fixed my gown and led him over to the table. He poured us both some wine.

"Where'd you come up with this idea?"

I shrugged.

"I don't know. You like?"

He nodded and lifted his glass to his lips. He was looking at me over the rim like he was sad.

"Something wrong, David?" I put my hand out for his and he held it.

"It just hit me on the drive over here that I'm not going to see you for a while, that's all. I'm going to miss you, you know."

I moved out of my chair and sat in his lap. His arms were around me tight.

"I know, baby. Me too. What am I going to do without you, huh?" I looked into those eyes and already I was tearing up.

"Hey," he said, "none of that. You promised."

I sighed hard and put my head on his chest. "I know," I said.

"I'll be back before we both know it."

"Yeah, yeah. At least you'll be busy doing stuff. I won't be doing anything but sitting around missing you."

"No you won't. You'll be working and doing all the things you do while I'm here."

"But David, I'm reminded of you everywhere. At work I'll have to see your office all dark and deserted. And at home, I'll have to sleep in my bed by myself. And then when I go over to your place for your mail and to water the plants, it'll feel strange not to have you there with me, chasing me around the house and getting on my nerves."

He started tickling me, and I almost fell off his lap.

"What do you mean, getting on your nerves." I turned to straddle him and we were laughing with our foreheads touching. The man had a gift for making me happy.

"I didn't mean anything by it. I'm sure I bug you too." This time I started kissing him and putting my hands where I had no business putting them.

"Woman, don't start anything you can't finish. I thought you told me you had this night all planned out."

"Don't you know that the best plans are the flexible ones," I said, unbuttoning his shirt.

"Oh well, in that case. . . ." He moved me off his lap, then picked me up in his arms like I weighed no more than a feather. I grabbed the wine bottle, and he took me into the bedroom, then set me on my feet in front of him, and my arms went up around his neck. We kissed some more and I rubbed my cheek against the stubble on his face. I don't know how we got undressed. David always made me forget to pay attention to what was going on. I was limp and lazy in his arms.

"I don't want you to go," I said, when we lay beneath the fragrant sheets together. Down the hall on the CD player I could hear Billie Holiday carrying on something terrible and threatening to jump in the river 'cause her man was gone. The languid music against her bare voice hit a chord in me, and I couldn't help but let loose some warm tears in response.

"Sweetheart," David said, kissing my tears, "you have to do better than this. This is our last night together for a while. I don't want to be on the plane thinking about you looking sad."

He was right. I wanted this night to be something that would take us both through the next few weeks, so I tried to smile for him. He palmed my breasts and kissed me lightly on the nose.

"I love you, Genie."

"I love you." His hands were working some serious magic between my legs. I had a sudden urge to get to know his body as well as he did. I kissed his eyelids. I ran my hand along his chest, then dotted butterfly kisses across his collarbone.

"I want to kiss you all over, honey," I said. He closed his eyes and I reached for the wine to add some flavor to that caramel skin of his.

There are places on the human body that are usually overlooked during lovemaking. I learned that from Eric. Just beneath the chin. The tips of ears. Elbows. The backs of knees. Inside of wrists. Achilles heel. Arch of the foot. Slowly, I explored every piece of David like I had never done. For the first time I tasted all of him. I'd never done that to any man. The oral thing. But I wanted that bond with David. That closeness. I wanted him to know that I would never belong to any other man, but only to him. At least I hoped he understood that that's what I was saying. I thought again about what Monica had said. No, it wasn't about lying on your back for an evening. What thing worth having could ever be so trivial as that? The sexual part was just my physical expression of something so monumental that it couldn't be explained in words. It was ineffable. All I could do was try my best to show the man that knowing him has enriched my life beyond measure.

David slept after we made love, but I went down the hall and ate some of that expensive cold-ass food I'd had the nerve to ignore earlier. My body felt well loved and brand new. Refreshed. I put in a John Tesh CD and took a long bath in the Jacuzzi. With David asleep or not, I was going to wear my eighty-dollar Vicki Secret gown. It was so pretty. It was a simple straight-cut with spaghetti straps and slits up both sides. It fell low in the front, but lower still in the back. It was see-through cream like the panels above the bed, but had handsewn flowers on it.

I lay back down beside David and rubbed his hair and messed with him to see if he was really asleep. He didn't budge except to fan me away with this irritated look on his face that made me smile. He had the most gorgeous lashes for a man. I thought about the pictures he'd shown me of himself as a little boy. Holding up his first fish. Standing on stage at a school play. Posing with his classmates on risers, looking serious and sure of himself even then. Little curly headed midget with big eyes. I lay there in bed and watched him sleep until I could barely keep my eyes open. There's a song that says don't say goodbye, say goodnight. My heart was so heavy about David's leaving that I think goodnight was the best I could do.

Genie

13

I'm going to tell David everything when he comes back from Africa. The whole ugly story. I've made up my mind. I think. Yes, we've only been together for five months. Yes, I'm scared shitless about telling him. But Tess is right. I have to make peace with my past if I'm going to have a solid future with him. Visiting Mama's grave had a lot to do with it. Seeing that place again, facing down that part of the pain in my life. . . . I know I have the courage to go a step further and show the man I love that I trust him. I guess the ring has a little to do with my decision too. I figure him giving it to me is a sign that he plans to stick around.

Paulette gave me some literature to read that she'd gotten from her mother-in-law that talked about how to tell loved ones that you've been sexually abused. I kept praying every night that I could find enough strength to talk to David about it. At least he'd be able to understand me better. More than that, I just hope I can live up to the woman he sees when he looks at me once he knows. There's nothing as important to me as that.

It was so hard being without my baby the first week that all I did was work and eat like a horse and cry and watch TV. I missed that boy to pieces. I sat beside the phone trying to will it to ring, knowing that

David had warned me that he wouldn't be able to call but once or twice while he was away. Then every morning when I got to work I would run and turn on the computer to check my E-mail. He told me he was going to try and get access. I guess not.

I got mad and jealous when I didn't hear from him by that next Wednesday. I kept thinking that maybe some beautiful African woman with hips and a headwrap had thrown some serious motherland booty on him. I was about ready to jump on a plane to go check things out, but finally Evelyn and Paulette read me my rights. You have a right to have a man, they said, but you also have a right to get a life. I was turning into one of those inert manless women that I hate, but I couldn't seem to stop obsessing for the life of me. Thank God he called on Friday before I bought myself that ticket.

"Babe!" he said, sounding like he was calling me from an airstrip, there was so much static in the phone. There was a delay, too.

"Hi, honey!" I yelled back. I was grinning like a chipmunk.

"What're you doing?" he asked.

I looked over at the clock. It was two A.M.

I said, "David, it's two here, I'm in bed. How's everything going?"

"Better than expected. The university's a wealth of information. They have an Institute of African Studies. I really wish you were here with me. I miss you."

"Me too. You been eating well?"

"Not really, babe. I've been too busy running."

"Honey, make sure you eat. And don't stay out in that sun too long. And try to get your rest."

"I will. Babe, you should see Michael's sister's village. I wasn't expecting it to be so modern."

"What's it look like over there, Doc?"

"Flat land. Not many trees. There's not an abundance of vegetation. The air's tropical. And the people, Genie—everybody's so warm and friendly to me. I'm going tomorrow for a tour of the castles and to some open-air market to find something nice for you and the kids."

"Oh, David. I miss you so bad."

"What you been doing? You remember to water my plants and take care of my mail?"

"'Course. I haven't been doing too much, baby. And you haven't gotten any mail that needs immediate attention. Although Dr. Winthrop wants a fax number for you, so he can get your approval on the changes for your book chapter. He said they're somewhat minor."

"Oh. Well, I'll try to call him sometime over the next few days. Go over to my house and send him an E-mail to that effect for me, would you?"

"Okay. David, it's so good to hear your voice."

"It's good to hear yours too. How's my kitty-cat doing?"

I started laughing and said, "I don't know, why don't you ask it and give it a big kiss." I put the phone down by my pride and joy.

"Did you talk to it?" I asked him.

"Yeah. I told it to stay warm for me. Listen, I can't stay on, babe, but I'll try to call you next week. I love you."

"Mkay, me too," I said, feeling the miles of distance of land and ocean between us.

We hung up and I hugged myself. I was wearing one of David's favorite shirts and it smelled just like him. I fell asleep with a permanent smile on my face.

• • •

I was standing in the kitchen about to fix myself some coffee and scramble an egg when the phone rang the next morning.

"Genie, I have something to tell you . . ."

"What?" I asked. It was Paulette.

"Have you read the paper yet?"

"Not yet. Why?"

"Edward's dead, Genie."

I dropped the phone and heard it bang hard against the floor. I heard some video playing on BET down the hall. But I was mute. And for a minute I was paralyzed. For so long I'd wished he were dead so I could forget, just like he'd never existed. I'd prayed a lifetime to be normal. I'd prayed that it would all go away. *Jesus, please just make it go away.*

"Genie?"

I could hear Paulette screaming my name. It snapped me back a little. I picked up the phone, but I got sick in the kitchen sink. I retched until I dry-heaved for a minute. Sweating and shaking, I turned on the water to rinse my mouth out while I held onto the edge of the sink. Once I finished, I wiped my mouth on the sleeve of David's shirt and sat on the floor with my knees up and my head down. I could see Marilyn's lips curled around her intense anger. I could see the knife and Edward looking afraid for a change. And me thinking how small and powerless he was all the time. And then Marilyn telling him, "I'll see you in hell, muthafucka! In hell!" That's where he was now. Finally. I was so glad he was dead, but then I still missed the other him, buying me a Slim Jim and a Cherry Smash and telling me I was his favorite girl. "Thanks, Daddy. Thanks, Daddy." I wanted to scream aloud. I wanted to be held and wished David was here. I gripped the receiver and started to cry.

"Paulette. How do you know this?" I whispered it. I was almost scared she would tell me it was a lie.

"That's why I asked you if you'd read your paper. It's in this morning's obits, G. There's a—"

I dropped the phone and ran to the front door, unlocked it and jerked it open. I picked my newspaper out of the bushes and tore through the paper until I found it. I didn't know how to feel. He was fifty-six. Only four years older than my David. I knew that with that throat cancer he must have suffered hard like Uncle Eugene did. He must have suffered like I did. I kept thinking about one thing. Water seeks its own level. I sat on the sofa and read what was written about him, and when I got down to the part that says so and so is survived by, it said a wife, Eileen Gatlin, and one son. I wondered what my brother's name was. I wondered if this woman Eileen knew anything about us.

Paulette came by my house and I asked her to run over to the 7-Eleven for two more newspapers for me. When she returned, I clipped the obituary notice out of both papers and put them in the mail to Marilyn and Tess. Then Paulette held my hand while I let loose and cried a river for me, Marilyn and Tess. For Mama too. Then I said a thank you prayer to God because I looked at how much good had come into my life when David came along.

"You feeling any better?" I had washed my hair and taken a long, hot bath to soak out all my pains. Paulette was feeding Porgy and Bess.

"Yes. I think I should tell David everything when he gets back here, Paulette. I have to."

"Good. I'm glad. You know I got your back every step of the way, don't you?"

"If I don't know anything else, I know that much." I brushed my wet hair and parted it so I could put it in french braids and let it air dry.

"You sure you're alright, Genie? You wanna talk to Tess or maybe . . . I don't know. You alright?"

"I'm fine. Now. At least, I will be."

"Well, how do you feel about it, sweetie?"

"Paulette, I'm glad he's dead; but at the same time, I realized just a few minutes ago that I don't have parents anymore. And I question what type of person I am to be glad that someone's dead, because that's not right. But at the same time, he got everything he deserved. It's too confusing to think about. Matter of fact, I just don't want to have to think about it anymore for a while. My brain's tired. I'm going to take a long nap. I've gotta go in for a checkup this afternoon and get my birth-control prescription refilled. Don't worry, Paulette, you can go on home. I'm okay now." She didn't look so sure.

"Well, you know where to find me," she said.

"Yes, I do."

"I love you, Genie."

"I know. I love you too," I told her.

I shut the door behind her. I needed a drink big time. I poured myself a nice tall glass of Sambuca. When I took a sip, I realized I didn't really want it after all. I poured it out and put the bottle back in the cabinet.

Sunday I went to church and prayed for Edward's soul. I don't know why I did, but I think God was proud of me for it. It's like ever since David came into my life, I've been on this continual upward climb. The dreams are gone. I don't cry like I used to. I feel like I'm learning to really live. David must be my guardian angel.

Later, after church, everybody came to my house for dinner. Paulette and Robert, who was speaking to me again, and Evelyn and Simon. As much as I love my godchildren, no kids were allowed. I fixed corn-bread-stuffed Cornish hens, brandied peaches, steamed carrots and cauliflower, and whipped potatoes. I set the table with Mama's thirty-year-old china. I needed to entertain like this. It was good for me.

When we all got settled around the table with dinner we plunged into one of our roundtable discussion. We hadn't gotten together like this in a long time and it felt good. I made a mental note to have another one when David came back home.

"Now I believe," Robert was saying, "that you can't help who you fall in love with. It's fate. Kismet and all that." He finished off his potatoes and took a quick sip of wine.

"Come on, Rob," Evelyn shot back, "Kismet is not why black men of status like Clarence Thomas, Barry Bonds and, need I say, O. J. Simpson have made the crossover to white women. I don't buy that."

"What do you think it is, then, Evelyn? I know I fell for you when I wasn't even looking for a woman, and it wouldn't have mattered to me what race you are, so how can you say they didn't just meet women that they felt they could make a life with?" Simon asked.

I chimed in then. "I'll tell you why." I dabbed my lips with my napkin, then poured myself a second glass of ice water. "See, most of the visible scars of slavery have disappeared, but that slave mentality is alive and kicking." I tapped the side of my head. "It's still the notion of Miss Ann being viewed as the white man's pride. She represents all that's good and pure and sacred. I believe black men think that if they can have a piece of her, they're not only trying to prove that they're acceptable as humans, but they're also giving the white man the finger for all the abuse and the shit black women went through back in the day. But what pisses me off is that you black men don't seem to see that you're giving the black woman the finger too."

"I concede to your ideas on the slave mentality," Robert said, "but I don't share your opinion on what motivates a black man to choose white. I agree with Simon on that issue. Like I said, I don't think we choose who we love. We have control over what actions we take once we love, but I don't think Clarence Thomas—and I hate using that poor excuse as an example—had as much choice about falling in love as anyone does."

"Excuse my Italian, but you guys are full of shit," Paulette said. "I'm with Genie and Evelyn. I think the only thing a black man loves about a white woman is what she represents. That's the attraction. Y'all know it's true. I'll bet these are men whose self-esteem levels are questionable." Evelyn and I nodded.

"Okay, fine, Paulette. But baby, lemme ask you this," Simon said, turning to Evelyn. "Why is it that when you see a black woman with a white man, you don't have the same hateful reaction?"

We all got very vocal on that one.

"Simon, first of all," Evelyn responded, "I don't have a hateful reaction. Angry, I admit to, but not hateful. There are too few good, available, straight, able-to-commit brothers out here for us to lose one-to-whitey. If a black woman chooses white I don't like it. It's a spit in the eye for every slave woman ever raped by her master. But a black man is worse, because he's the target. The Tuskeegee Experiment is one example. That's why I get so mad at black men."

"And I get mad at black women for being so judgmental. If the black man is guilty of getting a white woman to feel validated, then women in general are guilty of conniving to get a man for the same reason."

"Careful, Simon," Paulette said, "them's fighting words." She waved her butter knife in his direction like she was going to do something to him with it.

"I don't believe you, Simon. Just when I think you've gotten those idiotic opinions out of your skull, you come up with something else." Evelyn was pissed, and Simon looked very uncomfortable. It looked like he might be sleeping on the couch tonight, so I thought I'd rescue him.

"I didn't tell you guys I finally heard from David, did I?"

Paulette opened her big mouth up and said, "You mean you don't remember calling me at 2:30 in the morning just to tell me that the other morning?"

I glared at her. Sometimes Paulette should be seen and not heard.

"How is David over there?" I think Simon was relieved as quickly as he took up this conversation.

"He's good. He sounded good. And tired. We didn't talk very long, but he told me how nice everybody was being to him and that where he was staying was very modern."

"Where is he staying?" This came from Robert.

"With some extended family of a doctoral student of one of the professors. I can't wait till he comes home."

"How long's he been gone?"

"It'll be three weeks Friday. Then he'll be home the following Monday."

"Mmhmm," Paulette said, "and we won't see you till Doomsday, will we?"

"Sure won't," I told her laughing.

After we had cappuccino and pound cake, we played Uno for two hours. Tess had left a message on my machine, so I called her back after everybody left and we ran up a steep phone bill talking about Edward and the brother we never knew we had. It was strange having a sibling out there who I didn't know. But Tess and I agreed that we didn't want to know him. I'm not sure what her reasons were for not wanting to look him up; she didn't say. But for me, I only wanted to be at peace. To live in peace.

We had our book club meeting at Evelyn's house the night before David was due back home. I was glad, because I was so impatient that I needed something constructive to do. David hadn't called me again, and I was kind of upset. The next morning when I woke up I meditated for twenty minutes then got up and pressed my clothes for work. I squeezed myself some juice and ate some leftover orange danish from last night's dinner, then I showered and dressed. I almost burned my eye out trying to curl my hair with the curling iron. Then, when I put on my pantyhose, I discovered a hole in them and had to put some nail polish on the hole to keep it from getting any bigger.

My car was in the shop because it needed a new water pump, so I took a cab to the subway station, picked up a newspaper from the machine and hopped on the train. That's when it hit me that David was coming home today. A smile spread across my face. I rifled through the newspaper to find the horoscope section, and it told me that friends would seek me out today for advice and to show a touch of my natural objective ability. I looked at David's horoscope too. His I didn't get at all. He knew I'd kill him if he enjoyed any kind of brief flirtation with a Pisces. I wondered what sign Monica was. I didn't want to have to rumble with that big girl over my man.

I read the front page coverage of the campaign. I couldn't wait to put my two cents in for Bill Clinton. The last person I wanted to see in the White House was that one-armed bandit, Bob Dole. Boyfriend was so sure he was going to win that he even quit his day job. But we'd see about that. I thought it was stupid that he would rather give people the option of sending their kids to private schools instead of concentrating on making the nation's public schools better and safer. Something about the man just looked underhanded to me.

When I got to work I turned on some work music, made fresh coffee and checked my E-mail. Barbara had some mess on there as usual. Genie, you forgot to empty the coffee pot last night. Genie, why didn't you use yellow paper for the new change-of-advisor forms instead of brown because it's summer now, and brown is a late fall and winter color. The woman was Looney Toon. I erased that shit and went on about my business.

I started my workday by reviewing summer evaluations, and then I made some changes to Dr. Winthrop's manuscript. He was on my nerves. I guess because he was getting down to the delivery deadline, but every day he was in my face, all huffy and irritated, with bits and pieces of that manuscript. I felt like telling him to get the stick out of his ass and leave me alone.

"Hey, girl."

Justine walked into the office in a long, pretty peasant skirt and a tank top. Her straight blonde hair was in a french twist.

"Hey. It's hot out there, Genie."

"Isn't it? That's a pretty skirt. Where'd you get it?" I had turned back to the manuscript and was typing up a tornado.

"Nordstrom. They have a sale going on this week. Guess what?" I looked over my shoulder at her. She was smiling, so I knew it was something good.

"What?"

"Barbara won't be in today or tomorrow. She told me last night before I left. She's taking some of that nonexistent vacation time because her brother is here for the week."

"Yes!" I said. "Thank God. You know she had the nerve to send me some crazy note last night talking about my emptying the coffee pot and why didn't I use yellow paper for those forms I made up yesterday."

Justine shook her head.

"I know. You know, the little Wicked Witch of the East had me throw out the brown forms and recopy the shit on yellow."

"No she didn't, Justine. Oh God, why doesn't that woman do everybody a favor and just die from one of those damn diseases of hers."

"People like her will outlive all of us, Genie. Oh no."

We both looked out into the hallway because the alarm sounded.

"It's too hot to go back out there," Justine said.

This was a regular occurrence at Whitman. Somebody was always either pulling the alarm or calling in a bomb threat. I logged out of my computer and got my purse. A steady stream of people were moving up the hallway toward the stairs, and we walked down the ten flights and out onto the sidewalk. We stayed out there for fifteen minutes.

In the middle of the day, when I was back at my desk, I got four hang-up calls. The fifth time it happened I just gave up. I decided to get some sun, so I went over to the registrar's office for grad applications and then walked over to the deli for a soda and sat in the park across from my building like David and I usually did late in the day. Some homeless man asked me for money and I gave him a five. There were some kids rollerblading, and a few late lunchers were eating and talking beneath the cherry trees.

I sat watching the action and thinking about what I was going to tell David about me. What could I say? "So glad you're home. By the way, Edward, that no good molesting father of mine, is dead?" I didn't know what to do, so I changed my mind and decided not to tell David anything. Just let the past stay right where it was. Behind me. I chucked my Sprite can into the trash and went back to the office.

David

There's surely no place like home. When I finally touched down at Dulles, I felt like kissing the ground like I did when I came back from Nam in '71. I've never been so happy to see a place in my life. Despite my exhilaration at being home, I was exhausted. My body had a permanent tiredness that lay deep in my bones, making me sluggish even though I'd had enough sleep on the plane. Monica and the boys were there to pick me up. I was under the impression that just Devin and Mark were picking me up, but the first face I saw off the plane was Monnie's. She looked great. She'd lost a bit of weight, it looked like, and her eyes didn't look as hollow as I'd last seen them. It's amazing how much time she's got for me now that we're not together anymore.

She stood on her toes and hugged me. Kissed my face. Told me she'd missed me like we were still a real family. Mark liked seeing that, I think. I could tell by the look on his face. He and Devin both cracked my ribs a bit while Monica stood back smiling, watching us the way she used to when they were small boys, wrestling me in the middle of the basement floor. It made me kind of sad to remember that. I had to admit it was nice to see my boys happy, though. We went down and claimed my bags, and the boys helped me carry everything to the car.

"How was Africa, Dad?" Mark asked. I was so glad he was talking to me I almost missed his question.

"Beautiful. Sobering. Amazing. Different from what I imagined. Ghana's mostly farmland. Matter of fact, about fifty-five percent of the population is farmers. It's an agricultural country," I said, stretching out my legs in the front seat. "But Michael's from a family of weavers. Their village is called Bonwire, which is just outside Kumasi—the Ashanti people's capital. It's one of four craft villages, all of which are known for a particular craft. Now Bonwire's known for its kente cloth. Michael comes from a long line of weavers, and his uncle and brothers are amazing to watch. To do their weaving they take these looms that have two harnesses, see. They hold the strings between their toes, and that's how they move those things up and down while they weave. I took some pictures that I can show you when I get them developed. They're pretty poor, though, which is sad, because they're such wonderful, talented people."

"That where you stayed at?" Devin asked.

"One night. I mainly stayed in Accra—that's Ghana's capital—with Michael's sister Helene and her husband, Mohammed, and his family when I wasn't traveling about. Mohammed's family does well enough. They've got some mining interests."

"You saw wild animals over there?" Mark wanted to know.

"Matter of fact I did. I didn't go on a genuine safari, but we went over to one of the national parks. Rode through in a jeep. It was awesome, boys. Zebras and elephants. Antelope, monkeys. All types of birds. I wish you two could have been there to see it with me."

"What you got for us, Dad?" Devin asked.

"Ah. You'll have to wait and see, son." I rolled down my window and enjoyed the evening air on my face.

"You have a tan, I see," Monica said. She wheeled her Mercedes out of the parking lot.

"Yeah," I said, "The weather was pretty tropical. Mostly humid. It rained a bit my first few days there. But Monnie, the vibrant colors and the beauty of the people. The culture. I think that's what struck me most, apart from the poorness of Bonwire and some of the other villages I visited. The beautiful, richly colored skin. The women in their lapas and gailays with their babies on their backs. People with bundles on their heads. The drums and dancing. It was something else. And the open-air markets were so alive with people and activity. Crowded as hell. Goats and chickens everywhere at every turn. They sold dried fish and fruits and fabrics and all kinds of things. But the people. They were just so friendly. Always ready with a smile. I loved that part. But I got a lot of work done at the university while I was there too. It should only take me another three months to finish the manuscript."

"That's wonderful, honey," she said and patted my leg. Then she remembered herself and put on a cool look.

We stopped off at McDonald's, since the kids hadn't had dinner, and I ate a Quarter Pounder with them. I looked at my watch. It was seven-thirty. Genie was going to have to wait. I was having a great time with my kids.

"So, Dad," Devin was saying, " I wondered if it was okay if I go up to Jersey with Kelli and her folks next week. She gon' have her own apartment up there and everything. Her dad invited me to come, and it would be just for a few days. I want to get a look at Princeton anyway, see what it's like." He put more ketchup on his french fries.

"I don't see why not. What do you think, Monica?"

"I think it should be alright. Kelli's parents did invite him. I talked to Vanessa, Kelli's mom, yesterday, and she assured me that they'd treat Devin like their own."

"Okay. I guess that settles it then. So, Mark, what have you been up to while your Dad's been away?" I asked him.

"Nuthin. Sitting in my room staring at the wall. This the most boring summer in the world. Mom wouldn't even let me go to this party Saturday night."

"With those two hoodlums you call friends? David, you should see these little thugs. Scarves wrapped around their heads, pants hanging half off their little butts. One of them had the nerve to light up a cigarette on my front porch like he was grown and lived there. I was ready to make him eat it."

"But Mom, you smoke."

"And some people rob banks, but that doesn't mean it's the right thing to do."

Mark left it alone like I'd hoped he would. When Monica started talking about people robbing banks it was time to throw in the towel.

"Anyway," Monica went on, "I already told you I was letting you go to King's Dominion with Ida's boys on Thursday."

Mark smiled like he was satisfied with that.

"Oh yeah. Mom, I'ma need some funds for some new kicks and this bad shirt I saw at PM."

"PM?"

"Potomac Mills, Mom."

"I guess that's okay, since you did make the honor roll this term. How much is all this going to cost?"

"Couple B's, I think."

"B's?"

"Benjamins, Mom, dag. A couple hundred dollars."

"Mark don't take that tone with your mother. You know better, son."

"Thank you, David. Boy, if you would stop talking in acronyms, maybe I could understand what you're saying. You ready to go, David? I know you're tired after that long trip."

I nodded.

By the time I got home it was almost eight. Monica and the kids stayed at my apartment for an hour or so. I knew Genie would be pissed off, so I decided to tell her my plane was delayed. She was too sensitive about my being anywhere near Monica for me to tell her the truth.

I jumped in my car dog dead and drove over to her house. Her lights were off, but I could see the light from the TV glowing from her bedroom window. I parked the car and sat out there for a few minutes. I didn't want to go in yet. But I couldn't sit out there all night, so I made myself go up those steps to the house. I unlocked the door and crept in, just in case Genie had fallen asleep with the TV on like she sometimes did. I had jet lag but I'd gotten used to the time difference in Ghana, so although I was tired as hell from the plane ride, I was wide awake. So was my body when I saw Genie.

She was beneath the covers, watching an old movie on cable.

"Hey, babe. How's my sweetheart." I put all 196 pounds of myself on top of her and tried to kiss her. She turned her head. She was good and mad, I knew, but she was beautiful to see despite the confusion I was feeling inside. I reached over and touched the lamp on her night table so I could get a better look at that face. I hoped she wouldn't notice that I'd gained ten pounds and that some more of my hair had disappeared on top. I also hadn't gotten a chance to dye what I've got left. But looking at her eyes, even though she was angry, I could tell she still loved me anyway.

"I almost gave up on you." Her voice was like an ice pick, and I could smell liquor on her breath. I noticed the empty wine glass on her night table. She struggled to push me off her, so I moved and sat up beside her with my arm around her little waist.

"It's good to see you, too." I said. "It wasn't my fault I'm late, babe."

"Whose fault was it, then—and don't lie to me either, David because I know for a fact your plane got in on time. I cooked something special for you and everything. So where've you been?"

Some homecoming. I had thought of nobody but her the whole time I was away and here she was tripping off the line just because I was a little later than I said I'd be. Apparently absence doesn't make the goddamn heart grow fonder.

"Genie, time got away from me. You know I'm sorry. I missed you like crazy."

That softened her a bit.

"Me too," she said, looking up at me.

I leaned toward her, and this time she let me kiss her. There was four weeks of passion in that kiss. It brought me back to life and shrank the nagging thoughts inside my head. I had missed this. Coming home meant being in this beautiful woman's arms. I wanted to tell her just how much of my strength she is, but it was more a feeling than words. It was like we both had an urgent pulse inside that needed this closeness between us.

I pulled up the silky shirt she was wearing and got her panties off. She smelled so good. I knew I didn't, but I couldn't pull away to go get a shower to wash the staleness from me, because that lithe little body of hers had wrapped around me, twisting and tangling me up. We touched and kissed every familiar place we'd missed while I was gone until we were frantic. Then she climbed up on me, dug her knees into the mattress and rode me like she was possessed until I came hard with her name stuck deep in my throat.

I hadn't even caught my breath before she got up and went into the bathroom and locked the door. That confused me a bit. I guessed she was still mad. We always went in and showered together, then she liked for me to hold her until we fell asleep. I got out of bed and went to the bathroom door to see what was wrong. I could hear her crying. The fan was on, but I could hear her gasping for air in there, so I knocked softly.

"Genie, babe, are you alright?"

I didn't get an answer so I said, "Honey, I'm sorry I was late. I want to make up for it. I've got your presents in my trunk. Come on out and talk to me." I put my ear to the door. She was blowing her nose. I heard the water running, then the lock turned.

"Babe, why are you crying like this?"

Her face held no expression. She shook her head no like that made sense and walked ahead of me into the bedroom. I was ashamed of myself because the movement of her hips made me want to take her again. My body was on fire. Genie turned off the television and sat down naked on the side of the bed.

"David, are you my friend?" she asked. I stood in front of her with a hand on her face, wiping the tears away with my thumb.

"Your lover and your friend, babe. What's wrong?" I wondered if she could tell the difference in me.

"You were going to lie to me tonight, weren't you? About why you were late." I left that question right up in the air. I wasn't touching it with a ten-foot pole. I sat down beside her and noticed that she'd dyed her hair a bit lighter. It looked pretty. Her nipples were hard because the a/c had come on, and I wanted to lay her back and put them in my mouth.

"Do you still love Monica?"

I thought for a second about the things that had come to mind on the plane and on the ride home.

"Genie, what are these questions about? I love you and you know that. I don't know how I can show you any better than I do now."

She didn't say a word to that. She looked like she had something heavy on her mind, though. She kept sighing. She leaned over and reached into her drawer.

"Edward's dead, David," she said, and handed me some papers.

"Dead? Of the cancer? How do you know?"

"It was in the newspaper. The obituary's there."

I looked at it a minute and said, "What's this other stuff?"

I looked at the first piece of paper, then looked at her. I didn't understand until I got to the second one that said "How To Tell Your Loved Ones You've Been Sexually Abused." I looked at her again and she burst into tears and buried her face in the pillow like she was ashamed. I couldn't believe this was happening. Something reached down into my throat to suffocate me, and my stomach felt heavy. My eyes started to burn and I put a hand on her back, but she tensed and shivered like she couldn't stand my touch. I needed some air and a drink. The pages fell out of my hand. There were so many things about her that were beginning to make some sense. The dreams. That time she got so sick when she saw him. Her disdain for men. I had so many questions, but I needed to clear my head first and let her have some time to herself. I got on my pants and shirt and found my shoes under the bed, picked up my keys and went outside.

It was well lighted on Genie's street. There were some kids out on the corner, as usual, and they had their rap music going but it wasn't loud. I nodded to them when I walked by, on my way to the football field up the street where the club kids play every Saturday. I shoved my hands into my pockets and soothed the hurting in my chest with a few tears of my own. I needed to figure out what I felt about this thing. What the hell could I possibly say to her that would help us both? I couldn't begin to imagine what she'd been through.

It was so hot I walked up to the package store around the corner and got me a beer, then backtracked to the ball field. There was a ball court, too, and two young boys who should have been at home were out there playing basketball on the blacktop. I could only smile watching them.

"Check," the smaller one said as he bounced the ball at the other boy's hands.

"Check," the tall, lanky one with a wild afro answered, dittoing the move.

I sat down on the ground at side court and cracked open my beer and glutted down half of it. I kept trying to figure out what to say. I couldn't even figure out how I felt about the whole thing. What it meant. I already knew why she'd kept it from me. That was only human for something so horrible. The shame and embarrassment, the stigma attached to what that son of a bitch did. . . .

I thought about all the times we'd made love, and never once did I feel like she was frigid or tense about anything we did together. Actually, she and I are compatible enough in bed. Once we learned each other's bodies we were never awkward with each other since our first time together. We had a normal, healthy sex life. We had a normal, healthy relationship. There were times when she seemed overly emotional and possessive, but what woman doesn't?

I slapped my thigh when I felt something bite me. Probably a damn mosquito. That's when I realized I was deadly angry about this whole thing. Why hadn't the son of a bitch been rotting away in jail instead of casually sitting in some restaurant where Genie would have to see him? Had she gotten help so she could deal with this shit? I had a lot of questions I needed answers to. I got up and wiped off the back of my pants. I walked around a bit longer while I finished my beer and contemplated what the hell I was going to say when I went back. I always tell my boys to take responsibility like men. Look the hard things in the eye the same as you would the easy things. Sometimes I practice what I preach.

I tossed my beer bottle in the overflowing trash bin and walked back down the hill toward Genie's house. The lights were out. All of a sudden I thought about her mother and got scared as hell. Out of shape as I was, I sprinted for the door like I had all the energy in the world. Don't let my sweetheart be in there doing anything crazy, I thought. I'd been gone at least an hour. When I unlocked the door, I flung it open, calling her name, and half ran down the hall to find her. I cut on the light and I felt lightheaded, I was so scared; but then I saw that she was alright, and I was relieved. She was lying across the bed looking up at the ceiling. She didn't even turn my way when I sat down beside her and took her hand. Her face was streaked with tears.

"I guess you don't want me anymore," she said. She sounded so desolate I wanted to take all her pain on myself.

"Then I guess you don't know me the way you think you do, huh?" I squeezed her hand. I sat beside her and kissed her forehead, hoping it was okay to do that. She didn't flinch.

"David, I'm sorry." She turned her head away. She wasn't crying, but she looked like she might again any minute.

"Sorry for what," I said. I rubbed the back of her hand and stroked her hair with my free hand.

"For not being the woman you thought I was. For not being good enough for you. I wanted you to be so proud of me. Proud to be with me."

"Do you know how much guts it took for you to tell me this? If that's not something to be proud of, I don't know what is."

"I can't compete with Monica, David." She took her hand away and turned completely on her side away from me.

"I'm not asking you to compete," I said.

"David, I just want to be what you need, not just what you want." I didn't quite understand where she was coming from. I wanted to ask her to explain, but we had something more important we had to talk about right now.

"Babe, you have to tell me something. Why wasn't that bastard in prison?"

"I needed to forget it happened, David. That's how I survived. You have to understand that. All I've ever wanted is to be like everybody else."

"We need to talk about this, Genie. I need to know the whole story."

"I don't want you to think I'm a bad person. I couldn't stand that. I know that it was important to tell you about me. You have a right to know everything. But I just don't want you to think of me as a bad person."

"You're not a bad person."

She was silent for a few minutes. She was twisting the strings on the tassels of some extra pillows in the bed.

"David, I never even saw it coming. He was doing stuff to my sisters all along and none of us knew that the other was . . ."

"Them too? Tess and Marilyn? My God. The sick bastard." I cringed and lay my head down on her shoulder, wishing I could have protected her from it.

"Yeah," she said, like she was tired. "I was a regular kid, David. When I was little I was a tomboy. I would climb trees and play kick-ball with the boys and do all kinds of active stuff like other girls. And my sisters babied me. I thought I had it made. Edward, he was into all these different women. He took me with him for cover and we would pick up these women. And it was so sickening, David, because Mama loved him so much. You could tell she worshiped him. He would send her these flowers when he cheated on her. I felt like I was betraying Mama. David, you'd have liked her a lot." She reached out and put an arm around me.

"She was so full of life. Into everything. She was just so alive. But when those flowers kept coming, she had a breakdown. Tess thinks she found out that Edward was . . . bothering her, 'cause she heard Mama ask him if he was trying to touch her in an improper way. I guess that could have done it. She had Edward up on this pedestal that he never even tried to live up to. David, she turned into a whole different person overnight. She moved downstairs in the basement. She went to work for a little while, but then she called in sick one day and never went back."

Her voice was like stone. She stared off into space like she was talking to air, not me, so I lay down next to her. I wanted her to know she could look at me and she didn't have to be ashamed with me. I laced my fingers with hers.

"Did she go to a doctor? See a therapist or anything? Did Tess ever talk to your mom about what went on?"

"No. Nobody did anything. Tess went off to college with Marilyn. Edward was paying for that, so they kept their mouths shut. They were scared. They didn't even know about each other yet. Not until Mama's funeral, anyway. Edward sent Mama to her cousin Fitzgerald, over in St. Louis. He said she needed a rest. I think maybe they just didn't want anybody to know, because Fitz found Mama a doctor out there who gave her a bunch of medicine."

"When she came back she looked real good and I thought she'd be okay. She was taking all these pills, but she wasn't crying like before and she held a decent conversation sometimes. That lasted a good month. One morning she ran out in the front yard screaming and tearing her clothes off. David, it was bad. We were so embarrassed. The ambulance came and everything.

"Edward took her to some doctor over in Richmond who gave her some shots or something. She stayed out there for the weekend. He came into my room one night while she was gone and told me he would leave her out there if I wasn't nice to him. I wouldn't see her again, and he threatened me. I thought I didn't have a choice. David," she said, letting my hand go and turning away again, "his whole personality changed."

She started shivering like she was cold. I got the feeling she didn't want to be touched, so I took her robe from the pillow and spread it over her. I wanted to find some way to comfort her. But I could barely comfort myself. I was glad she'd turned away too, because I didn't want her to see my tears.

"He would come in there some nights, any night. There was no set time or anything. And he would say, 'I want you to watch TV with me, tonight.' First time it happened I was able to make myself forget. When it kept happening I couldn't. . . . I just kept repeating to myself that it wasn't happening to me. I started pretending I was somebody else. Mama was home and she had a nurse who came every day. And by then Edward had got meaner. I tried to fight him sometimes but he would pin me down and hold me till I couldn't fight anymore."

"I started doing anything to make it stop. I wet the bed. I would go without taking a bath sometimes. I hid sometimes. Some nights I slept downstairs with Mama, right underneath her bed. She would get all upset if she saw anybody but Nurse in her room, so I had to wait until she went to sleep and I'd crawl in under the bed. Edward bought me a lot of stuff and thought that made it okay."

"I went through that for a whole year, then it stopped all of a sudden. Edward had met this woman he was interested in, and for a while it looked like he might put Mama away anyway and bring the other woman in. But then that ended somehow. God, David, then the whole thing started with me all over again. I found that woman's phone number and I called her and begged her to come back, but I never saw her again."

She was quiet again. She knew I was crying, because I couldn't hold back. I could picture every damn thing she was saying and it was killing me. Just plain killing me. She sat up on the side of the bed and handed me a tissue off the night table. I felt so awful for crying. It seemed like she was being stronger about this than me.

"You know, with everything that man took from me, what causes me the most hurt is that he took my virginity when I was seventeen. That was the one thing I had been praying that I'd be able to keep 'cause I wanted to give that part of myself to my husband when I got married. I wanted to be like anybody else with a choice. But I couldn't even have that part. I swear, David, I was so far gone by then. I was just a robot when it came to Edward. I didn't care anymore. But I fought the night he raped me. I did. I screamed. I begged. I kicked and I bit him. I just wasn't strong enough. He just up and took it from me like it wasn't the most precious thing I had. And Mama. . . . David, she saw it. She saw him and she ran back downstairs and slammed her door. She heard that man rape me. She saw it. But she couldn't do anything. God. The next night she was gone."

"Jesus, Genie. I can't believe this shit." My voice was shaking. I shook my head and pressed my palm against my forehead, not really believing I had sat here listening to these horrible things. When I looked at her with the tears on my face, I still couldn't believe that the woman I was looking at was the same one who had dealt with so much pain.

"David, please don't hate me." She started to cry again with her head leaning against the wall and her hand covering her mouth. I didn't want her to think I wasn't on her side, so I ignored the heavy weight in my chest and reached out for her hand and said, "I don't hate you, Genie. I could never hate you. I love you, Genie. You're the bravest woman I know."

Genie

Telling David about my past was one of the most painful experiences I've ever gone through. It was devastating. I almost started to think I couldn't get through it once I started telling him about me, but somehow I managed. The only thing I'm ashamed of is that I didn't tell him about me for the right reasons.

I knew that his plane was due in at quarter of six, so I left work early and rushed home to make us some steak fajitas, grilled fruit and vegetables and a key lime pie. I set the table so pretty. I had cleaned the house up real good and had bought myself a pretty new nightgown for him. I was so excited that David was coming home I could barely keep still. I kept fidgeting and watching TV, looking out the window and then fidgeting some more.

When he still hadn't gotten to my house by seven-thirty, I figured maybe his plane was delayed, so I called the airline. Come to find out, his flight had arrived at Dulles a little ahead of schedule, so I thought maybe he was just really tired and had decided to go home first to get a quick nap. I called his house and got his machine, but I didn't leave a message. I just hung up and called his cell phone. No answer. As a last ditch effort, I called his office just to make sure, but he didn't answer there either, so I put on a pair of jeans and tucked my sleek black nightie in like a shirt, put on my Reeboks and headed over to David's place.

When I got there, I parked at the apartment building a little bit up from David's, because I didn't want his kids to see me if they were there. I noticed his car was covered up the way he'd left it. I went up to his apartment and used the key he'd given me before he left, praying that I wouldn't bump into his kids. Inside everything was the way I'd left it the day before, neat as a pin and smelling like a mixture of Pine Sol, Windex and air freshener. By then I was pissed, because I knew he hadn't been home yet, but I wondered if maybe nobody had showed up to pick him up. His kids might have forgotten he was coming home today.

I decided to drive out to Dulles, so I went back out to my car and that's when I saw them together: David and Monica, laughing it up with their kids as they grabbed his suitcases from the trunk of her big blue Mercedes. I felt like I had been struck dumb. David hadn't said a word to me about Monica picking him up from the airport. I just froze dead in my tracks and watched them together with those two tall, handsome boys of theirs, feeling small and stupid while I watched David peep at his car underneath the car cover, then wheel his big suitcase up toward the stairs with Monica next to him, her hand on his arm like she owned him. They disappeared inside and fear gripped me so tight that it numbed me.

I hadn't thought about losing David. I expected us to move forward together because that's what he'd made me believe we would do, but I didn't count on this woman's trump cards—her years of having been with him, her knowing what it felt like to carry his babies and raise them. If she played her cards right, I could lose. Then where would I be? *Who* the hell would I be without my David?

Somehow I got into my car. I was so hurt I couldn't cry. I just gripped the steering wheel and waited for a whole half hour while the sky changed, got dimmer. People came in and went out of the building, got into cars and went away, but the Mercedes was still parked right next to David's car. I wished it would just blow up. I wished she would just blow up. I finally gave up and drove home, telling myself that David wasn't worth shit anyway, knowing damn well I didn't believe that.

When I got home, I dumped the SOB's homecoming dinner in the trashcan and grabbed my trusty bottle of Sambuca. It wasn't until around nine-thirty that I heard a key in the front door. I was half asleep, drunk with the TV on the AMC channel. I wanted to run to David and put my arms around him, tell him I had missed him, but I couldn't after what I'd seen. So I just sat up in bed like I'd been watching *Key Largo.*

He came into my room and just looked so damn good to me. He had gained a little weight and had a serious tan that made his skin look a smooth deep golden. His face had a thin shadow of gray-black stubble on it and his hair was longer than I was used to seeing it. I just couldn't stop looking at him, even though I was upset; and when he started saying all the right things, of course I went softie and forgave him. The next thing I knew, we were kissing, and we started making heavy love like we hadn't been together for years instead of weeks. It was so good to feel him inside me again.

But there was a wall between us and I felt it. Something wasn't right. I went into the bathroom and cried. I was scared to death by what I had seen at his apartment and what I felt. I could see in his eyes that something was off with us. So when he asked me to tell him what was wrong, I switched gears. I had to let him know that I needed him more than Monica ever could, so I told him Edward was dead. I tried my best to tell him the rest, but I couldn't say it, so I handed him the pamphlet Paulette had gotten for me, along with the obituary clipping.

The look on his face when I told him was one I don't ever want to see again. All the color drained out of his face. He looked so hurt for me that I almost hated myself for using what I've been through like that. But what else did I have? Monica already had with him the things I want. We hadn't been together long enough for me to feel secure with our relationship. Telling him was my only way. I was ashamed of myself and didn't want to face him, so I was glad when he left the house for a while, because I needed to think.

When he came back to the house and wanted me to tell him the whole truth, I let it all out. Everything. Maybe the Sambuca gave me a loose tongue, but I couldn't stop talking. I just wanted that damn wall or whatever was between us gone. Maybe I was being paranoid, but I just knew something wasn't right.

David sat there, listening to me like he was out of it. Like hearing me tell him my ugly secrets was taking something out of him. I could see it in his eyes, and his body looked so lifeless. He was hunched over like he was feeling his age the whole time. By the time I finished telling him, he was crying like I was, and I felt so close to him and so loved that I knew that Monica couldn't hurt me. We talked until about three in the morning and I realized that I had done the right thing.

Tuesday when I got to work I called Whitman's Student Services Center and talked to the receptionist there, who told me that Whitman offered group therapy sessions twice a week for adult survivors of incest. David urged me to go, so I got all the information I needed about the group. The receptionist encouraged me to make an appointment with one of the psychologists on staff there first, though. I told her I couldn't get with sitting back and spilling my guts to someone who didn't understand my pain firsthand. But I could handle talking to other people who had walked in my shoes. So after work on Thursday night I hung around until seven and walked around the corner from the library building, where I worked, to the Blockton Center, where the meetings were held.

The Blockton Center was a decrepit little beige painted brick building, about three stories. Elevatorless and always stuffy, the building was nearly seventy years old and smelled like an old mothballed closet. This was where all of the student help services were. I walked up the uneven cement stairs holding the wobbly black railing, and went through a set of heavy double doors. The only real light in the building was the sharp sunlight streaming in through the panels on each side of the doors and through the windows from open offices. The ceiling lights in the building's narrow strip of a hallway were dim, making me feel like Hitchcock's first black leading lady.

I reached inside my purse for the yellow sticky I had written the time and place information on to check which room I was supposed to go to. It said 221. I turned a corner and went through a second set of doors and started up the stairs. I was nauseous. I was so nervous that my hands were sweating and hurting. I rubbed them together and took a deep breath and looked at my watch. It was almost time to begin. I found the room and stood outside the door for a few minutes doing some relax, relate, releases to get myself together and listening to the chatter inside the room. People sounded like they knew each other in there. Like they were comfortable with each other. I wanted to just go home, but David helped me understand that sometimes you have problems that are too big to work through alone. Sometimes you need help to get rid of old habits and fears so that you can be healthy. I thought about what this kind of help had done for Tess and about the confidence and self-assurance she has now. The bitterness she has let die with the past, since, she says, you can't go back and change any of it. I took another deep breath to quell the uneasy wobbling in my stomach and legs. Patted my hair and pressed my lips together to make sure my melon lipstick was on right. Then I walked in.

Two-twenty-one was a small, carpeted room with a blackboard and clock and a set of long windows, but not much else. Six of those student chairs were arranged in a semicircle near the front of the room and in the one chair that was facing the others was the psychologist, sitting cross-legged and wearing a turquoise suit with fringes hanging off the sleeves. She was Spanish, I thought, and young looking, with tasteful makeup, and her hair was hippie-style—parted down the middle and bone-straight. The smile she gave me was genuine and I liked her right away.

"Hello," she said and stuck out her hand for a quick, warm shake. "I'm Dr. Ortega. Are you joining us this evening?" Her accent was light and she had that soft, non-threatening voice that I've always imagined is prerequisite to becoming a head doctor.

"Yes," I said, looking at the empty blackboard instead of at her. I know it was pretty evident that I was nervous as anything. Behind me, everyone was seated and talking like they had known each other for years, and I felt like a complete outsider here.

"What's your name?" Dr. Ortega asked.

"Eugenia—uhm, Genie. Gatlin." I didn't know what the heck to do with my hands, so I put one sweaty palm on the strap of my purse. The other one I put in my pocket like I'd noticed David does when he's lecturing.

"Wonderful to meet you." She stood up. "Since it's your first time here, I just want to let you know that this is an informal group. We have about five or six people on a regular basis. Sometimes a few more drop in. You talk if you want to. When you feel comfortable about it. If not, you're welcome to just listen. Hopefully you'll take away something important you hear. Have a seat if you like and we'll get started in a few minutes."

"Okay," I said. I was meek as a lamb. The questions I had planned to ask somehow evaporated from my brain. I sat in the seat closest to Dr. Ortega, adjusted my short silk skirt so I wouldn't show too much thigh, and started searching through my purse like I was looking for something important until the man next to me hit my elbow.

With my hand stuck down in my purse trying to close in on a breath mint, I looked over at the good-looking, solidly built guy with, those long basketball hands that had tapped me. He was that beautiful Wesley Snipes dark chocolate, with brows as thick and straight as the hair on his head and long lashes like David's. I thought I just might like group after all.

"Hey, I'm Chris," he said. "Glad to have you here." He had a soft Jackson Five voice, but it was deeper. He was all in my face, but since he was so cute I didn't mind so much. I'd just finished a chili dog before coming here, so I took out my Certs and popped one in my mouth. I held up the pack of mints and said, "I'm Genie. Want one?"

"You trying to tell me something?" He was grinning at me like we were buddies from way back. Fine self.

"I'm trying to be polite. Would you like one?"

He shook his head no and pulled a stick of Double Mint out of his pocket.

"You a student here?" he asked me.

"Part-time. Nondegree. I work here too, though, in the English Department." I don't know why the man was making me feel this friendly. Especially in here. Sometimes a good-looking man has a way of making you talk too damn much.

Dr. Ortega looked up at the clock on the wall and got up to shut the door. Then she went over to those old-ass windows and fiddled with the blinds a minute before she could get one of the windows open halfway.

"I work here too," he said. "Over in the law library."

"You're a student, too, aren't you? I mean, this group is for students, right?"

"Yep. First-year law student. I got a masters in criminology here last year." He sounded so proud of himself. I wondered why he was here. What his story was and how this handsome and obviously self-assured man had wound up in group therapy, sitting next to somebody like me.

"Okay, everyone. I guess we should go ahead and get started now," Dr. Ortega said.

I looked at the rest of the people in the room. Two of the other women looked beaten and sad. I figured they were good friends since they had walked in together and talked nonstop about some business class they'd taken last semester. There was a slim Japanese girl sitting across from me on the other side of Dr. Ortega who had been talking off and on to Chris and the white guy beside him with a blonde ponytail.

The room got quiet when Dr. Ortega sat down, and I was scared to death to be here. I was glad I didn't have to speak unless I wanted to, but because I was new, I wished David was sitting beside me holding my hand for support. My throat was so dry and I felt like every eye in the room was on me, even though no one was really paying me any mind.

"Alright," Dr. Ortega said. "Last time we were here, we talked about establishing trust in adult relationships. If I remember correctly," she said, flipping through a spiral notebook, "Everett made some interesting remarks that we didn't really get to discuss. Everett, would you like to take the floor and reiterate those comments for us from Tuesday's session?"

The white guy with the ponytail was Everett. He looked a little nervous and pushed his glasses up on his face. Then he stood up and said, "Hi, my name is Everett and I'm an adult survivor of incest," just like they do in those AA meetings. I almost fell off my chair when everybody said "Hi, Everett." I looked around a little bit like I was in the Twilight Zone. It was weird. I sat there looking at what I could see of the buildings across the street out of the window, feeling uncomfortable because Everett gave a brief history of the brutal and ugly life in his father's house—I guess to fill me in, because he was looking pretty much at me. I kept feeling like I wanted to cry, but I was too embarrassed to do anything but sit there. I had to pee, too, but I was too scared to even get up to do that. Then Everett started talking about his boyfriend, Mel. That surprised the hell out of me, because Everett didn't look a bit gay. I was not ready for this shit. I really had to pee now.

"I just can't seem to trust anything he says or does," he said. "I try, but I always expect him to do something to hurt me."

"Can you give an example?" Dr. Ortega asked. I didn't really want an example. I just wanted to go home. I also wondered if cutie sitting next to me was gay. If he was, it was a true loss for our side. I was sick of staring out that damn window, and it was getting dark, so I found my hand lotion in my purse and started putting it on real slow like I'd rather be doing nothing else. I was trying to think of something else I could do to make the time go by.

"Well, like say he tells me he's going to the grocery store. Then he takes more than an hour because he stopped off somewhere like the dry cleaners or something. Well, the store is five minutes from home, so of course I'm timing him like a clock, and then when he's not back in an hour, I'm gettin' paranoid. I imagine he's out secretly meeting someone else while I'm left at home looking out the window every two seconds for his car to pull up."

That shocked me too. I had no idea that men waited around for other men. Ain't that some shit.

The Japanese girl piped up and said, "Hi. My name is Song and I'm an adult survivor of incest."

I was in on the secret now, so I joined everybody else and said, "Hi, Song."

She leaned back in her chair, crossing her legs and said, "What's Mel's reaction to this? Because my boyfriend has the same problem with me. For a long, long time I couldn't even have a relationship. I was too, like you say, paranoid about it. When I finally did get into a relationship, it was with an abusive boy. I stay with him two years." She put up two fingers like it was a lifetime. I guess for her it was. "I finally got out. Left New York and came here. Met this guy who is very good to me. But I cannot rest. I cannot let him be away from me very long. I accuse him of lies when he does not lie. I don't know." She shook her head sadly from side to side.

Dr. Ortega was silent. She just wrote in her notebook and let things play out.

"Mel's good about it, actually. Right now. He sort of laughs and lets it roll off his back. But I'm afraid that if I don't stop this, he won't stick around for the duration." Everett looked down at his feet like that would be the end of his world, and I felt sorry for him.

"Who else here," Dr. Ortega asked, "feels like they have trouble trusting in their adult relationships? Not just your significant others, but also in friendships, working relationships. . . ."

Everybody raised their hands.

"I would like to know," she said, "what some of you feel it would take to be able to trust someone. Not a textbook answer, but you personally. What would it take to get you to trust someone?"

That was a safe question. I was scared, but I wanted to feel like I was part of the group too.

"I guess," I said, with my voice cracking some, "I would need a lot of communication and reassurance, which my boyfriend, David, gives me."

"You didn't say the magic words," Chris said. I looked at him, confused.

"Hi, my name is. . . ." He gestured with his hand for me to continue, and I caught on, then I felt embarrassed and stupid. I had forgotten to say it, but then again, I didn't want to. It was like admitting my past to everybody here although everyone knew why I was here.

Dr. Ortega came to my rescue. "It's okay, Genie," she said and put her hair behind her ears. "When you're ready, you will say it. Who's next?"

"Hi, my name is Linda, and I'm an adult survivor of incest." This was one of the sad-looking girls. Looking at those two more closely, I noticed that they favored each other a good deal. They had to be sisters. They had the same drooping blue eyes, the same thin mouths and pert noses. The only thing that was different was one had frizzy auburn hair and the other's was honey blonde.

"Hi, Linda."

"I think what Genie said makes sense. A lot of communication and attention helps so much. But I need the support I get here too. I've learned that I first have to give myself the things I want to give other people. I have to love and trust myself before I can love and trust a man, or a friend. Even Leslie and I have had trouble trusting each other at times, even though she's my sister."

Leslie started to say something, but Chris was quicker. He repeated what he'd called the magic words and everyone responded. "I can relate to that," he said. "I don't have a girlfriend right now, but I've driven away the ones I've had because of lack of trust. Before I started coming here I think I saw my mother in every woman I came in contact with. I always accused them of using me for sex the same way she did." He looked down at his hands like he was very upset. I reached over and squeezed his arm to let him know I understood exactly, because before David, I looked at men the same way. I still did, really, but somehow I'd set David apart from other men.

Chris patted my hand as if to say thanks and continued. "I think I need infinite understanding and kindness," he said.

Song said she needed her boyfriend to be more reliable and Everett said he needed communication.

Dr. Ortega shifted in her chair and said, "Okay, I think Linda has touched on a very good point. Linda said that before seeking certain qualities in others, she first has to give them to herself. Now everyone here has said what it would take for them to be able to trust. Now think about your answer and take this a step further. I want you to ask yourselves if you've given yourself what you say you need. If you haven't given yourself any of the things you would like to have from others, I want you to take this weekend and do five things that demonstrate how you fulfilled your own needs. Write them down. And bring them on Tuesday so we can talk about it." She looked at her watch.

"But I said I need communication," I told her. I didn't get how I was going to do the assignment unless I sat around talking to myself all weekend.

"If I was hearing you correctly, Genie, what I understand you to mean is that you need the kind of exchange that is going to keep your eyes open. Not casual chatting, but the kind that reveals. You might not have noticed, but we all commune with ourselves in some form or another. For example, I can take a situation I'm confused about, sit down and think about it. Maybe figure out a few different ways of handling it. Then come up with the best solution. Believe it or not, I've just communed with myself. Just like if I have a problem that involves a person whom I love. We sit down and we talk about it. Discuss how we feel. We either compromise and fix it or we might even agree to disagree. But the lines of communication are open. Some people don't do that. Some people act blindly. Impulsively, without thinking about why they are doing what they're doing."

Everett said, "I still don't quite get it, Dr. Ortega."

"Okay, Everett, say in your case, Mel comes home a little later than you expect. You're angry. If you sit down and take ten minutes alone and ask yourself, 'Everett, why are you angry that Mel's late? Haven't you ever been late?' you may handle the situation differently because you've communicated with yourself about it. You're aware of what you feel. And you understand that you can control it."

I nodded, understanding completely now.

"Well," Dr. Ortega said, "we're out of time. I'll see all of you next week. And don't forget to continue with your affirmations."

I looked at Chris. "Affirmations?"

"Yeah. Each of us has written a personal affirmation that we say every morning when we wake up."

"Oh, that's nice. I'll have to write one, then," I said. I was feeling so exhilarated. So positive about this step. I couldn't wait to tell David about it.

"You wanna go have some coffee with me and I'll fill you in on this place?"

I shook my head no. "I don't think so," I said.

"Why?" He was looking down at me with those nice brown eyes.

"I—uhm. I have a boyfriend, Chris. And I love him." Too many men had come on to me and were not deterred knowing that someone was in my life, so I always added how I feel about David, just so they'd know they didn't have a chance in hell.

"I gathered that from the way your eyes lit up when you mentioned him. I didn't ask you to have coffee with me because I'm trying to hit on you, even though I probably should try. But," he whispered, "I thought since another black person finally made it here, I'd extend some group hospitality. What do you say?"

I couldn't help but smile at him. The man had charm like hell. Besides, David had started working on his book now like it was his new religion, so I looked at my watch and said, "That sounds harmless. I'd love to."

We said goodnight to Dr. Ortega and left the stuffy building.

It was after nine when Chris walked me to my car. I could have talked with him at least another hour, but I had made David some dinner this morning and I missed him because we hadn't seen each other for two days. I was getting jealous of that book of his.

I stopped by my house to pick up his dinner and pack a quick bag, then I drove out to Greenbelt, doing my first group exercise of communicating with myself. Something's wrong with David. For the past week I've wondered if it's me and I ask him, but he keeps telling me that he's fine. That he's just so into writing that he doesn't have much time to think about anything else. I try to act like I understand, but I don't, really. He hasn't laid so much as a finger on me since I told him about Edward. I just don't know what he's thinking. I'm guessing it's the Edward thing that's making him act strange, but it could be that he's so obsessed with writing this book.

He writes from early in the morning until late in the evening, sometimes without eating or even taking a shower. Nothing else seems to matter to him. Classes don't start again until the end of August, so he doesn't come in to the office at all now. He just stays in that apartment in front of his computer. So if I want to see him these days, I have to go to him.

I walked into his apartment with my weekender and the pan of lasagna I had made for him. I could smell the acrid scent of something burning. The air was foggy. The exhaust in the kitchen was on. The vertical blinds were pulled back and the balcony door was open to let in the fresh warm air.

"David?" There was no answer. I dropped my bag on the floor and took the pan of lasagna to the kitchen to heat it up. A singed pot was half full of water in the sink, sitting on top of a stack of dishes. The place was a mess. I went to find David in the room he used as his office. He had a big oak desk. One of those high-backed, ergonomically correct chairs, his computer, a printer, fax machine, and some nice pictures we had found at a yard sale I'd dragged him to. His bookshelf was full of reference guides on everything from writing to famous quotations. As usual he was bent over his computer looking exhausted, but his tired eyes were glued to the screen like he was in another place and time. He had on an old pair of shorts. He needed a haircut and a shave bad. He had three empty coffee cups sitting on the desk and there were papers and crumbs everywhere.

"Baby, what happened in the kitchen?"

"Oh. I, uhm, was trying to make some soup. Forgot about it."

"Well," I went over and put my arms around his neck, "come on and have some dinner. I made you some lasagna."

"Thanks, babe, I'm starved. I'll be just another minute." I kissed him on the neck.

"David, come on. I haven't seen you in two whole days."

"Okay. I'm coming. Fix me a plate and I'll be right there. I just have to read this over. I'll be five minutes."

That meant half an hour. I went in his bedroom and changed his disgusting sheets. Put his dirty things in the hamper and took all those dishes down the hall. The burning smell was dissipating, so I turned off the exhaust. I stacked the dishwasher, swept up and wiped off the counters. The man was a pig.

"David?" I yelled.

"Honey, start without me. I'm coming in a minute."

This Negro was getting on my nerves. I poured myself some fruit punch and put the lasagna in the oven on warm. Then I picked up the phone and dialed Paulette.

"Girl, what's up," I said. I leaned back in the chair

"Hey, lady bug. What's the good word?"

"I don't have any good ones, but I've got a few choice ones for David's ass."

"Still working on that book, girl?"

"Like he's married to it. Paulette, I don't know what to do with him. I can't get no satisfaction. He doesn't come to the office. He hasn't been to my house in days. I've never seen him like this. The man isn't even taking care of himself these days."

"You told me. But, Genie, give him his space. You know this is important to him. He'll write the damn thing and get it all out of his system and then you two will be up each other's butts like before."

I looked at my watch.

"Liar. He told me five minutes. Paulette, we haven't even made love since the day he came back from Ghana. He keeps saying he's so busy, but I think he's scared to try. What do you think?"

"Y'all still haven't been together?"

I shook my head like she could see me. "I want to, but he's hesitant, I think. He's still affectionate, but he doesn't take it further. And I do everything but come right out and tell him to give me some."

"Maybe he feels like you should have some time, Genie. You need to talk to him about it. No not that one, the other kind."

"Huh?"

"I'm sorry. I was talking to Robert. But like I was saying, talk to David about how he feels."

"I've tried, girl, but that's not working. He says he's just into this book right now." I hadn't told Paulette that I'd seen him with Monica when he came home from the airport. It would just be another reason for me to have to defend him to her.

"Maybe that's what it really is, then. Oh. What about your session tonight? Girl, I'm so proud of you. How was it?"

"Good. There's about five other people in the group. This one guy Chris is a total trip. I was scared at first though, P. I felt, I don't know, I guess kind of out of place. But then people started saying stuff that hit home, girl. I'm glad I went."

"Me too. You just stick with it and I know everything is going to work out."

"Wait. Here he comes. Lemme run."

"We still on for the movies tomorrow night?"

"Yeah. Meet me at Whitman after work and we'll hop the train to Union Station."

"Okay. See you then."

David came in and sat down across from me.

"Who was that?"

"Paulette."

"Oh. Where's dinner?" I wasn't even his wife yet and already he was sounding like I was his slave. I was the one who had worked all day, went to group, cooked his dinner, straightened up his house and still I was getting up to serve him.

"David, when are you going to get a haircut and shave that mess off your face? And you stink."

He took that in stride. He laughed, shrugged and put his long muscular leg up in the chair and drank some of my juice. I took the lasagna out of the oven and set two platefuls of it on the table. Then I sat in his lap, my favorite place to be.

"Thought you didn't like the way I smell."

"I accept all your bad points with your good ones."

He squeezed me. "Right after dinner I'll go in, take a shower and shave. I promise. How was your day today?"

"Quiet. Barbara wasn't there. We didn't do very much except cut up with Dr. Kemp. The man is a nut. You know you have eight people signed up for your section ten class already? And five in the second section. I checked this morning." I started feeding us both his lasagna.

"Great," he said, chewing. "I'm going to have to find some time between now and the end of August to prepare. How was your therapy group? Did you get something out of it?"

I didn't feel all that comfortable talking about it with David too much. He was so busy that I didn't want to really bother him like that, so I decided not to elaborate. I nodded and said, "It was good. Right now I'm mostly listening. But, David, it's so good to be around other people who understand because they've been there. Some of them have been through worse hell than me, I know."

He looked down at the floor. "Listen. Babe, I apologize for not being around more for you. I have to focus on this project."

"I know that. The group is something I need to do by myself anyway. I just miss spending time with you. I miss having fun with you."

"I know. I haven't been able to figure out how I can finish this book by September and live my life too. It looks impossible. I wish I could just freeze-frame everything and everybody around me until I can finish this thing."

That was a selfish thing to say, I thought. But I couldn't say that he hadn't warned me. I just had to make it a point to keep the faith like Evelyn told me to do. Outside of his job as an engineer, Simon was a closet essayist. And very good at it, from some of the stuff I read of his. I knew all about the changes Evelyn went through when he was writing. She told me that sometimes he'd wake up out of his sleep in the middle of the night just to get a thought down on paper. I just had to give David's creativity its breathing room.

"Come here," I said. I pulled his head toward me and kissed him. I pressed closer against him to let him know how much I wanted him, but he pulled back.

"I'm going to go shower."

"Okay." I slid off his lap, disappointed, and watched him walk out of the kitchen. I was so depressed. I went and closed the balcony door in the living room and shut the blinds. Then I reached for the remote to turn on the TV, but stopped myself and sat down on the sofa, deciding to commune with myself for a minute like Dr. Ortega said, to figure out what I should do. What was I doing anyway? Letting David just brush me aside like I don't need to be intimate with him. Since when had I let myself become docile and accepting? Shit. I wanted me some and it was up to me to get it.

I decided to strip off my clothes. The skirt and vest came off. I unbuttoned my top and flung it on the floor. Unhooked my bra and let that fall, then stepped out of my panties. I took the bobby pins out of my hair and shook it out. Then I marched myself down the hall to David's bedroom. He was already in the shower. His non-singing behind was in there grooving to "My Girl," except he was saying "my Genie." David loved to change the words to songs.

I busted right in that bathroom like Norman Bates would have and pulled back the shower curtain. There was so much steam in there I could hardly breathe. David had soap everywhere on his chest. His hair was slick and dark. His beautiful penis and those long hairy legs were glistening and dripping water. He looked so damn good I just wanted to rinse him off with my tongue. He was looking at me like he was surprised and didn't really want me in there, so I got all shy like an idiot and started fiddling with the shower curtain. You would have thought I was a virgin or something.

"Can I join you?" I asked him, looking down. The water from the shower curtain was hitting my feet and getting all over the floor. David put out his hand. I took it and stepped inside the tub in front of him. He adjusted the water for me, because it was a little too hot, and when he got it just right, I let the spray douse my hair and run down my body. It felt so good. I reached behind me and pulled David's arms around me so his hands could cup my breasts, but when he hesitated, I turned around to look up at him.

"You sure you want me?" he asked.

"You still want me?" I was scared of what he would say, but he looked at me like I was crazy and said, "Always. I just thought you needed to . . . I don't know. I thought I should wait until you told me you were ready to again."

That made me laugh. I moved all the way up against his chest.

"Doc, you mean to tell me we've both been missing out for nothing?"

"I guess," he said.

"Well, let me say this plainly. I'm more than ready."

I stood on my tiptoes to kiss him. The man lifted me and pinned me to the shower wall, barely giving me enough time to wrap my legs around him before he was inside me, making my head spin.

David

I've been having some small doubts about this new life I've chosen. Some small fears. I've started asking myself some questions that I'm not ready to answer just yet. Because I'm tired. The main question is, why am I letting Genie think that I've been writing this goddamn book, when all I've been doing is the same thing I was doing before I met her? Before I took the job at Whitman. Just hanging around the house doing nothing and feeling depressed. My sex drive is back to what it was before I met her. My energy level has, I think, fizzled. I've got a birthday coming up in a few weeks and I feel like I've got a foot in the grave already.

Another big question running around my head is whether Genie is with me because she needs a father figure in her life to replace the sick-ass, dysfunctional son of a bitch who . . . Every time I think about that shit I want to kill somebody. But she talked so much about that therapy group last night after we made love—the things she's realized about herself just after the one session, and how what happened to her has affected her adult life—that I'm wondering if she'll come to the conclusion that I'm nothing but a replacement father in her life. I couldn't handle that. That's why I haven't been making love to the woman since she told me what happened to her. When I touch her now that's what I think about. That's the only reason I can think of as to why she would want to wake up every morning to an old guy like me, with my wrinkled body and gray head. And I'm losing hair hand over fist too. How can she not notice that unless it's just her mind playing tricks on her?

I watched her get dressed for work while I lay there thinking about what I should do. She was so beautiful. Rushing around my bedroom in a sexy black slip, her hair thick from our shower session last night, with wiry strands working up out of those, what she called, french braids. She had on the dark pantyhose that make her legs look so smooth and touchable. She cut on the TV on her way to check on her coffee and I searched my night table for the remote so I could put on News4. I couldn't find it. I got out of bed and looked under and behind the bed and between the pillows. I was still looking when Genie came back into the room two inches taller. She'd put on her high heels.

"David, why didn't you just change the channel yourself, honey?" she said, and switched it for me. "You're already up."

"Because I don't want to have to look for the damn thing later."

She started putting on makeup. I watched her. She looked even younger than she is, in some short white getup she was wearing that looked like a dress but wasn't. I found the remote next to my shoes beside the bed. I caught a look at myself in the mirror above my dresser and just shook my head, wondering how I would ever hold onto Genie for the duration. She doesn't understand that this aging shit gets progressively worse. When I was her age, I thought I knew exactly what I wanted from life. But twenty-five isn't shit. How does she really know that I'm the man for her?

I went into the bathroom and took some Anacin because my shoulder was bothering me a bit after hoisting Genie up against that shower wall like I was some kid. Then I eased back in bed, watching her take those plaits out of her head and brush her hair back from her face. She wound it up and put some kind of white plastic thing with big teeth on it to hold it. Then she put on these nice, big gold earrings that looked like discs.

"I squeezed you some fresh juice, David. You want me to bring you some before I go?"

She leaned over to straighten her pantyhose, and for once it didn't give me any kind of rise at all.

"No, I'll get some later," I said, reaching for my glasses.

I just wanted her to go. I needed to be alone with the crazy thoughts swimming around in my head. I tried to act like I was interested in the banter between Katie Couric and Al Roker.

"Okay," she said. She leaned over me smiling and smelling fantastic. That armful of thin bracelets she was wearing was tickling my chest.

"Bye. I'll miss you today," she said. The kiss was a light one on my cheek. Then my neck. Probably because she'd just put on some lipstick. I was relieved when she left. I went to my office and turned on the computer, but I wasn't about to write anything. This was just part of my ritual. Once the computer booted up, I went in and got a glass of that juice and brought it into the bedroom. I stood in front of the mirror with the flashlight so I could really check my hair out. It wasn't too great.

I had to get out of here. I forced myself to go in and take a long shower. The pain in my shoulder was still there after I got out of the shower, but it was low grade, so I rubbed a bit of Icy Hot on it and put on a clean sweat suit. I felt like a good run. I put on my tennis shoes and did some stretches once I got outside. Wasn't a soul out. Most cars had already disappeared, since everybody in my building, except one young girl with a baby, works. I breathed in the heat and shook out my limbs and took off.

I started north toward the park faster than I normally run. My legs were really pumping. I guess I was trying to outrun my thoughts, but that was impossible. I couldn't grow old with Genie. I'm already there. She has a ways to go. But if I told her that, she would think I was having trouble with what she's going through. She would think I thought of her as damaged goods, which I don't. I love her. She has given me a new lease on life. Because of her I have grown in ways I'm still trying to understand. But I'm scared of her. People her age can afford to start and restart until they find what can make them happy or at least satisfied with their lives. I don't have that luxury anymore. Yet I feel obligated to helping her find her way beyond the things she's had to deal with as a kid. I'm between a rock and a hard place here. I'm beginning to think that maybe I didn't make such a good decision as I should have about this relationship, but she's so vulnerable right now, there's nothing I can do. And that's why I can't write even a goddamn sentence.

I've tried. I have ten filled notebooks, some audiotapes, photographs, copies of documents. An entire box of research. Chapters I've already written but need to tear apart. I can't do it, though. Just like I can't bring myself to sit Genie down and tell her that this thing between us might not work. She needs me and I need somebody. Something to hold onto that will make me want to wake up in the morning. I don't want to be all alone. I made the woman promises without knowing what I was actually saying to her. I was caught up in all the things she has to offer. But I don't have anything to offer her, really. I miss having a family. I'm a family man. There's so many sides to this shit that the pressure is depressing the hell out of me. But all I keep seeing is Genie some years down the road, wishing I would die already.

I got to the park and had to stop. My heart was beating out of my chest and I couldn't breathe right. I bent over and grabbed hold of my knees for a minute. I was gasping for air. Closed my eyes till I felt like I could at least make it over to the bench a yard or so away. My whole body was weak. Just sick. I had cramps in my side to beat the devil. I sat on the bench and put my head between my knees. A plane flew overhead and I wished I were on it, going somewhere far, fast. When I felt strong enough to get up again, I started back to that goddamn lonely apartment like I had things to do in there other than to sit in front of the computer feeling confused and stuck like hell.

Genie

"What are you doing for David for his birthday?"

"Not much," I said to Paulette. "He's been tripping more than usual about getting older. Keeps talking about his hair and his weight.

Keeps asking me if I think he's attractive. If I would ever leave him for a younger man. I don't know where all this is coming from. I thought he'd gotten over it." I was flipping through the jukebox selection on the table at the Silver Diner to see what I wanted to play. Paulette fished me two quarters out of her purse and said, "What brought this on? As close as you two are, how can he be so insecure?"

If I had given Paulette the unabridged story of my relationship, she'd know that David and I hadn't been hanging all that tough since he came back from Africa. She would also have known that we had been arguing a lot lately over small things that were definitely part of something bigger that neither of us could talk about. I knew I was on edge about him spending quality time with Monica in Atlanta, but my biggest problem was that I had no clue what was going on in his head, and that scared me.

I put the quarters in the jukebox slot and settled on "The Lion Sleeps Tonight" and "Twist and Shout," and pressed the selection button.

"I don't know, Paulette," I said. "For one thing, his anniversary with Monica came up. I think he had issues about that, and she may have dropped by to see him, for all I know. Now his birthday's coming and he's not taking getting any older very well. Plus, he's so buried in this book that we don't find a lot of time to spend together anymore, so you know I've been on my own a lot. Girl, I went out for coffee again with Chris the other night and mentioned it to David, and I think it bothered him. He asked me all these questions about Chris and everything."

"Why?"

"I don't know. Chris is that real sweet guy from group who I told you about who's been through a whole lot like me. You'd like him. Next time he comes by my house, I'll make sure you meet him. Anyway, David got all huffy and did everything but come out and accuse me of having designs on the man."

"Girl, men are ridiculous."

"I know. He should know I've only got eyes for him. But he's just sort of tripping in general, so I'm trying to deal. He has a lot going on."

Paulette drank some of her juice. "Don't forget you have a lot going on, too, sister. You make sure you're looking out for yourself."

"I am. I'm really trying to get myself in order, but David is not making it any easier. I just wish I knew why he's so upset and on edge all the time. What really concerns me is that he's not as sexual as before. You think he's having trouble with all this stuff I've told him about me?"

For some reason, I felt like eating everything on the menu.

"That could very well be part of it," Paulette said. "He's not being as supportive as I thought he would be. I know it must be hard for him, Genie. But I do think you did the right thing by telling him. Just keep trying to talk to him. What do you mean, he's not being as sexual? He still avoiding it?"

"No, girl. He just . . . He's not staying hard for very long at all. Last night he couldn't even get hard at all. Oh, God, he would die if he knew I was telling you this, but I don't know what to do. He won't talk about it with me. But he keeps telling me it has nothing to do with my past, and I think I believe him because he does encourage me with this therapy. I don't know what I'm doing wrong. I never had a problem turning him on before."

"I don't think you're doing anything wrong, Genie. It's him. Apparently, there's something going on with him that he's not talking about. He may have problems with your past and not be able to admit it to you for fear of hurting you, G."

"I've thought about that too. Well, here comes Miss Thing now, waltzing in here all late. Where you been?" Evelyn was all smiles. She had gotten some goddess braids and looked as regal as a queen with her long-legged self.

She breezed into the seat next to me and said, "Hey y'all. Sorry I'm late, but it was a man thang, so I know y'all understand."

"I figured that," I said, smiling, wishing I'd had the same excuse.

"You guys order yet?" She picked up her menu and started searching through it even though she always ordered the same thing every time.

"Not yet," Paulette said. "We were waiting for your hot behind. So I see Simon must still be talking your language."

"Paulette, I keep telling you to be patient. I'm making some headway with him, I think, but I have to be sure it's going to stick. But I did get him to register to vote, finally."

"For real? How'd you pull that off?" I was shocked. Simon was one of those warped people who thought his one vote couldn't make a difference.

"Girl, let me tell you. You know on Tom Joyner's morning show they've been trying to encourage people to get registered, right?"

Me and Paulette nodded.

"Well, Simon doesn't listen to the show, but for some reason he's religiously hooked on *It's Your World.* Anyway, a week or so ago I took him to work because he let his brother borrow his car, and y'all know how much I dig Tom, so of course that's what I was listening to. After *It's Your World* went off, Simon went to switch the station, but I told him not to, and that guy Tavis Smiley came on the program and talked about what our people went through just to have the right to vote. Simon seemed to respond to the message, so I encouraged him to call and register and he did."

"I am too impressed."

"Me too," I said.

We ordered breakfast and got another round of juice and coffee.

"Okay, guys. Dilemma. What am I going to do about the good doctor?" I looked over at Evelyn, who I knew was confused, and said, "I was telling Paulette before you got here how much David is tripping these days." Paulette understood that I wasn't going to tell Evelyn the whole truth.

"What's he doing? I thought you guys had ironed everything out and were acting all gross and in love and stuff."

"Shut up, Evelyn. He's just been asking me a lot of questions lately and acting weird."

"What kinds of questions?"

"Like, how do I see him and what do I think when I see younger men. Do I miss having sex with a man, or as David says, a fella, who can go all night. I told him he satisfies me just fine. The whole big production this morning was that he won't be around to see our kids grow up and that I have to be prepared to raise these children who we haven't even made yet on my own. And then he's still talking about going to see his doctor about getting a hair transplant."

"Lord. For what?" We made room for the plates our waitress was setting in front of us.

"Child. He is convinced that those few strands he's lost on top are a big deal. I don't know how to make him feel good about himself." I dipped my fork into my eggs.

"I don't know what to tell you, Genie," Paulette said. "The age factor is a real concern. I don't blame him for feeling intimidated by the fact that he's so much older. I mean, look at you. You can pass for a lot younger than twenty-five, girl. And he's sitting up there looking good, but looking his age none the less."

"That's not what I see when I look at him, Paulette. You know that. I love that man to death."

"Yeah, I know. I'm just saying there's no clear-cut answer to dealing with David's fears. He's got to do that. It may be a case of mid-life crisis. Sounds like it to me, anyway."

"David is not having a mid-life crisis. He knows what he wants. I believe he's just scared. But damn, I'm scared too. Doesn't he think I feel vulnerable with him still being married? And the dragon lady wanting him back?"

"I'm sure he knows that," Paulette said. "I think if the two of you keep the lines of communication open you'll do just fine, Genie."

I couldn't bring myself to tell them that my and David's lines of communication had recently shut down.

"Yeah. I guess. Provided Miss Lady doesn't make a play for him in Atlanta."

"From what you told me about how she looks, I don't know that you have much to worry about, Genie," Evelyn said.

"I don't know. She still has something I haven't got. His kids and his name. But I'm not going to keep worrying about it. We're supposed to be going on the *Spirit of Washington* dinner cruise tonight. Maybe he'll relax some out on the water and we can talk then. As long as he's not in one of those irrational moods."

"Well, Genie, I'm with Paulette. I think you guys have a special thing going and if you keep talking, you can get over the hump. You guys have been together, what? Six, seven months?"

"Yeah," I said. "Seven. And we haven't been able to relax and just be happy together yet." I lifted my coffee mug and went to take a sip, but realized that it was all gone.

• • •

By nightfall, my lips were poked way out. My arms were folded across my chest and I had attitude written all over my face. But I wasn't going to let that be the case for long. I refused to let David spoil my evening. I should have been having a great time. We'd had our cheesy teriyaki chicken dinners with rice and green beans, salad and dinner rolls. The dining room was all candlelit and we were sitting in a corner with a romantic portal view of the Potomac.

I was wearing a sleeveless red two-piece rayon pantsuit with wide legs, and black stack sandals. David looked sexy in a pale yellow cotton shirt and some tan Dockers. The band was playing Roberta Flack's

"Killing Me Softly" for the couples out on the dance floor, and that was exactly what I was wanting to do to David's ass. Kill him. An angry woman can do a lot of damage with a salad fork.

I had been trying to get him to talk to me about what was wrong with him. He hadn't told me a thing, but when I pressed the issue, the Negro had the nerve to blurt out that he's driving down to Atlanta with his wife. This shit was more than I could take. I wanted to feel like I could trust David, but he's still a man. And men are capable of some dog shit.

"You wanna go see the view from out on the deck?" I looked across the table into those eyes of his that seemed to have some kind of power over me, and I wanted to push him overboard.

"Okay." I slid my chair back and followed him across the burgundy carpet carefully, because my heels were sinking in. He stopped off at the bar near the exit and got himself a beer and me a white wine. I took my wine from him and we sat in some vacant chairs at the back of the ship. I took off my shoes. It was too beautiful out here. The endless waves. The sound of them roiling before and behind us. Even the air around me smelled wet. Water reminds me of life, the way it's always moving. I looked over at David, sitting with his beer in both hands between his knees. He looked lost in thought.

"David, what is it?" I don't know why I tried talking to the man again, because I knew I'd get no satisfaction from him, but something inside me wanted him to open up so bad. He didn't do anything but look up at me, drink a swallow of his beer, stand up to lean over the rail and look across the water. Inside they started playing the macarena song and it seemed like a thousand voices raised. Everybody sounded like they were having such a good time in there. I looked over at this couple in a dark corner of the boat, kissing and holding hands. Whispering to each other like David and I were supposed to be doing right now. It made me want to scream. I set my wineglass down and put my shoes back on. I was so fed up with this shit. By morning, this man was going to be hours away from me with his wife and kids. How cozy. I jumped up and started walking back inside toward the dance floor. David asked me where I was going, but I kept on going. He could just kiss my brown butt. I figured I'd see how he liked it if I shook my booty and ignored his black ass for a while.

The dance floor was down on the first deck. I walked toward the stairs on the second deck and inched my way between some people standing up over the rail clapping so I could see what was happening down there. It was packed. The woman and four men who made up the band were crammed onto a small step-high stage to the right of the brown and beige checkerboard dance floor. They were ending the macarena. The lead male singer, reminding me of Don Johnson in a pink pastel T-shirt and blue linen suit with the sleeves shrugged up, took the mike and started his intro to their next song. I made it down the brief spiral staircase and the group started playing Peaches and Herb's "Shake Your Groove Thang." That was my cue to get my groove on. I wasn't even thinking about that damn David. I eased out onto the floor and started moving double time to the music pumping in my ears.

It was hot and dark within the crowd. The ship had those cheesy spinning disco balls hanging from the ceiling, hitting us with silver lights. I lifted my arms and popped my fingers in time with the music. This was a great workout. This was the kind of fun David and I were supposed to be having, especially since by tomorrow he'd be spending a whole week with his wife. I don't know how, but I had a suspicion that he wanted to be with Monica and away from me. I refused to give a damn.

I did a turn and noticed this tall, dark-skinned brother. The man was really moving. He looked great out here on the floor. Like a real natural. He noticed I had some rhythm too because he worked his way over to me and we both smiled hello. Then he took my hand and we really started to work it out like we were in a seventies club somewhere. People noticed. A crowd formed around us and started clapping to the beat. The band had stopped singing and they prolonged the instrumental part just to see us work it out a little longer. I felt so good even though I knew my hair was flat as a pancake by now in all that heat. It kept flopping into my eyes every time he turned me. I hadn't danced like this since my days with Nick.

The tall brother spun me again, but I didn't finish the turn.

"What—?" I didn't know what was going on.

"Find your own woman to dance with."

"Sorry, man," the tall brother said, shrugged and started dancing to Rick James's "Superfreak."

David had me by the waist, dragging me off the floor like I was his errant child, and I was furious.

"Get off me!" I said, but when he refused to, I looked around at a few faces that seemed ready for a big blowup, so I stopped struggling. I couldn't have gotten away from him anyway. His arm was wrapped

around me so tight I was flush against his side, and I was already so hu-
miliated that I just let him lead me with my eyes on the floor. I wanted
to kill him. Just slap the living shit out of him for this. He took me up
the stairs and back out onto the deck where we had been sitting. Thank
God we were about to dock. I could barely wait to give him a piece of
my black mind. He half pushed me into the chair and stood up in front
of me, glaring at me like he was a cop getting ready to give me the
third degree. I rolled my eyes at him.

After a couple of minutes the ship began to slow. The motors were
throttled down and the captain made a final announcement to let us
know we were docking. Some guys and a few women on shore ran up to
pin the ship in place. God, I was fuming. I just wanted them to hurry
up with this boat so I could get away from here and just get home, because David was truly making me sick. He had the nerve to reach for
my hand as people rushed to exit the ship, once it was secure, in a big
balloon of a crowd, but I walked away.

"Wait a second," he said when we got onto dry land. He pulled me
by the arm over to the booth where they'd developed the picture we'd
taken when we got aboard. He found ours in the sea of pictures hanging up on some type of bulletin board and paid for it. Then he tried to
hand it to me so I could see it. I didn't want to see anything he had. I
just wanted to go home. When we finally got to his car and he unlocked the doors, I jumped in and slammed my door before he could
close it for me like he usually did. He looked as pissed as I was, walking around to his side. But so what. He had laid the truth about driving to Atlanta with Monica on me, and then had embarrassed the hell
out of me. He got in and started the car.

"What the fuck was that all about, David?" I was still so mad I
couldn't even look at him. If I looked his way I might spit in his damn
face.

"You'd better watch your mouth and learn how to talk to me the
right way," he said. He looked like he had been carved from stone.

I was about to explode, I was so angry. He was about to make me
hate him for sure. I was shaking, trying hard to keep from reaching
over and grabbing the wheel to wreck the damn car.

"Watch my—Who the hell do you think you are! Last time I
checked, your name wasn't on my birth certificate. You act like you
barely want to see me all week! Then when we do see each other, all you
want to talk about is how old you feel and losing your damn hair! I have
had it up to here listening to that shit, David!" I put a hand above my

head to demonstrate just how fed up I was. "Then on top of that, I come here with you tonight thinking I'm going to have a good time with you before you go gallivanting off on a fricking road trip with your wife, but all I get is the silent treatment! And when I finally do start having some fun on my own, your jealous ass ruins that too! What is going on here? Am I missing something or are you just fucking crazy?"

"No, you're the goddamn lunatic," he said. "Down on that floor shaking your damn ass with that young son of a bitch like you came with him tonight! What were you trying to do, make a damn fool of me out there, Genie?"

The man was insane. He was driving ninety and I wished I could jump out of the damn car to be away from him.

"First of all, you need to slow this car down. You're gonna get a ticket or get us killed. Second of all, I wasn't shaking my ass. I was dancing. A lot of people were dancing. I wasn't going to sit up there like a bump on a log looking at your sour ass all night!"

"Goddammit, Genie, I told you to watch it." He had the nerve to look like he was about to backhand me or something. If he did, I was going to whale his ass with the grandma purse I was carrying. But I figured I had better act like I had some sense while I was trapped in his car.

"David, I'm tired of this," I said. "You haven't been the same since you got back from Ghana. If you're freaked out about the Edward thing, then just tell me. Please."

He breathed in deeply and let it go.

"You really don't know me, do you?" he said. "How could you think I would be that insensitive? I would never hold what happened to you against you, Genie. Look, I don't want to talk right now. There are things you just can't understand." He turned onto my street and cruised down the hill.

"Oh, and Monica does, is that it? Is that why you've decided to drive down with her?"

He rolled his eyes and said, "Here we go again."

That really ruffled my feathers.

"You're damn right!" I said. "You wouldn't even let me dance with some stranger tonight. Matter of fact, you hit the ceiling when I went out for coffee with a friend. How do you think I feel about your spending all that time with your wife all next week?!"

He pulled up in front of the house and I jumped out of the car and slammed the door as hard as I could. I was so pissed about this whole thing that I started crying and couldn't stop.

"Why the hell are you always crying?" he said and I wanted to dig my fingernails right into his face.

"David," I said, fumbling for my door key, "just go, okay? If you miss Monica so much that you have to disrespect me like this, then fine. Have her. I don't care." I found the key and was about to put it in the door, but he grabbed my arm. The Negro had grabbed me one too many times tonight. I pushed him away from me but he shrugged me off and pushed past me into the house when I got the door open. I threw my purse on the sofa and turned on the lamp.

"David, I really think you should just go ahead and leave. It seems you're not happy without Monica, and I really don't need this shit." I was talking about his attitude, but he must have thought I was referring to our relationship, because he said, "You don't? That why you're suffocating me all the time?"

"What?" He was crossing the line now. He was obviously ready for a fight. I balled up my fist like I was going to do something with it.

"You heard me, Genie! You call constantly wanting me to see you, you're always sending goddamn E-mails and leaving voice messages or coming over to my place uninvited! All you ever worry about is if I'm doing something behind your back with Monica, and I'm really sick of your insecurities!"

That hurt the hell out of me. I plopped down on the sofa, put up a hand, shook my head and said, "Wait a minute. I think I have every right to be insecure, David! There's a woman you're still married to who told me that she intends to have you back! In the meantime I have to deal with your damn paranoia about getting older. On top of that I'm trying very hard with this therapy so I can try to get myself together, so you're damn right I'm insecure!"

He looked shocked. He put his hands in his pockets and stood in front of me and said, "What do you mean, she told you she intends to have me back?"

This was a can of worms I hadn't wanted to open, but he had pushed me into it. It was amazing, though, that out of all I'd said, *that* was the one thing he picked up on. I shook my head and said, "She approached me before you left for Africa and we exchanged a few words. There was really nothing to it. But that's not the issue here. I just want to know what the hell is going on with you."

He shook his head and said, "I don't know."

That bothered me, because I knew he was lying to me.

"Do you still love me, David?"

He looked up at me. "Of course I do," and turned away.

"You still want the same things I do?"

"Yeah."

I took a deep breath before I asked him, "You still love Monica?"

I didn't even get an answer from him, and a wave of pain ran through me. I didn't like the looks of this. I didn't like it at all.

"You know what, David? This is stupid," I said.

"What?" he asked.

"This," I said. "Us."

"What are you saying? You don't want to be with me anymore?"

"That's what I'm saying. I don't know about you, but I don't need these complications."

He sat down next to me, facing me.

"I'm not a complication, Genie. Despite some things I'm feeling right now, I know I'm in love with you. I want us to work."

I wasn't too sure he knew what he wanted, and that hurt.

"That's nice, David. That sounds really noble, but something's wrong with us, and if we're going to fix it, you have to tell me how you really feel."

"Genie, just leave it alone, okay. We'll be fine."

Frustrated, I jumped off the couch and put my hands on my hips.

"Something is wrong between us, David. I'm not blind, and I'm not stupid either. How am I supposed to leave it alone?"

He pulled height on me and stood up over me, pointing a finger in my face.

"Woman, I told you we'll be fine! Now just leave it the fuck alone"

I didn't believe this shit.

"Fine, David? Everything's going to be fine? If everything's supposed to be so fine, then why is it that the last few times we've been together, you haven't even been able to satisfy me? Why is that? Let's face it," I said, shrugging, "your sex drive just isn't a match for mine. A one-time Charlie isn't good enough for me, okay? I guess it was bound to happen sooner or later with a man your age."

I wanted that to wake him up to the fact that we needed to talk about this. More than that, I wanted to hurt him the way he didn't seem to realize he was hurting me. He was standing so close to me. I just wanted him to tell me that he wasn't going anywhere. I wanted him to prove that he didn't want any part of Monica, but he didn't say one word.

He looked shocked for a minute. But only a minute. Then he

grabbed my face and squeezed it like he was going to hit me, and I wanted him to. I know it was a sick thought, but I wanted some kind of passionate response from him. Anything. But he wouldn't even give me that. He let my face go. My cheeks were stinging where his fingers had dug into my face. Without another word he walked to the door and didn't even look back at me. He just left and slammed the door. I lay across the sofa and cried hard, hating myself for saying something so stupid, but at the same time, feeling like I was losing him anyway. Just like Monica said I would. He wanted her again. I could feel it in my bones the way he looked at me now and talked so much about our age difference, like he was completely paranoid. Once he even asked me what would happen if we didn't make it. I told him I would die if we didn't make it and he said, "you'd live," like being without him wouldn't be like physically taking my heart out of my body.

I thought about getting into my car and driving over to his place so I could stop him from going to Atlanta. I didn't want him to go. I fiddled with my ring and said a prayer. I don't know why. God doesn't support adultery. I couldn't let David leave like this, so I dialed his car phone number.

He knew it was me. He picked up but didn't say hello.

"David, I'm sorry I said that."

"No," he said, "you were right. You were absolutely right."

"David, I love you with all my heart. Please come back. Come hold me."

"I can't," he said. "I'm too tired and too fucking old to make it back over there."

He hung up right in my ear. I called back and got his voicemail three times. So I waited ten minutes and called him at home. I left him two voice messages there and gave up. I went into my bedroom with a glass of Sambuca and took off my clothes, leaving the pile on the floor. I got into bed and turned on the TV. *Dallas* was playing on TNN. J. R. kept me company while I cried myself to sleep.

Phase 14

David

"**D**avid. You remember the first time we drove down here together?"

"Mmhmm."

Dawn was just coming on. Monica and I had left the boys at the Morehouse College campus in Atlanta to rip and run, and now we were on our way to Moultrie to visit my Uncle Len and his wife, Rachel, for a bit. Rachel was Monica's first cousin, and she and Len had introduced us in '65 at their house. Len was only seven years older than I and more of a brother to me than Aaron. The three of us—Len, Aaron and I—grew up together in my grandmother's house in Chicago. Len taught me a hell of a lot about life. I hadn't seen him in over a year and couldn't wait to get to the house. My only nagging thought was that Monica and I hadn't told them we're separated. We hadn't told anyone, for that matter.

I set the cruise control at sixty after listening for an eternity to Monica's mouth going on about my speeding. Hell, I could handle a damn Caravan. I had forgotten my radar detector at home, though, so I guess it was better safe than sorry. Traffic was nonexistent. The windows were cracked and a breeze was tapping at my hat. Along that stretch of highway there was nothing to the view but miles and miles of trees and tall grass. An occasional car was pulled over by a trooper and maybe a rig or two rolled past us now and again like thunder. Otherwise the ride was dead calm. Monica was sitting next to me reclining in her seat. Her hair was covered with a blue scarf tied beneath her chin. And a straw hat was over that. She was always tired on the road. She still hadn't recuperated from the twelve-hour trip from Maryland three days ago, because we'd been on a constant run to get Devin settled when we got to the college. I knew she was fighting sleep because those tired eyes were on my face. Although my knees were protesting the long drive, I was wide awake and felt pretty good. I keep telling Monica a cup of coffee can do wonders, but she won't drink it.

"You asked me to marry you down here," she said. She put her hand on my bare arm and the hair there tingled. "Remember?"

I wondered what she was getting at. "'Course I remember, Monnie."

"You were so nervous. I didn't think you'd ever get the words out of your mouth. But you were so sweet and handsome. I knew what my answer would be even before you ever asked."

"Oh you did, did you?" I took my eyes away from the road a split second to glance over at her. Her hand fell off my shoulder.

"Yes," she said. "I never wanted anything more than I wanted to be your wife. Except for the boys."

That hurt. The absence of that bond between us made me feel so empty. She turned her body a bit and looked out her window like she didn't want to talk anymore, but she said, "What are we going to tell Len and Rachel?"

I didn't have a clue. Matter of fact, I didn't want to think about it. Or Genie, for that matter. I just wanted to feel good about seeing Len and Rachel again.

"I don't know," I said. "Maybe nothing."

She didn't respond to that. Just put her head against her window and was so quiet for the next half hour or so that I thought she went to sleep. I left her alone and thought about what I should do about my situation with Genie.

The dinner cruise had been a disaster. My plan was for us to leave our worries at the dock and just sit back and have a good time since I was leaving the following morning. I didn't even want to deal with what was bothering me. But Genie wanted to talk. Women always choose the wrong time for that. She wanted to bring up the age difference and kids, and it made me kind of tired. I know I hurt her feelings. I was cold and quiet the whole ride. But then she ditched me out on the deck. I thought she might come back, but when she was gone for more than a few minutes, I went to find her. Something told me to lean over the rail inside, and there she was, whirling on the dance floor below with some young, criminal-looking fella like she'd known him all her life. I mean, she was throwing that ass like a goddamn go-go dancer to that fast song they were playing. I went ballistic. I know it was wrong of me, but I wasn't thinking clearly. I just reacted to what I saw.

We fought in the car all the way to her house. Her big problem was that she didn't want me to drive down with Monica, but I had already decided. It didn't make sense for both of us to drive when we were headed in the same direction. But she was stuck on Monica wanting me back. And then she called me a one-time Charlie. What the hell kind of thing is that to say. Monica never would have said that to me. That shit cut deep. Doesn't she think I was starting to hear the disappointed sound in her voice when I come once and I'm ready to go to sleep? And that one night I couldn't even get it up, I could see the fear in her. I'm still embarrassed about that. She was probably asking herself if I was going impotent. Damn her.

I felt like knocking the piss out of her little ass when she said that I don't satisfy her. Her face was so close to mine I could have kissed her, but I had to go before I lost my temper any further. If that wasn't a sign that we can't make it together, then I'm not sure what more I need, short of a burning bush from God.

Once the sky got lighter, Monica came back to life.

"Excuse me," was the first thing she said. When I moved my knee out of her way she turned on the radio and tried for a minute to find something good on, but there was too much static, so she put in a B. B. King tape. I was in no mood for the blues. I had 'em already. She searched in some bag she had behind her seat and found the book she was reading.

"Monnie, what do you have good to eat in that bag?" I asked. We hadn't gotten breakfast, and the one rest stop we'd gone to hadn't had a food shop.

"Couple of sandwiches," she said. "Want one? Or some fruit?"

"What kind of sandwiches?"

"Your favorite. Ham and Swiss."

I put out a hand and she reached for her bag again and started rifling through it.

"You want something to drink?"

I nodded. The day was getting hot and I was beginning to sweat. I put both front windows up with the electric switch on my armrest and cut on the air. Monica handed me a smashed sandwich on wheat bread in some plastic and opened a cold can of apple juice and set it in the cup holder beside me.

"You know," she said. "I wish we had come down more often. We didn't have any excuse. We lived close enough. Maybe we should have taken some other trips together, just the two of us." She was starting again on stuff I wasn't ready to think about. I took a bite out of my sandwich. It was soggy with mayo and warm.

"I think this is our exit right . . . up . . . here. . . ." I veered off the main highway and braked behind a Camaro. Then I moved out onto a smaller highway and went up a few miles before I got off of it and drove toward the residential homes where Len and Rachel lived. The streets were bare of people.

"Ah," Monica said once we finally parked in front of the house. "I miss this old place. Rachel told me they've made some changes. Built on a Florida room last month and a new deck on the back of the house. Can't tell from here, though."

I downed the little can of juice and crushed it.

"Sure can't," I said. I switched off the van and took a good look at the place. The outside hadn't changed so much since the last time we were here. They had a ranch-style house with five bedrooms all to themselves. Their three kids were grown and gone. Rachel had their front yard looking beautiful as ever. They had a dogwood in the middle of the yard. Against the front of the house mixed in with the azaleas were hollyhocks and petunias, hosta and vincas. A rose bush was climbing the side of the house in front of the carport. Just beyond the carport was a pear tree. I noticed that Len had repainted the shutters white, and they looked good as new against the tan siding. The storm door was new—a heavy white one with a grape leaf design.

"Monnie," I said. "Let's keep our personal business between us, huh?" She looked at me and nodded.

"I think that would be best, too. I don't feel like doing a lot of explaining. Come on."

She took my hand and we walked up to the front door. It opened before Monnie could knock, and she and Rachel started screaming and making all kinds of dramatic noise.

"Aw, chile. I been looking out the window every minute this morning. Couldn't wait for y'all to get here." Rachel was trim and fit in a black sweat suit. Behind her thick glasses were a pretty pair of brown eyes. She was the same clear potato brown. She had the smooth-looking skin of a nectarine and her hair was black with white streaks and in a straight braid down the back of her neck.

She and Monnie hugged each other like they wanted to knock each other over. Monica's hat came off, then the scarf. I moved out of the way. I just stood back and put my hands in my pockets until Rachel was ready to notice me, standing inside the door, letting out the a/c.

"It is good to see you. Look at you, girl. Ooh." They hugged some more, laughing in between, and I wondered if I'd ever get a chance to get inside to take a piss.

"Well, you come on in here too, David Lewis," she said, giving me one of those pretty Rachel smiles. I still had a boyish crush on her from when I was fourteen and Len brought her home to meet the family, saying he was going to marry her. I think I blushed.

"How you doing, Rachel?" I said, smiling.

"Don't 'how you doing, Rachel' me. Come on give me a big hug."

I took my hands out of my pockets and hugged her tight. By then Len had made his appearance and was bear-hugging Monica. "Girl, you just get to be more beautiful every time I see you," he said, loud as usual. It was what he always said to her when he saw her.

"Ain't no flies on you either, Leonard. You know that's for sure," Monica responded with a smile. He kissed the back of her hand and she patted his shoulder, then he turned toward me. He was a bigger man than me. About six-foot-three and big-boned, with a head of thick black hair that I wished was mine.

"Heeey there, Doctor. What you know good, man?" Everybody in the family called me "Doctor" except Rachel and of course Monica. My grandmother started it because she had been so proud when I earned my doctorate.

"Len Lewis," I said. "My man. What's happening, man." I held out a hand, grinning.

Len and I went into a handshake that turned into one of those quick pat-on-the-back hugs, while Monica and Rachel went on down the hall squawking at each other like hens, they were talking so fast. Soon as they disappeared, Len leaned in on me and elbowed me like he was about to tell me his best kept secret and whispered, "Alright man. It's early, I know. But I'm about to get me a little nip. So what you drinking? Beer? Courvoissier? You know I got what you want. Even got some of that cheap-ass wine my old lady likes to sip on."

Len was a heavy drinker from way back. He drank me under the table many a night. Since we were going back to Atlanta tonight, I knew I had to watch it.

"Slow down there, bartender," I said, "we've got all day for that. It's ten a damn clock. I haven't even had a real breakfast yet. Let me get in here and sweet-talk Rachel into fixing me some of that country ham and grits and eggs first. Then you can fix me up after I've let it digest." I rubbed my hand down my stomach.

"Doctor, you drive a hard bargain. But since you're a guest, I guess I'll let my wife feed your black ass."

We laughed and he whacked me on the back.

"First I've got to get to the washroom," I said and found my way there.

I took care of things and we sat around the kitchen. Rachel's cooking was smelling like heaven to me. She was something else in the kitchen. Just like my grandma. I was sitting at the breakfast bar with the coffee Monnie had just given me, watching Rachel turn these thick slices of ham like a professional. The grits were simmering in a covered pot and she broke open two brown eggs on the griddle with the ham.

"So, Doctor, how's that job of yours treating you? You still on cloud nine?" Len had retired from the postal service and was enjoying life in the slow lane.

"It's a decent living, Len. I almost wish I'd have gotten into it sooner. The flexible schedule is exactly what I need at this point in my life. You go in to the office when you feel like it, you work at home when you feel like it. For instance, I haven't been in the office since I came back from West Africa."

"Well that's alright, then," Rachel said, setting my plate in front of me. She had sliced me a small piece of melon that I salted and started on first.

"Speaking of Africa, you remember ol' Swoop Johnson?"

I said, "Sure I remember Swoop. Had the frog eyes and the gap between his teeth."

Len laughed and said, "Yeah. That's ol' Swoop."

"We called him Swoop 'cause one day we were walking home from the movies and a bird swooped down and took a shit on him," I told Monica.

We all laughed.

"I know. I remember," Monica said and took a bite of my toast.

"Oh right," I said. "What am I thinking about? Of course you know Swoop." I had forgotten that Monica knows just about everybody I know. With Genie, I always had to explain who I was talking about.

"Anyway, Swoop done got himself an African woman now, man."

"Oh yeah? What happened to Sally?"

"Man, me and Rachel went up to Chicago in June and ran into Swoop. He finally got rid of Sally. Said he gon' marry this African gal, Esther. She a pretty little thing too." Len cut his eyes over at Rachel, who waved a hand at him and said, "She was alright, Leonard," and finished eating the heart out of the watermelon.

"'Member how Swoop and Sally used to fight?" I asked. I mixed my grits and eggs and kept eating.

"Fight," Rachel said. "Them two was World War One and Two combined, the way they went at it."

Len rubbed his knees and laughed. "Yep," he said. "Them two was something else. I remember that time when Sally whooped him for sneaking around with Francine."

I laughed hard on that one, because I remembered getting thrown to the ground trying to pull big Sally off the man.

"Man, she half killed that boy." I said. "That woman could box like a man. After she blacked both his eyes, I think she beat him with her purse awhile. Threw some rocks at him. Turned the waterhose on him. She was uncontrollable."

"What about the time," Monica said, "when we were all going to that club and they got to fighting in the car."

Rachel set a plate in front of Len and sat down across from him at the table. Len wasn't interested in the food. He had his gin and fruit juice in one of those small jelly jars Rachel used for canning.

"Girl, I was mad that night," Rachel said. "We all dressed up to have a good time and then they wanting David to pull over so they can fight on the side of the road. Mmm."

"She shot at him with her .22 that night too, didn't she?" Monica asked.

"Sure did. Child, the man was running so fast you could have shot marbles off his coattails. Then she had enough nerve to take him to the hospital after she shot him." Rachel remembered.

We laughed hard and I thought about poor Swoop limping and holding on to Sally for support.

"Now how are the kids?" I asked. "Last time I talked to Len he told me Rita was thinking about law school."

"Oh, child, they all doing just fine. Rita's applied to a few schools up north and is waiting to hear. And let's see, Kenny and his wife is having another baby. You know they give us a grandson already. And then Artis is in Germany now. He'll be there for another eight months or so, and after that he's hoping to get stationed in Augusta so he can be closer to us."

"Well, that's right nice," Monica said, making me smile. Her drawl came and went sometimes.

"Yeah child," Rachel said. "I don't have no complaints. The good Lord give us some fine children. Speaking of, what about the boys? I know you two excited as anything that Devin's going to such a fine school."

"Yes indeed. I just hope that Mark will follow in his footsteps."

Out of the corner of my eye, I could see Len giving me a signal with his jelly glass.

"Well, Rachel, you have not lost your touch, sweetheart," I said, picking up my plate to scrape it. I rinsed it in the sink and set it on the counter above the dishwasher.

"Thank you, sir. Thank you."

I winked, hoping that Monica wouldn't notice. She was hell on wheels whenever she saw me drink, especially knowing that we'd be back on the road soon.

"Come on, Doctor, let's go out back so I can show you my new deck." He winked back to let me know he had me covered. We started to leave the room but Monica caught me by the arm and said, "If I smell even a drop of liquor on your breath, I'm driving us back, David." Women must have some kind of antenna for this type of shit. I shrugged and said, "All I'm going to drink is some seltzer, babe." Damn. I kept slipping. I kept forgetting I wasn't supposed to call her that anymore, but I'd been doing it for so long it was second nature. Monica knew I was lying but she let me off the hook. She must have been in a good mood.

I followed Len through to the back of the house. Their new room was small and full of windows. It reminded me of the hot-tub room in the Outer Banks, without the hot tub. Rachel had put a whole bunch of white wicker and plants in the room. It was nice. Len stopped at a little refrigerator in an alcove to pour me a little glass of his pre-mixed "medicine," and I took a sip when he handed it to me. It was so strong it burned, but I didn't let Len know it. I'd have choked to death first. We went out through the sliding glass doors onto the deck and I was impressed by the workmanship. It was artistically done. There were two levels to it. It had fan railings. A set of curved steps. The works. It was so big they had two sets of lawn furniture with the big umbrellas and the long beach-like chairs.

"Now if you get in big trouble for this, you know I'ma lie and say you made me give you that drink. You want to pitch a few?" He gestured toward the yard where he kept his horseshoes.

"This deck is beautiful, man," I said, following him down the stairs. "Yeah, I guess you could use a good whipping. Seeing as though you were lucky enough to take out the master last time."

"Luck had nothing to do with it, brother. This here," he said holding up his right hand, "is skill. Pure skill."

He set his drink on the bottom rail of the deck and gathered the horseshoes so we could start our game.

"Okay, Doctor," he said. "What's going on with you and Monica?"

I scratched my head and tossed my horseshoe. Missed by a mile.

"What do you mean?"

"Man, I'm a lot of things, but I'm not blind. I know both of you too well and I can see something's wrong. What's going on? Oho. Nailed it, didn't you." He pointed toward the horseshoe I'd thrown and I smiled, nodding.

"We're just having some minor problems is all, Len. That's all. You ever feel like your whole life is spinning out of control, man? Like you woke up and you don't know who you are or . . . whether you're coming or going?"

"Hey, man. I been there. Don't think I haven't. Feel like you have no real direction and you wonder if the choices you've made in your life up to now were the right ones."

I shook my head. I didn't really feel up to horseshoes anymore. I walked back up the steps and found myself a seat among all that furniture. Took a bigger sip of my drink. Len came and joined me.

"Man," he said. "It's a difficult thing to deal with. Especially when you don't understand why it's happening."

"But there's this woman, Len and—"

"I know." He put a hand on my shoulder. "I've been there too." I was surprised, because he and Rachel seemed so perfect together.

"How do you handle this shit, man? Getting older. Feeling like life's got you by the balls. How do you work it all out in your head?" I looked up at him and hoped he could give me the answers I needed so much. He looked out into the next yard.

"Doctor," he said. "I'ma tell you like this. I don't care what else turns your head. I don't care how confused you get, how lonely, how discouraged or how depressed. Family is what's important. There's a woman in there that I know loves you. You've got two pretty good kids the two of you have worked hard to raise. Sometimes the few self sacrifices we make to maintain the family are the same sacrifices that will give you satisfaction in the long run. They will. And I think you love your wife and kids enough to sacrifice a little something you think you want because believe it or not, you've already got everything you need. I'm sure you and Monica have your problems. We all do. But Monica's a good woman and you know it. Don't let go of a sure thing for a mirage, man. You'll regret it."

I wondered if it was possible to love two women at once, but I didn't ask Len his opinion. Instead of helping me figure out what to do, he had confused me more. I thought about what he said the whole drive back to Atlanta. And I thought about starting over with Genie, and all the problems we were having. But I couldn't bring myself to think about officially breaking it off with Genie. Len was wrong about that. It would be no small sacrifice. If I decided to walk away from Genie for good, it would be the same as sacrificing my soul.

Genie

I've been trying to pinpoint what the problem is between me and David and how we got away from that feeling, that passion between us that made me feel so good all the time. David's in Atlanta now, and I haven't heard a word from him since that awful night of the dinner cruise. That was a scene right out of a bad movie. I've never been in love before, but I know it isn't supposed to feel scared like this.

I am trying to prepare myself for losing him for good. I keep wondering what my life will be like without David in it. The answer is, nothing. David has brought so much love, so much hope into my life that if he leaves, he takes it with him. Then I'll be here with no love and no hope. The two things you need to live and not just survive in this world. It makes me so scared to think about it, I feel like I can almost reach out and touch the fear. I need to talk to him. I need to hear him tell me he still loves me too and that we really are meant for each other.

I must have left the man a hundred messages at his house and on his voicemail at work. I wrote him a long letter, too, and left it on his pillow at his apartment. Now I'm just waiting to hear from him. Just waiting. Instead of falling in love with David, I should have stuck to my theory. At least then I was safe.

I've barely left my house waiting for that telephone to ring. I missed group Tuesday trying to get home to see if he called, and it worries me to death to think that maybe he hasn't gotten over Monica. I know she's just been waiting for some reason to get her hooks in him again. I just know it. This is her chance to try to turn David against me.

That was on my mind when I opened my door to get my paper Wednesday evening and saw Chris standing on my doorstep, grinning. Again. He was holding a pizza box this time and he looked just like he was delivering because he had on a Bulls cap turned backward, some jeans and an Ice Cube T-shirt.

"Hey, I dream of Genie," he said.

I sucked my teeth and rolled my eyes.

"Boy, get in here," I said, pulling him by his arm. I closed my robe over my nightie and belted it.

"You just want me for my pizza, don't you. You aren't fooling anybody, Ms. Gatlin."

I think Chris was taking it upon himself to take care of me now that David and I were on the outs. He hung around enough. I liked his company because he made me feel comfortable and he cracked me up. We had gotten into the habit of doing some of the things David had stopped doing with me. We went for morning coffee, did lunch, went to the movies sometimes, and twice he'd come by with dinner. I guess he was trying to be my surrogate boyfriend until me and David could iron things out. He had to know he couldn't steal me away from David.

I closed the door and Chris turned on the light in the living room.

"Damn, baby. What happened to you?" He put the pizza on the table and took my hand. He started raking my wicked hair back out of my face and I didn't say a word. I was too ashamed to admit that I'd been lying in the bed crying my eyes out since I got in from work.

"Still haven't heard from him, huh?"

I shook my head no and leaned my forehead on Ice Cube's left eye and started to cry all over again. I felt so powerless and stupid.

"Hey. He'll turn up sooner or later, baby. And if it is really over, you don't need him anyway. He's just being a coward, I think."

"But it was my fault, Chris. You didn't see his face when I said what I said to him." He cupped my chin and made me look at him, as ugly and screwed up as my face was.

"What'd you say?" he asked.

"That he couldn't satisfy me in bed." He let go of me and sat on the couch.

"Aw, baby," he said, patting the couch for me to sit next to him. "You know damn well you aren't supposed to attack a man's manhood. I don't blame him for going off the deep end. Was it true?" He gave me this side glance like he wanted some gossip from me. I wasn't about to give him any detailed information about David's dick.

"No, it wasn't. It was a big fat lie." I sat down next to him and he wrapped one of those long chocolate arms around me and kissed me on top of my head. I needed to be babied right now.

"Even if it's not true," he said, "you probably have the man going out of his skull worrying about it. There's not much you can do now, baby, but chill out and let him work things out in his head."

"You think he'll call soon, though?" I asked, wiping my eyes, but being careful because I'd just gotten my nails done yesterday. I didn't care whether David had to work something out in his head or not. I couldn't rest until I heard from him.

"I don't know, sweets. But I know it's no good sitting around here crying and feeling sorry for yourself. If you had made group last night you'd know that. Want some pizza?" He leaned forward and pushed himself up off my thigh. Trying to be slick and cop a feel, I knew, but I let him slide.

"Yeah I want some," I said, sounding all destroyed. My telephone rang and I ran to it with no shame, but it was just Paulette, so I turned on the answering machine to let it pick up.

"That's cold, Genie. I bet you do that shit sometimes when I call, don't you?" He reached into the pizza box and put two slices on each of the plates I'd handed him.

"No," I lied. "I'm only doing it now because you're here, C."

He shook his finger at me and said, "You talk a good game, baby, you know that?"

"Not good enough for my man, though," I said and flopped into one of the dining room chairs.

"No, that doesn't mean you don't talk a good game, that just means that you talk too damn much." I started laughing. The man reminded me too much of David Lewis. The way he used to be when we were first together.

"Thanks a lot," I said.

"You're welcome. Say, what you have in there to drink?"

I shrugged. "Cranberry juice, orange soda, milk, tea. Some bottled water."

"Okay, give me all that," he said, with this stupid look on his face.

I fell out laughing and said, "Shut up, please. And pour me some juice while you're in there."

We played Tonk for an hour and threw the rest of the pizza away because it was dry as a bone and downright nasty. Chris wanted to sit out in the lawn chairs on the deck, so I put on some Skin-So-Soft to ward off the mosquitoes, some long pants and a long sleeved shirt, and I lit two citronella candles.

"Yeah, this is nice," he said, stretching out in one of the chairs.

"I know, isn't it? David and I never really came out here too much. I don't know why."

"Genie, you think we can go two minutes without talking about the nutty professor?"

"Excuse me," I said. Even though it was dark, we both had on our shades like we were by the pool in Hollywood, soaking up sun. I crossed my ankles and watched the lightning bugs out in the yard.

"Don't be mad at me," he said and leaned his head against my arm.

"I'm not. I just miss him."

"I know you do," he said. He kissed the back of my hand and it made me ashamed of myself, because for some reason I wanted Chris to make love to me right in this chair. I felt so alone and I just wanted somebody to touch me because it had been so long. I leaned toward him and our lips touched. Then our tongues. His mouth was warm, but cool. Different from David's kiss, but good. It gave me a thrill that shot straight through me and lifted me into his arms, but it scared me to think that I could care for Chris, so I pulled away and found my shades where they'd fallen beside my hip in my chair.

"Damn, that was nice," he said and leaned back with his hands behind his head.

"Chris, you know I'm in love with David." I put my shades back on.

"I didn't say you weren't, baby. I just said it was nice. Not to admit that it was good would be a lie. Chill out. It was only a good kiss." He patted my leg like I was tripping.

"Yeah. That's why I'm in this mess with David now. An innocent kiss between friends."

"Baby, I've learned that it's best to make conscious decisions about everything you do."

I looked over at him above the top of my shades and said, "What do you mean?"

"I mean getting yourself hooked up like that with an old married man with kids is just asking for pain. Me, I would have avoided a woman like that. Period."

"And was kissing me just now a conscious decision?"

"Nothing but. I'm a single man with no kids, and I want a family of my own. I crave it. Despite how you feel right now, you're a single woman holding onto something that sounds pretty much over, but you fail to realize that it's not this professor you want so much, but a family. You need to face it, Genie. We're at the same place in life. I think we understand each other and we have a lot in common. So when you decide to get over this confused bum who's making you crazy like this, I'm here. That kiss, for me, was my way of letting you know where I stand. Unlike your David, I'm always man enough to say where I stand."

I was floored by what he was saying to me.

"I thought you said it was just a kiss and that I should chill out."

"It was just a kiss. Hopefully the first of many and a prelude to better things to come. It was also my way of making you aware of the possibilities. I think we could have something special together, Genie. I really do."

I believed that too. But there were so many hopes and dreams that David had awakened in me. I couldn't give that up. I loved David more than I ever knew I was capable of loving a man.

"What'd you guys talk about in group last night?" I asked, trying to change the subject and keep myself from asking Chris to make love to me. He was nice enough to play along.

"Building self-esteem," he said. "It was a good session. I spoke some about how my mother used me by telling me I was nothing without her. That no girl would ever want me because I was ugly and no good."

"Chris, you know that's not true."

"I know it now after being in therapy for two years. But for a long time I didn't. I was totally self-destructive for years."

"How old are you?"

"Thirty. You?"

"Twenty-five. Your mother still alive?"

"Yeah, as far as I know. I haven't seen her in about twelve years. Last I heard she was overseas in Germany somewhere. Had hooked up with some dude in the army or something."

"Mmm. Edward's dead now. He died of cancer last month."

"How do you feel about that?"

"I don't know. At first I was glad, because I always carried this fear around that he'd come find me and hurt me again. I felt relieved. Chris, you ever have bad dreams about your mother?"

"Used to. A while ago. You?"

"Yeah. A recurring dream. I keep dreaming about the day Edward raped me in front of her, but Edward's not there. It's just my mother and it's like she's holding me on the piano bench. She looks dead and then she starts taking her eyes out and stuff. . . . That part I can figure out, but when she opens her mouth to speak, all she does is groan. I know she wants to tell me something, but she can't."

"Damn, Genie. That's a terrible dream to keep having. Maybe she wants to apologize to you for not helping you. You know, the hardest thing to give someone sometimes is an apology. Maybe she wants to say it, but can't."

"Hmm. I never thought about that. I guess that's a possibility. What were your dreams like?"

"Crazy. She was always after me in these different disguises and different places. Like a chameleon. I haven't had those dreams since I've been in therapy, though. Once I broke through the fear."

"That's what I can't wait for. I just want to not be afraid anymore. I just feel like getting on with my life, Chris. Being happy. But now David's not acting right."

"He knows about what happened to you, doesn't he?"

"Yeah, I told him," I said and shook my head.

"He been supportive?"

"As much as it's possible for him to be, I guess. He has things he's been focusing on. He's writing a book, and he's stressed about that and about getting older. I guess he's been worried about me, too."

"Excuses, excuses," Chris said, but I ignored that.

"Chris, you think I lost him?" I asked.

"I can't say, baby," Chris told me. "I'm not inside his head."

I looked up at the stars and thought that if I'd had a million dollars I would have paid every cent to anybody who could have told me what was going on inside David's head.

David

When it rains, it pours, and right now it's coming down on my life like a cow pissing in the river. In four days I'll be a fifty-three-year-old man, and what do I have to show for it? A girlfriend I'm avoiding who looks more like she should be my daughter. A lonely apartment with no signs of life in it. Writer's block. And a goddamn balding head. I went in to see a doctor about the hair Saturday, but when he explained the process of taking some of the hair at the back of my head by the root and surgically implanting it on top, I opted out. It sounded tedious and painful. I'm going to look into getting some Rogaine instead.

When I returned home from the doctor's office all I did was lie in the bed and think all day. I had some decisions to make about my life. The rest of my life. I needed to get a handle on this whole situation. I needed to weigh the pros and cons.

First, I thought about the age difference. Genie doesn't understand anything about this getting-old shit. She has years to go before she can begin to see what I mean. Plus, she's working so hard, trying to get herself straight mentally. She doesn't need to deal with my baggage in addition to the luggage she's already toting. And I'm starting to wonder if I'm strong enough for myself to be there for her. I think she needs more attention and care than I can give right now. She says I'm a selfish man. I know she's right, but I don't know what to do to help me or her.

There are other small things that I learned about myself on the trip to Atlanta. I missed like hell that I don't have to explain to Monica who everybody is that I talk about from the old days because she already knows. I missed feeling like I could be myself and not having to dress a certain way or kill myself to run every single morning because I have to look the part for Genie. Monica understands exactly what I mean when I say I feel old. She's feeling it with me. Twelve years later she's still telling people she's forty. We both dye our hair. We've both got a few wrinkles. And what the hell am I going to do with a newborn baby when I'm fifty-four, with one son in college and one on the way to college next year? How ridiculous would a fella like me look pushing a stroller and getting up for two A.M. feedings? And Genie wants two kids. I'll probably be dead by the time they reach puberty. Dead and completely bald.

The pros to Genie's credit are the fact that I know she loves me, she gives me a lot of attention, she's a good and beautiful woman inside and out, and sex with her is better than a rich man's income. To me those are pretty good pros, so I made the decision to see if we could possibly work things out. Coming to that decision was several times easier than trying to find the words to say goodbye to Genie. Even though something inside me missed Monica like hell.

I finally went in to the office on Tuesday. I figured I'd take a minute break from my depressing apartment to prepare for this course and see if any students were looking for me. See Genie and tell her I'd read her letter and although I've got some reservations about us, I still want to try. I guess. I just don't want to feel like I've failed again.

It was good to see the old building. I hadn't been in since my trip to Ghana. I took the elevator up and went into the main office first. I didn't see Genie, so I went ahead and collected my mail and a cup of hot coffee.

"Hi, Dr. Lewis." Justine was coming down the hall from the back with her sunburned arms full of bulletins for the shelf out front.

"Good morning, Justine. How you doing?"

"I'm fine." She smiled and just did make it to the desk.

I looked in Genie's doorway.

"Where's Genie this morning?"

"She went over to the fellowships office."

"Thanks." I was relieved. I didn't feel like facing her just yet because I knew she was mad that I hadn't called her while I was away. I turned to walk across the hall into my office.

"Well, if it isn't Dr. Lewis."

It was that blimp Barbara. Another woman I had wished to avoid. She was standing in her doorway looking like she wanted to chat. I wasn't in the mood.

"Barbara." I nodded and spotted Winthrop walking past the door.

"Professor Winthrop," I said, making a big display of being glad to see him. "Hello, sir." I put a hand on his back.

"Lewis, my friend. Finally decided to make a personal appearance, I see. Where've you been? I tried to reach you all last week."

I unlocked my office and ushered him in.

"Had to take my son down to get settled in at Morehouse. He's starting this fall."

"Right. Right. I had forgotten about that. Listen, I'd like to have a word with you, if you have a few minutes."

"Alright." He looked pretty serious. He shut my door and my interest was definitely piqued. I gestured for him to have a seat and sat myself down behind my desk.

"David, I have come to think of you as a friend. I have a great deal of respect for you as a person and for your work."

My brow furrowed on that one. I couldn't for the life of me figure out what he was getting at.

"Ben, what is this all about?" He shifted uncomfortably like he had bad news for me.

"David, I believe you are going to have one hell of a career here at Whitman. You're publishing all the time. Your first course was a success. The faculty is definitely for you. Off the record, I believe I can safely say, even at this early date, that you are a shoo-in for tenure. More importantly, it has been my hope that another African American like myself, with a high degree of integrity and a natural gift for establishing good relations with students, can give our current faculty concrete evidence of the significant importance of having a diverse faculty. I would like for you and me to be, shall we say, the trailblazers in this department for people of color. And not only for African Americans, but for all people of color."

"I don't know about being a trailblazer, Ben, but I am one hundred percent for diversification. I think a faculty should mirror its students."

"So you're with me then?"

"I support your view, if that's what you mean."

"What I mean," he said, boring into me with his black eyes, "is that if you value your career, then you have to give her up."

My heart did a somersault, I think. I could feel the blood rising to my ears and I wanted to get out of that box of a room. I accidentally knocked my letter opener off the desk.

"I don't know what you mean," I told him, trying to save my crumbling façade. I gazed out of the window so I wouldn't have to look into those keen eyes.

"David," he said, "there's a neat little thing we have called a Code of Ethics. Not all people follow the Code, but it's there. Sometimes people blatantly break its rules. You've seen it in your short time here. I've seen it in my many years here. But the ones who get away with it have something that you don't. You are not a white man. And make no mistake, Professor Lewis. Your vitae and your work here may well call you a man worthy of tenure, but because you are black you are being scrutinized under the lens of a microscope. If there is but one bacteria found in your character they will crucify you. I'm telling you this as your friend, David. I want to see you do well here. Leave Genie Gatlin alone, man."

I gave up the denial. He seemed to have some inside track on my love life.

"How do you know about us? And does anyone else?"

"The gods be praised you've been very discreet. I don't think anyone suspects a thing. I only know because I saw the two of you together when I took my wife on the *Spirit of Washington* last week. How did you allow yourself to get involved with the secretary, David? She's very tempting, of course, but Monica's a lovely, mature woman. If you have to engage in extramarital affairs, then I advise you to do so outside this office."

How was I going to explain to him that it wasn't some sordid affair.

"Monica and I are separated right now."

He leaned across the desk.

"Because of this? Then this thing is serious then." He shook his head and sat back again and said, "I hadn't counted on that. What are you going to do, then? If Stevens gets a whiff of this you'll be out the door. Girls like that are liable to file harassment suits these days."

I was as uncomfortable as anything sitting there discussing my goddamn love life in the office.

"Listen, Ben," I said, "thanks for the tip. I'll think long and hard about what you said. I appreciate your concern."

I felt like death when he walked out of my office. I just wanted to run and hide somewhere, but my telephone rang. I almost let it go to voicemail, but remembered that my voicemail was probably full, so I picked up.

"This is David Lewis."

"David?" It was Monica, and she sounded hysterical.

"Monnie, what is it?"

"David, it's Mark. He didn't come home last night. He called and left a message on the machine, saying that he was spending the night with his friend Reggie. But then Reggie called this morning looking for him and . . . David, I checked his room and some of his clothes are gone and his suitcase is gone too. I don't know what to do."

This whole thing was not happening. It just wasn't happening. I sat on a corner of the desk, feeling weak. Why does shit always come up all at once?

"How much do you think he has on him, Monica?"

"He has two thousand dollars in his savings. I'm not sure what he had here."

"Shit. That's enough to take him pretty far. You call the police?"

"Yes. They told me that I could file a report, but a seventeen-year-old runaway isn't a priority. And he's only been gone overnight. I went ahead and filed the report anyway."

"I'm on my way."

I grabbed my briefcase and headed for the door.

By the time I got to the house I had a migraine and fear in my heart. It was strange pulling up in front. I hadn't been to the house since I'd left, and I really missed the place. I only gave that a minute's thought, however, because I was too worried about Mark. I used the key I hadn't taken off my key ring to open the door. Monica was sitting on the sofa looking like she'd been through hell.

"I'm so glad you're here." I got up the stairs and pulled her into my arms.

"Babe, everything's gonna be alright. We'll find him." I didn't want her to know I was just as scared as she was.

"I'm so worried about him."

"First things first. You have any idea why he would do this?" We sat on the sofa. I kept an arm around her.

She nodded and said, "Yes. I think he's taken what's happened between us harder than he's let on. I've been trying to handle it, David. I thought he was beginning to accept it. Mark acts like the tough kid, but he's much more sensitive than Devin."

I knew that. He was just like me. That hit me right in the gut.

"You know anybody he might have told where he was going? Any friends? What about Cheryl?"

"I called all the numbers on his caller ID. Cheryl's at her grandmother's in Newport News. Her mother's going to call me back once she gets a hold of her. I called Devin and he told me some places to check. I was just waiting for you so we can go look for him. I forwarded both lines to this phone in case he calls." She held up her cellular.

"And Devin hasn't heard from him?"

"Not a word."

"Dammit. Okay," I said, grabbing her hand. Let's go see if we can find him."

We drove around all day looking for him, but couldn't find the boy anywhere. We checked the three closest malls, the arcade places Devin told Monica about, the movies, the recreation center. We tried everywhere. Poor Monica was an even worse wreck when Cheryl's mother called her to let her know that Cheryl hadn't heard from Mark. We stopped past the police station on our way back to the house to find out if they'd come up with anythiing and to drop off a photo. They didn't have anything either, but the officer we spoke to was very patient with us.

We were both basket cases by the time we got back to the house. Monica fixed us something to eat, since we hadn't had anything all day. We went back in the living room to sit and wait. We tried to think of anyplace else he might be, but it was getting late. Monica was wide awake, so she went in the kitchen to make more phone calls, while I sat on the sofa and thought about the damage I might have done to my own son just because I was selfish enough to want to grab onto something that felt good to me. I never once really analyzed how terrible my actions would look to Mark.

Around eleven I heard a car door slam, so I got up and looked out the front window. In the streetlight I saw Mark's dark head and his long, lean frame in oversized clothes. He was carrying a shoulder bag and a suitcase. I was so relieved every drop of energy drained out of me, leaving me so weak I could barely get down those steps to meet Mark at the door.

"Monnie!" I yelled.

She came rushing out of the kitchen the same time the door opened.

"My baby," she said, even though he's two heads taller than she. She damn near tripped getting down those steps and she pulled him close to her and squeezed him. I wasn't for all the hugging. I was glad my boy was alright, but I was more than ready to whip his ass for doing something so stupid.

"Mark where have you been? You had your mother and me worried sick over you."

My jaw was tense. He looked up at me scared to death. He had every right to be, because I was beyond pissed off and looked it.

"Where in hell did you think you were going?"

"I'on know. I wasn't sure where to go."

"Where've you been?"

"I stayed up Marshall's house last night and hung out wit' him today."

"Who's Marshall?" Monica asked.

"Same dude that was having the party you ain't let me go to." Monica threw up her hands like she gave up and leaned against the front door. I was too pissed not to put my hands on him for a minute, so I grabbed the boy by the arm.

"Boy, what the hell possessed you to do something like this?" I said. I pulled him so close to me that I could feel his heavy breathing on my face. His nostrils flared like he was angry with me, and I was ready to deck him any second.

"David, please," Monica said. "Don't." Her hand was on my back.

I let the boy go, and he started crying and sat on the steps with his head in his hands.

"I don't know what I was doing, Dad," he said. "I don't know. I just know we was a family again for a whole week down in Atlanta. Mom ain't laughed like that in a long time. Dang. You ain't laughed like that in a long time either. Then we get back here and you go back over to that apartment again. And Mom, she try to be strong about it, but you don't have to listen to her crying at night when she thinks I'm sleep. I guess I was just doing like you did, Dad. I was running away from everything."

That shook me to my core. Tears came to my eyes. Monica took Mark in her arms and I just stood there unable to do a thing. What can you do when you're responsible for hurting your child? Ever since they were born, I had tried my best to protect my kids from harm. I realized I'd lied to myself when I'd thought that choosing a different life would make them happy.

"Mom, I'm sorry," he was saying, "I just couldn't take it anymore."

He cried harder than I'd seen him cry since he was eight years old.

"Sshhh," Monica told him, drawing his head into her lap. "It's okay, baby. It's alright."

Shit. I didn't know what to say, and I couldn't take hearing any more of this. I couldn't stand looking at my boy's hurt, knowing that

I'd put it there inside him. It tore me up so bad. I had to go off by my-self for a minute to get myself together or something.

I went upstairs and walked past the kitchen, then climbed the sec-ond flight and walked into my old bedroom. Once I closed the door, the room fell completely dark. I felt my way over to the bed. I took off my shoes to lie down on that bed I'd slept in for five years and pressed my face against the cool pillow where I used to lay my head every night not long ago. Aw, it felt good. Monica had the kind of sheets on that I like. Cotton. I'm not too keen on the satin ones Genie loves so much. I could smell the scent of Monica's perfume permeating the bedroom. My hand hit something on her pillow and accidentally knocked it off the bed. It was one of her books, I knew.

When did I become this person? How did I get to the point of con-doning taking away from my sons what they needed most? How did I trick myself into believing that I could be more a part of their lives by running out on their lives? Running out on my life?

I did have a life too. Being a husband and father weren't my defin-ers. It was the ways in which I carried out those roles that helped define me. As well as the actions I took as a man. That's what Len had been trying to tell me. To get me to understand. Winthrop called me a man of integrity. How much integrity have I lost in the eyes of my children for making the decision I made?

I pulled the spread up over my shoulders and stared into the dark-ness, sifting through the last six months of my life in my head. What I saw scared me. I gave up my wife and my home and my children, al-most jeopardized the career I love, for something that can never fulfill me. For a woman I hold great passion and adoration for, but with whom I can never grow with and who can never understand me, no matter what. Starting over wasn't the answer. I felt a sense of loss so deep, I just shut my eyes and let the tears come. I don't want more chil-dren, I told myself. I don't want to spend another day inside the silent walls of that apartment. I don't want to start a life with a woman who makes me feel like I have to prove that I am worthy.

The door opened and I knew it was Monica coming to check on me. For a second the light from Mark's room down the hall spilled into the room, hurting my eyes. But then the door closed again. I heard Mon-ica's footsteps as she moved across the floor toward me. She must have known what I was feeling, because she left the light off. Then I felt her body all warm against me as she sat on the bed near me and put her hand on my face. I didn't know how to tell her that I had been so wrong. I sat up in the bed, trying to find those words. My eyes had readjusted to the darkness, so I could see the silhouette of her face and I put my hands in her hair. I had loved this woman most of my life. She was as much a part of me as the children we had created together. I had become a man with her and because of her. There was no turning my back on that.

I didn't resist her mouth when she leaned forward to find mine. There are times when things familiar seem old and stale to the mind, but there are other times when they are a balm to your wounds. I felt like Monica's kiss was reconnecting me with my true self. I moved over to make room for her on the bed and she lay in my arms with hers wrapped around me like the protective mother she is.

"Is he okay?" I asked. I wasn't ready to face Mark yet.

"He will be. I talked to him and he understands that he did a stupid thing. I think it was his way of trying to make us take notice of his feelings. He asked me if we could talk about it in the morning, though. Said he was tired. I hate seeing my baby like this, David. He's so like you the way he holds in all his feelings."

I had nothing to say to that. All I knew was that I was the root of the problem and I wanted to fix it if I could.

"If you're blaming yourself, David, then you have to blame me too," she said.

I didn't understand that a bit. I was the one who'd walked out. Not her. She was the one who had tried so hard to hold things together for the kids. I kissed the top of her head and pressed my face into her hair.

"Why do you say that?"

"You didn't stop holding on to our marriage just because you were bored with it. You stopped because I had stopped. I had forgotten what's important, David."

"Apparently so did I."

I think that gave her a jolt, because she sat up, reaching for the lamp and turned on the light.

"What are you saying?" she asked. I saw the hope in her eyes and I wanted it there. I was so afraid that it might be too late for us. I remembered the day I had asked her to marry me with that cheap twenty-five-dollar ring I'd found in a pawnshop in New York. She'd had that same look on her face then. She still wore that ring even though I'd bought her an expensive one on our tenth anniversary.

"I'm not sure what I'm saying right now, Monnie. I need some time to think about it. But lately I've been wondering if our marriage can be salvaged."

She got out of bed and pulled back the blinds to look out the window. I wondered what she was doing.

"You know that's what I want, David." She turned toward me and her face was all red like she was trying not to cry. "There's nothing I want more than for you to just come back home. I told you that when we were in Atlanta. I've been telling you that since you left. But I wonder, David. What about her? I mean, it looked to me like you've made some strong commitments there."

Thinking about hurting Genie made me feel sick inside. She trusted me and loved me because I made her believe that she could. I made her think that we could have a future together because I made myself think it too. I thought about the hell that she's finally working her way out of and I knew I didn't want my life decisions to unravel all of her hard work. This would hurt her terribly. Hell, it was going to kill me too. My head was starting to throb from all the pressure. But down the hall I could hear Mark putting his things back where they belonged, and I had a strong urge to do that too. I slid from beneath the covers and stood in front of Monica. Put an arm around her waist and pulled her close to me and said, "Monica, I'm confused as hell right now. The only thing I know for sure is that I want my family back." She looked up at me like she needed me the same way.

"You never lost us," she said. "Do you still love her, David?"

I had expected that question. It seems cruel, but I didn't want to know what I felt for Genie right now. I didn't want to talk about her. I didn't want to see her even. I just wanted the whole ugly situation to disappear so I could get back on the right track. Write my book. Get tenure and make my family proud of me again.

"I love you and our sons," I said. And I knew it was the truth. Deep down, I had always known.

Phase 15

Genie

"**W**here the hell is he?" I said under my breath.

I was sitting at my desk trying to call David again. I still hadn't heard from him. I checked his apartment the other day when I couldn't get ahold of him by phone or E-mail, and everything looked normal. I knew he'd gotten back from Atlanta, because his bags were sitting in his bedroom and Justine had told me she'd seen him at work Tuesday while I was out running errands. This was so unlike David not to call at all. Maybe he was still mad at me. I wondered if maybe something happened with one of his sons or if he could be still upset about his birthday. That slipped by two days ago, and I'm at my wit's end trying to figure out where the invisible man has gotten to. But I know David loves me. I know it. So why do I keep thinking about that Toni Braxton song. Seven whole days. . . .

I hung up the phone. I hadn't felt fear like this in a very long time and I couldn't take it. I got up from my desk, rushed through the main office and dodged some students in the hallway, trying to get myself down to the ladies room. My face felt all hot and my throat was full. I knew I was about to cry again, so I picked up speed getting to the bathroom door. I had to cover my mouth with my hand because I started sobbing before I could even get into the stall. I flushed the toilet so nobody could hear me losing it like that. My throat was all tight and my mind was screaming things that I didn't want to hear. Telling me that he was with Monica. That he'd left me for good to be with her again. Somehow I could feel it.

I took a bunch of deep breaths to get myself together and wiped my face. My eyes were burning from the mascara and tears. I did so many relax, relate, releases that I lost count, and stepping out of the stall I was glad I was alone. That meant I didn't have to pretend that everything was fine until I got back to my office. Where the hell was he? How could he avoid me like this? I looked at my face in the long wall mirror, hating this red-eyed, weak-looking woman that I had become. Hating her. I didn't want to look at myself like this. My hair was a mess and my clothes looked like I had put on the first thing I'd found, which I had. My make-up was smeared and my eyes were already a mess from crying all last night and on the drive in to work. I asked God to help me before I went back to the office.

I looked at David's dark office and touched his door as I walked back down the hall, wishing I knew what he was doing. He had to be with Monica. I told myself not to worry, though. He wouldn't do that to me. He just wouldn't. I went back to my space and logged on to my computer because I hadn't been able to do a stitch of work. I checked my E-mail first, just in case, but the damn thing was empty, so I stuck in the disk with my letters on it and started writing a letter to a publisher requesting some text copies for the fall semester. Somehow I got through the morning without crying again. But, oh God, I felt like something inside me was dying.

Keeping busy wasn't helping. I made so many mistakes in the report I was doing that I deleted the whole document and rolled over to the phone.

I dialed Chris's office, but he wasn't in, so I dialed Paulette and hoped like heck she was there.

"Yes," I said when the phone was answered. "I'd like to speak with Paulette Beardsley."

It didn't take long for her to come to the phone.

"Paulette speaking."

"Paulette I don't know what's happened to David. He's not responded to my calls or my E-mails. I went past his house and he's not there. I don't know what to do."

"Genie, calm down. Where are you now? At work?"

"Yes." My voice was shaky and I knew I wanted to cry again, but I couldn't. Dr. Stevens had come into my space all smiles, waiting for his document to print.

"Sweetie, he'll show up sooner or later, I promise. Just be patient. From the things you said to him, though, I don't blame him for falling off the face of the earth, girl. You probably hurt him bad." Dr. Stevens left and I breathed easier.

"But I apologized a hundred times in my messages," I said. "He has to know I didn't mean those things. He has to, Paulette. I think he's back with Monica and he doesn't want to face me."

"Genie?"

I looked up from the affirmations book on my desk to see David standing in front of me looking like he'd seen a ghost. He seemed jumpy and very tired.

"I have to run," I said and hung up. I was so glad to finally see him I didn't know what to do. I wished he'd have come to my house instead of the office, because here I had to keep my professionalism about me. I wondered if that was why he'd chosen to come to me here.

"Where have you been?" I asked him. My heart was beating a mile a minute and the palms of my hands hurt like they always do when I feel overwhelmed or scared. I did a relax, relate, release in my head.

"Thinking," he said. His voice sounded so awful. He wouldn't look at me at all. He reached inside his suit jacket and withdrew a letter-sized interoffice envelope with my name on it. I didn't know what to think. I just took it and said, "What's this?" and pulled open the flap while I watched him. His head was bowed and he was shuffling his feet like he was nervous. I knew it was bad news.

"David, I'm sorry for the things I said to you." I put my hand on his sleeve. "Please forgive me. I love you. And I didn't mean to hurt you."

He just looked at me a minute. Like he was mute or something.

"Is this something I don't want to hear, David?" I asked. My heart was in my throat. I didn't understand any of this shit. I didn't want to know what the letter said. I wanted him to ask me to walk up to the Au Bon Pain and sit down with him over his cappuccino and my mocha blast to talk everything out. I wanted it to be easy like it used to be between us. But somehow, he seemed like a stranger to me now. How was that possible?

He still didn't open his mouth. He looked as if he was about to cry. Like he was choking on whatever he wanted to say. So he just nodded and walked away from me. I wanted to go after him, but a student came in to ask me a question.

"Genie, can you tell me if Dr. Kemp's still teaching this fall? I heard from a friend that he's not doing Am. Lit II because he's taking the semester off. He's not in his office and Justine doesn't know. I need to find out, because if he's not really teaching it, then I'm dropping it."

"Uhm," I said, moving away from my desk, "I remember him mentioning something to me about that. Let me look at something quickly." I left the envelope on my desk and went over to the shelves where we kept syllabi and flipped through to find the syllabus Dr. Kemp had given me. That jogged my memory.

"You know what, he's still teaching it. He's just going to miss the first two classes because he'll be on travel."

The student looked relieved and said, "Oh. Whew. I thought I was going to have to scramble for something else. Thanks, Genie."

"Sure, Julian. You have a good day now."

My charm turned off as soon as Julian left. I had to sit down. It was like there were weights in my legs forcing me down. I sat behind my desk and opened the white slip of paper folded inside the envelope. I assumed it was some kind of "space" letter. I assumed he was going to tell me that he loved me and forgave me but that maybe he needed some time for a while so we could figure out if we still wanted this relationship to work or not. It was less than any of what I was thinking it would be. Much less. It said: *From now on we can only interact on a professional level.* One sentence. There was nothing about love. Nothing about my confusion. Most of all, there was nothing about the pain striking bone inside my body.

This wasn't the way it was supposed to go. He was supposed to show up at my door. At home. I was supposed to be looking all fine in black lingerie and apologizing with every kiss. He would give me hell at first about my big mouth, but I would kiss his anger away. We would proclaim our love to each other again and head for the bedroom. Fade to black. That's how it was in my head every night. There was no one-line note in my fantasies. And no desperation within me to just open my mouth and scream like I have no sense. Let them carry me away on a stretcher in a fucking straitjacket, kicking like a wild animal. I wanted to die.

I sat there and stared at that note for a few minutes like more words were going to appear. I just couldn't believe David's ass. I was hurt, yes. But more than that, I was disappointed in him. I expected more from him. I expected to be treated with love and respect. My phone started to ring, but I made no move to answer it. It rang over to the front desk and I could somewhat hear Justine taking down the message that she brought to me after she ended the call.

"Message for you," she said. I barely understood her. "You okay?"

I was nowhere near okay. I balled up the paper and threw it in the trash can, then walked quickly out of the main office to talk to David. It couldn't be over like this. Not like this. How had we gotten to this point? His office was as dark and empty as me. Figured. The same coward who had run away after our first kiss was running now. I touched the ring on my finger and went back into my space to write him a note. I said the only thing my brain could come up with: *I thought you might feel this way, but I still love you.* I printed it off the computer and put the folded sheet of paper in the same envelope he had given me. Crossed out my name and put *Dr. Lewis* on it, slid it beneath his office door and went my dumb ass home to cry in peace.

David completely disappeared. He didn't call. Didn't come by. Nothing. There was a silence in my life so absolute, a sense of dissatisfaction and anxiousness in my skin so intense, that nothing could make it right. Nothing. I felt so stupid. So gullible for letting myself trust a man. For giving a man the part of me that feels. The part that is vulnerable and priceless to me. I hated myself for it, because I should have known better. I know what men are capable of.

I went through emotions like I change clothes. I was blue, so I cried. I cried so much that I had to schedule it just so I could make it through a day of work. I was angry, so I took out his picture and cursed him out. Called him an old son of a bitch like he could hear every word. I went berserk and ripped up and threw out just about everything he'd given me. I was lonely for him but too proud to let him know, so I went in his office early Thursday morning, lay my head on his desk and just cried until I couldn't stand those pictures of his family looking down on me. Damn I cried.

I know now why they call it heartbreak. There is definitely bone somewhere in this heart, because I have these sharp pains in my chest that remind me of the time when I was nine and fell out of bed one night and broke my arm. It's that kind of pain. Excruciating and all consuming. I remember the pain was so great when the doctor set my arm that I fainted. I wanted to faint now.

Friday night I was sick with missing David Lewis. Time went by in something of a blur. I felt like I had when Mama died, except worse because David could come back if he wanted to. I was grateful when Chris came by to hold me a while, because I didn't want to be alone.

"Genie, you can't do this to yourself," he said. He tried to get me to go out, get out of the house and go for a walk at least, but I refused. He was on the couch next to me, holding my head in his lap. I had Brian McKnight's "One Last Cry" on repeat in the CD player. It was my eighth time listening to it.

"Can't you see that my life is over?" I said. The pain just would not go away. I had a picture I took in North Carolina of David on a sailboat wearing his shades and his baseball cap. The sun was at his back and you could tell he was happy. It made me weak to remember how happy we both had been on that trip. Yesterday I had ripped the picture up and thrown it in the trash can after I couldn't get past his answering machine at his apartment. This morning I'd glued it back together.

"Your life is not over, Genie. It could be a new beginning if you'd let it be. You already know how much I care, baby."

Chris stroked my hair and kissed the top of my head. He had to be a saint to put up with me like this.

"Chris, you don't understand," I whined.

"Who says I don't understand. I've had my heart broken before. I'm human too, you know."

I started to cry again and said, "But the things he said to me, Chris. He told me he would never hurt me and I believed him. He told me he would always be there for me. I counted on that, Chris. He knew how much it took out of me for me to fall for him. I risked everything, all because I thought I could trust him. I really believed in him. I really believed he loved me."

"Like I said before, baby, he's a coward. I don't doubt that he loved you. He was just afraid of this whole thing. And you gotta know that a man that age with a wife and a family wasn't something to mess with. You had to know that, sweetheart."

I sat up and said, "But he made me fall for him. I told him it wasn't the right thing to do, but he pursued me. Now he's avoiding me like I'm some kind of awful person just because I still love him. I don't know why I let myself trust a man. I mean, a one-line note, Chris?" I shook my head. "What was that, Chris? How come he couldn't just talk to me. Why would he hurt me like this?"

Chris put an arm around me.

"You need to get over it, Genie. Now I'm sorry you got hurt and I'm sorry that he's such a cowardly asshole that he couldn't even face you like a man, but you know it's over. You knew it was over before he even came at you with the note. You knew, baby. You gotta pick yourself up and keep going."

After Chris left I pulled out the fifth of Johnny Walker I'd bought and a whole chocolate cake I'd made and took them to my room. My bed was too big, so I slept in a corner on the floor after drinking myself into a comforting forgetful stupor.

I woke up Saturday with a major hangover. I was such a wreck that I could hardly get out of my bed to go to the toilet. But I did manage to put Luther on the CD player. Luther understood my pain, because Chris damn sure didn't. Nobody I knew understood it. I didn't answer the door or the phone. I just lay there in a fetal position listening to Luther sing "Superstar, Until You Come Back To Me" almost all day. That part when he talks about loneliness being a sad affair? That shit is just too real. Then I switched to "A House Is Not a Home" because I had to hear Luther sing that part where he says, "it's driving me crazy to think that my baby wouldn't be . . . still in love with meeee . . ." I felt good for nothing all day long and I just lay there, scared, and listening for David's key to maybe turn in my door. Hoping.

I hit rock bottom by the time night came, and before I knew it, I was picking up the telephone to call him. I hit the memory key, hating myself but feeling like I couldn't help it, and I got another surprise that was really more a confirmation of what my common sense had already told me. His phone was disconnected. My emotions were so raw I could barely think straight. I knew exactly where he was, but I had to go see for myself to believe that it was true.

It had started to rain a little bit, so I put on my red jacket with the hood before I went out the door. I got in the car and switched it on, pressed the garage door opener and backed out. The rain beat against my windshield like rocks. So I turned my wipers on full-speed and put in Rose Royce's tape that David liked to listen to so much. I put on "Love Don't Live Here Anymore" and started crying so hard I could barely see to drive. I needed my David. I needed my baby, but I knew in my heart he was gone. I had to see it with my own eyes, though. I had to. I drove like the wind in all that rain, not caring if I crashed or not. I guess God does take care of fools and babies, because I made it all the way to Greenbelt, unharmed.

I pulled up to his apartment and remembered how bad I looked, but I didn't care. My head was uncombed and nappy because I needed a perm. I was soaking wet, because I hadn't looked hard enough in my closet for my umbrella. But I was hurting so bad it didn't matter what I looked like or if I got so wet I drowned. I went up the stairs of his apartment building and knocked on the door. There was nothing but silence. I knocked again. Harder. Nothing happened, so I used my key to unlock the door and went inside. I turned on the light in the foyer and walked around the corner and into the bedroom, but it was empty of his things. No cologne on the dresser. No mess. The bed was made. Everything was neat and in place. I rushed over to the closet and that was empty too. His dresser drawers, empty. My head was spinning and I thought the room was moving.

"Oh God," I said, and put my hand up to my temples. My stomach was flip-flopping and I couldn't breathe in here, so I ran back out into the rain, already wringing wet and got back in the car. I was shaking from the rain and my pounding heart. This couldn't be happening to me. It couldn't. David loved me. I started the car, knowing what I had to do next.

At night Whitman is still alive with people. Studying people, partying people and people just hanging out. Even in the rain there were students standing in front of the library building, beneath the overhang, smoking cigarettes and exchanging conversation in lyrical languages that I wished I could understand.

I looked at my watch. It was nine. The building was still open for another hour, so I went inside and used my magnetic card to get in through the turnstile. I knew I looked a mess, so I kept my head down and didn't meet anybody's eyes. I took the elevator upstairs and fumbled with my keys before I found the right one to open the door and went inside. The lights were on. It sounded like somebody was in the back, so I made sure I was quiet. I didn't need one of the professors seeing me looking like a hag. I looked over at David's mailbox and noticed that his mail was gone. He must have come in late Friday, because the mail was still there when I left for the day. Fucking coward.

I searched the front desk drawer for the list of professors and found what I was looking for. So I took a pen out of the cup sitting to the side of the typewriter and wrote the information I needed down on a yellow sticky. I put it in my purse and went downstairs to the eighth floor to get the other things I needed.

Thank God the eighth floor was deserted. I sat down in front of the computer there and typed in my search keyword. Several catalog numbers came up and I jotted them down on the back of my sticky. Then I took the elevator down to the basement and got off and went through the double glass doors into another reading area that was empty. I looked for the first catalog number on the sides of the shelves as I walked through the aisles, and found three of the books I wanted. On my way out of the building, I checked my books out, stuck them inside my jacket and ran back to my car.

The house in Cheverly was hard to find, but I was determined. I pulled over twice to read my map to make sure I was going the right way. But I still couldn't find it. By accident was how I came across Kitrell Lane. It was one of those no-outlet streets in the boonies, and I had backed into somebody's driveway ready to turn around when I saw David's car gleaming in the streetlight. Parked in the driveway as pretty as you please. A light was on in an upstairs room and I saw shadows of what I assumed were the two of them. I knew I wanted to die. Right then. I just wanted to be struck right through the heart by the lightning streaking across the black sky. I leaned my head on my steering wheel. I felt so powerless. Just me, compared with this beautiful, massive house with a woman in it who already had his name and his sons and twenty-seven years of togetherness behind her. I couldn't compete with this. Me. Just some young girl with a few bad breaks in life. Who was I to want a man like David? Why was I out here in all this rain staring at his car and his house like it meant something? Reality hit me like a ton of bricks and I took the ring, his fucking promise, and I threw it out the window.

I backed up in that driveway again and put distance between myself and that damn 90210 house of his as quickly as I could without crashing. When I got home I poured me some Sambuca and drank it like it was going out of style tomorrow. I was dead inside. I took Luther out of the CD player and put in Anita because the girl sang "Been So Long" in such a way that I felt like she was talking to David for me. I helped her sing it too. I belted out those words until my throat hurt, but I kept going. I scatted when she did and let my voice fall way down low until the last note. Then I harmonized with Sade a little bit on "No Ordinary Love," because she made that cut just for me. Just for a moment like this when this pain in my heart was suffocating me so bad that I had to suck deep breaths of air into my lungs just to breathe normal. I was so drunk I barely made it to the bed. I fell across it, cursing David out like a sailor and went to sleep.

On Monday when I got to work and saw David's office light on I thought I was ready to talk to him. I looked terrible. My hair was in a single nappy french braid. I had put on the ugliest dress in my closet, this psychedelic, Soul Train–looking thing Evelyn had bought me from Merry Go Round. It was short and hung funny on me and I had elephant ankles in the off-white stockings I wore because I didn't notice when I'd bought them this morning that they were queen size. I didn't give a damn. I wasn't even wearing any makeup and my face was cracked and dry from crying.

I walked into David's office with a thousand things on my mind to say. But when he looked up at me, I felt like a scared little girl. His eyes were so cold that I shivered when I shut the door. He looked just as bad as I did. I remembered how he had let himself go after he'd come back from Africa, and all of a sudden it hit me that maybe that was when he had decided that he didn't want to be with me anymore.

"Can I talk to you a minute?"

"Yes," he said. He sounded so horrible and he wouldn't look at me. He was looking out the window instead, and it hurt so bad I just wanted the floor to open up and swallow us both. My hands itched to touch him the way I used to, just reach out and run my fingers across that sheen of stubble on his chin and then through that soft hair. I wanted him to hold me the way he used to not that long ago. I wanted to see him smiling at me like he used to instead of looking so stone-faced and solemn.

I had gone over in my head so many times what I would say to him when I got a chance to see him again, but now every word seemed stupid. Insignificant. When I sat down in the chair across from him as he waited in silence, I let myself remember the first time I'd sat here like this. I remembered how I'd had to move all those books out of the chair to sit down and him giving me that play to read. That's the man I had come to talk to. I didn't know this other person. That's why I wasn't sure what to say. But I had to say something. I fiddled with my necklace because I was so nervous, but I managed to ask him if he got my note.

"Yeah, I did." That was all I got. He started shuffling papers like he didn't have time for me.

"David, why are you doing this?" I said, and was so scared of what his answer would be that I could feel myself start to tremble.

He looked down at his desk and gripped a cup of coffee with his left hand, and I noticed that he'd put his thin gold wedding band back on. It was like my heart started to balloon in my chest when I saw that. I wanted to run out of the room, but I had to hear him tell me something more than that damn note said. I wanted something to hold onto.

"Genie, I know this is difficult for you," he said after a long pause, "but I've gone back to my life and my family. You have to accept that and move on now."

Gone back to his life? What the hell was I, a break? A seven-month vacation? I felt so ugly and used up. I looked at this man as hard as I could, not believing that this was *my* David. There seemed to be no emotion in him at all. Not in his voice. Not in his expression. It hurt me so much that I began to feel that familiar heaviness in my chest and wanted to cry. But I would have died before I let him see me break down the way I wanted to. I gripped the chair arms so tight that my palms were burning.

We had been too damn much to each other for him to set me aside like I didn't matter. I at least deserved better than a typed sentence in an interoffice envelope. I had this urge to just take him by the shoulders and shake him and say, "It's me, David! It's me! The same woman who believed in you, who still believes in you! I'm the same woman you called beautiful and whose tears you kissed away when I was in pain! You idolized me, goddamn you. Don't hurt me, whatever you have to do. Don't just hand my love back to me like it wasn't the most precious gift that I could give you. Don't," I wanted to say. But the words were all jumbled up in my head. And the only thing that came out of my mouth when I shut my eyes a second to stop the tears and opened my lips was "David, how could you do that to me?"

He took a long breath and took off his reading glasses like he was about to clean them, but he laid them on the desk and said, "I think it would be better if we didn't talk about this any further. I don't want to hurt you any more than I already have."

I couldn't accept that as an answer.

"Do you still have any love left for me?" I asked. I was so damn hopeful it was a shame. I knew in my heart that even if he did feel anything at all, he wouldn't tell me.

"Genie, please. Let's not do this. You do understand that it's over, don't you?"

What I didn't understand was who this subhuman robot was that was sitting in front of me, looking like David but sounding like a pure stranger.

"No, David," I said, "I didn't know it was over. Matter of fact, I was just wondering when you'd be available to continue our relationship so you could have a chance to fuck me over again."

"Dammit, Genie, this isn't necessary. And please, it would be best if you started calling me Dr. Lewis again."

He might as well have spit in my face and called me a bitch. I didn't know what to say to that, so I said the first thing I could think up.

"I think I'd rather call you by your correct name. Backstabbing lowlife son of a bitch. How 'bout that?" I could barely get the last part out because I was sobbing, so I just got up and ran out of there. I ran down the hall and took the stairs down to the first floor and ran straight out of the building. On my way down the street I started remembering a few of the things I was supposed to have said to that scum, but I felt like it was too late now. I had taken my moment and had done a poor job of making him see that we belonged together. Or at least of making him feel my pain. I wanted so bad for him to remember that I needed him more than Monica ever could. That I was still the same woman he had held so many nights that they all seemed to blur together.

I ran all the way to the train station and rode halfway to the end of the orange line headed for New Carrollton before I remembered I had driven to work.

David

I had to do it that way. It was the only way I could have done it. How else do you tell somebody who is part of you that you have no room for them in your life? There's no way I could open my mouth and say it aloud. No way. I couldn't stand that. I'm not strong enough for it. I'm still vulnerable enough to tell her how much I still do love her if I don't keep my guard up the way I have. And if she knew that much about what I'm feeling, she'd only try to rekindle what we had.

Genie's so young. She has no idea what it's like to want something badly, have it right there at your fingertips for the taking, but choose the harder thing because it's the right thing to do. I care so much about that woman. What she thinks, how she feels. I want her to have a good life and find somebody decent who she can build it with. That somebody isn't me. That's one of the things I held myself back from saying to her when she came into my office this morning. She looked so lost, my heart just grieved for her.

I can't let her know I'm having a tough time with this. Therapy helps some, but I find myself thinking about little things I've experienced with Genie. Things I've learned from her. And I'll get tears in my eyes because I know that if this were a different life, if I were a different man, I would make Genie my wife. But my reality is that I have a wife I was once very much in love with who is willing to devote one hundred percent to us now. I have two sons whose respect I must have. A job I'm learning to love. My self-fulfillment. Those things are so much bigger than my selfish wants. So much bigger.

After Monica, Mark and I had a long talk together, I spent a few days by myself thinking about what my next move should be. Monica and I had a few more long talks and finally, after about a week, I got some of my things from the apartment and moved back to my house. That was more emotional than I thought it would be. It hurt me so bad to leave Genie behind that I didn't want to function for a while. I hibernated in Devin's room for two days. When I got my head somewhat together, I sat down to write Genie. I couldn't make myself call her or go to see her, but I had to end it somehow. I had to make a clean break, and yet maintain some sort of relationship with her. So I chose our professional link. I wanted Genie to know without question that there would be no more friendship, no more lovemaking, no more promises between us. But we had to work together, so that part would remain. As painful as it was, I had made my choice. A sentence was all I could write without losing my damn mind.

It was a bad move on my part, but I didn't feel like I had a choice. I promised Monica, myself and God that once I did this, I would never go back to it. I just hoped that Genie would see that we didn't have a chance in the first place and pick up and move on.

When I gave Genie that note, I wasn't even man enough to look at her. I just wanted it to be over. Done with. I wanted to hide again. I didn't stick around to see her open it because I was scared she'd make a scene or something. So I picked up and went home to hibernate some more for a while.

A few times I even picked up the phone to call her, but stopped myself from doing it. When I came back today I knew she'd seek me out at some point. I was on the alert. She came into my office looking so beautiful but so hurt. I was ashamed of myself for causing all this and I could barely face her. She asked me if she could talk to me and closed the door. I braced myself for her anger, but she seemed too shocked or tired for it at first. She just asked me a couple of questions, and I tried to keep it brief. I really just wanted her to get away from me. Yet part of me wanted to hold her and take that pain away. She'd been through so much hell in her life, and here I was adding to her pain.

I felt so bad I went home and closed myself up in my bedroom again so I could digest what had happened. I cried a long while about it because I felt so helpless. A long while. But what else could I do? I carved my life out a long time ago. Genie's is just beginning to take shape. We could have avoided all of this if I had only seen that sooner and listened to her in the beginning. But I guess there are some things in life that are bad for you, but look so good to you, you have to reach out and touch them anyway. Just so you can know for yourself what it feels like. Even if it risks everything that you are.

Once I let out some of the guilt and pain, I felt better. I was still hurting, but was relieved that it was completely over. I went downstairs and logged on to my computer, sat down and looked out of the window knowing I'd done the right thing. Somehow, while I sat there looking out over my yard, the dam inside of me burst and I was able to write again.

Genie

"Genie, why do you need all this?" Paulette asked. She and Evelyn had brought me the stuff I asked them to get for me. I looked too bad to go out and be seen in public and I didn't have the strength to get myself together.

"Because," I said, "I want my man back."

They looked at each other, then they both looked at me like I was totally insane.

"How is this going to get David back, Genie? What exactly are you doing?" Evelyn asked. Her pregnant behind was eating the last of a box of Twinkies and I wished her happy ass would just go back home to her little *Cosby Show* life. Her and Paulette.

"I'm working a root on him," I said and started whistling.

I took the stuff out of the bag. There were four candles. One red, one blue, one white and one pink. I put the clear quartz crystal on the table next to my natural vessel, which was a conch shell I'd gotten in the Bahamas, and I put the lavender oil carefully next to that.

"First of all," Paulette said, "that mess does not work. But just in case it does, crazy ass, you shouldn't be playing around with what you don't understand."

"Look," I told her. "I understand plenty. I've read four different books on the subject. I want my man back and I'm desperate, dammit. Now I don't care what you say," I said, pointing at Evelyn. "Or especially what *you* say," I said, pointing at Paulette. "I only know that that woman has him under her spell right now and the only way he'll come back to me is if I put him under my spell."

"But Genie, isn't it wrong to mess with the laws of nature and stuff like that? This is a selfish act on your part, girl. I expected better from you than this," Evelyn said.

"I wish her silly behind would stop all this mess. She needs to wake up and smell the coffee. Genie, David's gone and he isn't coming back. You have that fine-ass, very single Chris just waiting in the wings for you to come to your senses, and you're up here trying this stupid mess. I'm ashamed of you, girl. Especially your antics the other day." Paulette was preaching like she thought she was Yolanda King or something and I rolled my eyes at her.

"The psychic knows what she's talking about, Paulette. She said that me and David belong together."

I started to cry again because I wanted to believe that badly, but deep down I wasn't sure if David would ever come back.

Paulette waved her hand in my face. "Don't give me that," she said. "That heifer just wanted your money, Genie. She told you what you want to hear and took your cash, girl. I told you not to bother with any of those soothsayers. They're phony. Look, why don't you do yourself a favor and call Chris. I'm sure he's as worried about you as everybody else who loves you, girl. I'm sorry things didn't work out with you and David. Sometimes people come into our lives for other reasons. Maybe David came into your life to help you grow and help you realize that you needed to face your past so you could break out of that destructive behavior. Now here your behind is, working a damn root on the man."

I was mixing the lavender oil with some fresh parsley and putting it into my natural vessel.

"Why don't you two just go," I said. "You're messing up my concentration." I sniffed and wiped the tears off my cheeks.

I had two of the spell books I'd checked out from Whitman open and was following the procedures in the best one I'd found. This had to work. This one was to make your sweetheart come running back to you.

"Genie why can't you be sane about this?" Paulette asked. She took both my hands in hers. "I'm worried about you. I've never seen you like this."

"Why are you so worried about me, Paulette?"

"Because, Genie, you've gone crazy. Why can't you be like any other vindictive woman. Any other woman would have cursed David's ass out, slashed a few of his tires and called it a day. But you—you're screwing up all around. You haven't gone to work. You've stopped catering. You haven't gone to group. You look like something the cat dragged in and you're drinking like a fish. And now you're trying to do voodoo on the man, Genie? I swear, I'm too through."

"Paulette, this is not voodoo. Voodoo is a religion, thank you very much. This here is black magic," I said, bringing the full glass of water closer to me. "You don't understand, okay. You have a man at home and a beautiful little girl. All I had was David. I love him and I can't live without him. I understand how you feel, but I'm having a damn breakdown right now, if you don't mind. All I want is my man back. If my spell works out, the man won't have a choice but to come running back here and I'll be back to my old self again."

Evelyn shook her head. "If you only knew," she said, "how off the wall you sound, girl. But I'ma leave you alone because y'all were there for me when I was putting on my sunshades and wig trying to see what Simon was up to when we were apart."

"Well at least somebody finally understands," I said, looking at Paulette. Paulette just turned away from me.

"Genie," she said, "I'm not saying I don't understand, sweetie. We've known each other forever and you know I've had my heart broken before. You held my hand the whole time when I was getting over Drew. If I had been so stubborn that I refused to accept that Drew and I were over, I'd have never met Robert, and you know it. Now you knew when you got into this thing that David was married and had been for a long time. You knew that he was going through some shit that he needed to work out. Hell, you were going through your shit and still are. You knew that you two were friends and you knew that you two work together, but you let it happen anyway. You are a grown woman and your eyes were wide open.

"I warned you to watch it a bunch of times because these office romances can only get you into trouble. But you were happy and I could see the changes in you, so I didn't say anything. But David's gone back home now. And where does that leave you? You still have to go in there and see the man every day. That is, if you ever go back to work. You have to see this thing for what it really was, Genie. I think you need to let it go and just try your best to move on."

I was getting sick of everybody saying that to me. What the hell did that mean anyway? Let it go. Move on. How could I let go of something that had slipped away from me already? And then move on to what? To whom? There was nothing and no one that I needed more than my David. Neither of these fools seemed to understand that. So I ignored Paulette's ass and unwrapped my candles and put them in the candleholders to light them. I guess she and Evelyn gave up on me, because they up and left. I was glad. I went ahead and started on my spell.

I held the clear quartz in my hand over David's picture and said the incantation that was supposed to seal the spell, then I drank down the water and blew out my candles one at a time. And I swear, I felt better all of a sudden. Hope can be a beautiful thing. I followed the instructions to the letter on closing out the spell. Then I took a long shower and put on a pair of unironed jeans and a shirt. I went down to the shop to let Arleeta have her way with my head. She was so glad to see me that she bumped another walk-in just to get her hands on me. She permed my hair and cut the dead ends for me. Arched my eyebrows and gave me a lecture for staying away so long. Then the manicurist, Faye, did my nails.

I got home around four and checked my messages thinking that maybe my spell was working on David already. It wasn't yet, so I did some laundry, cleaned up the mess I'd made over the past week and cleaned out Porgy and Bess's fish tank for them. I could tell they were happy about that. I sat down to eat a light supper when the telephone rang. The caller ID said out of area. I picked up anyway.

"Hello?"

"Genie? Hi, girl."

It was Tess. I had been avoiding her happy ass too because I wasn't in the mood for it. I just needed to be alone with my thoughts. But at least she caught me on a good day.

"Hey. What's up?" I said.

"I wanted to ask you a favor," she said.

This was surprising. Tess had never asked me for anything. I tested the heat of my pasta with the tip of my tongue, then ate some.

"Ask away," I said.

"I was wondering if you had room for me."

"Room for you? What are you talking about?"

"I've always missed it up there, Genie. You know I only moved away because of Edward. I would like to come back."

I thought it was a wonderful idea.

"What about Alex?" I asked.

"Oh, that. He relocated to Colorado last month. He's got family there and was pretty miserable here. That's what got me to really thinking more seriously about coming back to Maryland. I miss you and I miss it up there. Plus, I hate my job and there's a million hospitals up there. What do you think?"

I was smiling into the mouthpiece. It felt so good to be able to smile today.

"Girl," I said, "You don't know how much I needed this good news right now. When can you have your behind packed and up here?"

"Hey, I'll give my notice tomorrow when I get to work. My lease'll be up in a couple weeks, so I'll let my landlord know. I already have a girlfriend who said she'd take my furniture for me if you let me come stay, so I guess I can wrap things up and be up in, say, two weeks."

I let out a scream.

"Tess, I am so glad."

"Good, girl. Me too. How's David?"

That name made me feel like a knife was in my chest.

"We broke up," I said.

"What? You did? What happened?"

"Long story," I said. "I'll tell you about it when you get here."

"Not because you told him about Edward?"

"No. It's not that. It's . . . I don't really understand exactly why. He's not talking to me at all. He's avoiding me like the damn plague."

"Oh, God, Genie, I'm sorry. I know how much you loved him. I just knew the two of you were getting married some day."

"Me too." I crossed my fingers hoping my spell would work.

"Did he go back to his wife?"

"Yeah. And didn't even have the balls to tell me that's what he was going to do. I just walked into an empty apartment Saturday night.

Well, empty of his clothes, anyway. But look, I'm not going to bring you down with this crap. I'm just excited that you're coming."

"I am too, girl. Listen, we'll have us a serious male bashing session when I hit town, you hear me?"

I laughed and said, "I hear you." My pasta was like cardboard in my mouth all of a sudden. I pushed the plate aside.

"Well, I guess I better get off my long distance money and start taking care of my business. You take care, Genie, and try not to be too depressed. You have to believe that if David isn't the one, then there's someone else who's going to come into your life who's just for you. Okay?"

"Okay," I said. But my heart told me David was the one.

"Good. I love you, sis."

"I love you too," I said and hung up the phone. That terrible pain came over me again and I closed my eyes, trying to fight it. I walked around the house a while just remembering so many things. I thought about our first night together. How afraid we both were to even get involved. I thought about the look in those eyes when he took me into his arms. No man had ever looked at me like that and made me feel that way.

I walked down the hall and I could see myself running from him without a stitch of clothes on, laughing as he chased me into the dining room. The two of us cooking together. I went into the bedroom and walked over to the bookshelf. I wanted to burn every last book there. How many nights had he and I sat up in bed reading together? How many nights had he tried in vain to teach me to write poetry? The times we'd sat up all night just talking or singing off key to each other but just enjoying the sound of our love anyway.

Everything in the house, everything at work, was a reminder of David. I opened the Bible on my night table to try to read some Psalms for comfort like Ms. Henley always told me to do, but I remembered that another David had written most of those, so I put the good book down and lay on my stomach just looking at the wall, thinking that if my spell didn't work, if David didn't come back to me, Tess could have the house, because I was better off dead.

Phase 16

Genie

I guess my little dabbling in the black arts didn't work after all. I walked into the office with the birthday gift Dr. Kemp had given me under my arm and David breezed right past me and into his office. This is how it's been since August. I took a leave of absence in September just because I couldn't make myself strong enough to face this kind of shit. Now here it is October. I'm back now, and he's still acting like I don't exist. Every time he's around it hurts the shit out of me when he does that. But then when he's not around that hurts too, because I feel like he stays away so much now because he can't stand the sight of me. I keep wondering the same thing over and over: Why are we strangers now?

I heard from Justine that David's gotten a second office down the street in the Lifner Building, which houses the African Studies Department. That's where he spends most of his time now, his students tell me. All of this shit makes me want to just fly at his throat with my teeth and rip it open, because that's the only thing I can think of that's equal to my suffering. My damn pain that doesn't seem to let up. Ever.

It seems like overnight I've turned into this terrible woman that I can barely look at in the mirror. I can't respect her. She's my ugly alter ego. I call her D.A. for Dumb Ass. She's the woman living inside me who talks me into all the dumb-ass things I've tried doing to chase down this man I love who does not want me anymore.

D.A. does things like convince me that if I just have one more talk with David, he'll remember that he used to love the hell out of me. He'll remember that he said he'd never hurt me. That he idolized me. So D.A. gets me to walk into his office armed with every shared moment between us that will press his buttons. And she sits me down, and makes me open my mouth even though David sits there like wood with those gray eyes looking right through me and acting like he would rather be sweeping the streets of D.C. than talking to me. D.A. makes me keep talking anyway, singing the same song over and over. The song is called "but baby, I still love you and I don't understand why you are treating me this way, oh, baby, why are you doing this to me?" The shit doesn't work. All it does is make me seem more pitiful, while he seems like he doesn't have a care in the world.

That's not all she does. D.A. gets me to write David E-mail notes, telling him what he already knows. She somehow talks me into writing him three-page letters sometimes that I slip under his door before leaving at night and am embarrassed about later on. Of course, David doesn't respond and never will. His silence makes me feel like my heart has imploded. And yet I must be a glutton for punishment, because D.A. is still able to take my fingers and get me to dial his number to leave him these sad-ass voice messages. I don't understand why she thinks she gets any satisfaction out of these desperate acts. I hate that woman. She's ruining my life.

It's to the point now where Tess, Paulette and Evelyn have already told me that if I keep talking about David the way I do and doing all the crazy, obsessive stuff I've been doing, they'll be forced to perform an exorcism. I don't blame them. I've turned my own life upside down for a man who doesn't want me, and I know it. But knowing it doesn't make me give a damn. All I've been doing is crying over him and sitting in my bedroom. I don't cater on the side anymore. I haven't gone to group since August, even though Tess goes now. It takes every piece of energy left in me to be able to function at work every day. I never knew that getting up and putting on clothes every morning could be this difficult and I see why Mama found one damn house dress she could put on and stuck with it. Sometimes you wanna look just like you feel. I drink these days like nobody's business. Now I'm having that damn dream again. Poor Tess doesn't know what to do because I've refused to seek professional help. The only help I feel like I need is help getting my ex-man to understand that we belong together.

I turned twenty-six today and I told myself when I got up this morning that I would try hard to make it a good day despite the fact that I feel like stepped-on shit. The staff and some of the faculty took me to lunch at an upscale Italian spot on Penn to help me start my celebration. It bothered me that David didn't come. Or even wish me a happy birthday, even though he knew. He had to know, what with the dozen red roses on my desk from one of my students and the three huge silver balloons with *Happy Birthday* written on them that Justine had tied to the back of my chair. But what did I expect? It still hurt though. The Negro had even given Barbara, who he hates, a damn birthday card when her birthday rolled around. But I was trying not to think about that.

I sighed so hard. I decided to try to do a little bit of work, since I hadn't gotten anything done all day. I needed to finish my spreadsheet on the fall enrollment figures, so I found my disk and popped it into the drive. I sat in front of my computer with my mouse in my hand and rolled the arrow over to the Excel icon and double-clicked. Then I pulled up the spreadsheet I'd created and took the page I'd written the enrollments on in pencil and put it in front of me.

I heard David outside the door of my space talking and laughing it up with one of his students like he was having the time of his life. I forced my eyes back to the computer screen. That didn't work, so I got up and walked down the hall for a cup of tea. That didn't help either. I was still restless. The man was standing there looking so beautiful to me in a tan linen suit that I burned myself with the hot water when I poured it on the back of my hand instead of into the cup.

"Ow," I said, and knocked my stupid cup on the floor. David and his student turned my way to see what had happened, but then resumed their conversation. I acted like I didn't pay them any mind. I wiped my hand and cleaned the water off the table, got myself a bag of Constant Comment to calm my nerves. I walked back down the hall to my space sipping my tea.

The tea didn't help either. David was still standing there cheesing like fucking Jimmy Carter and I just didn't feel like trying anymore, so I logged out of my computer and turned it off. Put my phone on send calls, got my purse and carryall and walked into Barbara's office.

"Hi, Genie." Barbara was on E-mail as usual. The woman used E-mail like crack addicts use their pipes.

"Barb," I said, sitting down and trying not to cry, "I think I need to go home." My hands were trembling, my face felt hot and the waves of pain washing over me made me want to lie on the floor.

"What's wrong, hon?" She asked. She looked up from her computer and turned toward me.

"I don't know," I said. Lying like a big dog. But what else was I going to say? It wouldn't do to come out with "that no good Professor Lewis told me he loved me then stabbed me in my back and now I can't get no satisfaction." I squirmed in the chair, wanting to be out of there before I burst into tears in front of this wench.

"Well, you look all upset about something. Is there anything I can do?" She looked genuinely concerned, but that was Barbara's way. Mother you when you're sick or upset. Kick you in the teeth all the times in between. She took her glasses off and patted my hand.

"No. I just think I need to be alone," I said. The tears escaped my eyes and I hoped to God David couldn't see me crying.

"Okay," she said. "Take all the time you need. Let me know if there's anything I can do."

I nodded, because I couldn't talk anymore. I would have really lost it then. Something inside me felt crazed and tired at the same time. I just wanted to lie in my bed and cry as hard as I needed to. Ask God why David was doing this to me. Maybe he could give me the answers that David refused to give. I clutched my things against me and rushed out the door without telling Justine goodbye.

Somehow I made it to my car. I felt completely irrational and out of control. I couldn't find my keys, so I had to dump everything out of my purse on top of the car to find them. Pennies and stuff fell all over the ground but I didn't care. I just wanted to be alone. Away. I got in my car and drove off, ran a red light out of the garage and sped down the street.

There was a backup on Route 50 because of an accident. I sat in the traffic looking down at my steering wheel trying to hold back the tears. I just felt this emptiness inside. And the pain that I was getting so fed up with. Why couldn't David understand that we belong together? That I need him?

Traffic started moving on slowly. The rubberneckers were braking every step of the way, but finally I got past the accident, which was only a minor fender-bender, and drove like a she-devil. The radio was on and the Average White Band's "Schoolboy Crush" went off. I. B. Love, the dee jay on 94.1, told all the listeners it was him on the mike and then went into the next song. I wanted to crash my car right into a barrier getting off at my exit when I heard the beginning strains of "If This World Were Mine." That sent me completely over the edge. I couldn't even cry anymore I felt so dead inside. I was twenty-six today and hadn't accomplished shit except learning how to love and lose a good man.

When I pulled up in front of my house, I half parked my car. It was pretty far from the curb and somebody could have come along and hit it, but who really cared anyway. I looked at my watch. Tess wasn't due in for another three hours. That was plenty of time. I went straight to the bathroom, not even thinking about what I was doing and took the bottle of sleeping pills my doctor had prescribed out of the medicine cabinet. My tears dried up and I just went on auto pilot.

This was it. I couldn't do this anymore. I couldn't stand this pain another day. I refused to. And wouldn't his ass be sorry when he came in to work tomorrow and Barbara told him that she'd gotten a call from my sister telling her that I was dead. That I had killed myself. Nobody else in the office would know what had driven me to it. But he would know he was responsible for it. He would know and would have to live with it the rest of his life, haunted by the fact that he'd ruined the life of a good person. A person who never did him any harm. Whose only fault was loving him. And what good was I when I couldn't function without his love to sustain me? My future was David, and now that he's gone, I might as well disappear too.

I went back down the hall to the kitchen to pour myself a tall glass of Sambuca and dumped the pills onto the kitchen table and sat down. Trembling, I took a handful of pills and put them to my mouth.

"Shit. What the hell are you doing, Genie?"

Surprised and shocked, I let the glass slip out of my hand. It shattered near my foot. Shards of glass and liquid littered the floor, intermingled with blood seeping from my heel where a piece of glass had sliced me. I couldn't feel the pain from the cut, but my head hurt bad. My whole body was thick with fear and my heart beat so fast it boomed.

"Genie, why?" Tess started to cry. "Why would you do this to yourself?"

I just sat there with my face to the wall, moaning because I couldn't cry. The pain was too overwhelming. She opened my hand with the pills in it and said, "He's not worth this," taking them from me.

And all of a sudden I remembered myself at Mama's funeral standing over her waxy face, so destroyed that I was numb. I had started to shout in the quiet church sanctuary, "Was he worth it, Mama? Was he worth your damn life?" and before I collapsed, hands were reaching for me and pulling me out of the room. I didn't stop screaming even when they draggged me outside the church. I just couldn't stop and I didn't stop saying those words until I lost my voice.

"What are you doing here, Tess?" I said finally. "You weren't supposed to come yet. Not yet."

"Genie." Her voice pleaded with me.

"You weren't supposed to come yet," I cried. I lay my head on the table.

"I called your job and Justine told me you got upset and left. I came to check on you. Oh God, Genie, can't you see. You aren't Mama. You aren't sick. We can fix this."

"Tess, I love him. I don't think . . . I'm not strong enough to keep going without him. Please just let me do what I need to do."

"Genie, I love you. What about that? What about Marilyn? We've all seen too much pain to lose you, Genie. Not like this. Oh God. You have to realize that you need help. You don't need David. You need to fix what's inside you, sweetheart."

I was shaking my head and said, "It's too hard. It's just too hard." I was so tired of fighting and I didn't know how to explain that to Tess.

"Genie, I've been to this point. I know how it feels to want to give up. Dammit"—she gripped my wrist—"I've thought about ending my life before. But what turned me around, what got me back on track, was when I made up my mind to focus on learning how to live, Genie. There's so much good that will come, if you just hold on and don't give up. If I can do it, I know you can too. Just look how far I've come."

I thought about the magnitude of what Tess was saying to me. She was saying the same thing I'd said to Mama's cold body nine years ago. *Is a man worth that much? Is a man worth your life?*

I was twenty-six years old today. I didn't even have a family yet. So much had already been taken from me in the past that I just wanted to experience some love in my life. I never realized how much I wanted to be loved until David. David helped me reopen the places inside me that I had kept closed for so long. He helped me understand that I was worth loving. That I was capable of loving. If I committed suicide like this, I would lose my chance to prove to myself that I deserve the same things that other people have. And David wasn't worth taking that away from myself. He wasn't worth my life. My life is priceless. I was so scared of what might be ahead of me, but I realized that I was even more scared of never knowing. Hot tears slid down my face as I took Tess's arm. Clenching my teeth, trying hard to fight the horrible pain within me, I let myself trust her and I said, "Tess . . . Help me. . . . Help me. . . ."

She didn't say a word. She just hugged me close for a long while. Then she reached across the table for the phone and dialed Dr. Ortega.

Epilogue

It was a busy Saturday afternoon and trying to maneuver through the mall crowd was on my final nerve. All I had wanted was a new pair of black leather pumps, but I hadn't been able to find the right pair to go with my new Sunday suit. I'd already hit Rack Room shoes, Parade of Shoes, Hecht's and even JCPenney.

I'd gotten the suit at BeBe's. It was black pinstriped and had this fierce cut on the jacket that somehow made me seem more slender and taller. I'd found the perfect hat, too. I figured if I could find just the right shoes, I could strut around the offering table and out of the corner of my eye, catch jealous women cutting their eyes at me. It's almost like I can hear them saying, "She is not all that."

I decided to try Nine West as my last resort, but then as I was about to pass the Crown bookstore, I remembered that I needed to pick up a copy of Gloria Naylor's *Linden Hills*—the latest choice for my book club.

I walked in and made my way toward the African-American section. There were a ton of people in the narrow aisle, mostly in front of the fiction section. I waited a second until a wide-hipped woman in spandex made her way further down the aisle, then I took her place and began searching the rows of books.

I saw it when I reached the *L*s and for a minute I stopped breathing. *Song of Freedom* by David Lewis. I couldn't hide from the flash of old hurt that stirred within me. Or from the pride that filled me from knowing that he had conquered one of his dreams. I hoped he was happy. I hoped he was kicking himself for letting me go. It was as if a million conflicting feelings were battling inside my head.

It took me a while before I could even touch the cover, and when I did, I put my fingers to it lightly at first like I thought it would burn me. I saw my hands shaking and I looked around me before I lifted the book from the shelf, just to make sure that no one else could tell that I was struggling within myself to keep my composure.

"Put it back," my mind told me. But I couldn't. I couldn't *not* run my hand across the smooth, heavy book jacket, the stunning cover depicting a muscled, determined black man breaking the chains that held him captive, and a ship in the background, imbedded within a map of Africa. I couldn't *not* read swiftly through the acknowledgments and breathe a sigh of dissatisfaction that my name was not there. I couldn't *not* flip to the back of the jacket to find David's picture. And he was there, smiling. I could tell it had been taken in his office because I could see part of James Baldwin's framed snapshot behind him. It had been nearly two years since I'd seen David, and though I tried to fight it, I found myself devouring the sight of him. He looked so well. So at peace.

I let myself remember his laughter for just a moment. I allowed my fingers to drift across his cheek and remembered how his eyes had once loved me so well.

"There you are. We've been looking up and down this mall for you, woman."

I turned to find Chris standing beside me.

"Honey," I said, "I thought you said we were going to meet at the car."

"I did say that, but our daughter is getting a little fussy and I don't think this pacifier is going to work for long. You okay, babe?" he asked.

I looked up into my husband's eyes and at that handsome face of his that I love so dearly. Chris had seen me at my worst, and together we had worked hard to help each other heal. I looked at our beautiful baby in her carrier, all wrapped up in her blanket with only her silky black hair and little round face peeking out. She was so tiny and new. It overwhelmed me to think that Chris and I had created something so perfect and pure. Looking at the two of them, I realized that they were my future, and that I wouldn't have had it any other way.

"I'm fine. It's just that I feel so blessed. I love you, Chris," I told him, and meant it from the bottom of my heart.

He looked at me strangely for a second, but said, "I love you, too, baby," and touched my face.

And then I was able to do it. I felt strong and empowered with my family beside me. So I took the book that held my past somewhere within the folds of its pages, and I put it right back on the shelf where it belonged. For some reason, that one simple act made me feel completely alive. And when I took my husband's arm, I felt my own sense of freedom, and together we walked away, headed in another direction.

About the Author

Patty Rice is cofounder of My Sister Writers, a writers group for African-American women. A poet as well, she has published a chapbook, *Manmade Heartbreak*. Ms. Rice resides in Maryland, with her two daughters, where she is working on her next novel.